Duty and Delusion

Duty

and
Delusion

Malevolent Mantras

Shawna Lewis

Matador
9 Priory Business Park,
Wistow Road, Kibworth Beauchamp,
Leicestershire. LE8 0RX
Tel: 0116 279 2299
Email: books@troubador.co.uk
Web: www.troubador.co.uk/matador
Twitter: @matadorbooks

ISBN 978 1789017 205

British Library Cataloguing in Publication Data.
A catalogue record for this book is available from the British Library.

Printed on FSC accredited paper
Printed and bound in Great Britain by 4edge Limited
Typeset in 11pt Sabon MT by Troubador Publishing Ltd, Leicester, UK

Matador is an imprint of Troubador Publishing Ltd

*This novel is dedicated to
the doers of thankless tasks.*

Prologue

Blue, electric icicles dangled from gutters, flashing arrhythmically. Hoar crystals ferned the windows of the drab community building. Tiny flickers of light showed through the roughly-drawn curtains. It was Christmas morning, but only just.

At the roadside, three police vehicles drew to a halt, one a normal squad car, the others multi-passenger. More than one arrest was anticipated. Resistance was unlikely. Intelligence had been passed from a trustworthy source embedded within the community. Incriminating evidence had already been examined *in situ* and would be confiscated as part of the raid.

The officers approached the building, catching faint strains of music as they climbed the steps. There was no other determinable sound, yet a sense of life within. Breath, perhaps. Of the movement of limbs. Snowflakes began to fall.

The door banged open. Lights blazed.

"No one move!"

Male and female officers strode in, spreading out between the sponge yoga mats and tea -lights placed around the floor, frost from their boots dotting the bare boards as skinny young men and plumper women struggled to cover themselves and comprehend what was happening.

The party was over. Over, too, for the organiser, arrested and soon to be charged, under Section 53 of the Sexual

Offences Act 2003, with running a brothel and recruiting others into prostitution for her own gain.

Not a very festive turn of events.

The participants were given time to dress before being led, shamefaced, down the icy steps and into the vans. The brothel-keeper was handcuffed and shown to the car. Those in custody, including a Country and Western singer fresh from a gig at the Working Men's Club round the corner, were exhorted to join in with the officers' hearty rendition of *"Dashing through the snow..."* broadcast countywide on the police radio frequency. The remarkable nasal twang of the lead singer was given more air time than he had ever dreamed of.

The lads were let off with cautions. The women, mothers and grandmothers some of them, would receive further, non-custodial attention. The Madam pleaded her case: that she was fulfilling a demand; offering an ancillary service to the regular keep-fit classes she ran in the hall; creating an earning opportunity for women in this area of low employment. She argued compliance with the hall's constitution by providing tuition which benefitted the community. Testimony from those entrusted with managing the building, however, confirmed that the night-time partner-work sessions were un-booked, unpaid-for and most certainly unauthorised by the committee.

Marina Thorne was sent to prison for one year and one month.

1

Between the wardrobe and the foot of the bed there was just enough space to do it; where the pile of the yellowing carpet had been flattened by years of footfall, vacuuming and a fair bit of rolling around. One advantage of this flattening was that she no longer got fluff in her nooks and crannies.

There was plenty of room for stretching out lengthways if she flicked the wastepaper basket onto the landing with an extended toe. Lateral extension was trickier: too sudden a move and she'd crack her head on a sharp corner or be skewered by the key of the 'secret' under-bed drawer, hidden by the faded valance.

Lying flat, with her back to the carpet, she felt that one lone floorboard which had never quite lain flat over the copper pipework beneath. The pile of the carpet softened the sharpness of the ridge but she was always aware ... always aware. But then, life is full of uncomfortable obtrusions, isn't it? She tried to bear them stoically, aware that, however miserable she sometimes felt, there were millions of others who would rejoice in such tepid emptiness.

She liked to begin gently; kinetic; beat by beat; moving towards the transcendental rush that made her gasp for air. She always remembered, now, to keep her eyes shut. Once a woman has given birth, it doesn't do to come upon your intimate reflection in a dusty wardrobe mirror. There are some things it's better never to think about or look upon. She had never been one who thought 'the more the merrier'. To her, this was a private ritual, almost religious – heavenly at times, for sure. It held her life in place as surely as a silken cocoon shrouded the larva within, protecting those she protected. It enabled her to shelter, to support, to love. To shrink, unnoticed.

Only when it was over, this day, did her ears open to the clatter of the window-cleaner's ladder as he struggled it through the side gate. Had the bedroom window already been done? Had he been a witness?

A polite tap on the front door signalled that the man was expecting payment. Leaping up she grabbed her husband's flung-aside trousers, scattering loose change across the carpet. She scrabbled around – 50p, a £2 coin, 20p – not enough to pay the man. No good shouting down for Doug to fork out: he was already on his way to work. She'd heard the rev of his van's engine before she'd got her breath back.

What if she went down as she was and answered the door smiling enigmatically? What if she told him she couldn't get her hands on any *cash*, today?

He wasn't bad to look at – always a grin and a cheeky wink. Maybe if she ditched the motherly air he'd find a way of letting her off the eight quid. He'd already had his money's worth, perhaps.

She would just have to brazen it out. Sleeking her hair into place with her left hand, with her right she reached for her dressing gown. By the time she opened the front door she was almost decent.

Breathlessly: "Hi! I'm... er... I'm afraid I haven't got any *cash* today."

"I've got change! He rattled his pocket. "Or – I can come back later...?"

Was that a glint in his eye? His eyes went to his wrist, glance resting just a microsecond on her half-exposed thigh. Their eyes connected momentarily and Belinda froze.

"Never mind, love. Give me it next time."

With his trademark wink he turned on his heel and whistled his way back down the path, bucket bouncing off the ladder. By the time Belinda found her voice, the gate had clicked behind him. She closed the door, turning the key in the lock to be sure. The new woman next door was younger, more athletic and quite forward...

*

Thinking back later, she realised that the interruption had come before she'd reached the experiment. The plan she'd been working towards, the one that was to change her life, had never been given voice. And it was to be all about voice. This had been the day, the day of the first utterance, but it had not happened. Yet, incredibly, even without utterance, the plan had provoked change: brazenness.

OK, so the window-cleaner had not noticed her brazenness, but for her it had been the first leap into her new self, the start of a work in progress. It had nearly worked, the chance of delivery following hard on the heels of conception, with no gestation period. Therein lay danger – but what if it was too late to backtrack?

A fine, silky thread tickled her arm. If she pulled it, the golden cuff of her wrap, Doug's gift, would unravel. She dare not pull the thread...yet.

To care for; to compromise; to take responsibility; to endure. These had always been her options. "A Guide smiles and sings under all difficulties": one of the defining maxims of her childhood, and one which she had failed, always, to live up to. Known as a crybaby, the question for Belinda had ever been, "Why isn't everyone else crying too?" The window cleaner had responded as she'd expected: "Never mind, love. Give me it next time. Don't catch cold." This is what she'd remembered.

Belinda Lowe (Mrs) had found herself disappointed but not surprised. No man would ever try to take advantage of her in that way, even when she laid it on a plate. They all knew her, you see. And anyway, how would she ever have faced him again?

Did she feel spurned by the window-cleaner's rebuff? No. Maybe she should. Maybe she should get her own back. She knew his wife by sight ... but to cast aspersions would be an unkind thing to do, and Belinda had not been brought up to be unkind. Sometimes, she thought, life must be easier if you had. If you allowed yourself to hurt others, maybe they would take more notice; would do their share; not take for granted that whatever needed doing would be done by someone else.

The water in the bath ran as hot as she could stand it. Eyes closed, she exhaled sparingly until her breathing slowed. On the in-breath, she filled every lung crevice to bursting point. With the controlled exhalation, unbidden, came the *Ohmmm* nasal in her head, her pharynx, tingling her soft palate. On the third breath she made the change which began the experiment.

The sibilance at the start was easy: pushing the rest of the syllable up into her head took effort. *Self* is such a short word, easily missed, difficult to hum, but she persevered until it came out with a nasal quality. With practice, she felt, it might work, but it would not be enough on its own.

If Belinda was to disappear, something stronger would be needed.

*

Over time she experimented with different sounds and words. *Vile* worked particularly well, but other suitable vocabulary did not quickly spring to mind. Duty drove her daily round, as before. The idea of the experiment faded. When the window-cleaner next visited, a month later, she remembered to pay him but almost forgot to be embarrassed – though she did wonder why he'd brought a helper with him this time, an assistant who stared leeringly up the stairs while she was paying.

She couldn't help turning to see what he was looking at and in doing so, let the coins fall from her hand. The bearded assistant bent first to pick them up. She noticed he had black hairs on the back of his hands before the bilious, two-handed touch as he placed the money in her upturned palm. *Doug was not a hairy man.*

After closing the door, she climbed up thoughtfully, prompted to recover the experiment from the back of her mind. If only she'd had someone to discuss it with, to bounce ideas back and forth. She had women friends, but they were all busy and it was hard to find time to meet up. Maybe she needed advice on how to do it. Were there self-help books, she wondered? She stripped off her clothes and lay down on the carpet. The ridge of the raised floorboard was discomforting.

'That's like me,'she thought. 'Slightly annoying but does the job.'

Not worth sorting out, just something you'd prefer not to be there. That was almost certainly how Doug felt about her, though he never said.

Soon they'd have been married for twenty years, but there had been no mention of a celebration. Not like Diane, whose husband Alan had booked a world cruise for their Silver Wedding. Diane, secretary of the village hall, had been a committee colleague for years. As with Belinda's other friends, the closeness had weakened as women re-embarked on careers, were laden with grandchild-minding duties or husbands took early retirement. Life had become lonely, though she was rarely alone for long.

No, there would be no world cruise for Belinda and Doug; the most she could hope for was a long weekend in the caravan somewhere. She'd bet her bottom dollar on Doug suggesting

Appletreewick as a change from Pateley Bridge, to make it special.

Not that she'd complain, of course. They had no money for world cruises and anyway, who would look after Mum and Dad? They were fond of Doug and he never complained about the hours she spent with them. As long as his tea was ready when he came home from work, there were clean clothes in the wardrobe and he could go to the match every Saturday, Doug was sound. He didn't ask for much, everyone agreed.

On her back, she shuffled herself along a little to a place where the carpet pile was thicker over the ridge, and began to slow her breathing, readying herself. A new technique involved simple leg-lifts. On the upward move she would inhale to the word *not,* then very slowly lower the stretched limb, exhaling, to the word *nice.* She did forty with little effort and knew that it was too tame. She didn't want to be *not nice.* Bel wanted to be *nasty.* It was *so* difficult to change one's personality, yet she must change or go under, for sure.

Rolling over onto her stomach, she felt a sharp stab from the carpet. Her fingers rummaged in the compressed pile until she found the cause: bloody Doug's toenail clippings – big toe again, by the look of it. Why did he do this? Why was picking up *his* detritus *her* responsibility? Had he always been so thoughtless? It would be easy to blame his mother, but Belinda had a son of her own and was reluctant to take the blame for his shortcomings, so her mother-in-law must be absolved.

The stabbing nail had given her pause for thought. How much better to be a sharp pain than a minor irritation! Working up some speed in her movements, she found herself punching the air to the refrain, "Hit! Hurt! Punch! Pain!" Perhaps if she began with the physical it would be easier to move on to the emotional, psychological and unlawful. That's where the real power would lie.

The phone rang. Someone wanting to make a booking for the hall: a kids' party a week on Saturday, 1p.m. till 4. She asked if it was OK to hire a bouncy castle for the event. Bel explained, as was her duty, the need for the bouncy castle proprietor to have his own Public Liability Insurance and to show the PAT test certificates relating to his equipment. God, she was bored of saying this.

She took the booking and agreed to show the hirer round the hall … NOW!

The woman, Candy Dunne, had been insistent. It was her four-year-old's first proper birthday party and she wanted to be sure everything was *just right*. Candy had taken a few hours off work (she was a 'P.A.') to make all the arrangements. Her time was *so* precious. Candy's brain was innocent of the notion that the person whose number she'd got from the village notice board might, actually, *have a life*. That it might not be convenient *just now*. You could tell by her voice that she would never ask; would just assume that 'that woman from 'village hall' had nothing better to do than Candy's bidding.

Having done just that, Bel reached the hall panting hard, keys rattling in her hand. The glossily-groomed young woman sat impatiently in her car, parked facing the 'Please use the car park at the rear' sign on the front of the building. Bel's hackles rose higher as she forced a smile and led the visitor up the six concrete steps and through the blue front door.

Candy peered round, making little comment, though Bel knew she'd spotted the single cobweb which dangled from the metal roof girders, too high to reach without a scaffolding tower. Having paced the space, she decided that yes, one of the smaller bouncy castles would fit. She would go ahead and book it. Her blonde hair gleamed as she flicked open her smart-phone and started to talk into it while her eyes rested, unfocussed, on Bel, who, it seemed, was both inconsequential and invisible.

A garbled conversation later, Belinda once more had Candy's attention. The mother explained that her little boy, Job, deserved the party and the bouncy castle. He was such a star! Her blue eyes widened, as if surprised that his stardom had not yet made its mark on that woman from 'library who, it turned out, was also that woman from 'village hall.

Bel's attention froze as she imagined the child's name in a school register. *Job Dunne! Surely not?*

"We're having grown-ups at 'party too. All my family are coming, and Tyson's. And I'm going to invite everyone in Job's class at nursery."

"Mmm ... Nice," murmured Bel.

"I think I'll ask 'teachers too. Job's ... well, he's so special they all love him. They wain't want to miss his big day."

"Has he been poorly?" asked Bel politely. *What was so special about this child?*

"Oh, no! He's fine. Just really, really bright, and so lively 'e runs 'em ragged. 'E's got enough energy for a classful," she giggled. Candy believed in building a lively child and was proud of her darling's hyper-activity, so amply supported by fizzy energy drinks and food additives.

Did Belinda think they'd need to hire an entertainer, she wondered?

"Why not?"

Twenty-four four-year-olds on a bouncy castle, a load of young adults necking down cans in the back room, some clown you've never met before scaring them witless with God-knows-what tales while you're getting trolleyed. Bellyfuls of pizza and ice cream. What could possibly go wrong? Heaven forbid that you should entertain the little ones yourselves.

Once the experiment had worked, this was *exactly* what Bel would say to women like Candy.

She turned to continue with the tour of the building and entered the small kitchen. Here on the wall was Belinda's favourite thing. She'd ordered it herself off the internet after some lout had thieved the whistle, which the fire service had deemed an adequate warning device for such a simple building.

It was fire engine red, a round metal dome fixed to the wall at head height. It had a black handle and carried instructions in bold black print. Candy stood inspecting the sink and crockery. Bel, behind, reached her left hand over the woman's shoulder, grabbed the handle and rotated it at speed. The noise was fit to wake the dead. The jangling clangour of a past century's fire appliance gonged around the tiny space. The walls shook.

"And this is the fire alarm," Bel mouthed, still rotating its handle. She stopped, smiling. "Quite effective, isn't it?"

Candy, paler now, and clutching her ear, fought her way past Bel to a larger space. "Mmm ..." She fumbled in her bag - couldn't get away fast enough - and thrust over the £10 deposit.

As the Saab zoomed away, Belinda, with some satisfaction, saw Candy slapping at the side of her head with her left hand.

"Round One!" Bel laughed and shook her fist in the air. "Winner: Belinda Lowe, the Sharp Pain."

2

It came to pass that Bel's middle age, like a bank balance in a recession, became pinched and spare. It still worked, still had enough reserves to tide her over, but there was no slack.

Job Dunne's party, at which only his mother's heart had been broken, became a distant memory. Party bookings were down overall. It is a little-reported truth of the children's entertainment scene that, when times begin to get tough, parents spend a higher proportion of their monthly income on giving their kids what they want. Rather than hire the village hall for young Tamla or Tyler's birthday, parents will put themselves in hock and hire minibuses to take the party to MacDonald's or Harvester, which give away goody bags to seal the deal.

Keeping everything up and running sapped energy from charities, businesses, local authorities and individuals alike. It had come so suddenly – a generation had grown to whom notions of thrift and making-do were absurd. A generation of young parents were bewildered; unbelieving.

The village hall's finances were in a pickle: expenditure exceeded income and alternative sources of revenue must be found. Belinda dipped a digestive in her coffee and sucked out the liquid, concentrating on preventing the biscuit from disintegrating. Her experiment had stalled once again, but the time she had nearly deafened Candy Dunne remained in her memory as a triumph. Weeks later, she'd heard that the woman had suffered a burst eardrum, which people thought to be the result of the very loud disco music played at Job's party and, always, in his dad's vehicle ... whichever he was using at the time. Bel thought that she knew otherwise and grinned with satisfaction at the knowledge. She frowned at the still, small voice which murmured, "It's your fault," at the back of her mind. Best not dwell on repercussions.

Family life was changing for Belinda and Doug. Decision-time lay ahead for Aidan, their firstborn. Would he go or would he stay? His mother longed for him to stay, but knew he must go. She must not let on about the dread that churned her bowels at every thought of his departure. She worried about his sister, too. Melanie, over-sensitive, relied too heavily on Aidan's presence – at home, and even at school, where her brother had reached the stage of prefect-hood and status. The bullies had backed off from him now, but Melanie was just warming up to be fair game.

Each night, her mother would fall asleep imagining envious, hoyden girls encircling her sweet-natured angel with yells and taunts. In dreams, her child wept softly, longing for her mother's loving embrace. In dreams, those arms encircled and clasped, sheltered and protected, held close: strong; constant; ever-present.

She worried about whether her son would cope without her constant attention and support. She'd made sure he could cook an omelette and use the washing machine, but she'd heard that university campuses offered a wide range of diversions not available in Sallby. There was always the risk that he'd be distracted from his studies. On the other hand, he had to understand that he needn't spend every spare minute studying.

When she wasn't worrying about her children, Belinda had a rich seam of alternative subjects to mine. Her parents lived not too far away – just close enough for her to be on constant call but too far to pop round. Mum was losing it, but to voice the truth would be more painful than could be borne. Dad soldiered on, keeping everything looking normal from the outside.

Then there was Doug. Always a bit detached, somehow, now constantly pre-occupied with finding enough work to keep the business afloat. Self-employed electricians were ten-a-penny nowadays, with Poles and Estonians getting the work that the locally-born tradesmen used to rely on. Doug's bottle green van had spent more time on the drive than off it, this year. He never said much. How worried he really was, she had no idea. He'd never been one for discussing problems. "Talking solves nowt," he'd say.

Belinda did often wonder what made a rather dull, middle-aged electrician with few social skills transform, on Saturday afternoons, into a singing idiot in a green nylon wig, face paints and giant hands made from sponge, for his one weekly foray into 'normal' society. His team usually did badly, home or away, but she had to give credit for his loyalty. He was a loyal man, give him his due.

With the downturn, even libraries were closing, and her three afternoons a week looked like disappearing. She would miss the superficial chats with users and the escape from her real responsibilities, although it hadn't been the same since the council turned the outlying libraries into One-stop Customer Service Points. The old air of studied quiet had gone; there were squabbles about why someone's green bin was un-emptied, whines from council tenants about dripping taps and, always, people queuing to search for jobs on the internet. The library now had more DVD's than books, and encyclopaedias were things of the past. Belinda missed them.

The village hall was still standing but would soon be in need of another facelift. Over the years, many committee members had come and gone, putting in their two-penn'orth as and when. Some worked wonders but burnt out quickly. Others attended meetings month after month but had lives too full for hands-on volunteering. Nowadays, only a couple of old lags like Belinda really knew how it all worked. She was waiting for someone else to offer to share the load, but they all had good reasons not to.

And in moments of rest, there was always the issue of Dorothy to consider.

*

One of Belinda's tasks at the library was to keep the *What's On* displays up to date, taking down old posters and putting up new; making sure all the leaflets were current and plentiful. One Wednesday in April, at 14.20 exactly, she took delivery of a pack of new publicity material from the Central Library Service. By 14.30, Belinda had glimpsed the golden gate of opportunity.

The poster was stark, with a grey-green background. It showed a dark, bulbous shape which may have borne some resemblance to human form, but equally, may not. Beneath the image, in a green so dark it was almost black, the words *Yorkshire Sculpture Park*.

A school visit years before swam at the back of her mind. She knew she had been to the YSP; remembered sitting under the trees with the rest of her fifth form Art class, while the teacher, handsome, young Mr Edwards, told them of the brilliance of Barbara Hepworth. Belinda remembered her own puzzlement. Would Dad think these sculptures were brilliant? She could almost hear him saying, "A load of arty-farty rubbish if you ask me." But Mr Edwards had been different – gorgeous dark blue eyes which seemed to understand what you were thinking. And you often caught him *actually thinking* himself. Dad hadn't seemed to do much of that, when she was fifteen.

She looked at the poster again. It advertised a wood-sculpture course during the summer. Her open-mouthed gasp caused Tim, her colleague on the Council Services desk, to call over, "Everything OK Belinda?" before turning back to his monitor.

Her eyes were fixed on the poster. Why had she never seen these things advertised before? She wondered how many places there were; how much it would cost.

Not that she could go, of course. It was Aidan's A Levels soon and then he'd be on edge waiting to see where life would take him come September. He needed her to be there, although he did have his holiday job to keep him occupied. Melanie was another matter.

The afternoon wore monotonously on. She found herself returning to the poster repeatedly to check the state of the Blu-Tack holding it up. When her break came, she sat at one of the public computers and ran YSP through a search engine. She soon found the details she needed. Mmm ... a lot of money for five days, but she'd only have to use up one afternoon of her holiday entitlement. Maybe she could do an extra shift the week before. Then Doug wouldn't be able to complain about interfering with his caravanning plans: although he never made any until the last minute, he liked to think he was well-prepared.

3

Four months later, having spent an uneasy night at the B&B, Belinda ate a full English breakfast alone in the chintzy dining room. Hepworth House's landlady, Maureen, a cheery woman of sixty, seemed unfazed by accommodating someone going on a course at the sculpture park. It seemed a completely normal thing to do ... nothing outlandish at all. Not like when she'd raised the possibility at home. Doug had shaken his head in disbelief but said,

"If you feel like it, go. Don't see why you want to, but they say women do strange things at your time of life."

Can he not see himself in his green wig and sponge hands? Belinda wondered.

That had been more or less his last word on the subject, except to ask who would look after the kids and, later, to insist on a reconnaissance trip ahead of the date. Maybe there'd be a caravan site where he could pitch the van for her to stay in. It would work out cheaper than a hotel.

Stuck on my own in a tin box in the middle of a field? Lovely!

There was no caravan site. Mum and Dad had offered to pay for a B&B for four nights as a joint birthday and Christmas present, though Dad, like Doug, had been bemused. Bel reckoned that, behind closed doors, Mum had put her foot down. Despite her failing memory and intensified emotions, she still had intuition, and sensed that this adventure was necessary for her daughter. Melanie would stay with Gran and Granddad, who lived on the same cul-de-sac as a friendly classmate, so it was OK.

Belinda arrived on site on a misty, grey morning. The puddles in the parking area were rapidly evaporating, though the sun had yet to make up its mind. Between mature trees she could not name by species, a number of nylon gazebos had been erected, the sort of thing she'd seen in catalogues. Further away stood a circular pavilion of faded cedar wood.

Following the path towards the gazebos, Belinda saw that each shaded one, if not two, large plinths of wood, rough hewn at the sides but smooth-topped, and standing within six inches either way of an average man's waist height. Here and there, smaller slabs of stone lay singly or stacked one atop another.

A figure approached through the trees, eyes on Belinda. The man's body was long, narrow and fluid as a ribbon, this impression heightened by his hair. Unevenly streaked with white and steely grey, its primary shade was somewhere this side of mustard. It hung clean, in cords, ending in wispy tails just beyond his waist. His beard grew sparsely, the product of neglect rather than cultivation. His teeth, when he spoke, were tinged with yellow.

Smiling, the figure stretched out a sinewy hand.

"Hello there. I'm Ambrose. Welcome to the sculpture park." His accent was posh, Belinda thought, with a slight West Country burr.

"Oh. Hi. I'm not sure if I've come to the right place." She felt so twee, so out of place, so ordinary.

"I'm the tutor." He put down the chainsaw he'd been carrying. "You're in the right place – just the first to arrive. Good to meet you."

His eyes didn't signify that he'd noticed anything odd about Belinda. As if it was perfectly normal to be standing in a woodland setting with a married, middle-aged mother and library assistant of mousy demeanour. He seemed quite nice, actually.

"Come up to the pavilion. Let's make a brew."

She could not imagine this man in any other habitat. It seemed that he was of this place, the shades of his gaunt features mirroring the flickering shadows of the foliage above, a creature of the trees under which they stood. They strolled towards the building, where Ambrose placed a neat tick against her name on the list. His hands, she noticed, had power, grace and precision.

The space was rimmed with trestle tables supporting a number of tool boxes, of both battered wood and grazed plastic. They were filled with mallets, chisels and gouges of various cross-sections. Some were fine and tiny; others spoke of larger sweeps and scars to come. Hard hats, yellow and white; gloves; plastic goggles with green elastic; sand-paper; sanding discs, and unidentifiable mechanical tools lay orderly, waiting. Reels of extension cable stood on the planked floor. The place smelt of sawdust and herbal tea.

Another table, set slightly apart, held a chrome urn emitting the sounds of water coming to the boil. A row of chipped mugs and plastic teaspoons stood neatly on an ancient tray, in front of boxes of teabags and fruit infusions, a jar of cheap instant coffee and a blue tin labelled SUGAR. A flowered biscuit-barrel added a domestic touch, which drew Bel forward.

This was a different world. What was she doing here?

The rest of the group arrived in dribs and drabs, some timidly, others surging onto the scene. A surprisingly large proportion of them were women; Bel wondered if any might become her friend. Most looked quite ordinary, which was reassuring. The men it was easy to imagine wielding the tools, but not the women.

Ambrose's introductory talk was lots of common sense about Health and Safety, (which made everyone groan inwardly), the use of the tools and the types of wood available for sculpture. At no point so far had there been any mention of size. She had imagined herself carving a small box or figurine, but others were asking about garden benches and full-scale nude figures. Her nervousness welled up again.

"Let's go and take a look at some wood," suggested Ambrose. "I'll show you what we've got and you can take your pick."

They followed his long stride down a path until he stopped, pointing to a pile of fallen or felled tree trunks, some three or four metres long, ranging in circumference.

"These are oak - some lovely pieces. If you think you want to work with oak, take a look at each log and see which one speaks to you."

The idea of being 'spoken to' by a log seemed a bit bizarre to Belinda, though Bel thought it just fine.

"The whole trunk?" one woman ventured.

"Decide which length you want – look at the shape, where the branches might have been – some have bits left. Imagine the grain and think about what you intend to create."

Create. Not make. How lovely to be about to create something. Even if it turned out to be rubbish ... as it was bound to do.

"Once you've decided, let me know." He stroked and fondled the timber as if it were his child. "Paul here," pointing to a pleasant-looking young man who had just arrived, "will help with the sawing. It might take us all morning but don't rush your choice. Decide which part of the log you want. If you've any worries about lifting, get us to do it for you. Just ask me or Paul there."

Grinning, Paul waved his chainsaw in their direction. Ambrose led them further down the path, introducing haphazard piles of cedar and birch logs. The men seemed to find it easy to stroke tree trunks, or haul logs from where they lay. The women were more tentative. Belinda had never imagined going so far back to nature: she'd somehow expected the wood to come ready-prepared by B&Q.

For the rest of the morning there was a lot of hanging around, and the tranquillity of the setting was riven by the ZZZZ...ZZZ of the chainsaws. Having chalked her name on a hefty, forked bough of cedar, Belinda killed time by wandering up to the pavilion. Another woman joined her. Of the group, Marnie seemed least comfortable with the proceedings: clothes less practical than showy, shoes more slippers than the recommended sturdy boots, yet the smile was friendly enough as she asked if Belinda would like a roll-up.

Mistaking the question for the offer of a chocolate caramel, Bel nodded.

"Ooh, yes please. I'm quite peckish."

"Won't do much for your peckishness," retorted Marnie, with a smoker's voice, holding out a pack of Rizlas and a tobacco tin between black-lacquered, diamante-studded fingernails. "It's all a bit slow, isn't it?"

Belinda murmured agreement and, feeling silly for her mistake, drew comfort from sucking a mint taken from a tube in her fleece pocket. The other woman rolled a flimsy cigarette and lit up, while Bel made them both a cup of cranberry and camomile tea. She had often seen similar teabags in the shops but, knowing Doug's tastes as she did, had never experimented with them. She felt a bit disloyal, but Doug need never know.

Marnie had never had them before either. "What the hell's this? Looks like watered-down blood. It smells nice, though."

They sat together in shy silence, but not for long.

"Have you done any sculpture before?" Belinda took a tentative sip.

"Nah. Just fancied having a go. Used to like Art at school though."

"Me too. I came here once when I was in the fifth form. Have you been before?"

"I had this chap used to bring me. Classy, 'e were. Educated. Knew all about artists and sculptors and that. Lovely smooth hands 'e had. You could tell 'e'd never done a day's 'ard graft." Her eyes had a faraway look as she remembered.

"Didn't he have a job?"

"Yeah. 'E were a vicar or priest or whatever they call 'em. Minister: that was it. Don't know what the difference is. Do you?"

"I think it's something to do with which church they belong to," Bel explained. She did know, but didn't want to seem too clever.

"How long were you together?"

Marnie laughed and probed her right ear with a manicured talon. "Together? We were never 'together'. 'E just used to go with me sometimes. You know, for a bit o' fun. *You know*." She jerked her arm suggestively.

Actually, Belinda didn't know. She looked down, abashed, but Marnie seemed not to notice. She gazed reflectively out at the trees, taking slow drags on her cigarette, by now flattened and drooping. She examined her nail-art.

"There was no harm in it. 'E just wanted company – a woman on 'is arm. Mostly, I listened. 'E were ever so interesting... and kind."

"What happened to him?"

"Don't know. 'E just stopped getting in touch. It were about four year ago. Nicest bloke I've ever been with – showed respect, if you know what I mean?"

Belinda nodded.

"I missed the money, I can tell you. It was nice to get paid for being treated right."

"He paid you?"

"Well, yeah, of course. Usual 'escort' rates, though I were a bit more than an escort, I suppose. To be honest, I'd've gone out with him for free. Not much to look at, but when you've lived the life I've 'ad, looks mean nothing."

"Well yes," Bel murmured. "Anyway, looks don't last, do they? My Doug was quite a handsome lad with curly hair when I met him, but now he's nearly bald and has a bit of a paunch. Still the same bloke underneath, though."

"If he makes you 'appy, you 'ang on to'im, love." Marnie sounded so much older and wiser than Bel felt, though she guessed they were pretty similar in age. Her mind flitted briefly to her abortive dalliance with the window-cleaner some months earlier. She wondered what would have happened if she'd gone through with it and Doug had found out.

"This chap, Mick, used to bring me to places like this, 'n' restaurants for lunch. We even went to York once. I loved The Shambles – I could have spent all day poking round them little shops. We went in 'Minster, too – first church I'd ever been in. It were a bit scary though – all them dead people carved out of stone. I liked the coloured windows."

"You mean the stained glass?"

"I don't like to call them that. Stains are summat you try to get rid of. Them windows was beautiful."

She leant out of the pavilion door and poured the remainder of her cranberry and camomile tea onto the ground in a crimson stream. "See that colour? It reminds me of them windows. I love it. Not keen on the taste though."

Belinda emptied her mug and they set off towards the sound of the chainsaws. It must be their turn soon.

Within an hour, Belinda was staring at her own piece of wood, wondering what on earth to do with it. The log nestled on its side, on a saw-horse, her plinth being too high. All her ideas had fled.

*

Under their individual gazebos, the rest of the group had started work. Some people had clear ideas about their intentions. Others, like Bel, were still waiting for inspiration. She couldn't get beyond thinking, '*Where will I put it?*

Ambrose strolled over and looked thoughtful. "A lovely shape, that. What do you see in the wood?"

Bel was embarrassed: she couldn't really see anything.

"Well, maybe a snail just here," putting a finger to the tree rings where the trunk had been sawn.

Ambrose nodded thoughtfully. "I can see it too. Why not work with that idea and see what happens? You'll need to take off the bark first anyway. Remove it all and let's see what else is revealed. It could be a garden ornament."

Relieved that she'd been given a definite task, she ran to the pavilion and kitted herself out with goggles, gloves, a range of chisels and a mallet. Then she set to, chipping the bark from her log.

It was hard work, but satisfying. Bel found her mind emptying of everything but the task in hand. It felt so good to be here: free but focussed. The trees; the gentle sun glinting through the leaves; the sound of mallets on chisels; the occasional murmur of voices, and everyone in the group absorbed in their own creation. She wasn't interested in what anyone else was doing. It was enough that she was here. Ambrose would pay her some attention to make sure she was OK but beyond that, she could do what she liked. She forgot to think about the village hall, the kids and her mother. She even forgot to worry about Dorothy.

She smelt Marnie's smoky breath before she heard the soft tread of her sequinned slippers.

"Coming to the café for some lunch?"

Actually, Bel had brought sandwiches from home but she was ready for a sit down, and nodded her head. It was all part of the experience. Money being tight, she and Doug did little eating out. She checked her purse and followed her new-found friend, smiling at the thought.

It was the school holidays and the café was crowded with families. The atmosphere was affable and friendly, as if the patrons had absorbed communal good cheer with the fresh air and tranquillity. Small children sat well behaved, sucking milk shakes through straws and swinging their legs happily. Mums and dads smiled and joked and rummaged in rucksacks for tissues and cups with spouts. Grandparents struggled to manoeuvre all-terrain baby buggies between the tables; those already seated smilingly hutched in their chairs to open up the aisles for new arrivals bearing trays.

As Belinda followed Marnie to a small table that had become vacant near the window, she stooped to pick up fallen paper serviettes, but was ignored by the chatting adults. Her eyes widened to engage with each child; she smiled in envious sympathy with wind-blown adults trying to spoon-feed reluctant toddlers. She was sorry to have grown out of that world. Those had been her happiest days.

Once seated, she surprised herself by ordering a seafood salad and a flapjack. Doug couldn't stand anything that came out of the sea and his favourite cakes were jam doughnuts; for convenience, Belinda's own diet tended to reflect his tastes.

A little bit rebellious of you, Bel! You'll be trying hummus soon!

The women chatted about Ambrose, the other people on the course and how they came to be there. Marnie had noticed that one chap had knuckles crippled with arthritis. They wondered how he'd cope with the tools. Marnie, it turned out, had done a couple of months' relief work behind a bar, cash in hand, and had taken her time deciding how to spend the money, a bigger sum than she'd ever had at any one time. She'd seen a poster advertising the sculpture course on the wall of a smelly underpass in Leeds.

It was clear that this woman had lived a life totally unlike her own, yet Belinda found Marnie's openness comfortable.

"Where did you grow up?" she asked.

"Not far from Leeds, though I moved around a lot. I stayed with different people – foster homes sometimes – or with people my mam knew."

"Is she still alive?"

"Nah! Don't think so at any rate. Last I heard she were going off to Crete wi' some chap who ran a bar. Then I got a text to say she were in 'ospital wi' serious head injuries and never heard any more. That must've bin… ooh… eight or nine year ago now."

"Can you not find out?"

"Don't particularly want to. She were a crap mother. Didn't give a damn where I wa' or what I were doing, even when I were right small. It's a wonder I grew up at all."

"That must have been awful. What about your father?"

"Never met 'im. She 'ad me when she were fifteen and I don't think she knew which lad 'ad got her pregnant."

Belinda thought of Melanie. Poor little girl; how would she cope with pregnancy at fifteen? God forbid that it should happen. She made a mental note to have 'that talk' with her daughter when she got home. It was difficult to imagine the life Marnie described, though it revealed a glimpse of thrilling uncertainty which Bel thought could be liberating. Her own life, second child in a stable family, married mother of two, dwelling in only four houses in her forty-three years – seemed yawningly dull. It was almost criminal, really, to let it be so uneventful. She was wasting her life. Her only achievements were her children, and once they were grown…what would she do?

When Belinda fished out some snapshots of Aidan and Melanie from her purse, Marnie looked at them with longing and regret.

"They look right clean and healthy," she said. "I bet you're a good mum. Let's see one of Doug."

Bel didn't carry one of those around with her and, for the first time, wondered why not. Maybe she didn't feel such a strong need for him as she did for the kids. She supposed he was her rock, as they say, but her mind came up with an image of a large, immovable boulder blocking her path. Then a line from the old song 'I am a Rock', by Simon and Garfunkel: Doug was a rock, but also an island, separate, though fed and watered from the mainland that was Belinda herself. She felt guilty at the thought and changed the subject quickly. Doug, after all, *was* the breadwinner.

※

Although Marnie was good company, Belinda was beginning to think that perhaps she was not the sort of woman an assistant librarian ought to be hanging around with. Some of the details she was letting slip made her past seem quite seedy, rather than exciting. Her new friend, though, viewed Belinda's life as a charmed one.

"No, my life is really dull. Yours might have been tough but at least you've lived."

Marnie smirked.

"Shows how much you know! 'Ave you ever 'ad to go on t'streets to get enough food to eat? Or ever 'ad to sleep rough?"

"No I haven't. Sorry. I didn't mean to offend you. It's just that, sometimes, I'm afraid that I'll live my whole life looking after other people and not doing anything for myself."

"You're 'ere, aren't you? And your 'ubby let you come? And your mam and dad are looking after your lass for you? Seems to me you don't know when you're well off."

Belinda felt ashamed as she poured another cup of tea from the pot and smiled at the glances from the couple at the next table.

Back at the site, they separated and returned to their own mental worlds, chiselling bark and studying the form of their pieces. Occasional glances around showed that most others were a little further on, but nothing seemed to have taken shape yet. Ambrose and Paul moved quietly among them, offering help or advice, lifting a heavy piece into a different position or, occasionally, making sweeping cuts with a chainsaw to help a sculpture move towards its creator's vision.

Belinda emptied her mind. It was wonderful to be able to concentrate without fear of interruption, yet she was not really concentrating. It was more just *being and doing*.

So Marnie had once been 'on the streets'. That meant, surely, that she'd been a prostitute? Belinda had never met one before. What was it like as a job? She couldn't imagine there being much call for it round Sallby.

At the end of the afternoon, bone-weary, Belinda checked in at Hepworth House, a tidy B&B in a detached villa half a mile from the park. She settled in her room before undressing, in readiness for her exercises. The carpet here was thick and heavily patterned... serviceable rather than attractive, but it felt good under her skin, with her eyes closed. She tried to remember the 'not nice' mantras, but it was difficult to summon up any enthusiasm for her experiment just now. Just let things flow, she decided. Her breathing slowed, her muscled limbs relaxed, her mind drifted to slumber.

*

Awaking with a start and pangs of hunger, she noticed gobbets of carpet fluff between her bare toes and wondered where else she might find them. Another shower, fresh clothes, a dab of lipstick and perfume and she slipped gently downstairs into the dining room to eye up the other diners while she waited. There were a couple of lone men, both of them around her own age, both quite presentable. If she had been Marnie, she would know how to create an opportunity.

She tried to imagine how it was done: flirting. Did one toss one's hair coquettishly and gaze into the man's eyes, fluttering false eyelashes whilst exposing some cleavage? She'd have a hard time to do the last of these, being a 34A cup on a good day. Mostly she just wore a sports bra so there was nothing much to look at. "Seduction in a Sports Bra": could be the title of a cheap novel. In real life, she thought, it was unlikely ever to happen.

Her hair was too short to toss coquettishly, and the thought of a middle-aged coquette was nauseating anyway. Seduction, rather than coquetry, she decided, but immediately her head was filled with images of Dad during his short-lived craze for marquetry. And once Dad was in her head, he stayed, glaring at her with disapproval as he shaped tiny bits of veneer into a picture of a wolf in a pine forest.

The moment had gone. When her prawn cocktail starter arrived, Belinda concentrated on not letting Marie Rose sauce drip onto her lemon BHS top.

Later, as Dad's image faded, she gained enough confidence to acknowledge the other diners. One of the lone men, seated at the next table, actually smiled and asked if Belinda had stayed at Hepworth House before.

"No. Have you?" Her voice came out too high-pitched and she was conscious of a strand of cress lodged between her front teeth. She dared not smile back.

"Yes, I'm a regular," the by-now-charming man replied.

He was tall and thickset, with a shaven head. The charcoal grey suit and white shirt looked incongruous on him: he was built for Rugby League and hod-carrying. The black tie escaped her notice.

"Here on business?"

"Family business. Not anymore though. This might be my last visit."

She looked at him quizzically, wishing he would turn away so she could fish out the cress.

"It's been my father's funeral today."

Belinda noticed the black tie at last and tried to look sympathetic.

"I'm sorry..." as if it were her fault.

They each finished their super-rich bread-and-butter pudding at the same time. During an awkward silence, Belinda got up to leave the room and remove the cress. As she passed into the hallway, Prince Charming followed. He tilted his head towards another door.

"There's a bit of a bar in the lounge. Can I get you a drink?"

A jangling in her head like the village hall fire alarm made her gape. This man, this *hunk* (there was no other word for him), wanted to buy her a drink! Her face burnt but she tried to look serene. *Forget seductive; concentrate on avoiding ridiculous.*

She asked for a dry white wine. This was the only alcoholic drink she ever asked for. He stood by the tiny semi-circular glass-topped bar and pinged the brass bell while Belinda wiggled the strand from between her front teeth.

The landlady's husband, Ron, came through from their domestic quarters to serve them where they sat on chintzy armchairs. She found it difficult to relax, though Charmer seemed OK. Belinda supposed he was emotionally drained. It had been a sad day for him.

In a short time he had revealed enough about himself for Bel to know he was neither rugby player nor hod-carrier, but that he worked at two or more night-clubs and casinos in the city. His name was Bud Baxter, but on his birth certificate it said Daryl. His dad had been a bugger and treated his mum like a doormat. But when all was said and done, "Your dad's your dad and you have to do right by him."

So there'd been a nice funeral package from the Co-op, hymns at the crematorium – *Jerusalem* and *Bread of Heaven*, his mam being English and his granddad Welsh – and a finger-buffet wake at the pub in the village. His sons had given him a good send-off, which was more than the old sod deserved.

Bud didn't ask Belinda much about herself, which she didn't mind. His life was much more interesting than hers, anyway. Despite this, her eyelids were drooping with weariness and she needed to go to bed. At last, she took advantage of Bud nipping to the Gents' to gather up her handbag and get to her feet, waiting until he returned to wish him, "Goodnight."

She just didn't have the energy for anything else. She fell asleep as soon as she climbed between the polycotton sheets.

*

A gentle knocking on the door roused her enough to look at her watch. 1.30. Sleepily concluding that there must be an emergency, though there was no sound of alarm, she opened the door in her gold-coloured dressing gown.

Whereas in his funeral suit Bud had looked well built and firm, the baggy jersey cotton of his night attire revealed his wobbly bits. Wobbly lots, actually, she noticed. Tears rolled down his cheeks, coming to rest on his darkened jowls. (Bud was a two-shaves-a-day man, as a rule.) His shoulders heaved with sobs. Bel stepped aside to let him in. Her brain was jangling again.

Bud did not take her in his arms as men do in films and TV soaps. Instead, he sat on the green velvet stool facing the dressing table, staring at himself in the mirror and stroking his five o'clock shadow. What he saw was not pretty.

Distressed to see this grown man crying, Bel approached behind him and laid her hands gently on his shoulders in a gesture of comfort. It was impossible to see such grief and remain aloof. He leant back against her. She could smell the beer on his rising breath.

It all felt terribly racy.

Her hands moved slowly from his shoulders to his neck. She stroked as she would to comfort a hurt child, graduating her touch, adding pressure as her fingers swept round his ears, tugged gently at the lobes and round again to his nape. Hands moved tenderly, caressingly over his skull, stroking then kneading, pausing to increase the pressure where she felt tension, and finally round the rim of each eye socket.

She'd learnt how to do this at the village hall, when they'd run an aromatherapy course with a final session on Indian head massage. Bel knew she wasn't following all the rules, but it always calmed Melanie down when she was in a state after other girls had been cruel to her. Melanie's horrified face appeared in her mother's head at the same instant that Bud spun round on the stool.

He buried his wet face in her midriff where the cord of her wrap had come loose. Strong arms wrapped forcefully round her hips. She could feel his tears through her nightie. Thank goodness she was wearing the new one she'd got for Christmas.

"I wish I'd had a mother like you!" he blubbered through snot and tears.

Aghast, she pulled away and stepped into the tiny en suite bathroom to compose herself.

A mother like her? How old did he think she was?

By the time she returned, Bud was sprawled on his back on the plum-coloured counterpane, asleep.

Top Tips for Boys:
1. *Never mention your mother during foreplay.*
2. *The one exposed testicle is not a good look on a recumbent man.*

From her vantage point at the foot of the bed, Bel could see that the sole of his right foot bore a tattoo. Twisting her head, she was able to read, in blue lettering intertwined with red roses, the word *Mother*. So, Bud's father was not the only one who treated the poor woman like a doormat! Her sympathy evaporated. No excuse could cut the mustard with her.

She eyed the man with distaste. There was to be no seduction, though she *could* claim to have had a strange man in her bed if anybody asked…well, *on* it. Desperately tired, her every sinew burning, awash with fresh air, she slipped between the sheets on the other side of the bed. No-one would know.

As she reached to turn off the bedside lamp, the pleasant scent of deodorant and talc wafted from her own body. She buried her face in her armpit to block out the stench of belched beer fumes and flatulence. *Doug's underpants always fitted snugly.*

She reached out again for her phone and typed in the text, "Great day. Missing you. Love you all." She pressed SEND and fell asleep.

*

Some time around 4.30 she became aware of someone urinating from on high into the en suite loo, but turned over and slept on. By the time her alarm sounded, Belinda lay alone. Embarrassment flared, but if she could play it cool she might get away with it. At breakfast, feigning nonchalance, she helped herself to cereal. An oddly-matched elderly couple at the next table nodded politely and continued with their scrambled eggs. The woman was tall and large; her husband short, slight, with a tonsure-like bald patch set amongst hair of a wiry pale grey.

When Ron came to take her order, he eyed her cautiously.

"Tell you about his father, did he?"

He knew! Belinda's face turned puce; her breath caught in her throat.

"Don't worry about it. He's cremated four fathers to my knowledge. A bit of a regular, is our Daryl."

"Nothing happened!" she whispered, shamed.

"Never does. I reckon his mother was a serial monogamist. Our Margaret works at the care home she's in nowadays. Reckons she's always climbing into some old geezer's bed. No wonder Daryl's a bit of a mess. You have to feel sorry for him. Never had much of a chance, from what I can tell."

Bel sat silent.

"Listen, love, don't worry about it. We get all sorts in here, each with their own tragedies and problems. No-one tells tales and we've all got skeletons in the cupboard." He poured her tea and went back to the kitchen.

So that *was her hunk! He must be given his comeuppance. Wished he'd had a mother like her, did he? Well, she'd show him just what a mother like her was capable of.*

Belinda found herself increasingly belligerent nowadays; outwardly mousy and compliant, in her head she was a harridan. The experiment begun months ago was having some effect, although it wasn't making her happier and as yet was barely visible to the outside world. Candy Dunne had been her only victim so far, but Bud-bloody-Baxter was next on the list.

He'd very nearly attempted to take advantage of the mother of Bel's children, and tacitly insulted her by not following it through. Her very honour had been sullied: it seemed to be common knowledge at Hepworth House that, semi-naked, he'd come to her room at the dead of night. His sobs had been heard through the walls. The creaking of the bed, the bellow of his snores and even the cataract of his urination had resounded through floor and ceiling and along the landings. She had been shamed.

Even worse, according to Ron the proprietor, she hadn't been the first.

She hadn't encouraged him. She'd been nothing short of demure. No – Dashing Daryl would have to learn that he'd messed with the wrong person. He had messed with a woman who knew how to handle a chisel.

*

Like raindrops falling on an upturned bucket, the tapping of mallets on chisels rang through the woods next morning. Belinda, chastened, gathered her tools from their place and resumed work on her project. Others, already in full concentration mode, acknowledged her with a smile or raised eyebrow.

Few masterpieces were yet in evidence, although it was plain that some were destined to be sculptures, while others would remain chunks of carved wood. Belinda already recognised that her own work would fall into the latter category.

It was relaxing: good to empty the mind again and let the shame seep away. When she imagined the chisel against Bud's shaven head, her action with the mallet intensified. It felt good. Food for thought.

Marnie arrived late, fag dropping trenchant ash as she passed Bel's area with a wave but without stopping, en route to collect her tools. Ambrose and Paul wandered by from time to time with words of guidance or praise. Otherwise, the morning passed in quiet concentration. At lunch, a few of them gathered round a larger table in the café and discussed the current exhibitions in the galleries. The decision of whether or not to discuss Bud's conduct with Marnie did not arise, although Bel would have liked the more worldly woman's take on events.

At the end of the day, it was easy for Bel to slip a chisel into her bag.

Bud had booked into Hepworth House for another three nights, allowing time to sort out his late father's affairs. Hoping to avoid another meeting, Bel stayed in her room, watching back-to-back reruns of *Antiques Road Show*, *Dad's Army* and *QI*. *Does no-one make new TV programmes nowadays?*

The late summer evening was sultry; dark by nine, and clammy. She watched from her window as other guests returned from cooling bedtime strolls or turned in after a last cigarette on the terrace. By eleven o'clock, all was quiet.

She waited a while before she slipped on her cardigan and left the building, silently. Curtains were all drawn, windows closed against moths and midges. Circling the building, she searched for one particular vehicle. Bud had mentioned, nay, bragged about his car, a silver four-wheel drive with blacked-out rear windows.

The main parking area contained no such motor: her own red hatchback; a newish mini; a nice blue sports job and a back VW, but no four-wheel drive. She found it tucked away beside the bins, furthest from the road and sheltered by a thick bed of laurels.

From her cardigan sleeve she extracted the elegant chisel, its edge narrow but keen. Already aching from the day's labour, her legs shook as she gently placed a folded towel on the gravel drive and knelt down beside the driver's door.

Bel had been thinking about this all day. Her artwork would be stunning.

It took about half an hour to complete by the light of Aidan's headtorch, slipped into her suitcase at the last minute 'just in case'. A hedgehog shuffled by, searching for slugs among the rotting vegetation. Her legs and feet stung with pins and needles by the time she stood up and tucked the folded towel under her cardie. The chisel she slipped back up her sleeve, holding it in place with a flexed middle finger as she crept back to the house, keeping to the side of the drive where the gravel was silenced by moss and last winter's leaf mould.

She skirted the cars quickly and quietly. From inside the blue sports job she discerned a red glow, moving a little, tiny, just bigger than a pinhead. Then a second glowing dot appeared and a faint whiff of cigarette smoke mingled with the night scent of damp earth and herbage. Bel moved deeper into the laurels, chest constricting.

There were two people in the sports car. In time, its windows opened with an electronic buzz and the glowing dots were jettisoned on either side of the car, their light fading slowly. An owl hooted somewhere nearby; unidentifiable squeaks, barks and wheezes responded. Moments later the sports car began to rock. Bel took her chance and darted up the front steps, slid her key into the lock and slipped into Hepworth House.

As she climbed into bed, she felt a satisfying sense of revenge fulfilled. Tomorrow she would set her mind to recompense, but tonight she would sleep soundly.

*

The soft light of an English summer's morning washed into the room at Hepworth House. Birdsong trilled and echoed through the single-glazed window. Bel woke with Browning's lines running through her mind:

"God's in His Heaven,
All's right with the world."

Extending her fingers to draw back the curtains, she felt the pull on each muscle and nerve in her upper body. Though she ached to her very bones, her heart sang for love of life and liberty.

She knew that she had achieved half her aim. Soon, if not already, Bud Baxter would learn that he'd got his comeuppance. Bel would have claimed her second deserving victim. He would not dare to admit any suspicion of the perpetrator's identity.

She lingered between the sweet-smelling eau-de-nil sheets, musing randomly. Laundering this bed linen would not be her responsibility. Preparing breakfast; clearing the dishes: not her job. Worrying about Bud's reaction: not her problem. Another day beckoned, a day of creativity and contemplation, of the loveliness of trees and the fellowship of kindred spirits. What freedom was promised by this dawning?

By the time Bel made her way to breakfast, the other guests were going about their business. The elderly couple, Sheila and Gordon, stopped in the hallway to tell her about their plans for a day in Knaresborough, visiting Mother Shipton's Cave. It was to be a trip down Memory Lane: their first visit since Gordon had, beneath the petrified boots and bags of several generations of visitors, proposed to his shapely sweetheart fifty-one years ago. They were all smiles and happy memories.

Alone at her table in the window, Bel watched them help one another down the steps towards the parked cars and out of view, her eyes misty with sentimental fondness. They reminded her of her parents, each living only for the other. The thought of Dorothy flitted across the back of her mind but she would not allow it headroom, instead savouring the sharpness of fresh orange juice in preparation for an onslaught on the full fry-up she'd ordered. By the second sausage it was hard going, but she persisted with her second pot of tea. Her parents had paid for this. Besides, she had a hard day's work ahead and would need the fuel.

She wiped her lips on the gingham napkin and smiled. Hunger for both food and revenge had been satisfied.

As Bel passed through the hallway, Sheila Tickton sobbed her way back in through the front door. Her tiny husband shuffled up the steps, lugging a picnic basket and protesting loudly.

"After all these years I thought I could trust you!" Sheila wept. "My mother was right all along. She said you'd never change!"

"Sheila, love, I don't know what you're talking about. We need to call the police – this is going to cost us a fortune. I wasn't happy about borrowing our Tony's car in the first place but you all insisted. It's too big for me to handle – but would you listen? Now look what's happened. Who on earth could have done such a thing? And the insurance won't pay up if we don't have a crime number."

"Don't change the subject. I know who did this: that floozy's husband."

"What floozy? I don't know any floozies! When have I ever had chance to meet floozies?"

This argument had been rehearsed many times before.

"There are always floozies," Sheila complained bitterly, without divulging any specifics.

At the commotion, Ron appeared from the private rooms.

"Is something the matter?"

"He's betrayed me again." Fury and grief fought for supremacy in Sheila's emotions.

"Someone's attacked my – our Tony's – car. That's what's the matter!" Gordon clarified, standing as tall as he was able.

Bel drew closer to Sheila and sat her down on a chair with barley-twist legs. This mention of a car was disturbing.

"Just come and have a look. Then we must ring the police."

Bel followed as they trooped down the steps, crunched across the gravel and round to where the silver four-wheel drive with the blacked-out rear windows stood. Her blitheness dissipated like the morning mist.

It really was quite something, gleaming in the sunshine, effectively a coat of arms, carved in shining steel on a bed of silver. Argent, they called it in armorial circles, she believed.

Within a shield-shaped outline, each top corner held a St Andrew's cross. In the centre, what seemed to be a rat *couchant*. Neatly, though not expertly engraved beneath was the single word "*Pilgarlic*"!

The group stood, shuffled, stared and wondered. Except that Bel didn't wonder – she knew that Bonkers Bud had lied to her. The silver-four-wheel-drive-with-the-blacked-out-windows in the car park did not belong to him.

She joined in with the bafflement as the group discussed the significance of the graffiti. Sheila was adamant: the vandalism was proof of her husband's infidelity right up to this anniversary day. The perpetrator must have been an angry spouse in search of revenge. No-one knew what the word *pilgarlic* meant, yet. Gordon, with trembling chin, tried in vain to argue his innocence as he looked up, pleadingly, into his wife's ravaged face.

These unreasonable accusations were getting him down more and more. He knew that the event on Sheila's mind had happened in 1954, in a shelter on Blackpool promenade, before they were even courting, when she'd seen him necking with Pamela Turner. It was only during the last year or two that his wife, the one love of his life, had dredged up the name from the depths of her memory and become obsessed. He knew it was a heart-breaking precursor to the dementia with which Sheila's mother had been afflicted.

Back inside, the guests clustered round the desk while Gordon used the house phone to call the police. They detected a certain reluctance to send out a car – or even an officer on a bicycle – all the way from the nearest station ten miles away, just for a spot of criminal damage. A crime number was issued but the victims were not to hold their breath waiting for a visit. The two female PCSOs carried out a weekly foot patrol in the area but that had been yesterday, so it would be next week before they were back. But if a car happened by, maybe it would call in.

As Gordon maintained his innocence and Sheila accused, Bel set off for the sculpture park with the chisel firmly wrapped in her apron at the bottom of her bag. Detouring round the

4WD, she could not resist another look at her handiwork. A glow of pride sat uncomfortably with the clutch of fear at her midriff; a trace of guilt, too, at ruining the Golden Couple's day.

Hepworth House was only a five-minute drive from the park, down a quiet country road which became the main street of a tiny, scenic village. Slowing down between the parked cars which narrowed the road outside the church, she spotted Bud Baxter. He stood at a bus stop. *The real pilgarlic*. She drove by without a second glance.

Her log was by now looking recognisably snail-like in form and Bel was hopeful that she would end the course with a usable garden ornament, at least. The tranquil atmosphere of diligent concentration continued on the third day, and the learners gained confidence enough to stroll around the site to see how the others' pieces were progressing, inwardly comparing their own works of art to the rest. It was in this spirit that Marnie came over to Bel's space during a fag break.

"Want to see the exhibition this lunchtime?"

Bel waited until she'd executed a particularly tricky manoeuvre before asking,

"What's on?"

"Don't know but I'd like to have a look. Might as well make the most of the chance."

Bel agreed. As long as no-one expected her to make pseudo-intelligent comments about bits of wire or unmade beds, she'd be glad to tag along. They arranged to knock off early for lunch in an hour's time.

The new criminal wondered how much to share with the other woman. After all, she hardly knew her. Yet she felt an affinity with, even admiration for Marnie, who, after all, was even further from her comfort zone than Belinda herself.

When the time came, the subject turned quite rapidly to Hepworth House. Marnie had been travelling daily from the city, but with some of her savings still unspent, she fancied treating herself to a couple of nights' en suite accommodation. Belinda handed over the B&B's promotional card, Marnie touched the numbers on her shiny pink mobile and the room was booked.

The gallery was large and geometric, a stark contrast to the classical balustrades which edged the terrace outdoors. Large rooms contained monumental shapes: bald, expressionless heads; gongs of bronze vibrating massively in different tones when stroked with sheepskin-covered mallets; a corridor of chains suspended from the ceiling, rippling and ringing as they swung. The women were awestruck. They felt strangely excited, as if seeking the true significance through a veil of ignorance. This excitement spurred Belinda on to tell her tale of Bud's 'seduction'. She knew that Marnie was no angel herself and once the course was over, their paths were not likely ever to cross again. It would be a relief to talk to someone who understood fleshly matters, and it seemed pretty safe.

The other woman laughed as she described that first night away from her husband, but failed to see why Belinda had been so offended. The way Marnie saw things, Bud had been drinking all day, the victim of suppressed grief, of lost childhood and opportunities, overcome by guilt and regrets. In all honesty, she didn't understand Belinda's response. As for the "cremated four fathers" jibe, maybe the first three had been step-dads and this was the real one. Regarding the 'artwork', why would Bel put her good name and her nice, quiet, safe life in jeopardy by such a vindictive act against someone who had turned to her for comfort?

Bel bridled. *She* was the *nice* one, the one who offered comfort and reassurance! OK so she had been vindictive, but wasn't that what strong people were like? The ones who didn't get taken for granted?

"You see, that's exactly it," she protested. "You have no idea how dull my life is. People take me for granted. There's always something to be done for someone. I wanted to make a point."

Marnie smirked. Her expression hardened.

"Do you know what it's like not to have anyone? To have no-one to care for? *You* don't know when you're well off."

Belinda was disappointed by the turn the conversation had taken. She'd expected a bit of help from Marnie. Some advice on how to become a bolder person, less of a dogsbody, wouldn't go amiss. Marnie seemed to think that being hard and calculating was a character flaw. To Belinda, it was a trait to be cultivated.

She tried to explain what it was like to be 'that woman from 'village hall'. She tried to explain about the responsibility, the worry, the work, the always being blamed when things broke, of not wanting to be the last in the line of volunteers. She asked herself, and Marnie, why she bothered. Why did it matter so much? Marnie seemed to envy her involvement, the knowing who lived where and who could or could not be relied upon for what.

The two women had left the galleries and were strolling round the park, pausing as they came upon more sculptures which seemed to have become part of the landscape.

"I did some work in a village hall once," Marnie reminisced. "It were a nice little place and I had a good thing going till someone grassed. Put me inside for months."

"Inside?"

"Prison. For what? For earning a crust and helping people out!" Marnie was getting angry. She'd come to the YSP to get away from the harsh realities of her life, not to be reminded of its lowest ebb. Her explanation was curt and brief, leaving Belinda only half-informed.

They walked on in silence. Marnie rolled another cigarette on the move, scowling. Her demeanour had changed. Now she looked hard.

Belinda felt awkward. She'd spoiled Marnie's day, on top of ruining the old couple's anniversary. This vindictiveness lark was not a bed of roses, especially when you missed your target.

"It's really hard to get enough hirers to keep the place running," Belinda explained. "We do it voluntarily but there's always someone telling you where you've gone wrong. They never attend fundraising events or donate raffle prizes – just point out that the place belongs to everyone in the village."

This silenced Marnie for a while. She'd never thought about who kept these places running.

"When it's the Annual General Meeting we're lucky if anyone turns up, though we drop leaflets in every house."

Belinda's committee had lives of their own to lead. They were not professional fundraisers or buildings managers, cleaners, decorators, accountants or impresarios. She wished she'd never mentioned it.

"Well, let's forget my troubles." She was trying to placate. "Sorry for spoiling the day. Just let me know if you have any other good ideas I might use."

They walked in silence back to their pitches and back to work where one or two of the group were experimenting with power tools. Harsh sounds of electric grinders converted the glade into some surreal giant's dental surgery and set Bel's teeth on edge. She remembered that Melanie had an appointment with the hygienist that day, and hoped Doug would not forget.

Gradually the grinders ceased and peace seeped back. The women lost themselves in their work, stroking and smoothing, feeling the textures, tracing the whorls and knots in their individual, small piece of creation. Spirits soothed, each fell to musing privately.

Marina Thorne's schooling had been fragmentary; her acquaintance with mathematics, science and literature less than rudimentary. Her historical and geographical awareness was limited by what she'd picked up from various foster parents and social workers, until one of her fellas had, in the days before sat navs, taught her to map-read.

Had the ball bounced in her favour from time to time, Marnie may have developed her innate entrepreneurial talents and led a different life, but balls had never bounced to her advantage. Whenever she looked like finding some stability, some security, maybe even a deposit on a place of her own, fate had come in with a sidetackle and put the boot in. The attack on her VHB business was a case in point. She had worked hard to drum up trade from the villages around the city, trying to make sure the punters could arrive on foot and alone.

She'd befriended women and girls on her nightly walks through the parks and back lanes, offering them access to sexual health checks from a registered practitioner (only debarred on a technicality) whom she knew, and a warm, clean, safe place to work. OK, so it hadn't been what you'd call private, but privacy was a luxury these women could not afford and the boys didn't care about. And they had mostly been boys, the punters, or young men with no confidence or personal graces but a few spare quid in their pockets. She hadn't made a fortune, just taken a twenty-five percent share of the girls' earnings. Sometimes there were eight or nine at a time, offering half-hour sessions over the three hours each night. Marnie had an appointments diary and always insisted on cash up front. She kept her accounts in a proper book she'd bought from WH Smith and got the girls to sign for their money at the end of each shift. It had all been done properly, by her own lights.

Sometimes, during that winter, one of the coldest on record, she had been forced to turn on the central heating, though she worried that the increased usage might be spotted and arouse suspicion. She kept the lights off. With curtains drawn, and just a few tea lights placed here and there, the atmosphere was subdued and subtle, making up for the lack of privacy. The yoga mats had been a bit thin and narrow but they would have done until she'd made enough money to invest in some of those high-quality inflatable beds and an electric inflator pump. She would have been able to take them home with her each night. But that was destined never to happen.

Admittedly, she had never contemplated paying rent for the hall. She already paid for her keep fit classes and assumed she was entitled to come and go as she pleased. In any case, the committee would have to have said no. Some goody two-shoes would have looked down her nose. They wouldn't have given her houseroom and she'd have lost the little bit of keep-fit income as well.

Marnie craved respectability. Husband, children, home, love: she had been denied these things. From childhood, her focus had been on survival. Now she knew that her future survival would depend on her ability to make changes. No one wanted forty-three-year-old pole dancers or glamour models. She'd always been a bit scrawny for that anyway, but there had been a few backstreet photographers who weren't too demanding.

Now the ones she knew were retiring or going legit, offering soft-focus wedding packages in padded white albums, in which the bride, always plump, looked unrecognisable from her daily self and the groom, even plumper in his tailcoat and pink cravat, gurned uncomfortably under spiky, gelled hair. These packages, priced to undercut the upmarket firms, managed to include the DVD and CD of the 200 wedding snaps. *Technology is a wonderful thing*, thought Marnie. If she'd ever had a wedding, one of those albums would have done for her.

Respectability: how to make that change? She knew so little of the life she longed for – had only caught brief glimpses of normal family life when billeted in foster homes for one of her longer stays.

She remembered one couple around the time she was eleven, who had actually seemed to love her. Each one fat and cuddly, they'd worked together as comfortably as her own two hands. Marnie shifted position as she thought of them, observing her grip on mallet and chisel. That was comfortable, too. They'd had children of their own: two boys who had enjoyed having a younger sister for a while and treated her as someone special. Smiling, she recalled how they'd all gone together to choose wallpaper and curtains for her tiny room. How thrilled she'd been.

That was her ideal... yet it was strange how she'd forgotten their names – all of them. She had longed for this to be her real life, but even then had known it couldn't last. If she had lived that life, Marina could have blossomed.

After an absence of almost a year Marnie had, without explanation, been reclaimed by her mother, who had set up home with some Joe from the Caribbean not averse to having a pre-teen daughter about the house. Normal life had resumed for the twelve-year-old.

Her name had always puzzled her. The only other Marina she'd heard of had been royalty, though it was unlikely she'd been named after some princess. It was too late now to ask, but the obvious conclusion was that her mother had been ahead of the trend whereby the child is named after the location of its conception. If it was good enough for the Beckhams...

Britain's coast is lined with marinas. Had it been one of those, bobbing with small yachts and motor cruisers at the edge of a seaside town? Or somewhere seedier, like the rundown, flooded canal-side clay-pit on the edge of the city, where dads taught their kids to tack in Mirror dinghies and teenagers tumbled into murky water from sailboards hired from the council-owned sports centre? Probably the latter.

She had been called Marnie for as long as she could remember, except by school teachers and social workers before they'd got to know her. At some schools she'd been given the nickname "Mardy Marnie" even before the first day was over. It was difficult not to appear mardy when you knew no-one, in a strange building which roared and heaved with even stranger, noisy teenagers and odd, inquisitive teachers with unfathomable whims and quirks.

Some people still thought her a bit po-faced, but what was there to smile about? *The here and now*, she answered herself. This place and these few days were the best thing since the fat foster family, apart from Mick. She let the sounds of the place fill her ears, breathed in its smells and concentrated on her work. A gaggle of elderly people walked along the visitors' path, stopping every few feet to point at the works in progress and pass the time of day with the sculptors. Marnie hoped they wouldn't want to chat, and turned back to what was beginning to look like a swaddled infant roughly carved in cedar wood.

Ten yards away, Belinda was developing some pride in her art. She had managed to chisel out a snail-like shape from the forked log, with the smaller branch signifying a head. That still needed work. At present, following the tree rings with a gouge was creating a whorl effect which pleased her. The work took time, concentration and a steady hand. Her forearm was numb, her back ached, but her mind was at peace. She did not dwell on her *faux pas*.

Easing her muscles, she caught the eye of a grey-haired chap in a smart beige jacket, flanked each side by two elderly women with cardigans and leather handbags, obviously part of a pensioners' coach trip.

He complimented her on her work in progress and smiled happily. It was so nice, Bel thought, to meet people when they were enjoying themselves.

In an instant her mood changed. Standing next to him, stony-faced and looking straight ahead, was Dorothy. Belinda's heart pounded. She felt invaded.

46

The pleasant-eyed man continued. "We're the Cup of Cheer Club," he said wryly, "though you wouldn't always think so." He nodded towards his two companions, who had walked ahead rather than converse with an outsider. "Dorothy, there, saw a poster in the library and thought this would be a change from Chatsworth and Filey. We try to have a trip out once a month during the summer." He nodded, and moved on to offer an arm to each of his waiting companions.

At the next break, Belinda was bursting to offload her fury. She sat on a log, rough through her jeans, drinking rose hip tea.

"What's up?" Marnie hitched up her denim mini-skirt to sit down.

"I've had a shock. One of those old women on the path."

"What about her?"

"I sort of know her."

"So?"

"Well, you'll never believe it, but… I think she's my dad's bit on the side."

Marnie laughed out loud. "What? She must be eighty at least!"

Belinda brushed splinters of wood from her trousers. "Maybe not now, but it went on for a long time. She's been stalking me for years."

"Go on." Marnie was doubtful.

"I was ten or eleven, on my way home from school, and I saw my dad coming round the corner of a house on Station Road."

"So what?"

"When I got home, I told Mum and she went all quiet. When Dad got in from work I could hear them arguing in the kitchen but couldn't make out what they were saying. They kept their voices down, so it must have been something secret. We had sausage and mash for tea that night – I can still remember it – and when I told Dad I'd seen him coming out of a gate on Station Road, he just denied it. Said he'd been at work all day, nowhere near Station Road. But he was lying. I could recognise my own father.

"Later, I told Fiona, my sister. She used to treat me like a kid and not take much notice of me, but this time she said, 'Oooh! Maybe it's his bit on the side,' and giggled. Older than me, Fiona is – she'd have been around fifteen at the time, and very keen on boys. I didn't know what 'bit on the side' meant, but I didn't like the sound of it.

"Mum often seemed sad after that, as if there was a weight on her mind, but I never asked why."

"You're making a lot of assumptions. Maybe it was just grown-up stuff they wanted to keep private."

"Hmm. Perhaps. Over the next few weeks I hung around Station Road on my way home. There was sweet shop on the corner and I'd take my time choosing a ten-penny mix-up each day. I liked listening to the chat. One day a woman left her purse on the counter. The shopkeeper, said, 'Run after her. Catch her up and say I've got her purse. Her name's Dorothy.'

"I caught her up just as she reached a white gate – the same one I'd seen Dad come out of. I walked back to the shop with her but she didn't speak. The shopkeeper gave me a stick of liquorice but there wasn't even a thank you from Dorothy."

Marnie kept quiet, remembering the joys of a ten-penny mix-up. There'd been few of those for her, as a child.

"And another thing," Belinda was winding down now, "Mum and Dad don't live anywhere near Station Road, but every so often I see *her* walking past their bungalow. Never speaks. Always looks the other way."

"Maybe she's visiting."

"Hmm." Her gut feeling persisted, but maybe it was time to give the old woman the benefit of the doubt. It would be a shame to spoil the holiday with negative thoughts. After all, Belinda herself had displayed the poster in the library for others to see. *Some yoga this evening,* she decided, as she returned the mugs to the pavilion.

*

At the end of the day, Marnie, unlicensed and unconcerned, followed in a tired, borrowed grey Nissan as Belinda drove back to Hepworth House, wondering if they'd meet up with Bud this evening, and what Marnie would make of him if they did.

Avoiding his eyes, she introduced the new guest to Ron, picked up her room key and left them to it. There were two hours before dinner, in which she would do nothing but soak in scented water, snooze and think positive thoughts about Dorothy.

For fifteen minutes she emptied her mind, drifting towards sleep despite the cooling bath. She hooked her foot around the plug chain and tugged, lying there until only the bubbles were left. She had not yet reached the 'understanding Dorothy' phase.

Her phone rang as she stooped to dry her toes. It was Melanie: according to the hygienist, she needed to buy some tiny brushes to clean between her teeth in order to prevent gum disease. The mention of the word *disease* had spooked the girl. Convinced that she would lose her teeth like Granddad and need recourse to dentures within the year, Belinda's daughter was close to tears. Grotesque images of naked gums and false teeth in a glass on her bedside table filled her imagination. *How would she ever get a boyfriend now?*

Belinda made reassuring noises and managed to convince her daughter that the problem would wait a few days. Then, certainly, they would seek out and purchase the recommended product. After a quick word with her mother, she ended the call and lay on the bed.

In vain she tried to recapture the tranquillity. What was she doing here when she ought to be at home, safeguarding her daughter's oral health? Why had she not phoned Doug? Why had neither he nor Aidan bothered to ring her?

She had to face up to last night's 'adventure'. There would have been no remorse if it had actually been Bud's car she'd decorated. He was a double-crossing, bald-headed rat, despite Marnie's comments. But it hadn't been his car, had it? The 4WD didn't even belong to Gordon and Sheila, but to their son. And because of what she, Belinda, had done, the anniversary of their wedding was turning into its funeral. Should she do something... or nothing?

Who could say what Ron and Blondie might throw into the mix if she started stirring? It was best just to wait and see.

*

It had been arranged that the two women would share a table at dinner, so when Bel entered the dining room at seven she was surprised to see Marnie seated at a table for four. Alongside her sat Bud Baxter. Each looked relaxed and happy as they chatted to a third person at the table.

She was disconcerted, but sat in the spare seat, smiling weakly. She would have to be polite to the *pilgarlic* in front of the new chap. He too was tall and thickset, though he had more hair on his head than Bud: a bushy rim of faded auburn curled round his ears, growing forward onto his cheeks as impressive ginger sideburns.

Very seventies.

It was explained that the other man was Bud's brother, who'd come over from the coast for the funeral and was staying around a day or two longer to help with the legal stuff. He was at Hepworth House for dinner and a chat with his brother. Bel tried to look nonchalant. *How much does he know?*

She was desperate to avoid a conversation with Bud but needed food. He returned her smile faintly. She felt embarrassed. She tugged at her skirt and fiddled with her earrings; rummaged in her handbag for a tissue and checked her phone for no reason.

Marnie was looking less tarty than usual, in a blue smock dress of floaty blue printed muslin. *Very seventies*, Bel thought again. She was slim enough not to look pregnant in such a dress. In fact, everything about Marnie looked different: softer, gentler, happier than when they'd first met. As she exchanged banter with the men, Bel began to understand how the woman attracted men without effort, never mind her status or situation. How natural, then, that she should seek to please them in ways that kept a roof over her head.

Belinda didn't feel much like talking. It was all too awkward. Not until they were on the dessert did Bud speak directly to her.

"Marnie was telling us about your village hall, before you came down. It sounded quite interesting."

He was clearly trying to make up for his rudeness the other night. How could anyone possibly find Sallby Village Hall interesting? He needn't think he could win her round so easily.

"Anything but!"

"Why get involved if you don't like it?"

"Well, someone has to." She sounded prim, snooty. *Invaded. The village hall was her domain. It was not up for discussion with these… these… ne'er-do-wells.*

Bud's brother, Miles, piped up, "There have been some very interesting studies on the importance of village halls in maintaining services in rural areas."

We seem to have an expert in the room!

He went on, "With the new emphasis on the Big Society, government is looking at ways of supporting these volunteer-led facilities without taking them out of the hands of the community. There's been too much Big Government over the past two decades. Now it's all about handing power back to the community."

Who was this guy? She didn't want any more power, thanks. What outsiders saw as power was actually *responsibility. Less of that would be welcome, not more.*

This bloke was a prat who didn't know what he was talking about, but now was not the time to tell him. She repeated her weak smile.

"You seem to know a lot about it," she said without enthusiasm, as she lifted the last spoonful of raspberry pavlova to her lips.

"I'm on a parliamentary subcommittee looking at the rural economy," he replied, as if she ought to have known that. Bel looked up, only slightly more interested. Was this another fantasist?

Bud interjected quietly, "Miles is a Member of Parliament."

Bel was stunned.

"Miles Baxter-Hatton, MP for Uttering South." He rose slightly and reached his hand across the table in a formal handshake.

Belinda found herself rising from her own chair as she took the hand and almost bobbed a curtsey.

"He's my half-brother," muttered Bud.

"Daryl's mother was Dad's first wife," Miles smiled. "He soon realised that she was 'not a keeper' and took up with Amelia, my mother."

Bud was not smiling. "They were divorced by the time Miles was seven, but Amelia made another good marriage." His voice was tinged with resentment.

"Yes, Mother is still alive and living in Harrogate, quite comfortably, with her second husband, Edward Hatton, who played the father's role in my life."

Belinda was trying to take this all in. She felt instinctively that she wouldn't like Amelia.

She felt sorry for Bud, protective almost. No wonder he'd wanted a mother like her, someone normal.

Daryl/Bud spoke up. "Our dad was a charmer. He could charm the birds from the trees, but he had a hard upbringing and not much schooling. Managed to get by without, mind, because people believed in him. He had kind eyes, but there was only so much kindness in his heart."

This was the most thoughtful thing Belinda had heard him say. Both sons had in some way taken after him; each had a warm expression. Even Bud must have displayed some charm to convince her that a second drink had been permissible the other evening. Only when he was drunk and crying had he become a slob. And give him his due, he *had* been crying for his dead father, no matter how tough his childhood had been.

Miles was speaking again. "The way forward is about rolling back the state. Letting people take charge of their own destinies and communities. That's why we're encouraging volunteerism. There's been too much nannying from the state. People have the right to stand on their own two feet and regain self-esteem. Communities are longing to come together, decide what they want in their area and make it happen."

Bel noticed that the other diners had gone silent. Political speeches were not often heard in Hepworth House.

"Take the Yorkshire Sculpture Park." He warmed to his theme as on the hustings. "If the community wants to change it, there should be nothing standing in the way. Community needs should not be restricted by Arts Council diktat about what constitutes art. They could display artwork produced by schoolchildren and pensioners, the local painting classes and photography clubs if art was what they still wanted. The whole place could be run by volunteers, if only they were organised enough. They could even sell off some of the land to developers, to build local homes for local people. The place would become a truly local facility, run *by* locals *for* locals, what we in government call the Localism Agenda. This would free up valuable funds, enabling Arts resources to be directed towards the cultural centres, where visitors want to be."

Ron broke in. "Local people round here have got homes already. It's selling them that they have trouble with nowadays."

Bel was reminded of Candy Dunne, whose home had been on the market since soon after young Job's party.

"What cultural centres? What visitors?"

Miles sailed on without answering.

"To be of economic value to the nation, the greatest works of art must be easily accessible to overseas visitors. Those visitors almost all arrive via Heathrow. Hence, the art and culture of the nation needs to be co-located in the south of England, within an hour's travel of Heathrow. Think of the jobs created. Think of the income generated. Overseas visitors bring money and they're prepared to pay high prices for British culture. Think of the lure of London's bright lights, the royal parks and historic buildings. Add to that the entirety of Britain's most precious and challenging works of art, and we would create a world treasure. The wasteful policy of free museums and art galleries for the masses would be a thing of the past."

"But what about the people here? What about all the money spent on the new galleries and restoring the parkland? That would all have been wasted." This was Marnie.

"Not at all. We'd be giving this wonderful resource back to the community, as I said. It would be theirs to maintain and use as they saw fit. If they wanted to use the buildings, say, as a hostel for the homeless, government would not stop them."

Miles had indeed made an impression. The room was quiet. The single spat whisper,

"Prick!" hissed out. Everyone stared at their plates, silently concurring.

The noise of cutlery chinking against china bowls resumed, and forced, inconsequential chat shielded the diners from their embarrassment. More than embarrassment: it was fury.

Bel was sorry she'd returned the chisel to the pavilion. Half of her wanted to tell Miles that she and Marnie were 'visitors' to the cultural hub of the YSP, who were spending their money there and thus supporting the local economy. She herself had bought half a dozen postcards and stamps, plus several drinks and sandwiches in the café. She wanted to ask where these volunteers would come from and why they wouldn't be at work, now that no-one was expected to retire at sixty-five but to work until they dropped?

The other half of her wanted to sink a chisel in his skull.

This man had given up living in the real world. *How long had he ever lived in it?* she wondered. Was Edward Hatton a more desirable role model than Al because he was a good father, or had young Miles been brought up and educated amongst the privileged classes to ensure that he lost track of his roots?

After coffee, she had no polite reason not to cross the hall to the sitting room. Ron came through from the kitchen and took up position behind the kitsch little bar, eyes narrowed above gritted teeth.

Miles found the set-up rather quaint and did his best not to patronise; his best was poor. The MP's most outstanding feature was his voice. He knew this, and loved its sound, imagining that his audience was equally smitten.

Touching on a range of political topics, he lectured Bud, Belinda and Marnie through two rounds of drinks. No other guests joined them. From time to time Ron moved back into the kitchen, where Maureen's nephew and his pal were enjoying the leftovers of that evening's boeuf bourguignon. After an hour, Miles returned to the theme of volunteering, and village halls in particular.

Bud seemed to have shrunk, somehow. Recalling coyly how she had first thought him a hunk, Bel saw now that he was just a bald, middle-aged chap with not much to say for himself. For all the brothers' parity in height and build, Miles appeared the larger man.

When at last he paused for breath, Bel got up to visit the Ladies'. Ron intercepted her in the hallway.

"The police did call round this afternoon," he said quietly.

Her heart jumped in her chest.

"And…?"

"They were quite impressed." He grinned. "Took lots of photos and had a bit of a laugh about it. Went off to look up that word up on the internet." He looked her in the eye, raising one eyebrow.

"What about the old couple?"

"Sheila calmed down eventually after she'd spoken to their son. He told them to hire a car for the rest of the week so I got on the blower and sorted out a Corsa for them. Rentamotor delivered it around lunchtime, so they were able to get off on their trip. Gordon was relieved to be driving a car like his own, so they went off quite happily."

Bel breathed more slowly now, regretting the upset she'd caused.

"And did the police find any clues?"

"A couple of tab ends in the car park but they weren't near the 4x4. They asked which guests were smokers, but of course, I don't know that. This is a non-smoking building. Those fag ends could have been left by anyone – the window-cleaner, even."

Their eyes met, both faces deadpan.

Ron held in his hand a business card. Hearing the handle of the lounge door turning, he quickly dropped it into Belinda's palm, signalling that this was private. She closed her fingers and turned away as Miles came through the door.

"Aha, caught you at it! In flagrante!" he jested loudly. "And what are you two talking about?"

"Only the unfortunate vandalism that occurred here this morning."

Leaving Ron to explain the rest, Belinda moved along the corridor to read the card. On a background of vibrant stripes were the words: *Bronte FM, your local news and music station*, followed by email and website addresses. There was also a phone number.

Puzzled, she tucked it in her purse.

Back in the lounge, Miles was giving the low-down on the morning's events to Marnie and his brother as if he had witnessed them himself. Bud had already set off for the bus stop when the crime was discovered. Marnie kept quiet. The defaced car was still on the drive, so the three of them went outside, briefly, to inspect the damage by the light of Miles's keyring torch.

Back in the bar, Marnie and Bud were even quieter than before. For him, one or two things had fallen into place. The window of his room overlooked the bed of laurels beside the silver car's parking spot; he had lain awake, unable to sleep, listening to the exchange of hoots and wheezes between two owls. He recalled a vague sense of the sound of movement on the gravel and a soft, intermittent scraping that he couldn't identify. He hadn't bothered to get out of bed to look and was soon asleep again.

"Ah yes, *The Pilgarlic*!" Miles declaimed. "Came third in the1980 Grand National! I was just a lad at the time but I was there at Aintree, with Mother and Edward. Stood me in good stead, too. I had it as a nine-letter word when I appeared on *Countdown* some years ago. It clinched victory for me."

"Never heard it before," said Marnie.

"Ah yes. It's archaic of course – meaning bald-headed, or alternatively a *worthless fellow/ a poor creature*. But it proves two things: one, the perpetrator is a betting man, and two, he is not young. Maybe also he is a *Countdown* aficionado who recalls my contribution. But it was his victim he labelled a *pilgarlic*. Ergo, the victim must be thin on top."

'Ergo'?

Miles looked around him. His brother was shaven-headed; Ron had a silver comb-over Brylcreemed down over a freckled scalp. His own wiry locks surrounded a pate as slick as a domed skating rink. "What about the old chap?"

The others tried to remember, but Gordon had not struck a memorable figure. Between them, eventually they put together an identikit description of a small, bespectacled septuagenarian with thick hair of steely grey covering most of his head. There was a round hole in the centre like a comic-book monk's, but he wasn't really bald.

"No, but bald enough, and a miserable creature, by your description." Miles clearly wanted to take the reins of this investigation. Marnie had been very quiet, with a sense of doom that was familiar. Trouble had always followed her, but when she'd decided to spend the remainder of her savings on a couple of nights at Hepworth House, she was aiming to build a moat around her precious time away from real life. Yet as usual, Trouble had crept unnoticed into her suitcase and come along for the ride. And this Miles chap really got on her nerves.

She looked at Bel. "Whoever is responsible for the graffiti knew what they were doing. As a piece of art which carries a message, it's quite effective." Her eyes glinted. "And it must have been someone educated, to use a word like that. I've never heard it before. Have you?"

"It rings a bell," Belinda smiled. "I probably saw Miles on *Countdown*. I used to watch it every afternoon when I worked mornings." She struggled not to smile.

The chat was interrupted by the clang of the old-fashioned brass doorbell hanging from a bracket outside. Seconds later, two police officers walked in, wearing full kit. One was talking into his radio.

"Don't bother getting up. We'd just like a word with you, if you don't mind," said the other.

Miles stood to introduce himself, volunteering his own opinion on the crime.

"Thank you, sir, but we'll do the investigating if you don't mind. Now, can I take your names and addresses?"

One by one the group gave their details, some with more misgivings than others. The officers asked the whereabouts of each guest the previous night. There was no way of corroborating Bel's or Bud's statements that each was in their own bed and heard nothing. Marnie had stayed in her bedsit on the outskirts of the city. Miles had been 'at a friend's'.

"Can you give us the name and address of this...'friend', sir?"

"No I can't. I don't intend to drag anyone else into this. A man in my position has to be beyond reproach and you have my word that I was there all night."

"Indeed, sir. Beyond reproach," repeated the officer slowly, scratching his ear. Against Miles's name, he wrote in his notebook: *Declined to give whereabouts.*

Without a pause, the second police officer took over. "Any of you know the word *pilgarlic*?" He looked benignly round the group. All eyes turned to Miles.

"Well of course," he blustered. "Any racing man will have heard of it. Third place in the 1980 Grand National."

Rocking back on his heels and flexing his knees slightly in stereotypical plod style, PC Pete Manton gave a small cough.

"Archaic: meaning – a bald-headed man; a miserable creature." He looked handsomely around the assembled company while ruffling his own thick blond hair.

After a few more questions, the two officers left the room to speak to the lady of the house, returning ten minutes later.

The taller one asked to speak to Miles in the hallway. Miles agreed with alacrity, certain that the plods wanted to pick his pretty special brain to aid their investigation. They even asked him to come down to the station with them to assist with their enquiries.

"As you seem familiar with the word *pilgarlic*, sir, and with your well-known interest in policing, it could be beneficial all round. You might be able to shed some light on the situation... able to spot something we've missed."

One of Miles's pet themes was the fight against crime, it was true. He supposed it was his duty, as an elected member, to assist the law enforcement agencies in any way possible. It would be interesting, at any rate, and no doubt get some positive coverage in the press, so he acquiesced with a show of reluctance.

Pete Manton's colleague Dale started the car, then remembered something.

"I left my notebook in the kitchen when I was speaking to the lady of the house. I'll just pop back." He strode round to the back door, out of sight, walked in without knocking and winked at his Uncle Ron.

"Thanks for the beef, Aunty Maureen," he said. "We'll just give this bloke a little ride. Seems a right tosser. S'been a quiet night so far." He retrieved the notebook from the dresser and disappeared with a wave.

Back in the lounge, Ron told the group that the other gentleman had been called away suddenly. As Bel got up to leave, he followed her out and lingered in the hall.

"That card," he murmured. "Local radio always welcomes snippets of news."

She looked puzzled.

"You know, such as 'County MP taken in for questioning ... criminal damage...' Get my drift?"

He turned away, leaving her to ponder his meaning as she climbed the stairs.

She undressed and set a bath to run as she did her exercises. No need for the malevolent mantras tonight. There was no doubt in her mind that Miles was an obnoxious Hooray Henry who needed bringing down a peg or two, and on the dressing table rested her means of making that happen. There was a brief demur as the memory of Candy Dunne's hearing affliction flitted through her mind, and then of the mistaken identity of the car's owner... and maybe Bud hadn't deserved it after all... but in all honesty, she knew she *had* to do it.

Naked by the side of the steaming, scented bath, she took her phone and adjusted the setting to *Number Withheld*. She pressed the digits with the thumb of her right hand, not taking too much time in scripting her speech.

It was soon answered.

"Bronte FM."

"I have some breaking news. The Member of Parliament for a constituency in this county is helping police with their enquiries into criminal damage to a vehicle parked on private land. He was visiting Bronte FM's coverage area for family reasons. The MP in question is an outspoken critic of what he sees as ineffective policing and lenient sentencing by the courts."

Questions followed.

"Check it out," was her only reply.

Putting down the phone, she stretched out in the foaming bath and drifted into a reverie. Miles Baxter-Hatton: sorted. Comeuppance: delivered. A smile settled on her lips as her muscles relaxed until she was close to sleep. Thirty minutes later she stirred enough to climb out, wrap herself in a towel and fall across the bed, totally soothed and at one with herself.

*

61

Miles did not sit comfortably in the back of the police Range Rover, although the officers took him on a scenic tour of the country lanes of the county's more westerly environs, all the while lamenting the darkness that prevented their passenger enjoying the best that rural England could offer. He noticed the road was gaining altitude. Pete explained that the Farm Watch squad had reported some suspicious low-loader activity in the vicinity of a tractor shed, so a detour round a few moorland lanes might just be worthwhile. Miles's impatience to reach police headquarters and share his wisdom was quite understandable, the officers agreed, but these rural areas were hotspots for large-scale poaching and farm-vehicle theft. It would be more than their jobs were worth not to visit a few of the remoter agricultural buildings, since they were so close.

The rutted tracks, potholes and forded streams were beginning to bring on Miles's motion sickness, and he found it difficult to make sense of the chatter back and forth over the radio. Pete had reported in that they were bringing in a witness for further information, and would be back at HQ as soon as convenient, but an hour had elapsed since then. Dale once more tried to elicit Miles's whereabouts on the night of the crime.

"I told you. I stayed with a friend."

"You're a lucky man, Miles. It's a lucky man who has friends he can lean on...in times of trouble, I mean." He paused, thinking. "Known him long?"

"Yes. We were at school together."

"What school would that be, sir? Not one round here, I don't suppose..."

Miles named a famous public school in the West Midlands.

"A boarder were you, Miles?" Was that a snigger coming from the front seat?

"This friend: was he in the same year as you?"

"No. Somewhat younger."

"Your fag, was he... sir? Ever read Roald Dahl on the subject of his public school days?"

Miles couldn't say he had. (Dale had enjoyed the writer's account of his boyhood when Miss Clements read to them every Friday afternoon in Year 8, although it's possible that his enjoyment had been intensified by the young teacher's warm eyes and short skirts.)

"About this *pilgarlic*, sir. When did you first hear the word?"

"I told you. It was a racehorse – won the Grand National in 1980."

"You must only have been a lad then, Mr Haxter-Batton."

"Baxter-Hatton. Yes, I was."

"Strange that you can remember something like that from your childhood."

"As I said earlier, I had the opportunity to use it on *Countdown* when I appeared. Got right to the final but was beaten by *innuendo*."

"And who was making the innuendo, sir?" The constable concealed a smirk.

"No, no. You misunderstand. Anyway, are we nearly there yet?" He was getting tired of all this. His opinion of the police was sinking even lower. "I don't have time for idle chat about racehorses. I think I've given you enough of my time and now I really must insist you let me out of this car."

"What, here, Miles? Miles from anywhere?" Both officers guffawed at the pun.

"I'll call a cab."

"Not many cabs round here. Doubt you'd get one to come up onto the moors, a lonely spot like this, on a Friday midnight. Not unless it was pre-booked and with a definite address."

This was Dale.

The radio came alive again, this time to pass on intelligence from the police chopper. A low-loader had again been spotted, moving suspiciously along a narrow lane in the direction of another tractor shed. The team, who unbeknown to Miles had been driving in circles never more than five miles from Hepworth House, decided this was more important than the MP's intelligence.

"Sorry, sir," said Dale. "I think this *pilgarlic* business will have to wait. We're needed to prevent a crime. We'll drop you off at Hepworth House and see if we can catch this low-loader."

They were there in minutes.

Stiff and pale, Miles swayed as he stood on the verge and watched the Range Rover disappear. He relieved himself among the laurels, took his keys from his jacket pocket and vomited over his shoes. He had never been able to travel in the back of a car.

*

Next morning, in the dining room a small digital radio on the sideboard was playing popular music from the past few decades: easy listening, mostly. At 8am, the DJ interrupted the music with a time check and a reminder that listeners were tuned to Bronte FM, bringing them local news from coast to dales. This was Bob Oglethorpe bringing the latest stories from round and about.

There was concern about the level of unemployment throughout the region, and an interview with someone from Jobcentre Plus. Next came bad news about the closure of a glass factory, once predicted of being capable of sustaining the local jobs market for generations to come but closed down within a decade. The third item cut through the muted conversations.

"Reports are coming in that one of the region's up-and-coming Members of Parliament, Miles Baxter-Hatton, was last night one of several people questioned by police. It is not clear at this stage whether an arrest was made. Details of the circumstances surrounding the case are sketchy, but reports from those close to the scene suggest an act of serious criminal damage was involved. It is believed that the MP, who represents the Uttering South constituency on the coast, was visiting the Dales area on family business. We'll bring you more on this as it comes in."

Neither Marnie nor Bel heard the rest of the news. Bel was stunned into silence. But what had she expected? She avoided Marnie's eyes.

"Well, that's a turn-up for the books! Wonder how they found out."

"Mm. Don't know."

Bel's tone aroused the other's curiosity. "You know something, don't you?"

"Least said, soonest mended."

"Was it you? I know he was a right pillock, but... It *was* you!" She lowered her voice but couldn't suppress the laughter. "I were expecting a nice quiet few days among refined people... the sort I never get to meet as a rule. Instead, I've got tangled up with some madwoman determined to cause trouble."

"I'm not mad," shushed Bel. "Just shaking off the shackles of domesticity."

Though the thought was new to her, the words rang true, and the room was filled with their laughter. They laughed till they could taste their own tears.

*

On this penultimate day of the course, the sculptors focused on their work. The vague ideas they'd arrived with had either taken shape or been abandoned. For many, the joy had been in the peace and liberty to create; for others the satisfaction was physical. One or two had glimpsed possibilities for an artistic future.

Ambrose was playing a stronger role now: he knew when to suggest, when to back off, and when to step in with a decisive stroke of the grinder or chainsaw. His manner never changed – the man of wood in both senses of the word.

He sat with Marnie on a log, smoking a roll-up (as usual of Marnie's making and provision), contemplating her swaddled abstract and calling it a beautiful thing. She tried to conceal the elation she felt at his response: to think that she had created something beautiful filled her heart with a new gladness. They were easy company, recognising in each other a coasting attitude to life, a resistance to set boundaries and routines. Both were lackadaisical followers of ideas and dreams: neither had a regular income; each relied on happenstance to get by. For Ambrose, happenstance had brought some big breaks and valuable commissions. When these ran dry, he relied on a bit of craft teaching to adult learners and, when times got really tough, he'd do anything the job centre could find him. For Ambrose, life was about his art and whatever turned up.

For Marnie there had been no high-end commissions. As a younger woman her face and figure made her a popular photographic model for some seedier publications, which did not pay well. A one-time erotic dancer, waitress, hostess in the city clubs and, for short periods, she'd been a kept woman. These relationships had never lasted, being based on convenience rather than affection, and never on love. She worried, sometimes, about coping in old age if she survived long enough, having rarely paid National Insurance. It was likely she would live in penury and die young. A few times, money had been so tight that she'd had to go on the streets. This neither horrified nor pleased her: it was a necessity to be dealt with, in the same emotionless way she had learnt to do everything else since her mother's liaison with Joe of the paedophiliac tendencies.

Yet Marnie knew she had much more to give and to receive. When she allowed herself to look into her heart, she imagined a caged starling yearning for the open sky, yearning to swoop and swirl in synchronicity with the myriad flock, to create that fluid, marvellous, mysterious beauty, acting as one with its fellows. Marnie longed to be one of the crowd, but the crowd always seemed to be in a place that Marnie could not reach.

Ambrose rolled another Rizla as they touched on these things, languidly, neither wanting this pressureless week to end. Marnie spoke of the difference between her life and Bel's; how she envied the other's home, family and sense of duty. Marnie had never felt the call of duty – she had no one to feel dutiful towards – but felt the capacity was within her. She wanted to belong. To be needed.

They discussed their habits when no-one else was nearby, acknowledging the range of substances that could be sampled within the Rizlas. Neither had a compulsive habit, but nor were they strangers to the softer drugs. They had both been lucky enough to grow up and move on before addiction conquered sense.

At dinner that evening, Ron served the celery soup in sombre mood. Calling their Pete's mobile had been a bit of a lark at the time, but his wife's nephew seemed to think that the MP might want an investigation into why he was questioned and how the local radio station had got hold of the news. Worry about Pete's career and his own reputation blunted the satisfaction he'd felt about bringing the pompous git down a peg or two. Belinda had also come down from her high and dreaded the possible repercussions of her actions. Marnie had had enough of the madness for now. She steered Bel's thoughts towards home, asking more about the Lowe family members. She wanted to learn what a normal, average family was like.

Over coffee in the lounge they chatted comfortably, defences down. Bel told of how she dreaded an empty nest once the children had flown, of her daughter's over-sensitivity and desire to be a physiotherapist ever since she had broken her leg as a youngster. She spoke of Aidan's love of the outdoors and rock climbing, and what fear she felt when he was up on the crags with his mates, even though she believed him to be a sensible lad. With greater dread, she dwelt on Mum's precarious state of mind and how, in spite of Dad's blind devotion to his wife, she was convinced that the marriage was a sham, because of Dorothy. Falling silent, Bel realised that her heart was pounding with fear. Her eyes were moist with unfallen tears. There would be so much loss to endure in the coming years. And she was no closer to knowing what to do about her father's other woman.

Seeing the clouded eyes, Marnie regretted making her confront the future. Like herself, Belinda had come away for respite, and there was one more day of it ahead. As a diversionary tactic she ventured,

"Tell me more about your village hall."

Another bag of tucked-away concerns was unzipped: the state of the wiring – who knew how old it was? How to find the money to have it updated? The constant pressure to find regular hirers who not only left the place clean and tidy but also paid up on time; of who would take over her role if she fell ill or just packed it all in. How important it was to her not to be the last of the long line of volunteers who had kept the hall going since the second decade of the twentieth century.

"Once you're back at home, Bel, may I come over some time and have a look at it? Maybe I can come up with some ideas." Marnie's mind had been working.

Bel raised her eyebrows quizzically. "Are you thinking of setting up a business?"

"No, no. I don't want to go inside ever again. But I know a lot of people in the leisure and entertainment business and

d visit Bel some time, take a look at what made *her* tick.
surprised them that their paths had never crossed before,
erating as they did in that mid-world of society that moves
st above the illegal and just below the socially acceptable.

Certain names, places and characters were known to both
them, if only by repute. It wouldn't be difficult to maintain
e connection. Each had found a new friend, in a world where
endships were scarce.

Bud had more work to do clearing out his father's OAP
ngalow before the council repossessed it on Monday. The
gal stuff would be taken care of by little brother. It wasn't
ely that Dad had left any money above the few pounds in
trouser pocket when he died, so whatever Miles did about
e will, or lack of one, it wouldn't affect Bud. It was his
her's personal effects that bothered him more. Bud was too
ntimental to bin them all, as Miles had suggested. On the
her hand, he was unlikely to make use of anything, though
would keep the photo albums.

Taking the scraps of furniture and clothing away by bus
s out of the question; it was agreed that Marnie would drive
d and Al's belongings back to his lodgings in the city, only
o or three miles from her own bedsit.

*

nday came: the final day. Belinda's spirits were low. The
e had gone even faster than she could have imagined. She
d fluttered the wings of independence and caused some
bulence, but had not yet had the chance to soar. That it
uld come, she had no doubt.

Her day was spent soothing and smoothing her snail. She
d grown to love it; almost dared to believe that it might look
d in the tidy back garden at home and be sturdy enough to
rk as a stool; ideal for watching the birds build their nests

72

it might help to get ideas from a different perspective. I expect
a village only needs one or two keep fit and dancing classes.
Maybe there are ways you could branch out. And you're only
fifteen miles from the city, which isn't that far."

They tapped each other's numbers into their phones. Bel
needed sleep: criminality was an exhausting business, she
realised. Bidding goodnight, she left Marnie alone in the
room. With closed eyes, Marnie sank back into the soft, floral
cushions. She liked it here and wished she could afford to stay
longer. OK, so it wasn't the Ritz, but it smelt good; it was
clean and comfy and homely. The food was decent, the people
friendly. What more could anyone ask for?

She too faced the future with dread, but her dread was of
not being able to afford the rent on her bedsit, and of what she
might need to do to find it. Things were getting tougher all
round, but Marnie had glimpsed something better and, eyes
closed, she let her mind play on ways she might make it her
own.

The door opened quietly. Soft footsteps trod the carpet.
Thinking that Bel had come back, she murmured, "Forgotten
something?" without opening her eyes.

She heard the squish of cushions close by, peeped, and saw
Bud sinking into the armchair on her left. She thought about
rousing herself. It was their first meeting since Miles's exit
with the police.

Unaware that he was being watched, Bud stretched out and
closed his eyes. A tear gathered at the corner of his eye. For all
his hunky-thug appearance, Daryl was a sensitive man, prone
to melancholy even in better times. One of the few permanent
features of his life had gone. Although the marriage of his
parents had been short, Al had been a constant presence,
sometimes at a distance but oft-times close at hand when
trouble called. He had tried to do right by the only son he was
allowed more than perfunctory access to. After the mistake of

69

it might help to get ideas from a different perspective. I expect a village only needs one or two keep fit and dancing classes. Maybe there are ways you could branch out. And you're only fifteen miles from the city, which isn't that far."

They tapped each other's numbers into their phones. Bel needed sleep: criminality was an exhausting business, she realised. Bidding goodnight, she left Marnie alone in the room. With closed eyes, Marnie sank back into the soft, floral cushions. She liked it here and wished she could afford to stay longer. OK, so it wasn't the Ritz, but it smelt good; it was clean and comfy and homely. The food was decent, the people friendly. What more could anyone ask for?

She too faced the future with dread, but her dread was of not being able to afford the rent on her bedsit, and of what she might need to do to find it. Things were getting tougher all round, but Marnie had glimpsed something better and, eyes closed, she let her mind play on ways she might make it her own.

The door opened quietly. Soft footsteps trod the carpet. Thinking that Bel had come back, she murmured, "Forgotten something?" without opening her eyes.

She heard the squish of cushions close by, peeped, and saw Bud sinking into the armchair on her left. She thought about rousing herself. It was their first meeting since Miles's exit with the police.

Unaware that he was being watched, Bud stretched out and closed his eyes. A tear gathered at the corner of his eye. For all his hunky-thug appearance, Daryl was a sensitive man, prone to melancholy even in better times. One of the few permanent features of his life had gone. Although the marriage of his parents had been short, Al had been a constant presence, sometimes at a distance but oft-times close at hand when trouble called. He had tried to do right by the only son he was allowed more than perfunctory access to. After the mistake of his first marriage and Amelia's urge to rise up the matrimonial ladder to a more prosperous status, he had become dour and ungiving. Two failed marriages promised a lonely old age, but by keeping faith with Daryl he had maintained the emotional insurance payments.

For Bud, three legal stepfathers had come and gone, plus countless casuals. From his mother he had inherited a restless spirit, but he lacked her recklessness and needed some stability in the background of his life, and Al had been its only source. For that, if for no other reason, Daryl was bereft. The meeting with Miles the other night had only emphasised the loss.

At their father's insistence, the half-brothers had met on an annual basis throughout their childhoods – blood being thicker than water was one of his maxims. The meetings had never been welcomed by Amelia, Edward or Miles but each year, on his birthday, Al had arranged a day out for the three of them. When the boys were younger, they might go to a theme park, bowling alley or ice rink, always followed by a pricey meal. By the time they were both adults, this had mostly reduced to just the meal. Since Miles's election to represent the Uttering South constituency, Bud and Al had travelled to London, to be granted a lightning tour of the House of Commons or some other sightseers' haunt, followed by a very rushed but exotic and expensive sandwich at a backstreet gastro-pub somewhere near Parliament Square.

By the time of his death, Al could not recall how he had come to fall in love with Betsy in the first place. In those heady sixties days, free love had just been invented. Although the newsreels simultaneously celebrated and condemned the new libertarianism, for Al and Betsy, as for so many others, the much-vaunted sexual freedom had led straight to matrimonial imprisonment and the shackles of teenage parenthood.

Bud mused on all this, wishing someone would offer him a little comfort. He did not think of Marnie as a possible source.

Although he'd warmed to her, there was no physical attraction. The memory of his trip along the corridor to Belinda's room that first night was blurred, and he was unaware of the loss of his scant dignity. She was definitely fanciable, but maybe the motherly air was the attraction. Anyway, she was married, and he was no Edward Hatton-style marriage-wrecker. As if she'd be interested, anyway... No, he'd reached the age of forty-one without a steady girlfriend and looked likely to stay that way.

Marnie opened her eyes and saw his sorrow.

"Want to talk?" she asked.

Bud gave a watery smile.

"Nah. Not really. Just like to wallow in a bit of self-pity now and then."

"Don't we all?"

Slowly, a conversation of sorts began. They each struggled to express the cause of their own self-pity, although the common links between them gave understanding beyond words. Gradually, what emerged was a longing to be like other people, people with homes and partners and children, even with all the ups and downs that would inevitably come too. Each knew, instinctively, that the other party in this conversation was not the one to deliver the goods. Each needed someone more committed and stable, someone with the stamina to help them change.

"Someone like Belinda," Marnie suggested, "for you. For me, maybe someone like her Doug, though I've never met him. Bel seems to find him boring, but I'd settle for boring any day."

They agreed that they must look further afield for love and boredom.

Talk turned to Belinda's life and preoccupations, which were foreign lands to Bud and Marnie. Bud had never even been into a village hall, being an urbanite through and through, while Marnie skated swiftly over her own experiences in such facilities. Between them, they made a vague pact to meet up and visit Bel some time, take a look at what made *her* tick. It surprised them that their paths had never crossed before, operating as they did in that mid-world of society that moves just above the illegal and just below the socially acceptable.

Certain names, places and characters were known to both of them, if only by repute. It wouldn't be difficult to maintain the connection. Each had found a new friend, in a world where friendships were scarce.

Bud had more work to do clearing out his father's OAP bungalow before the council repossessed it on Monday. The legal stuff would be taken care of by little brother. It wasn't likely that Dad had left any money above the few pounds in his trouser pocket when he died, so whatever Miles did about the will, or lack of one, it wouldn't affect Bud. It was his father's personal effects that bothered him more. Bud was too sentimental to bin them all, as Miles had suggested. On the other hand, he was unlikely to make use of anything, though he would keep the photo albums.

Taking the scraps of furniture and clothing away by bus was out of the question; it was agreed that Marnie would drive Bud and Al's belongings back to his lodgings in the city, only two or three miles from her own bedsit.

*

Sunday came: the final day. Belinda's spirits were low. The time had gone even faster than she could have imagined. She had fluttered the wings of independence and caused some turbulence, but had not yet had the chance to soar. That it would come, she had no doubt.

Her day was spent soothing and smoothing her snail. She had grown to love it; almost dared to believe that it might look good in the tidy back garden at home and be sturdy enough to work as a stool; ideal for watching the birds build their nests in springtime. What would Doug think of it? For him to call it rubbish would be devastating; even worse, he might mock.

As the day slunk towards its close, adjustments and finishing touches were made to the artworks. Reluctant to leave this oasis, the sculptors hung around in small groups admiring one another's work, eventually huffing and puffing their creations into the boots of cars, where they were wrapped, propped, wedged, protected as preciously as new-born babes. Awkward glances encompassed those remaining, quick waves, and one by one they were gone.

Bel and Marnie lingered, not wanting it to end, although Ambrose was clearly anxious to see them off the premises. He shook hands with Bel and waved her off. As she pulled away, reflected in her wing mirror she could see he was still in conversation with the other woman. He stretched out his hand and passed something into hers. With her other hand, Marnie was tapping at her phone.

5

Of course Belinda was glad to be home, she supposed, though in reality the time away had been too short for strong emotions. She hadn't been much missed. Melanie's scare had been resolved with a visit to the chemist's shop with Granddad, who purchased a pack of the minute blue inter-dental brushes which could save the girl from a toothless future. Aidan had been climbing during time off from his part-time job at the garden centre.

Doug had some news: in partnership with other local tradesmen, he had landed a contract to renovate a rundown block of flats in a city further north. This would mean working away from home, Monday to Friday, for several months. She could cope with that. He would take the caravan to live in, perhaps sharing with one or two of the other guys to keep costs as low as possible. The money would be good, and with Aidan's exam results only a few days away, his parents could now view the financial future with a little less dread. No parents of their generation had ever dreamed that, in order to take advantage of the higher education their children had been told was their right, they would have to choose between disappointed dreams or nightmarish debt.

The threat to her afternoons at work had receded, for although the council had closed down eight of its sixteen small suburban libraries, Denswick's survived for now. But looming with both threat and promise, like a storm cloud over a desert, was the imminent departure of Belinda's son. (Doug's son too, she reminded herself.) She wished he'd been a school refuser, that she had never nagged him to do his homework, or spent her salary on private tuition when he'd struggled with a particular mathematical concept in Year 10. She almost wished he'd got some local girl pregnant and married her at seventeen, so he would be tied to home and parents for advice and support. She wished these things, but loved too generously to want them in reality.

When they came, the results were better than expected and Aidan's place secured. Bel acted the part of a delighted and proud mother. Inside, she screamed.

Melanie withdrew into adolescent angst. She had never been alive without her brother and did not imagine that she could survive such a change. She watched the heightened activity and preparations with dread, not knowing what it was she feared.

Doug had made a plan for the family to take a weekend away together in the caravan, delivering Aidan, his books and paraphernalia to his university on the Welsh coast at the end of it. Belinda said little, knowing that planning complicated itineraries was Doug's way of coping with difficult situations.

*

One Friday in late September they pulled onto a pitch on a small campsite betwixt sea and mountains. The scale of the vistas made the family's business seem small and timeless, made them aware of their own insignificance in the grand design. With this came a release of pressure. *"As it was in the beginning..."* The words came to Belinda's mind unbidden, from Sunday School days and prayers in assembly, though not many schools had them now. They had given her a sense of a greater power, which was reassuring. *Are we any better off now these things have been lost?* she wondered. *"As it was in the beginning, is now and ever shall be…"* seemed to sum it all up. She must come to terms, silently, with the umbilical severance, as all mothers must.

Behind the caravan was the entrance to a wood; the coolness of its shadows beckoned the family inside. They sauntered leisurely, solemnly, into the gold-glinting emerald light, all aware that this weekend marked the beginning of an ending: the ending of the eighteen years of family since Aidan's birth had created this unit. Even Melanie recognised that she had hatched into an existing nest, built in the childless years of her parents' marriage in preparation for the joys to come. The girl knew that she and her brother *had* brought joy; she knew she was loved without ever having given it thought. She kept pace with her brother and father, as they talked of football and rock climbing and which university clubs the lad would join.

Belinda fell behind, and soon she could no longer hear her family's voices or the snapping of twigs beneath their tread. It seemed that she had been drawn off the path at a predetermined angle, drawn by familiarity, a sense of *déjà vu*, overtaken by calm and ease; a certainty that this was where she was meant to be.

Leaf mould, centuries old, softened tread and clung to boots. Grey-green blocks of worked stone – slate, maybe – ancient, lichen-splashed, leant or stood together like last guests at a wake. Angular gaps, raggedly framed by rotting wood, defined form between saplings; nettles and brambles dropping with moist fruit gleamed blackly where a single ray of sunlight shone through the leaves. Unseen, badgers would stride at twilight over slate slabs patched with moss and sharp wild garlic.

Joy, rushing, kept company with the gushing stream, which leapt and forced its way between a confinement of boulders, before falling free and haphazard to a dark pool. Where shafts of sunlight glinted the surface with topaz, peacock-blue damsel flies hovered, staying or going as they pleased.

Inside the ruins, Bel was consumed by the absence. This was, or had been, or could be, her home. A home it had been once, for sure, before comfort and commercialism had seeped into the pores of the nation.

She dropped to her knees on a mossy slab, smelt the leaf mould. Plucking at the wild garlic, she rubbed its leaves and flower on her hands and face. Eyes closed, her ears tuned to the returning birdsong, sometimes distant, sometimes close by. *What mysteries of birdlife were sung through the canopy above?* she wondered. She longed to take part. To be free as a bird seemed such delight, but was it really like that? Did every hen bird feel the wrench of loss as each chick fledged and flew the nest?

Raising her head, she discerned jerky, spasmodic movement on the bark of a giant conifer. She stiffened, stared, watched, until the shape of a small bird emerged. It was flat to the creviced bark and seemed to be crawling up the trunk. The name *treecreeper* came to her mind – from whence she did not know. The bird reminded her of herself: barely visible in her natural habitat.

She sat on tumbled stone beside a gap which had once been a window, gazing through it, a part of the forestscape, feeling more tranquil than she could remember. Never here before in *this* life, she knew it was her home. From this she absorbed the certainty that we are more than physical beings: that each of us has a soul. Aidan would always be with her, wherever his life took him, and even after death she would be a part of his very existence. Her soul, if not her body, had known this place before, and she had been drawn back, secure that the spirits which dwelt here would look after her boy while he was in their land.

Belinda heard them calling her name and left the rocky seat, brushing moss and twigs from her jeans as she made her way back to the path. She would be able to leave Aidan without tears, she believed.

When they left him in the rundown hall of residence, there were a few. From Doug, hearty handshakes, warnings about drink and to make sure he phoned his mother, as she would be worrying. Belinda gave her son a soft kiss, a squeeze of the hand and an unspoken prayer with a false grin. Melanie wept, and sulked all the way home, not knowing how to deal with things in any other way.

*

By late October Belinda was growing used to Doug's absence during the week, but not to Aidan's. He responded tersely to his mother's texts. His life was moving on. There was work, play and girls aplenty, and he rarely thought about home. Family security ran parallel to his current life like a banister up a flight of stairs. For his mother, Christmas seemed far too long to wait to see him again. Maybe they'd visit, soon.

6

It was Friday afternoon and almost dark outside by six o'clock. Bel was returning books to the library shelves. One old chap still sat at the computers reading *The Mail* online; she often had to send him home when she locked up at seven. It was his winter habit to use the council's electricity to keep himself warm during the day, complaining about fuel poverty at every opportunity.

The sound of traffic from the street surged in briefly and faded again, telling Belinda that another customer had come through the door. She moved from between the stacks. A smartly-dressed woman stood at the desk; it took seconds for her to recognise Marnie, who looked different, somehow. Her hair was longer and more subtly toned; she had filled out a little and there was no sign of the tarty dress sense. The woman Belinda saw looked businesslike in dark grey coat and trousers, with a vibrant jade-green wrap around her shoulders. A tilted cap in the same shade added that extra something.

With a surprised laugh, Belinda gave Marnie a hug. "What on earth are you doing here?"

"I got tired of waiting for you to invite me!" the other replied in mock indignation.

"I wasn't sure that you meant it when you said you'd come – and anyway, there's been a lot going on at home… But never mind… it's lovely to see you."

Disgruntled that his peace had been disturbed, the old man snorted and logged off. As the door closed behind him, Marnie said,

"Actually, that brings me to one of the reasons I wanted to visit you at work." Bel was puzzled. "The computers. People can use them for free, right?"

"Yes, for an hour a day, but you have to be a member of the library first."

"I want you to teach me how to do it. I haven't a clue." It was all part of her plan to become more like other people: to become a proper, respectable member of society.

Marnie eased herself into the still-warm chair and stared at the screen. Hands hovering above the keyboard, she stared at the desktop icons on screen. They meant nothing. Bel used her own login code and brought up a search engine.

"What do you want to know first?"

"This interweb thing. People talk about it a lot but none of it makes sense to me."

The quiet lull at the end of the day gave Bel time to demonstrate the basics to Marnie and let the student find some information for herself. Taking back the controls after half an hour, she typed in the name of the city authority's library service. Within seconds she was able to hand Marnie a printed schedule of IT tuition close to her bedsit.

"Get yourself down there on Monday morning and put your name on the list."

Marnie was excited. The sculpture course had cost an arm and a leg; this was free and in a warm place. This internet thing might be the means of delivering her plans; she had these and schemes aplenty, but it was not yet time to share them with Belinda.

"I'll be closing up soon," said the librarian. "Why not come home with me? We can have a catch-up and something to eat."

Marnie nodded, with a smile.

After sharing a meal with Melanie and her mother, she seemed keen to discover more about the village that they both took for granted, and asked to be shown around despite the threat of frost and a chill breeze.

Typical of ancient English townships overlaid with industrial-level housing schemes of the twentieth century, Sallby was an uneasy mix of the picturesque and the brutally banal. Behind darkling yew trees, the Norman church hid from the ruffian, sixties, concrete working men's club, now in its last throes. Detached and porticoed estates of the boom years interlocked with rows of brick-built, between-the-wars semis and OAP bungalows. Here, a scruffily hedged field, with two horses and an upturned bath for a drinking trough. There a ragged farm, spewing straw or fodder; a stone barn conversion too expensive to sell; ample, lumpy, white-washed cottages, and a soon-to-be-shut-down post office. Odd-looking houses that had once been shops spoke of the commerce and convenience stolen away by the all-providing, all-destroying supermarket five miles away. Hefty chunks of mud from the treads of tractor tyres reminded passers-by of the rural belt encircling the village, and metal posts bore plastic housing for unfathomable bus timetables to places nobody wanted to go to. It was a village closer to nowhere than its own demise.

Four centuries old and boarded up, the pub was hung with *For Sale* and *To Let* signs. Four centuries of hubbub and ale, wars civil, wars of the world, wars between neighbours; four centuries of shove ha'penny and darts, fruit machines and tobacco, buxom barmaids and funeral teas. All finished, polished off in a decade by cheap supermarket booze.

Set a little apart, alongside a field, was the drab village hall, built in memory of The Fallen, at a time when a numbed nation realised that building for the future was the only worthy memorial, the only way to cope with the loss of those who died securing a future they would never enjoy. It was this unprepossessing construction to which Belinda had given so much time and effort over the past fifteen years, and Marnie loved it at first sight.

She loved it for its plainness and its permanence. It represented much that she had missed out on in life. She loved the idea of community. In that, she shared a politician's rainbow-tinted idealism. Community was something she had always been excluded from. Whereas the politicians spoke in generalities and pipe dreams, Marnie believed in the myth. She wanted to be part of it.

After much urging from the visitor, they walked down to the hall, where a dancing class had just finished. It smelt of little girls and their scented mothers. Belinda walked round dispiritedly, picking up odd, forgotten socks and sparkly hair slides jettisoned from tumbling curls.

"It's so... lived in," Marnie enthused. "I love it." She experienced a brief flashback of her days as a rural Madam.

While it was always heartening when people showed an interest, Bel couldn't quite understand the attraction, or why her friend was so interested in the booking procedure, licences and charges.

Marnie, meanwhile, was slotting the place into her plans, but this time she would do it properly. She had no intention of going back inside. There were contracts to pursue, services to promote, suppliers and clients to be found. But for now, there was no need for Belinda to know.

An hour later, Marnie was on a grimy bus back to the city, her mind swirling with possibilities. There was no doubt in her mind that she would make a success of this; any doubts concerned getting away with it.

7

<hr>

A month had passed since Marnie's visit to Sallby. Melanie and her mother were slowly adjusting to life without menfolk in the house, though it seemed more like a half-life. The girl threw herself into school work – or so she told her mother. Her preference was to spend evenings in her room on 'assignments': i.e. keeping in touch with her 2,147 Facebook friends. Belinda had subsided, almost, into the role of a numbly mechanical functionary. She cleaned the house when it didn't need cleaning; did the laundry, the shopping, the cooking, her job; supported her parents, and relaxed by dealing with village hall matters, which were thin on the ground. In her spare moments, she found time to worry about Dorothy, last seen following her in Denswick marketplace.

Bookings for the hall continued to decline, the dancing class having folded because few parents had the money to pay. The young women who had started their dancing days in this same room and gone on to train as teachers returned to the dole, their certificates stuffed at the backs of drawers, with little hope of future relevance. No-one wanted to use the building because no-one could afford to pay. The committee and Belinda continued to meet, but whereas in the past meetings had been friendly and relaxed, now they became worrisome, imbued with a sense of failure and despondency. Dully, they discussed the latest blocked drain or faulty heater. A hastily-organised jumble sale raised a scant £67, hardly worth all the effort, but it would help pay the refuse-collection charge, payable whether the bin needed emptying or not. The long-term outlook seemed hopeless. The previously-unthinkable step of boarding up the hall and referring themselves to the Charity Commission for dissolution had to be considered. 'After Christmas,' the committee decided; after submission of the online annual return to the Commission in January. They'd see what happened when the accounts were examined. There were no actual debts outstanding as yet, but it would only take one powerful storm...

The winter nights were long and dreary, and Belinda was missing Doug. Her mood lightened a little when he came home at weekends, but it was a forced gaiety. The gap where Aidan had been, the knowledge that life would never be the same again, followed her round like the smell of sour milk.

Already beginning to weather, her wooden snail looked good beside the tiny garden pond. The pale cedar had taken on a richer hue after Bel applied the preservative mix of boiled linseed oil, white spirit and malt vinegar Ambrose had insisted upon. She stood at the kitchen sink, watching a robin hop in the grass, then flutter onto the snail's head to sample some scattered titbits. The bird's perkiness cheered her for a moment. The robin had come to represent Aidan; diligently she put out the breakfast crumbs each day in an attempt to fill the gap.

The ringing phone made her jump. Someone wanted to book the village hall for six hours on a Saturday night for a private function, the nature of which was hazy. Something about Sallby being a central meeting place for like-minded individuals from different parts of the county. Belinda wasn't too inquisitive: £60 was £60, after all. She agreed to post out the hire agreement to an address in the city and await the deposit. Payment would be made in full before the date and she would meet the caller on his arrival.

Ending the call, Belinda returned to the sink with a little skip. She rested her elbow on the draining board, chin in hand, trying to remember where she had heard that man's voice before. The robin had gone

✽

At five o'clock on a dark December afternoon, a large box wagon drove along Sallby's main street and pulled gingerly onto the field next to the village hall. Behind the wheel, tense with concentration, was a tall, thickset, shaven-headed man unused to driving any vehicle at all, let alone a hired van of these proportions. Beside him sat a slim, blonde-haired woman in her forties. Having parked, they climbed out and walked round to the already-lit building.

Waiting for them, keys in hand, was Anita Su, who had agreed to open up for the unknown hirer in Belinda's absence. Tetchy when the hirers arrived ten minutes after the agreed time, Anita was in a rush. The Su family ran the only oriental fast-food outlet in the village and that day were working on a pre-paid order: a takeaway banquet for sixty-five. All hands were needed in the kitchen.

"When you finish, drop the keys through the letter box of 18 Dapple Grove." She handed over a sketch map of the route to Belinda's house, quickly pointed out the facilities and fire exits, collected the fee and jogged away, no questions taken.

The couple sped into action, the woman closing the curtains while the man returned to the van. He reversed it out of the field and round to the side fire exit, where the activity would be less visible to passers-by. The rear loading doors opened and several people, women mostly, clambered out. They worked as a team, unloading wheeled metal contraptions and boxes, heavy but manhandleable, then suitcases, briefcases, folding screens and finally, cases of wine, crates of lager and a barrel of beer. They worked quietly for two hours, readying the place.

Clothes rails heavy with garments both smart and glitzy divided the place into individual boutiques, offering a range of female apparel for both night and day wear. Shoes, from stiletto-heeled ankle-breakers to pomponned slippers, together with the fitting paraphernalia still occasionally found in the higher-class footwear establishments, took up one corner. From another, the scents of a well-known brand of party-plan cosmetics wafted the scent of luxury and wellbeing. Strings of costume jewellery dangled and glittered from display stands; dazzling rings of knuckle-duster proportions lay on velvet cloths; studs and dangly rings for pierced ears only were hooked onto cards which hung beneath a tiny mirror, for purchasers' self-inspection.

A third corner had been more privately set out: a cubicle formed from the blue folding screens housed a small table, winged mirror and an upholstered chair. The outside of the screens showed pictures of well-coiffured women. Only on close inspection was it possible to read the text beneath the photographs; this explained the materials from which the hair was made. On a small table, wigs adorned four blank-eyed model heads, hinting at the contents of the red velveteen ottoman at the side of the cubicle.

In the back room, polished glasses stood ready in rows on the bar. The barrel had been linked up to the rarely used pumps, bottles of spirits slotted into optics and the bottled liquor conveniently displayed, along with tiny packs of savoury nibbles. A Temporary Events Notice from the local licensing authority was pinned to a notice board: Marnie had been determined to do most things right.

She and Bud were satisfied with the finished effect, and praised the traders' efforts as they handed out mugs of tea and coffee before opening the doors. They also collected £200 from each stallholder, as agreed in writing and backed up by a £50 deposit when the initial invitation to take part was accepted. A cheque for the £60 hall hire fee, signed illegibly, had been posted in advance to the bookings secretary along with the completed hire agreement. It had aroused no suspicion: Belinda and Marnie had never got round to sharing surnames.

Shortly after seven-thirty, a fully occupied fifty-two-seater coach drew up outside Sallby Village Hall with a shush of air brakes. The door swished back. Passengers alighted. Conversation ceased. The party passed into the building in silence. The coach moved away, to park up at the motorway services three miles away.

They filed up the six steps into the building: the strutters and the waddlers; the neat-boned whippets with short, cocky steps, and the porky snub-nosed, who swayed when they walked; the long and lean, hatchet-faced, and slender, cherubic teens not quite sure which side of the line their future lay. An observer might have been hard-pressed to explain the presence of such a disparate band of men in an English village hall so early on a Saturday evening.

An aura of shyness descended on the party as they viewed the bounty before them. For once, they would be able to do their specialised shopping without fear of mockery or abuse. Here were ladylike shoes in manly proportions; corsetry for concealment and enhancement; floaty dresses designed to hang from brickies' shoulders; rings for fitters' fingers; make-up to make the rugged radiant, and cleavage-making brassieres in rich-hued satin and lace.

For half an hour, the shoppers browsed and murmured among themselves, admiring or rejecting the merchandise displayed. Slowly, confidence increased. A few took advantage of the bar for Dutch courage. Then the serious shopping began. Still wearing some of their everyday attire, the shoppers piece by piece accumulated entire outfits. The effect became increasingly bizarre as items were tried and kept on or discarded, each purchaser aiming for his own individual style. Behind screens and in the cloakrooms, jeans and sweaters were thrown aside or stuffed in rucksacks.

Like butterflies drying their wings in the sunshine, the unprepossessing body of men transformed into a bevy of beautiful women, comfortable in their glory and their alter egos, gender distinguishable only by hands, feet and voices.

Arms folded across his chest, Bud Baxter had fallen into bouncer mode. Changing location from time to time, his role now was to stop trouble before it happened. The punters might have looked and moved like women, but a swung punch would land with a heftier crack than most female fists could deliver. There must be no damage to the building's fabric or furniture: Marnie insisted upon it. Therefore there must be no fighting.

Even here, footwear for the larger-boned transvestite was difficult to find. It was inevitable that competition would break out, and it broke out over a pair of Size 12, stack-heeled, cream leather lace-up brogues.

In one corner Vicky, a beefy body of fifty-five in a stylish, bronze wrapover dress with three-quarter sleeves and a ruched waist, was after an elegant, mature look. The dress fitted well over an impressively sculpted bosom and less convincing hips, but was not complemented by the black socks and trainers Victor had arrived in. No make-up had yet been applied: the five o'clock shadow was disconcerting.

The attractive displays so carefully arranged by the shoe stallholder had been turned upside down as the customers riffled through boxes in search of a perfect fit. While Vic was thus employed, he came upon the single shoe that stole his heart. It was the right size and colour and had the classic elegance he was looking for. He bared his right foot and slipped on the pop-sock provided. The shoe was just right and looked as good as it felt. The search began for its mate.

Vic found it on the foot of his arch enemy, Sam. Polite requests to hand it over were ignored, and the interchange became more physical. Bud left his station outside the Ladies' and made his way towards the raised voices, arriving just as Sam's brogued left foot made forceful contact with Vic's private parts.

Vic doubled over, on the way down inadvertently nutting a slightly built dental technician named Ashley just as he bent forward to pick up a pair of four-inch stilettos.

Ashley went down like a dropped brick, landing on an upturned heel which pierced his flesh just beneath the ribs. As he lay stunned and crumpled on a mess of crushed cardboard, blood seeped through his new batwing top.

Bud reached the scene as the red blotch spread. He was used to other people's blood and a pretty safe pair of hands when it came to breaking up a fight. He grabbed Sam and slung him through the front door, with admonitions to wait outside. Vic was still folded and in no condition to cause more trouble. Ashley needed attention.

Marnie, appearing from nowhere, clambered over the boxes to look at the wound. She was very afraid, but wore her harshest expression to deter further aggression. The other shoppers backed away and returned to their own purchases. Bud fetched a First Aid box from the kitchen but ignored the Accident Book stuck through the handle. Marnie took the plastic gloves from their tiny sleeve and slipped them on before lifting Ashley's voluminous top. The puncture wound was the diameter of a drinking straw, hardly bigger, and a centimetre deep, no deeper, thank goodness. Heart in mouth, she cleaned the wound and applied a folded gauze pad held in place by a length of sticking plaster. The bleeding slowed and Ashley, pale and shaken but coming round, was anxious not to draw attention to his situation. Bud sat him on a chair with a cup of water and left him to pull himself together.

Turning his attention to Sam, the bouncer went outside to find the instigator smoking a cigarette by the bus stop, one foot still wearing the high-heeled, cream brogue.

"Nice shoe, but one's no good, pal."

Sam nodded sombrely. No violence had been one of Marnie's most explicit instructions when detailing arrangements on Facebook. The evening had begun so well, but now it looked as if Sam had barred himself from future jaunts. And the shoe was pinching his bunion, anyway.

"Sorry, mate. Tell Marnie it won't happen again. Old habits die hard and all that…"

He bent and untied the fine lace, removed the shoe and handed it to Bud. They walked back up the steps and into the hall. With a handshake and a grunting apology to the recovering Vicky, the shoe was handed over.

As if by some silent signal, at 9.45 the stallholders began to pack away their merchandise. Most shoppers were by this time barely recognisable from their arrival selves. Whether their adopted persona was a blousy broad, bronzed bodybuilder, whore or housewife, the clients worked as a team to move tables and folding chairs into a line down the middle of the floor. White paper from a banqueting roll covered the scuffs and stains on the table tops.

Soon, the stalls' remaining merchandise had been boxed and transferred to the back of the van, which was then reversed end-on to a blank wall for security. At 10.15, Lee Su's takeaway delivery van drew up outside the hall's disabled access. Lee, Anita and their staff had sweated long to prepare this feast, which had been a handy way to use up leftovers as well as a nice earner.

The village hall's stock of plates was spread out on the tables and the guests seated – almost all women, it seemed to Lee, who felt a little uneasy. Lee liked his women petite in the Chinese fashion; these ladies were well built with thick necks, and many had hair on the backs of their hands. Although he'd come from Hong Kong with his parents when he was just a child, he would never get used to the strangeness of the English.

He carried in trays laden with polystyrene containers, and willing hands distributed them evenly down the line of tables. Spiced sauces, of chilli and black bean, ginger and oyster, released their aromas into the air. There was everything on the takeaway menu that you could think of. Plates of prawn crackers, bowls of rice and noodles and tubs of curry sauce were shared between diners. The odours of hairspray and beer fumes were doused by these new smells. The guests all tucked in.

There was an occasional spillage on floor and frontages, but nothing that couldn't be sorted by a mop and a damp cloth. The atmosphere was comfortable, the earlier upset forgotten. How good it felt to be well dressed, well fed, in good company as women together. Bud and the barman were not rated highly as 'babe magnets', so faded into the background.

While the meal was in progress the coach had returned and drawn onto the field. The driver was busy unloading something from the under-floor luggage hold and stacking more boxes by the side door. Then the contents were carried in and set up down the sides of the room ready for the next activity. It was this that caused Marnie most disquiet, for the simple reason that, according to the premises licence, the building had to be vacated by midnight. She was keeping her fingers crossed that any chance passer-by would not know that. She was also hoping that no one would spill the beans about the law-breaking she was about to aid and abet.

In a darkened hall, angled lamps shone cones of light onto baize-covered tables, eight in all. Roulette wheels, chips, rakes, cards and other gambling paraphernalia were arranged ready for play. Low music played on a continuous loop to create a relaxing ambience. The DIY Casino Outfit from Kitty's Mobile Casinos had been delivered to Bud's flat a week ago. He knew the games well enough, but this portable equipment was a bit tackier than he was used to. He'd make it work somehow, confident he could make this part of the evening profitable, as long as the licensing authorities didn't get wind.

Bud had opted for the Superior kit, hired at £260 including delivery and comprising eight games of roulette, poker dice and blackjack. Bud's venture differed from the usual DIY casino system in just one respect: instead of the 'fun money' supplied, real cash would cross the tables. Marnie and Bud had argued about this. So far, there had been nothing illegal about the night's enterprise, meaning no prospect of court appearances or prison. They had read up on the legal side of things, and knew that by allowing real money to be used, they were breaching the terms of the prize gaming provisions in Part 14 of the Gambling Act 2005. Contrary to this regulation, there would be private gain. Most of that would be Bud's, though the stallholders he had quickly trained as croupiers would get a cut.

For the new trainees it had been a long night. It was difficult to sustain the atmosphere of fun and laughter when everyone was tired. The punters already looked jaded – wigs askew and lipstick smeared – but the opportunity had presented itself and Bud had been unable to resist. On reflection, he thought as he was stacking the chips, a separate event might have been better, though more likely to be rumbled.

Nevertheless, the red and green baize, bright beneath the lamps, exuded an allure that few of the guests could resist. Roulette wheels caught the light as they spun and there was something about the noise that drew a crowd. Few knew much about the games but their remaining cash yearned to be spent. With the primary colours of the chips on the blackjack tables, the cards in their shoes, the music, the clothes... it was easy to get drawn in. The stud poker tables attracted the more reserved characters.

Being an experienced croupier, Bud had taught his trainees well. Leaving behind their shopkeeper selves as they donned tuxedos, they became smarter, more suave and sociable. Fools and their money were as soon parted that night as always. The more sensible transvestites stayed in the bar.

As he moved from table to table, Bud got his first real opportunity to study his clients properly. He was struck by the range of accents he heard and the social backgrounds suggested. He knew from his work on the doors at city clubs that drunkenness is a great social leveller; beyond that, he'd never given class much thought.

In these parts, Received Pronunciation stood out like a crow in an aviary. In Sallby tonight, a few jarring tones and snatches of caught conversation hinted at professions and high status. Bud was watching a game of hold 'em poker when, from the bar, one voice in particular caught his ear. Its owner was out of sight but clearly identifiable.

At the first opportunity Bud changed position so he was facing the bar. It was difficult to keep his eyes on the game. His chest constricted. He foresaw disaster.

By this time, many of the colourful outfits and stately hairdos were deranged and unkempt but, still in pristine condition, a silky, strawberry-blonde bob sat atop impressive shoulders draped in a stole of bronze voile appliquéd with butterflies. Beneath the voile, a low-cut evening gown in velvet of the deepest green stretched across a broad, masculine back.

Millicent was engaged in a tipsy conversation with a meagre, bored-looking crowd. As she turned, Bud made out the slight, gingery fuzz on the jowls, for Millicent, like her brother Daryl, was a two-shaves-a-day man, and it had been twelve hours since the last one. There was no doubt about it: Millicent and Miles Baxter-Hatton were one and the same person. Self-absorption being a trait common to both personas, neither had paid any attention to the bouncer. This evening had not been about other people, after all.

Daryl Baxter was shocked and, initially, not amused. What would their father be thinking as he looked down from his cloud on high? Never a tolerant man, the idea of his poncy, public-school son also being a cross-dresser would be explosive... would have killed him if he hadn't pre-empted the discovery by dying a few months earlier. And how did Bud himself feel about this new facet of his half-brother's personality? Disturbed, bewildered and, yes, happy that fate had dealt him such a winning hand for a change.

Miles had certainly not been on the original list of invitees, compiled by Bud and passed to Marnie. Email addresses had been elicited as Bud worked the doors of the clubs. After a quiet word in the ears of a few regulars at the tranny nights in town, the social networking sites had done the rest. Each had made individual contact with thornymarina@exconmail.com to ask for an official invitation to this private function.

Try as he might to resist, Bud's eyes were drawn to Millicent's lustrous bob as she pontificated about the classless society to a dwindling group of loners. Eventually, that feeling of being stared at won out over the pull of an audience, and she turned. Eyes locked with her big brother's, recognition undeniable.

Both men were rigid with uncertainty. How to respond? Who had most to lose from an outing? Like the icons on a fruit machine, calculations spun in each brain. With uncanny synchronicity, Daryl and Millicent strengthened the stare, inhaled, stood tall, and turned away. Millicent strode past her brother, brushing his shoulder with her stole. Daryl tried to become Bud again, but in all honesty, his grasp of the game had gone.

He wondered if Marnie had spotted Miles, but couldn't leave his place to find her.

Marnie had in fact spotted Miles early on in the proceedings and had taken him outside for a stern talking-to. The MP had made compliant assurances that he would keep schtum about the event in return for similar discretion on her part. Marnie had not mentioned Daryl's presence – it would only have muddied the waters, especially as the illegal part of the night was Bud's responsibility. So she relied on crossing her fingers in the hope that the brothers' paths would not cross.

Activity at the gaming tables slowed down in the early hours of Sunday morning, and by one-thirty they were being stowed away as the passengers boarded for the return journey, laden with carrier bags and rucksacks full to overflowing. They sank into the plush-covered seats, no chat left and, almost to a man or woman, fell asleep. Miles was a little longer dropping off, and when he did, he dreamt of Sunday headlines and dirty linen. The driver looked forward to a peaceful drive up the motor-way, back to the city and a Sunday morning snuggle with his missus.

In the empty hall, Bud and Marnie swept and mopped the floor, washed glasses and stuffed rubbish into the wheelie bin outside. Neither had much to say. Counting the profits and talking things over would wait till the following afternoon. At last they climbed into the truck's cab and pulled away from Sallby Village Hall.

As the van headed for the motorway, a half-full tub of curry sauce fell from the overflowing bin and rolled down the path to the gutter. Half a dozen rats galloped after the chicken chow mein clinging to the polystyrene container blowing in the wind. Later, a vixen found the open bin and strewed its contents along the road.

8

The visit to Wales had been a disappointment. Deep down, Belinda, Doug and Melanie had to face up to it: they were not essential to Aidan's happiness and wellbeing. The boy seemed happy. He loved the place, the people, the staff and even his chosen course. The accommodation wasn't up to much but it was the best his parents could afford and he accepted that. The prices in the union bar were a bit steep too, but hey! He was an eighteen-year-old, well-balanced lad, away from home, footloose, fancy free and happy to stay that way.

It had been nice to see Mum, Dad and Mel, but, "My parents are always a bit of an embarrassment," he told his flatmate Jude when they'd gone. Jude was quite posh and Aidan wished his dad was something more impressive than an electrician.

"Yah, mine too. My mother's on so many committees that people think she's Prime Minister of Bath or something, but she's never had a job or read a book in her life."

That sounded quite cool to Aidan. Jude thought Aidan's sister looked a cute kid.

It was a subdued journey home that Sunday evening as the family tried to come to terms with the student's independence, but he would be home for the Christmas vacation in a couple of weeks' time and all would be well.

It was dark when the car passed the village hall. Belinda had no intention of inspecting the building that night – surely Anita would have done that already. But she couldn't help noticing the litter, and that no one had put the refuse out for tomorrow's collection.

"Stop the car," she told Doug.

She stepped out and dragged the wheelie bin to the kerb.

*

Long before 7am, Doug shouted goodbye on the way to his van and another week of work and chilly caravan nights further north. The mood in the house sank lower. Melanie had to be prodded out of bed, then slunk off to school breakfastless, complaining that her weekend homework had not been done, thanks to her mother's insistence on dragging her all the way to Wales when she didn't even want to go in the first place. Belinda watched through the front window as her daughter pattered off down the street, still moaning as she met up with Chelsey from a few doors down.

Nothing to look forward to, Belinda made herself another round of tea and toast. It was a sunny winter's morning. Slipping her coat over her pyjamas, holding the toast between her teeth she carried the hot mug into the garden. The wooden snail was weathering now: it looked a more natural part of the scene. She sat on the snail's back warming her hands on the cup and stared into the little pond's black shallows. There was no sign of the five or six goldfish put in when Doug re-stocked back in the summer. Maybe the heron had been back. Belinda sometimes thought the money they spent on fish was a waste: they might as well feed them to the herons direct. All efforts to keep the birds at bay with nets or decoys had failed. Just as everything Belinda touched failed, she thought to herself, sliding into depression.

She hoped the robin would appear to peck up her toast crumbs, but no. She remained totally alone in the garden, wallowing in melancholy. Stiff and weary she sat, getting stiffer and wearier as the chill entered her bones. There must be a way forward, a way less lonely.

Leaning to the side, she laid her face against the snail's head and stroked along the grain of the wood, recalling the lovely days of summer and the exultation of creation. Memories of her criminal act made her smile. She had got away with it, and for a time it had brought her alive, yet the experiment had fallen into abeyance like her pre-Christmas diet. Even her exercise regime had slipped. It was time to pull herself together. Picking up her plate and mug, Bel walked purposefully back inside.

She cleared space at the end of the bed and lay on the carpet, which was grubbier now. Stretching gently, limb by limb, she extended muscles still cramped from the weekend's journey until she was ready for the more testing moves. Clothing was jettisoned piece by piece until she reached a frenzy of exertion. At last, spent, she draped herself forward over her dressing-table stool, eyes closed, head, arms and breasts hanging forward and legs extended behind. Her breathing slowed until, gradually, she reached that state of relaxation which is not quite sleep.

*

Bare buttocks catching the morning light greeted Dave the window cleaner as he reached the top of his ladder that morning. Was that a dead body slumped over the stool? He could see his own reflection in the mirror behind, so it appeared that he was not only viewing the scene from both sides, but examining his own reactions as well. He wobbled unsteadily on the rungs, bracing himself before taking another look. It was a strange pose and he could see no movement. The face was out of view. He wondered at the possible cause of death. There was no blood. The woman had been strangled, he surmised.

The ladder shook as he descended and signalled to his oily assistant, Steve.

"Take a look through that window." His voice trembled.

Steve went up the ladder, caught the same eyeful, and quickly came down again.

Dave took his phone from his pockets, but decided to have one more look. His heart was pounding. What if he had a heart attack or a stroke up there?

Reaching the top, he braced himself. The corpse had not moved. He was sure now. It was dead, but he rapped on the window with his phone anyway.

The body convulsed and fell sideways, toppling the stool. The head hit hard on the wardrobe corner. Nude legs flailed rudely in mid-air as Belinda struggled to understand what was happening.

At the first, horrifying convulsion, Dave's instinctive backward jerk yanked the ladder from the wall just an inch or two. At the same time, its right foot slipped on the mossy path beneath. The window cleaner teetered, gasped, and clung to the toppling ladder, managing to jump at eight feet from the ground. He landed awkwardly the other side of the little gate, one foot on the wall of a raised bed, the other on concrete. The falling ladder dealt a glancing blow to his left shoulder, and felled him proper.

Steve was quick off the mark with his own phone, dialling 999 without delay. He mentioned both the naked female body upstairs and the fallen fenestrator, but didn't know the house number. He would stand at the gate and wave as the emergency services arrived. Having checked that Dave was conscious and not bleeding, he jogged to the roadside to wait.

The double glazing provided effective soundproofing; Belinda, in her somnolent state, was unaware of the drama outside. It seemed that she had fallen asleep and fallen off the stool as she relaxed... she'd been using images of the summer sessions in the sculpture park in her visualisation, with the tap-tapping of mallets on chisels in the background. Her head was sore where it hit the wardrobe but she was quite comfy on the carpet. She rolled onto her stomach, dragged her discarded dressing-gown from the bed to cover her middle, and fell asleep.

*

"Squeeze my hand if you can hear me."

What was going on? Belinda struggled to remember where she was, let alone comprehend why she was lying naked on the carpet with a dark-eyed paramedic holding her hand. Had she been taken ill? Had a stroke? And how had he got in?

Eyes rolling, she squeezed the hand.

"That's really great. Can you tell me your name, love?"

"Belinda."

"That's a nice name. Now try not to worry, Belinda. Can you tell me what day it is?"

She paused for thought.

"Never mind, Belinda. It will probably come back to you. Now, Belinda, take it slowly and tell me what happened."

"How do you mean, what happened?"

"Well, Belinda, an ambulance was called because you were seen to have collapsed over a stool and appeared to be unconscious."

"I was asleep."

"Hmm. Asleep? Do you think you can sit up now, lovey? Slowly does it."

Belinda's yogic calm was fleeing.

"I've got a colleague from the police here with me, Belinda. He helped us break the door down and sort out one or two other issues. He'd like a word if you're feeling up to it."

Feeling up to it?

"How did you get in?"

"Like I said, Belinda love, this is Constable Stuart Willis and he broke the door down."

PC Willis leant forward, clutching his notebook and taking care not to look at Belinda's nipples.

"It looks as if there's been a spot of bother here, Belinda. We just want to help, that's all."

"I don't need help. What sort of bother?"

"Well, the furniture is in disarray, you have a big bruise on your temple and your husband seems to have gone AWOL. Just tell us the story from the beginning."

"He hasn't gone AWOL!"

"Your neighbour told us his van headed off in a hurry at around five o'clock this morning. Then at approximately 10.15am, Mr David Simmons, your window-cleaner, witnessed what he thought was a naked corpse through an upstairs window. The shock caused him to fall from his ladder, sustaining injuries to his leg and shoulder. The emergency services were called and a forced entry made. Happily, Belinda, they found not a corpse but an unconscious woman, namely yourself, with severe bruising to the temple, and the furniture in some disorder. Are you telling us that your husband is not responsible for your injury?"

"Of course he's not! He wouldn't hurt a fly!"

"Can you tell me his whereabouts?"

She pulled the dressing-gown higher. "Why should I?"

"Because this is an official enquiry, Belinda." She was beginning to hate the sound of her name. "The emergency services were called and it's our duty to investigate the incident. Now, where is your husband?"

"At work."

"And where would that be?"

"Up north."

"That's rather vague, Belinda. We'll need something more precise than that."

And so it went on. Belinda realised that, actually, she did not know her husband's whereabouts. She knew he was rewiring a block of flats with a team of independent tradesmen from around Denswick, and that they'd travelled up to the north-east. With mobile phones these days, it wasn't necessary to have an address to stay in touch. And why should she give them his mobile number? No reason at all.

"So you say Doug is in the north-east but can't be more precise than that?"

"It might be Sunderland. Now I'd like to get dressed, please."

The paramedic persuaded her to remain where she was until he'd assessed her condition. Satisfied at last that she was OK to stand, the two men withdrew onto the landing while she dressed. As bafflement faded, fury filled the space. Was it a crime to head off in a hurry at 5am? Was it a crime to sleep naked in one's own bedroom? And she'd known there was something *iffy* about that window-cleaner's mate!

It was obviously him who had put her dearest Doug in the frame for wife-beating /attempted murder. She'd known he fancied her back in the summer by the way he'd pressed her hand, but had never imagined he was such an obsessed fantasist.

And what about the neighbour? She must have been twitching the curtains every five minutes to spot Doug setting off so early. The woman, Patricia, had only moved in four months ago and they'd not yet got comfortable with one another, but Belinda had suspected a malicious turn of mind from the start.

The police at last decided to pursue their investigations back at the station, having taken note of Doug's van registration and mobile numbers, reluctantly provided by Belinda to get rid of them. The paramedic encouraged her to pop along to A&E to get her skull X-rayed, or at least have the bruise looked at. He didn't want any comeback for leaving a wound unchecked.

Meanwhile, the greasy assistant had accompanied his employer and the second paramedic into the ambulance, which arrived at the scene within ten minutes of the call. Steve was in a state of some shock, though whether the shock was occasioned by the buttocks, the corpse or his boss's fall was difficult to say. Dave was in both shock and pain. His shoulder was tender, his ankle was killing him, and he feared his dancing days might be over. Belinda joined the two men in the ambulance.

On arrival at A&E they were triaged and sent to a large waiting area full of seats upholstered in lavender vinyl, with a payphone under a hood on the wall and a drinks machine. Behind a curved reception desk of pale wood, a bored receptionist took their details and told them to sit down. Dave remained in the wheelchair while Steve – or, rightly, Stevan – tremulously did his bidding. Belinda sat in a daze, trying to understand what she was doing here. She came to understand one thing quite clearly: her new neighbour, Patricia, had messed with the wrong woman. It was once more time for the malevolent mantras. She could do some in her head while waiting. Unobserved, she closed her eyes and relaxed her breathing, which calmed her down and made the pain in her head fade into the background. It also meant she didn't have to be polite to Dave and Steve.

*

Two hours into their wait, an old woman in a faded beige coat and a furry hat arrived. She spoke to the receptionist at the desk before turning to scan the seated, waiting wounded. Her face clouding with a look of recognition when she saw Belinda, she smiled stiffly as she spotted Dave Simmons. The woman squeezed past with a glare, indicating that Belinda should move along. Plonking her large, rigid handbag on a seat to create a barrier between them, the woman turned towards Dave and kissed him on the cheek.

The old woman was Dorothy.

She started talking to the man, whining about the difficult bus journey to the hospital, only asking about his injuries after a good five minutes and pointedly ignoring the woman on her right, who sat bemused by this latest revelation.

If Dorothy was the window cleaner's mother, as seemed likely, and Dorothy had been her father's bit on the side, as she believed, the man she'd tried and failed to seduce last summer could be her own half-brother! Had the window cleaning been a front, a cover for stalking his half-sister? Was Dorothy behind this morning's fiasco? Dave had seen her bare behind that very morning! The thought brought colour to her cheeks. She squirmed in her seat. Her vow to think more kindly forgotten, more malevolent mantras followed, this time encompassing the ubiquitous Dorothy.

*

Maybe the mantras were working. The old woman was looking uncomfortable, undoing her scarf, removing her coat and cardigan, fanning herself with a copy of *Take a Break* pulled from her handbag.

When Dave's number came up on the digital display above the desk, Stevan wheeled him through purple double doors. Dorothy picked up her bag and moved into the vacated seat, glancing evilly at Belinda. She continued flapping her hands in front of her face. Her breath came in short, rasping heaves, open-mouthed. Under normal circumstances Belinda would have offered assistance, but now, she watched in amazement at the impact of the venomous vibes she was emitting.

*

A chap sitting on the row behind called out. "Nurse! Nurse! This lady needs attention."

The nurse scuttled on, deep in her own responsibilities. Someone else attracted the attention of a porter.

"Tell the triage nurse." He pushed on with the squeaky-wheeled trolley he was manoeuvring. A disembodied female voice called out from a speaker next to the digital display: "Number ninety-three, please."

Belinda walked through the swinging doors unaided. What a waste of time this all was. And why was Dorothy still stalking her?

A tired, plump nurse asked her a few questions and examined the bruised temple, making it obvious that, in her opinion, Belinda was a time-waster. A white-coated Asian youth, possibly a junior doctor, sidled in for a quick glance at her notes and a nod and sidled out again. She was free to go.

There was no sign of Dorothy or her handbag when Belinda walked out. No sign of Dave or Steve either. It was by now 2pm and Belinda had no way of getting home. The dozy ambulance man had not reminded her to take purse, phone and keys to the hospital.

She sat on the low wall of a bare, raised flower bed which bloomed only with fag packets and tab ends whatever the season. It was eight miles back to Sallby. She was tired, hungry, angry and stranded. There were so many people to blame for her predicament: her own family, for being somewhere else when she needed them; Greasy Steve for phoning the ambulance; Dave Simmons for peering through windows at naked women (were all window-cleaners perverts?); the woman next door for sharing unfounded assumptions with PC Willis; Dorothy for stalking her and seducing her father. Bel needed to strengthen the mantras, though of course she would not include her own family members.

She'd lost track of how long she'd been sitting on the wall when a taxi drew up opposite. As soon as the occupants climbed out, she climbed in, explaining her predicament to the driver and agreeing that he would take her to her parents' bungalow. They were bound to have some cash in the house to pay the fare.

Not until she was seated did she think about how much she should tell her parents. They mustn't find out that Dave, the window-cleaner and possibly her father's by-blow, had seen her naked, or that she had been sitting next to Dorothy in A&E. Even after all these years, she could not be sure if her mother was aware of the other woman's existence.

Melanie, by now on her way home from school carrying her own back-door key, was summoned to her grandparents'. Another taxi ride with more borrowed money, and they were home, exhausted, embarrassed and depressed. Bel's temple was quite sore, too.

She'd forgotten about the policemen battering the door down. It had been made safe, as in, not usable in the normal manner. However, the state of the front entrance meant that Belinda could not conceal the morning's events from her daughter.

Melanie was not that interested, as it turned out. Ben Jepson, the topmost, fittest, dreamboatest boy in the school, had sat next to her at dinner. Not only had he pinched a couple of crisps from her plate (the standard first step in canteen-based foreplay), he had touched her hand accidentally-on-purpose whilst pouring a glass of water, *and* said she had nice teeth. Hurrah for the inter-dental brushes! In her dreams, a diamond ring and mountainous wedding dress would lead to a house full of good-looking, well-behaved and incredibly brainy children, though she had the sense to keep those dreams to herself for now. No, her mother's hospital jaunt didn't even register on Melanie's radar of significant events.

Too tired to think, Belinda rang the takeaway and ordered a home-delivery meal for two. Soaking in the bath before the food arrived, she replayed the key scenes of the day. Her breathing slowed and deepened, eventually giving nasal voice on the exhalations. A mental image of Dorothy in her mind's eye, she watched as the old woman shrank, withered and collapsed like a blow-up doll punctured.

Depletion completed. Her attention shifted to Patricia next door.

9

A tight-muscled woman, hair dyed unnaturally black with orange streaks, the new neighbour affronted Belinda on many levels. Foremost were her insensitivity and superior air. The two had met in September as Belinda picked roses from the rambler which clambered over the fence separating their gardens. The house next door was on the market, though she'd heard rumours that a buyer had been found.

Belinda said a friendly hello. Instead of returning the greeting with a smile and an outstretched hand, the woman had looked at the flowers, then at the bush, and said,

"That'll have to go. It's an eyesore."

Belinda adored the mass of shocking pink blooms and shiny green leaves. The plant's enthusiasm for life gave hope for the future. She loved to fill vases with its blooms. She loved the way the fading petals changed colour before they dropped or lay where they fell. She loved the memories – of her parents' garden in her childhood, of the scent of roses carefully pruned and tidied by Dad; of gathering bowlfuls of petals to make pot pourri or 'perfume' with the children. Dad's garden was neat and tidy; her own taste was for rampant growth. She chose plants with vigour, which thrived on neglect.

"It's an eyesore. I can't abide flowers. So tasteless."

"Then why buy a house with a garden?"

"We're going to gravel it over. We've got a big caravan and what with three cars, we'll be taking down that hedge as well." She pointed to the dense run of copper beech which ran between their houses and down the first half of the front boundary.

"That's our hedge." Her voice came out faintly. Inside, Belinda was all disappointment. She'd hoped the newcomer might fill some of the gaps in her life – provide friendship and chats over coffee. This was clearly not to be.

The woman let her eyes rove over Belinda, her garden and house front... a little faded, maybe; not quite freshly painted. Certainly past their best.

"You want to get PVC windows put in. I bet them wooden ones you've got are all rotten. They'll devalue all the property in the street! They look a right mess."

Belinda had thought for months that they needed painting, but she'd let them rot now just to spite this interloper. She thought fondly of Mr and Mrs Benson, who'd lived in the house since it was built back in the 1930s, raised children and grandchildren and died in their own beds just weeks apart. She gave a watery smile and stretched out her right hand.

"I'm Belinda Lowe."

"Oh. Patricia (she pronounced it *Patreesha*) Street." Ignoring the offer of a handshake, she nodded her head towards her own new dwelling. "The way some people live! We're going to be gutting this place. You should see it... like something out of the ark."

Belinda *had* seen it, many times. Had seen it the day Mrs Benson died; helped organise the funeral; found Mr Benson dead in bed before the floral tributes had faded. It had been a true family home and she missed them all.

Patreesha was continuing. "All the inside walls are coming down – we'll have everything new. Our Jermyn's going to turn the garage into a studio. He's got his own band."

Belinda's heart slumped even lower. That garage stood between their two houses. She asked the age of this young musician.

"Thirteen. Our Sloane's twelve and Harley's eleven. Their dad, he's called Gerrard."

"Hmm. Unusual names. Anyway – must get on."

"Ta. Oh, do you want us to see about taking this hedge down or will you see to it?"

Belinda pretended not to hear.

✳

The transaction had taken months to finalise, but Patricia Street was soon included in the malevolent mantras. Sloane's nasal voice, screeching along to her brothers' unsynchronised drumming and strumming like a dentists' drill above the sound of heavy traffic, became a familiar earache. With Doug away for most of the week, there had been no autumn trim for the offending hedge and the dry, russet leaves, dispersed by November gales, gathered in heaps along hedge bottoms, gutters and driveways. The milkman kicked his way through drifts each morning as he marched past the six-berth caravan parked between the hedge and where next door's lawn used to be.

✳

Belinda had been waiting for the mantras to kick in even before the day's ambulance trip and associated traumas. Now, as the water cooled in the bath, her mood became colder, more resentful, as if she had entered a spiritual zone of malice. She seemed to stand outside herself, observing the shift in her aura. Thinking about the hedge, she realised how much she loved it, though she had often complained about the fallen leaves herself. Now, she would defend it at all costs.

She called upon the hedge to protect her family. Defend and protect – surely the true purpose of any boundary. She thought of the row of copper beech as a barricade, now. She envisaged herself manning that barricade against the enemy.

Drying herself with a warm towel, she looked out of the window overlooking the parked caravan and the breeze-blown leaf piles. A fat rat strolled calmly from one heap to another. It was joined by another, and another, even fatter. Belinda smiled, and pulled down the blind.

Later, noticing a chilly draught as she walked downstairs, she paused to draw the curtain over the front door. An unexpected weight impeded the drag. Stopping, she found a brown, padded envelope holding down the hem. It was addressed in block capitals to Sallby Village Hall.

Puzzled, Belinda took the package into the kitchen to open. At her first glimpse of the contents, she sank onto a chair at the breakfast table and up-ended the packet. A stack of bank notes fell out: twenties, some tens and fives – even a couple of fifties, all jumbled together haphazardly. A plain postcard carried the message in blue felt pen: *For the village hall. From a Well-Wisher.*

She sat at the table sorting the notes into piles, baffled, her mind swirling with possible mystery benefactors, motivations and uses for the money. The last was easy: there were bills to pay, for a start, and any left would buy toilet rolls. She was sick of buying them out from her own pocket for half the village to take home.

£630! This was the equivalent of 126 week-day hours of hire, with none of the associated outgoings. But where had it come from? How long had the package been behind the curtain? Belinda thought back. It had not been there when she vacuumed last Friday before setting off for Wales. When they'd returned on Sunday evening, the weather was mild for December and she didn't remember pulling the curtain shut.

Today had been frantic. Her head was spinning. Logic told her that the salsa teacher, who had disappeared owing a lot of rent, was trying to assuage his guilty conscience.

A ring of the doorbell signalled the arrival of the chicken chow mein for two. It smelt good as she set out the container and called Melanie, who was, mercifully, uninterested in her mother's life. She asked no awkward questions about the sealed-up door, being more bothered about Jermyn Street's scrap with Ben Jepson. While her mother was in the bath, a call from Chelsey had destroyed Melanie's life. It turned out that her friend and Ben had been 'an item' for nine whole days. He'd told Chelsey she had nice teeth too, and held her hand on the bus. Chelsey had kept the relationship secret because she felt sorry for Melanie, who now wept into her noodles, convinced that she'd be single for life.

Bel was sympathetic to a degree, whilst the phrase *self-centred drivel* in her head couldn't be ignored. A box of chocolates bought as an emergency Christmas present was unearthed and they ate till they both were sick, tired and ready for bed. The money slept under Doug's pillow.

Maybe things would be clearer in the morning.

10

The first thing was to get the money paid in to the village hall's bank account, a job normally done by the treasurer, John Spinks, for the last few years the only man on the team and the one to whom hire fees were paid. One of the old guard, John had served even longer than Belinda – since 1970, according to the old minute books stored in the hall's oddly shaped loft. Now over eighty, John only occasionally attended meetings, due to indifferent health and dodgy legs. He had been treasurer for nearly all his time with the hall and kept beautiful account books in copperplate handwriting. No-one had ever stood against his re-election to the committee at the Annual General Meeting or put themselves forward as treasurer. As for suggesting computerised accounts, no one would dare. When the time came, John would be a hard act to follow and no-one had a clue as to who might be willing to try. His mind was still as sharp as a tack.

At the moment, John was in hospital having veins removed during a rare good spell for his varicose ulcer. An intensive spell of home visits from the district nurse had improved the leg's condition sufficiently for the operation to take place. John's wife, Sybil, now mentally quite frail and hard of hearing, had resisted efforts to take her into respite care while her husband was away from home.

Belinda needed to bank the money before she started work at two that afternoon, so as soon as Melanie had clattered off to the school bus, she dialled John and Sybil's number.

"Hello Sybil. It's Belinda, from the village hall."

"You'll have to speak up a bit." The line crackled. "Did you say you're coming to mend the wall?"

"It's Belinda, from the village hall. How's John?"

"John? I don't know where he's got to. I thought he'd gone to make me a cup of tea."

"His operation. Has he come out of hospital, then?"

"Oh, he's out, is he? I don't know where he's gone with my tea."

"Sybil, listen. I've got some money to pay into the village hall bank account and I need the paying-in book. Could you ask John if I can call round and collect it?"

"Who are you? John's not here. Don't know where he's got to. I'm not giving you any money."

"No, I just want the paying-in book. Could you ask John where he keeps it, please? There might be some bills that need paying too, so if I could collect those and the cheque book, it would make things a lot simpler for John when he's back on his feet."

"Are you the chiropodist?"

"No. I'm Belinda from the village hall. It's to do with some money."

"I'm not giving you any money. You sound like a con-man to me. I'll call the police if you call again."

Belinda scratched her head, perplexed. Nice woman, Sybil. What a dreadful thing to happen to anyone.

❋

John and Sybil's son Derek lived an hour's drive away and Belinda knew him only vaguely. Their other children had emigrated years ago to Canada and New Zealand. Only Derek could help, but it took an hour of phoning round known relatives and associates to track him down.

She explained the situation and begged for his help. John's summons to hospital had come after a cancellation, leaving little time to transfer responsibility and the village hall accounts. Derek would need to persuade his mother to part with the cheque and paying-in books. He would do what he could, but it might take a few days.

*

Belinda was left with the stash of bank notes. If she'd had the bills, she could have paid them. Instead, she hid the money in an old calico shopping bag and hung it on a coat hanger in her wardrobe, so full of old clothes that the bag was well concealed. She really must get round to having a clear-out.

There was no message from Derek when she got home from work so the money stayed where it was. Easy to forget.

*

Christmas decorations were everywhere, brash and fragile, fooling no-one. Belinda went carol singing round Sallby with a group of local women and children – no men, as usual – raising funds for the county's air ambulance again. It always seemed to be her job to make the arrangements but no-one could remember why. This year, contributions were smaller, many donors tipping coins collected in socks into the concave bucket-lids. The coppers and silver made a satisfying racket as they slid through the slit and landed on those beneath.

Soon the buckets were too heavy to carry. Damp and cold, the singers drifted home after only an hour. In the past, carolling had always ended in the pub, extracting money from drinkers with repeated threats to keep on singing just one more chorus. Then someone would buy them all a drink while they sat at a table and counted the takings. This had been one of the high points of Belinda's Christmas.

Now, with the pub boarded up, the singers drifted away in ones and twos to their own homes, leaving her with the blue-lidded bucket. No-one was keen to stop by and supervise the count, as legally required. She lugged the bucket home, feeling cheated, and stuck it in the wardrobe beneath the calico bag. A red blouse of artificial silk slipped from its hanger to cover the bucket, which balanced tipsily on a pile of spare coat hangers and old shoes.

*

There were only a few more days before Aidan came home for the Christmas vacation, so it was necessary for his mother to clean his room several times, tidy his drawers and sanitise the personal possessions he'd left behind in September. The next five weeks were going to be wonderful. He would bounce home, long-haired and dishevelled like the students on TV commercials. The house would smell of delicious home cooking; she'd produce his favourite meals at the drop of a hat, and boys who had been turning into men under her eyes would make themselves at home with hugs and warm looks, and gasp with pleasure at Mum's sausage stew. The washer would be full of underpants and sports gear. Aidan would sit and watch her cook, picking her brain and cracking jokes. From time to time, he'd exclaim how much he'd missed all this. Melanie would start to smile again, and follow her brother round, once more the adoring puppy.

Doug would be home for the full ten days. She would get him to replace that piece of cracked guttering that let the rain through onto the conservatory roof, keeping her awake on wet nights with its constant drip, drip, drip. Maybe they'd even have time and energy for a cuddle or two. She'd bring Mum and Dad over for tea and maybe a game of Monopoly or Cluedo. Something traditional. The Wii would be put away... Granddad had still not got over the smash on the jaw he'd given Melanie when 'boxing' last year. Belinda couldn't wait.

Meanwhile, at the library there was Story Time to prepare for. Part of a national scheme, Belinda found this part of her job a trial. She didn't mind the preparation too much – finding attention-grabbing stories or poems was something to relieve the boredom of shelf-tidying and book-stamping, but the vacant countenances of the half-dozen regular attendees made her cross, suspecting as she did that they were only there to save on the heating at home. What with the library's future under threat, there was no money for professional storytellers or performance poets. Belinda was *it*, even though her rendition of *"'Twas brillig, and the slithy toves..."* sounded banal even to her own ears. The expressions on the faces of young Charlie, Jacintha *et al.* told her she was useless at it, yet delivering these sessions was a box to be ticked by the Chief Librarian, so deliver them she must.

*

Afternoons were dark and damp. Street lamps glowed orange, reflected in puddles already a-glimmer with junction lights. Navy skies pressed downwards, shrinking the days. Moribund spirits made feeble attempts at regeneration by drinking, partying, and drinking again; self-abusing challenges sought to imitate enjoyment, and failed.

But Aidan was coming home. For his mother, nothing else mattered. The time since his departure (and Doug's, of course) had seemed like an aeroplane journey flown at a height of a hundred metres. You looked down from inside a sealed capsule at life carrying on oblivious. Nothing had changed: everything had changed. Almost like a death.

Now her lifeblood began to flow again. It was Thursday, and the boy was expected at some unspecified time over the weekend. He insisted on travelling by train.

There was just one lender in the library by 6.30, a middle-aged chap in a balaclava and cycle helmet wanting the latest Dan Brown. It was not in stock. As the man continued to browse between the stacks, with a change in air pressure and a surge of street noise, Marnie Thorne walked in, shaking raindrops from her cream, caped gabardine. She folded a neat, emerald green umbrella, throwing droplets onto the counter top, and inspected her purple nails.

Concentrating on the computer monitor, the librarian barely registered a presence until, looking up at last, she smiled with genuine pleasure.

Marnie, it seemed, had been in Denswick "on business". What sort was anyone's guess – she was certainly not going to tell – and on her way back to the bus station, she'd decided to pop in to say hello.

Already in an optimistic frame of mind, Belinda gushed with life and warmth.

"I have so much to tell you!" she laughed, thinking of the ladder, ambulance and hospital episode. "There isn't time now or you'll miss your bus."

"Well, I'm not doing much over Christmas." Marnie tried not to sound too much of a Jilly-No-Mates, but just enough. "Maybe you could find time for an hour or two?"

Belinda wouldn't hear of 'an hour or two', insisting that her friend should spend a day with the family.

Parents and grandparents would take up Christmas and Boxing Days and no buses would be running, so the date was set for 27th December. The hostess would be able to parade her happy family to her lonesome friend. Not that she felt smug.

The man between the stacks approached the desk as Marnie left, and ordered *Digital Fortress*. Through the glass he saw the cream gabardine waiting at the bus stop before his view was blocked by the double-decker. On the bus, Marnie watched the glistening streets and smiled. Mission accomplished.

*

Patricia Street was on the doorstep when Belinda arrived home. Behind a half-open door, Melanie's relief at the sight of her mother was evident. The girl had been struggling with her Maths homework and resented the intrusive Patricia, dangling a set of keys in the air, speaking at volume about some Goan holiday paradise the Streets were off to the next morning.

At the news, Belinda allowed herself a laugh.

"How wonderful!" The enthusiasm was genuine. "Wonderful for the children," (meaning her own). "Wonderful for everyone!"

Two whole weeks without the twang-bang-screech of the Street Fytas, who had recently 'only just' failed an audition for *Britain's Got Talent*.

"Have a lovely time, all of you!" Bel called after Patricia's tottering heels. She couldn't wait for them to be gone.

*

Her plan had been forming for some time. Now, execution was imminent. She heard next door's car rev away in the early hours, but forced herself back to sleep. She must wait until Melanie had gone to school and other neighbours were about their business.

At nine, she dressed in old clothes before extracting a length of plastic pipe from the garage, where it had lain for years. She found a small hacksaw and removed a metre from one end. That would be ample for her needs. Rooting in Doug's tool box, Belinda unearthed a pointed, toothed gadget and a pair of pliers, then an off-cut of old carpet that Doug would lie on when examining the underside of his van. Hidden away on the cobwebby top shelf was an ancient, half-empty tub of rodent-control preparation, used once, years ago.

She carefully dropped the equipment over the fence onto next door's drive, before walking out of her own front gate and in through the Streets'. Bel looked from side to side, calm but alert, making sure she was not watched.

Hidden between the caravan and the fence, she pushed the carpet under the trailer. Belly down, only calves and feet protruding, she wriggled to reach the saw blade, which she took in her right hand. She had to twist her torso uncomfortably to stick the pointed end up into the caravan's underside. After the first incision, she worked patiently until she'd created a small hole. Then the pliers were used to nibble away at the orifice until the floor looked chewed. Satisfied, she raised one end of the piping and forced it into the hole, wedging the other end against a wheel with a half-brick. (She must remember to move the pipework before the Streets' holiday was over and install some fallen twigs in their place.)

She took a paper bag containing bits of bacon rind, stale bread, corned beef and cheese from her pocket. Crushed into a paste and laced with a few grains of Ratrid, the mix was laid in a trail under the van and into the narrow entrance to the pipe. As an afterthought, she pulled this out of the hole again, put a good handful of the mixture up onto the caravan floor, and replaced the pipe.

The rats would love it.

11

The Reverend Michael Batty had some interesting habits unknown to his flock at the grey-rendered Wesleyan chapel on Hooker Street. He had been on the Denswick circuit for three years now, but somehow he had not gelled with the chapel-goers.

Denswick folk were not the sort of people he had ever seen himself ministering to. Nationally, churchgoers of any denomination were thin on the ground, doddery on their pins and, increasingly, bewildered in the brain. To make things worse, for centuries this county had been renowned as stony ground for preachers, prophets, priests and pastors, and sadly, Michael was not a man known for personal charisma or persistence.

But Reverend Batty was a good man, though his left eye edged inwards towards his nose during conversation. His secret vice was not really a vice. Every Thursday he would roll up a frayed pair of black Speedo trunks in his favourite stripy towel, conceal them in an Asda carrier bag, and cycle to the swimming baths, which were housed in a 1960s concrete monstrosity a mile from the manse.

There he had his half-hour of tuition from Samantha, the newest of the pool attendants, who had just achieved her instructor's certificate. Samantha was unaware that the Reverend had been able to swim since he was seven.

It was only a small lie. He had never said he couldn't swim – just enquired about one-to-one lessons at the desk one day and found himself signing up for a twenty-week course. It was something to do to break the midweek monotony of funerals, hospital visits, prison chaplaincy and cups of tea with the housebound infirm.

From the start, Michael had managed to tense his body in a way that made him sink in the water. It was no good Samantha teaching from the poolside. The man needed hands-on support.

*

Contact was light and slight, but it gave Michael a frisson rarely experienced since the death of his lovely wife, Sylvie, some nine years earlier. He craved physical contact. This was not about lust, but loneliness. Michael was a man born to love. He loved all God's children; sadly, those who had loved him in return were dead or distant. Time was when it had been natural to hold the hand of a grieving widow, or take a small child on his knee during a home visit. Now, constant warnings about 'inappropriate physical contact' meant that every adult lived in fear of unwarranted allegations of paedophilia or other perversions.

The Reverend Michael certainly loved children, but not in *that* way. After the death of Sylvie, their lack of offspring was his greatest sadness. For Sylvie had just begun to suspect she was pregnant, after ten years of hoping, when a hit-and-run accident had wiped out their future. Michael had so much love to give, but no-one seemed to want it.

He was on the verge of falling in love with Samantha, her shapely bosom and gentle ways, but knew that it would be inappropriate. She was, after all, a pretty, comely, twenty-one-year-old girl, while he was a forty-three-year-old man with a cast in one eye and a calling that few people respected nowadays. Being the wife of a Methodist minister was no life for a young woman. Not that she would even look at him as a potential suitor in any case...but he couldn't help dreaming.

*

On his way home from the swimming lesson, Reverend Batty sometimes stopped off at the library to borrow secular reading matter, for not all his lonely evenings were spent preparing sermons or calling in at the youth club. He liked to escape into a fictional world to combat the emptiness in his soul that, sometimes, not even the Lord could fill, and had recently taken a shine to Dan Brown's novels. They might be far-fetched, but they certainly raised plenty of 'What ifs' that made one challenge past certainties.

This dark, damp Thursday, he was browsing along the shelves when he heard a familiar voice; a voice he had not heard for almost four years; a voice which had played a large part in his move to Denswick. It was the voice of Marina, the escort whose company had brought him comfort and pleasure until he fell foul of tittle-tattle.

Yes, he had been so desperate for female company that he, the Reverend Michael Batty, had paid for it. Not for sex, mind you. There was never any of that. An arm-in-arm stroll, a peck on the cheek, touching hands across a dinner table – this had been not quite, but nearly enough. He had tried other women from the agency, but they had been too full-on and out for a good time. Marina, despite her brassy appearance, had been more thoughtful and, yes, he had imagined that he might show her another way, broaden her mind and, God willing, save her soul.

Their happy enjoyment and companionship had come to an abrupt end when his relationship with an erstwhile prostitute came to the attention of the more judgemental members of his city congregation. It didn't take long for rumours to spread and for Michael himself to be vilified. It mattered not that he was innocent of everything but befriending a woman of dubious moral history.

"Did not the Son of God do the same?" he challenged his accusers.

This led to further accusations, this time of putting himself on a par with Jesus Christ. Michael had been in a hole, and every time he spoke, he dug it deeper.

In the end, he had taken up the offer of a position on a different circuit, in a small-town location some thirty miles to the south. He never contacted Marina again for fear that events would repeat themselves, but he missed her company and knew he had behaved badly in not explaining his departure.

*

A lonely Christmas stretched before him. Michael would enjoy the Carol Service and the Brownies' Nativity Play; the hymns and carols, so joyous to the contented, so mournful to the sad and lonely. Since Sylvie's death, Michael had made moan to the Lord through many a bleak mid-winter. The hopes and fears of all the years weighed heavily on his spirits. He was saddened by humanity's fall into the claws of mammon; grieved by the commercialisation of this holy festival and appalled by the dominant equation for young people, in which *celebration = drunken debauchery + chemical enhancement.*

The 'sports centre' was closing for two weeks, so there would be no Samantha to look forward to and he could find no excuse to refuse Mr and Mrs Lovejoy's kind invitation to Christmas dinner. If last year's was anything to go by, a gravy-less chicken wing, some barely thawed roasties and sprouts from Iceland would be it. There would be no Christmas pudding, which Michael loved, because it gave the Lovejoys wind – this last explained to him *sotto voce,* with exaggerated lip movements and nods of the head. He sometimes daydreamed of going away for Christmas – on a cruise maybe – but for a clergyman, that was just not on. Sylvie and he had loved their Christmases spent with her sister, brother-in-law and their four children. He rarely saw them nowadays.

But now! He had glimpsed his Marina once more! Had overheard her conversation with the assistant librarian; had knowledge that she would pass through Denswick again on the 27th. He would stand at the bus stop all day to catch a glimpse of her, if necessary. He would try to talk to her. Explain things. Maybe it would all be possible this time. Surely nobody in Denswick could know of Marina's history? And maybe the Dan Brown novel would arrive before Christmas. He could bury himself in that to help time pass quickly. Waiting for the 27th would keep Reverend Michael warm this Christmas, for sure.

٭

The minister did not cycle straight home from the library but braced himself to call on one of the most acerbic members of his congregation. A regular worshipper and bun-baker extraordinaire, the eighty-year-old had just been sent home from hospital following heart surgery. She was one of his flock: more importantly, one of God's children, so Michael loved her unconditionally. That is not to say he liked her.

Leaning his bike outside the window of her little front room, he threw back his shoulders, fixed a smile on his face which failed to reach even the wandering eye, and rattled the door-knocker. He saw light and movement through the glazed panel. A huffing and puffing grumble approached. The door opened a few inches.

Recognising the minister, the woman unhooked the chain and let him in. Without a word of welcome, she turned and shuffled back down the hall to a kitchen that smelt of cats and fried fish.

On a chair pushed back from the floral-clothed table, Dave Simmons rested an ankle trapped in a plaster cast. A pair of plastic and aluminium crutches lay askew on the floor.

"Dorothy! David! Good to see you both on the mend after your trying times! Looking forward to Christmas?"

Dave Simmons raised an eyebrow and grunted. His ankle was refusing to mend and he had no time for optimism. Dorothy sat down with a wheeze and a thump, dabbed at her forehead with a crumpled tissue and groaned.

"Oh, Mr Batty! It was very nearly the end of me, I can tell you. The things I've seen in that hospital… It's a wonder I got out alive."

Michael rearranged his face into an attitude of concern. Dorothy dabbed her upper lip with the tissue.

"It's not going to be much of a Christmas. David here can't work and he's having to stop with me… and I've only the folding bed for him to sleep on with his bad leg and all!"

Michael chanced a quizzical look at her son.

"Been thrown out," Dave grudgingly admitted. "Daft bat of a wife went off her rocker. A misunderstanding."

Michael's earlier cheer waved goodbye and disappeared down the hallway, but it was another fifteen minutes before he was able to follow suit. After a short prayer, he was glad to be out of there. Dorothy and Dave were glad to see the back of him, and returned to their self-pity.

*

The minister forced himself to whistle 'Joy to the World' as he pedalled the final half-mile back to the manse, and by the time he dismounted he was singing at full Methodist throttle, *"Let Heav'n and nature Sing!"* Not only was the joyful celebration of Christ's birth imminent: he had glimpsed his Marina and would be near her again on the 27th. Pushing his wet bicycle through the front gate he stopped, took a penknife from his pocket, and cut a sprig of holly from the tree at the side of the path. This year he would deck the hall… fa-la la la la! …for now he had reason to be jolly … fala, fa-la!

Not forgetting, of course, the birth of Our Lord.

That evening, he settled down to plan his Christmas services with fresh gusto, renewed faith and glowing satisfaction. He remembered why he had chosen this path in life. His congregation would, this Christmas, see him through unclouded eyes.

12

Aidan rang as his train pulled into the city, news having reached him of a lightning strike by bus drivers – something to do with a case of unfair dismissal. The branch line to Denswick had been axed long ago, so the student was stranded.

Belinda didn't drive much, beyond the library, supermarket and her parents' home, all in Denswick, only three miles distant. It was years since she'd taken the car into the city. It was easier to let her husband do all the driving than listen to each sharp intake of breath whenever she took the wheel, but Doug was still in Sunderland so today she must do it herself.

She must brave the heaving high roads and surging city streets. She planned her route, psyched herself up, calmed herself down, equipped the car with shovels, chains, blankets, hot drinks, torch and a brand new sat nav, and set off. Her boy needed her.

Reaching the city was not too complicated, but the correct exit from the ring road eluded her until the fourth circuit. Her head pounded. She suppressed the urge to stop the car mid-carriageway and shout, "I give up!"

At last she spotted the opposing arrows denoting a railway station and, following the signs, found herself under a Victorian stone canopy at the tail-end of a fifteen-long queue of black cabs. Other cabs followed hard upon the hatchback, trapping it in.

He was there, behind the queue and the haphazard standers-around-with-luggage. She stepped one foot onto the tarmac, waved and coo-eed at her son, swelling with pride and relief that he had survived and come home to her all-consuming love.

Aidan continued to look the other way. She couldn't catch his attention, and the taxi drivers were getting agitated, gesticulating and swearing in a multiplicity of languages. The hand holding the mobile phone to the young man's ear was not visible to his mother, who, seeing the movement of his lips, fondly imagined her son to be singing Christmas carols along with the Salvation Army band ding-donging merrily on the station concourse.

The chorus of taxi horns drowned out the voice in Aidan's ear. He spotted his mother making an exhibition of herself by parking on a taxi rank and coo-eeing so everyone could hear. God! She was such an embarrassment! Pretending they weren't related, he threw his rucksack and bags into the boot before climbing into the back seat. Not even a kiss for his desperate mother – just a grunt of acknowledgement. She searched for his face in the rear view mirror, but he avoided her eyes by closing his. She fired questions at him in surging disappointment, while Aidan feigned sleep. Belinda told herself that the poor lamb was exhausted; all would be well when they reached home.

Once there, her son barely looked at his sister, who had washed her hair and put on new mauve eyeshadow for the occasion, but went straight to his room. There he lay on his bed, headphones on, hoping to recover from his end-of-term hangover and longing for the girl he'd fallen in love with the previous evening. If only he could remember her name! Maybe he'd put it into his phone but he was too tired to check through his 214 stored contacts just then. Zoe, was it? Or Chloe? Or even Joey? His longing was not enough to keep him awake.

Downstairs, Melanie and her mother drank coffee in disappointed silence.

*

Doug returned for Christmas and things seemed almost normal. Their son was preoccupied, but not hostile; the gap which had opened up between him and the rest of the family grieved everyone but the young man himself. When gifts were exchanged on Christmas morning, his thanks were tepid and no recompense for the hours spent searching for the perfect present. His own offerings had been purchased from a single website, delivered in a green van on Christmas Eve and handed out in their original packaging. Effort expended: minimal. Belinda pretended not to notice, but she did, and she minded terribly.

The family celebrations followed their annual pattern: the grandparents frailer each year, less jolly, more complaining or confused. For Belinda, there would be three big meals to cook, for nowadays they took the Boxing Day meal ready-prepared to Doug's family in Derbyshire. With Marnie expected on the 27th an extra feast was needed, and Belinda was excited by this divergence from the norm.

13

The first bus to Denswick left the city at 9.15, arriving outside the library fifty-five minutes later. It was a chilly morning. On a bench across the road, Michael Batty waited, well wrapped up against the cold. When the bus arrived, no-one alighted. Michael helped a young woman on with a baby buggy, and the bus surged away. It would be an hour before the next one. He was not disheartened but cocked his leg over the crossbar and pedalled home to get warm.

Fifty minutes later he was back, and this time he was in luck. Sitting on the bench was Samantha from the swimming baths, fully-clothed in cherry-red anorak and jeans. Meeting someone out of context is always a puzzle, but after a few false starts they established each other's identity and cracked the traditional joke about not recognising people with their clothes on. An awkward pause followed, for Michael was positive that when he first sat down, Samantha had been weeping quietly.

He had joined the ministry partly because of his faith, but also because he was a compassionate man who wanted to help mankind. He was not one to pass by on the other side of the road, although it is true that mankind sometimes crossed to the other side to avoid *him*. Samantha, however, had become acquainted with him in a manner not reliant on eye contact, and felt his honest concern. When her tears returned, the minister gently asked if he could help.

A tale of lost love and lost child emerged. Samantha had fallen in love with a man from Serbia, who had entered this country in the back of a lorry full of timber. They planned to marry – indeed the man, Drago, had moved into her one-bedroomed flat above a hairdresser's and a child was conceived.

*

Sadly, the trauma of Drago's arrest, detention and subsequent deportation had brought on a miscarriage, which happened just three months before Michael began his swimming lessons. It was not only for Drago and his child that Samantha wept, but for her brother, gone to work on a North Sea gas platform with no intention of ever returning to his young wife, of whom Samantha was very fond.

Reverend Michael felt moved to suggest a prayer, there on the bench in the cold and damp. He held her hand for Samantha's comfort, not his own. She was at first embarrassed, not being practised in *al fresco* religiosity. Then came relief and reassurance that the lost child was safe in heaven; that she was still loved in the earthly world and the spiritual. These things were what she needed to hear and Reverend Michael's appearance on that bench, at that moment, on that morning, seemed to Samantha like divine intervention, or would have done had she known the term. "God's timing," would have been Michael's explanation of choice.

They raised their bowed heads as the bus pulled up. After a rapid, embarrassed leave-taking, the grieving girl disappeared between folding doors that swished shut behind her. Michael had failed to notice Marnie alighting from the vehicle, but spotted her climbing into the passenger seat of a small red hatchback parked fifty metres away.

He determined to follow the car by bike, which was fine as far as the traffic lights, but he fell behind when it met the open road to Sallby. His pace slowed as the bus disappeared in the distance. Freewheeling to rest his aching legs, he made up his mind to buy a racing bike and get fit in the spring. Then, maybe, he would be worthy of a woman like Marina.

*

Pondering, he pedalled on through hamlets and villages in search of the red hatchback. He found it parked in Denshill, outside the only surviving corner shop for miles. Marnie was still sitting in the passenger seat; the driver was behind a queue of six inside the shop.

A rap of knuckles on the window made the visitor jump. A dishevelled man in a dog collar and cycle helmet stared down at her. The face, so red and shiny, looked vaguely familiar. She looked again as he removed his headgear and mouthed, "Marina! It's me!" through the glass.

She saw that it was Mick! The nicest guy she'd ever been out with.

Carrying fresh milk and cut-price Christmas crackers, Belinda emerged from the shop to find her friend locked in an embrace with some random chap who stood straddling a battered sit-up-and-beg bicycle. Thoughts of Marnie's old trade raced through her mind.

She coughed discreetly. As the four lips parted, the man's face revealed itself to be that of the Dan Brown fan from the library.

Marnie swung to greet her, smiling happily.

"Bel, this is Mick – an old friend. I think I told you about him back in the summer."

Shaking the minister's hand, Belinda gave a watery smile, exchanged seasonal pleasantries and tossed the shopping onto the back seat, waiting for the lovebirds to decide what they were doing. Happiness radiated from them like sparks from a log fire and singed her pride. Belinda felt sore.

After a few minutes the couple exchanged phone numbers, shared another lingering kiss and parted. Marnie re-joined Belinda in the car and the man pedalled slowly away, humming the 'Hallelujah Chorus' under his breath while inwardly thanking the Lord for His goodness.

For Belinda and Marnie, the rest of the journey passed in near-silence. Belinda was disappointed that her festive good deed had been outdone by a chance meeting. Marnie was in a spin. She had intentions for today, and must make sure that her excitement over the reunion with Mick did not deflect her from them.

*

At 18 Dapple Grove, the second Christmas turkey was roasting gently in the oven. Introductions were stilted, with Aidan and Melanie keen to get back to the digital devices in their own rooms. Doug put on a good show of being the genial host, but would much rather have been dozing in front of the TV. Marnie was keen to get to know Aidan: she had a proposition for him, so feigned an interest in his collection of technological wizardry. He thought that, maybe, she was marginally more interesting than most of Mum's friends.

The chance to introduce her topic of the moment came during the pre-planned after-dinner walk. The day was crisp and blue, with frost crunching underfoot. As their path crossed fields and twisted through a wooded vale, Marnie managed to fall behind and stopped to lean against a slanting tree trunk. Realising she was no longer with the group, Aidan was asked to jog back in search of their guest. He found her, as she had intended, rubbing a supposedly sprained ankle and wearing a pained expression.

"I'll be alright in a minute," she said matter-of-factly. "It's a weak ankle, and I'm not used to walking on rough ground."

Her stoical manner won more sympathy from the youth than tears would have done.

Actually, Aidan was curious about this new friend of his mother's. He knew that they'd met on the wood-sculpture course, but Marnie was very different from other mature women he'd come across, who had mostly been teachers or the mothers of friends – plus those weird village hall women Mum was always on the phone to, talking about toilet rolls and light bulbs.

This one was quite fit in a scrawny way, and lacked the motherly fussiness he was used to. He bet she knew a thing or two as well. He found her... not exactly seductive... but fascinating certainly, even in this winter woodland setting.

Marnie played it cool, knowing exactly how to get her man.

Gallantry to the fore, Aidan offered his scarf as a bandage for the ankle and his arm to steady her progress. It felt manly to have such a woman on his arm. He just knew he would learn something from her.

As she hobbled along, Marnie asked disingenuous questions about his life at university, assuming the ignorance of a woman not bright or fortunate enough to have enjoyed such an education while Aidan exaggerated his successes, both academic and social. Gently, feigning coyness, she nudged him towards the subjects of sex and money.

In truth, Aidan had partaken in none of the former and had very little of the latter, although some of his flatmates enjoyed both with abandon. He was on the outside looking in at the student high-life. Sensible and strapped for cash, he both abhorred what he had seen and wanted to taste its pleasures. Marina knew instinctively that this was so.

Changing the subject, she asked him about earning opportunities for students. In Wales as elsewhere, they were thin on the ground.

"I've seen some adverts about sperm donation, have you? I should think handsome, intelligent young men like you are in demand for this, aren't they? I bet you're all doing it."

Aidan blushed. This was not an opportunity he'd heard of – and he wasn't sure he wanted to share his personal habits with Marnie just yet.

"My uni's a bit of a backwater. I've heard of it, but at other places," he lied. He wasn't quite comfortable with the idea.

Marnie changed the subject. The metaphorical seed had been sown. The literal would follow in time.

Changing the subject again, she embarked on a tale of three thirty-something women she knew, all respectable, none in a permanent relationship. Her aim was to make them appear respectable but deprived: how they were moral enough to eschew casual sex or marry an illegal immigrant wanting right to remain, but how this morality condemned them to live without the joy of children and a family life. As a footloose young man, these joys meant nothing to him. He took for granted what he had always known: that he would seek these things in years to come. Right now, for Aidan, family was on the hindmost of back burners.

Marnie herself had never known a father; this gap loomed larger with every passing year. Even a photograph or a name would have helped her feel complete. The life she lived as an adult had always been hand-to-mouth, rootless. None of the men she'd lived with were father material and much as she would have loved a child, she would not bring a baby into the world without some stability to offer. Her feelings were genuine and her delivery unaffected: as a persuasive speech, it worked big time. Aidan was convinced.

The women she described to him were mature, stable and not entirely penniless. Internet purchase of sperm was increasingly popular, but risky. Enrolling with a private human fertility organisation was beyond their means. Such treatment cost thousands… what with all the tests and screening… and it might not work. She bet the profits were massive, and painted a picture of fancy scientists and doctors living in luxury while ordinary women were denied their right to a child, simply because they hadn't got thousands of pounds to blow on a long shot. Using library computers and her new information technology skills, Marnie had researched the facts on donated sperm for her own purposes, and dropped carefully-selected truths into this 'discussion' diffidently, as if the topic had cropped up in passing.

When Aidan replayed it in his mind that night, he could not recall how the conversation had taken such a turn.

∗

Slowly the pair hobbled across the frost-whitened field towards the stile, where Belinda, Melanie and Doug were stamping their feet against the cold. It was decided that Doug and Aidan should jog back home for the car while the women made their way slowly to the garden centre-cum-café, which had been their original destination.

Once there, on only the third day of Christmas, the baubles and tinsel were gone. In their place stood racks of cagoules and fleece jackets, patio heaters and bowls of dried up hyacinths, all marked down by thirty or forty percent since Christmas Eve. The elves had been at work.

In the aquatics section, koi carp and shubunkins swam listlessly in the bubbling water, some on their sides as if snoozing. Concerned grandparents stood pointing out the dead fish to tiny children, who wept at the sight.

There were customers aplenty, stir crazy after two days of domestic jollifications, getting their fix of commercialism or handing over presents, gift-wrapped with receipts included, for a speedy exchange.

In the café, Belinda queued with the tray for coffee and cakes as Melanie settled Marnie at a table. It was difficult for the woman to maintain the pretence of suffering; as soon as the coffee arrived, she used it to swig down a couple of painkillers to look convincing. If she forgot to limp later, she could give credit to the pills.

Melanie was glum. Unlike her brother, she did not find Marnie interesting. Why had her mother invited this stranger to their home at Christmas? Melanie's own friends were cool or pretty, witty, clever or just *amazing*, according to her mood (when they were in favour), but it was a mystery why a woman of Mum's age should need a friend. What on earth would they have to talk about? They knew nothing of celebs or fashion! She supposed they might chat about recipes or getting stains out of carpets, but what else could two middle-aged women have to say? Did they discuss *Countdown*? Or *Jeremy Kyle*? Weird. She sipped her latte and nibbled a chocolate-chip cookie in silence. What sort of a name was Marnie anyway? And she looked a right slapper. She hoped Mum wasn't following in Gran's footsteps and going loopy already. Melanie would just *die* of embarrassment if that happened!

Watching the girl, Marnie began to see the downside of having kids and wasn't going to pander to *this* little madam. Belinda was embarrassed by her daughter's unwelcoming posture. What had become of the sweet, compliant, pre-puberty child?

"Doug seems to be taking a long time to fetch the car," she ventured, to break the awkward silence.

"They've gone to Gran's," offered Melanie, with no explanation.

"How do you know that?"

"Got a text."

"Who from?"

"Aidan."

"When?"

"While you were queuing."

"Go on!"

"That's it."

"Why didn't you tell me before?"

A shrug. There was something else going on with her phone which demanded her attention.

"What does it say?"

"'S from Chelsey."

"Aidan... what did he say?"

"Sshh... Hi Chels! What did he say...? He didn't...? You didn't...? Hang on a sec, babe..." The girl stood and walked away, animated at last, gasping and giggling into the plastic box, relieved that the purgatory of festive isolation had been breached.

Belinda's embarrassment flared, yet as a doting mother she tried to hide it under a veneer of pride.

"That Chelsey! I don't know how she'd cope without Melanie. Always turning to her for support... got a bit of a hang-up for some boy who actually fancies Mel. And I don't think her parents are that stable, from what I hear. Mel's always there for her..." She smiled weakly and tailed off.

Marnie adjusted her position on the shiny chair of moulded beech, and winced in pseudo-pain.

"Don't you think you should find out why they've gone to your mother's house?"

"I didn't bring my phone and I doubt if Doug's carrying his."

"I've got mine," Marnie volunteered. What a chance! "Do you know Aidan's number?"

The youth's mother rattled off the eleven digits, then repeated them slowly as Marnie tapped them into her *Numbers* list, pressed *Save*, then *Dial*. At the ringing tone, she handed the device to Belinda.

This stroke of luck accomplished the true purpose of Marnie's visit, which was to find a way of contacting Aidan in private. Now she had it. Her thoughts could turn freely to the happy chance of her meeting with Mick the minister. She was excited. Bel was speaking quietly into the phone, beneath the clatter of trays and piped background carols. She walked to a quieter place, away from her daughter, her expression concerned. Marnie twiddled the empty cookie wrapper in her manicured fingers and looked about her. This was her first visit to a garden centre; yet so far, she had seen no plants. She quite fancied having a pot of flowers or even a window box on the ledge of her dingy bedsit. Even this short time in a proper family home had nudged her dormant nest-building instincts towards wakefulness.

The call ended, Belinda sat down, face pale, hands shaking.

"It's Dad. They've called an ambulance. Looks like a stroke."

Her breathing was controlled; exhalations came through pursed lips. This was the dreaded moment: the moment that proved her parents were not invincible.

It had been Mum who answered the call – quite lucid, rational, controlled even. She'd had the presence of mind to dial 999 when Dad had suddenly stopped talking mid-conversation, struggled to carry on, but failed, one side of his face drooping, his arms unmoving.

"It was just like that advert on the telly," she'd said.

She'd wrapped the throw from the settee round his shoulders and phoned Enid from next door, who'd run round to give moral support. The paramedics had been wonderful and taken Dad off in their ambulance to the hospital. Doug and Aidan were going to take her there now. She must dash as they were waiting in the car.

Melanie was still wandering round oblivious, engrossed in her conversation with Chelsey. At Marnie's approach, she turned away. Marnie grabbed the girl's shoulders and spun her round. There was a scuffle, during which the phone clattered to the floor.

Aghast, Melanie shrieked, "Get off me, you perv!" and staff came running.

"Your granddad's had a stroke! Your mum needs you!" Marnie yelled, and the staff backed off.

"Selfish little cow didn't bother passing on a message," she explained.

The staff backed off even further and other customers tut-tutted at the crassness of youth nowadays. The girl was scrabbling on the floor in search of the pink sliver. It was found, accidentally, by a passer-by, who kicked it under a stack of aquariums and related equipment.

✳

Belinda was still seated in the café, dazed and shaken, only dimly aware of the kerfuffle in the fish aisle. The stomp of muddy trainers roused her: she expected her daughter to come running up in tears. What she got was a teenage tantrum over the potential damage to an essential piece of electronic hardware.

"Your granddad's had a stroke!" she interrupted.

"So? Get a doctor! What is a stroke, anyway? Can't be serious."

"It is very serious, Mel. We have to be prepared for the worst."

"The worst is that my iPhone... the one that *you* bought me for Christmas... has been kicked under a load of fish 'n' stuff. It's that tarty cow's fault!"

Her mother couldn't believe what she was hearing. Knowing that her legs wouldn't hold her, she remained seated, silent. The café manageress came over and led Melanie away, speaking in soothing tones. Marnie asked someone for the number of a local taxi firm, dialled and ordered a ride to the hospital. A fine day this was turning out to be.

After dropping Melanie off at Chelsey's, the two women travelled in silence to the hospital, where Marnie stayed just long enough to reunite the rest of the family in the A&E waiting room. She was an intruder now, not a guest; anxious to be of service but in the way, and sensitive enough to recognise the fact.

"I'll leave you now. Thank you for a lovely day – I do hope your father will be alright."

"But how will you get home?"

"Don't worry. I'll call a taxi. God Bless…" and she was gone, wondering what on earth had made her say that. It had been a useful day. Shame about the old man.

With Doug and her son close, Belinda just wanted to think about Dad. Sitting on the turquoise vinyl seats they waited, in trepidation.

14

Despite the sprig of holly in the hall, the manse was not a welcoming home, lacking as it did any signs of a feminine touch. Heart pounding, Marnie stood in the porch and pressed the bell. The sound echoed through the house. Peering through the stained-glass panels of the Victorian front door, she could make out a tiled floor, a newel post of dark-stained wood, and the bottom six treads of a flight of stairs gaudily carpeted in the old-fashioned way, with brass rods and dusty edges.

She rang again; heard sounds of water draining from a bath, footsteps descending. Michael, in tartan dressing gown, opened the door. Neither of them spoke. With both his eyes smiling into Marnie's, the minister stepped back, held open the door, and gestured her inside.

Overcome with emotion, he leaned his back against the closed door, opening wide his arms. It mattered little that his dressing gown fell open as Marina moved forward and laid her head on his chest; it was a joy just to hold someone close. That it was this woman he held was enough to wipe out the doleful ghosts of ten Christmases past. He could begin to live again, and for this he thanked the Lord – even as he felt this woman's teeth nuzzle his right nipple. All the Hallelujahs and Glorias of the Methodist hymnal rang in his head in glorious exultation at God's goodness.

Many issues were resolved on the night of 27th December: importantly, no consummation outside wedlock. It seemed odd to Marnie, but Michael insisted that everything must be done with complete propriety and she accepted his resolve. They were each carried on a tide of relief towards a haven of love: relief that at last things could be explained and understood; love that would make sense to no-one but the two people involved.

*

By seven o'clock, Michael had gone down on one knee and proposed. When Marina accepted, he went down on two, in silent and thankful prayer.

This whole prayer thing was a mystery to Marnie. She remembered *"Our Father..."* from the few school assemblies she'd attended, but the concept of belief and religion was a blank. Michael's explanation of God's love as *ineffable* was to her just that: beyond understanding.

"I can learn," she told Michael. "I need to find out what it is that you believe in, and why you're so sure. I'll give it a try."

Never before had she cared what people believed or thought of her... or had that been an illusion? Now, she wanted to be approved of, for Mick's sake.

*

The sparsely-furnished second bedroom in the manse was cold and unloved, so after the elation of the proposal and acceptance, practical matters had to be dealt with. Donning his bike-riding outfit, Michael set off for the cash dispenser and late-night supermarket, leaving Marnie to sit in his old armchair and smell his absence.

First in importance was bedding. Thrift was second nature to the clergyman: he eyed the prices of duvets and examined the tog ratings, imagined Marnie cocooned in their warmth, of waking her with a morning cup of tea and chaste kiss. Duvet chosen, he moved on to pillows, covers and cases. Should he go for plain or patterned, subtle or cheery? He stood for a long time, gazing and dreaming, eyes glazed over, smiling happily. He stood in that aisle and composed the announcement he would make to his congregation: should it be before or after the wedding? Reaching out, he grabbed a cellophane-wrapped duvet cover of vibrant red and yellow. It was impossible not to smile. He swapped the cover for a plain one of pale green, and then again for one of a blue floral design.

*

The store detective watched this odd-looking guy in the balaclava and cycle helmet with mounting suspicion.

Michael pushed his trolley to the display of scented candles: so many, prices slashed. So tempting. He had often weighed up the likelihood of enduring power failure, and moved on, but now he fondled and sniffed with sensuous delight. Bubble bath, toiletries, fluffy white towels – his Marina would need all these. The trolley was overflowing.

The detective followed at a distance. He had not felt a collar since before Christmas Eve and his productivity statistics were in need of a boost. This chap was a shoplifter if ever he'd seen one.

Michael moved on to Food. They would need a hot meal this evening. The only things in his cupboards were teabags, a couple of eggs and multiple tins of baked beans. Looking for something quick but wholesome, he opted for the supermarket's own-brand Luxury Shepherd's Pie. A pineapple pavlova for dessert, some fresh bread, milk and breakfast cereal, and he was done.

There being no more room in the trolley, Michael lifted out the plastic-wrapped quilt so he could add the foodstuff. The duvet went underneath, balanced on the wheel supports.

This confirmed the suspicions of the security man. He edged nearer to the checkouts, watching from behind a display of Australian wine. The hooded man was pretty clumsy, dropping merchandise onto the conveyor belt as he chatted cheerily to the girl on the till, paying finally with cash fished from an ancient wallet.

Michael started towards the door with his trolley, only now wondering how he would get the goods back home. In a bubble of perplexity, he paused at the entrance. There came a tap on his shoulder.

"Excuse me, sir. I'm from the store's Security Department. Would you come with me please?"

"Yes of course. Is someone ill? I am a First Responder, you know. How can I help?"

He made to leave the trolley where it was.

"Bring the trolley, sir. No, no-one's ill. I think we have a problem with your shopping."

He was led to a small office, where sat the store manager and another security officer.

"Could you give me your receipt, sir?"

"Which receipt?"

"For the shopping in this trolley, sir."

Michael dug into his pockets and finally found the crumpled strip. He handed it over. He was beginning to feel uncomfortable.

The security guard unloaded the items onto the manager's desk as the manager ticked them off on the receipt. Michael was puzzled but not afraid. He had done nothing wrong. Why had he been singled out thus, on what had been one of the happiest evenings of his life? When the trolley was empty, the men did not smile in apology. Instead, the security guard bent to retrieve the duvet from underneath.

146

"Just check again will you, Mr Martin?" he asked the manager. "Is there £59.99 for a SupersoftSnuggles microfibre 15-tog king-sized duvet on the receipt?"

The manager scanned the list and confirmed the item's absence. Only slowly did understanding come to Michael, so convinced had he been of his own innocence and, this night, of the goodness of God and the justness of all mankind.

"Didn't I pay for that?" he blurted. "I'd forgotten it was there!"

"Indeed, sir?" said the store manager, a bitter man who had recently been passed over for the Area Manager's job. "I'm just calling the police. The company has a policy of reporting every shoplifter apprehended." He sighed impatiently as his call went unanswered.

All four men waited in silence listening to the ringing of the phone. Michael, getting hot and bothered, took off his helmet and balaclava. He had remembered the recent debate on the inadvisability of wearing hooded garments in shopping centres. Surely no one would take him for a hoodie!

"While we're waiting, sir, for our records, would you tell me your name please?"

"Yes. It's Michael Batty. Actually, it's *Reverend* Michael Batty. Look, I haven't stolen anything... not deliberately."

"Well you *would* say that sir, wouldn't you?"

"What can I do to make you believe me?"

"Now you wouldn't be offering an inducement there, would you, *Reverend*?"

The security chap was enjoying this. Reverend! *As if!* The guy looked like a cross between a tramp and a psycho. Wouldn't be surprised if he'd escaped from some sort of supervision, psychiatric or penal.

At last the call was answered. An officer was on his way. The group sat and waited, Michael with mounting hysteria and loss of faith.

Marina would think he'd abandoned her again! And if he were to be found guilty of shoplifting, his career would be over...unless he pleaded temporary insanity. There were people who would take satisfaction in testifying to that effect, though Michael still contended that the sermon in which he'd drawn a parallel between a wind farm and a community at prayer was one of his best ever. The congregation had laughed when he told of the Windfarm Prayer Movement in the USA, and quoted Ezekiel 37 at them.

He'd told of the resurrection of the dry bones and how the Lord commanded Ezekiel to summon the winds. "Thus saith the Lord God: Come from the Four Winds, O breath, and breathe upon these slain, that they may live... and the Lord breathed his spirit in them and led them to their own land." Just as wind-generated power could breathe life, hope for the future and clean air into communities blighted by fossil-fuel pollution, so the power of mass prayer could bring guidance and enlightenment to benighted souls and rogue nations.

'As a sermon, it rocked!' Michael had thought, but others disagreed.

"This new minister's a bit eccentric, isn't he?" they'd mumbled to one another on the way out of church that first Sunday morning in Denswick. "A bit 'off the wall'? Not sure I could follow his reasoning, though he probably meant well."

And the old ladies had shuffled off home, reminiscing on the simplicity of the old minister's sermons and his preference for cheery hymns rather than the mournful ones favoured by Reverend Batty, though those who knew of his sad loss put it down to grief and felt his pain.

*

That evening of 27ᵗʰ December, the only police patrol vehicle on duty in the south of the county happened to be parked up on the edge of a country estate three miles from the supermarket. The officers were officially on the look-out for under-age drinkers and over-age drug dealers who'd been littering the woods with cans in their hundreds and crack bongs by the dozen. In reality, on a cold December night, the odds were long. The coppers were bored, cold and tired. When the chance of a change of scene came up they were off like a shot, siren blaring – "Just to show it were still working, like".

On arriving at the supermarket they adjusted their dress and assumed their most authoritative demeanour, walking the length of the checkouts glaring at staff and customers alike just for the hell of it, before heading to the manager's office. The shorter one tapped on the door.

"PCs Stuart Willis and Robert Daley," extending their right hands. "We're here in response to your call to HQ. I believe you've apprehended a shoplifter." Stuart spoke ponderously.

"That's right, officer." There was self-importance in Mr Martin's voice.

"Where is the suspected thief?"

"Right here." The manager pointed to Michael.

PC Daley looked round the room. Catching sight of the minister, his eyes lit up.

"Hey up, Mr Batty! How're you doing? Grand carol service you put on last week – one of the best, I were telling Stu, weren't I, Stu?" Stu nodded.

"You know this man?" asked Mr Martin.

"Know him? He married me and my missus a couple o' year ago, and baptised t'babby nine months later. Actually, Michael, I were meaning to ask when you can do the twins. They're two-month old now."

In his mind's eye, the store detective saw his productivity graph descending.

"What are you doing here anyway, Michael – er – Reverend Batty?"

What Michael was doing was struggling for breath. He had not had an asthma attack since his teens, but was now wishing he still carried an inhaler. Oblivious, Mr Martin interrupted.

"This man here is the shoplifter, officer."

Both policemen guffawed. "Nice one! Is this our Christmas present? Were you feeling sorry for two lonely coppers sitting in the cold and thought you'd invite us over for a warm-up and a laugh? Any mince pies going?"

Mr Martin remembered why he was an embittered man. That these buffoons should represent the long arm of the law; that despite their idiocy they were afforded respect and deference by the bulk of society; that he, educated, focused and man of principle, should be passed over time and time again in favour of go-getting upstarts, was just too much to stomach.

The flow of the manager's thoughts was interrupted by the noise of Michael's wheezing. The more he fought for breath, the more he worried about what Marina would be thinking. Words came out singly. His lips, his earlobes were blueing, deepening. He hunched forward in his battle. A call was put through to the store's First Aider, who set off from the canteen at a fast waddle. A wheelchair appeared from somewhere and Michael was wheeled into the cold night air. This seemed to help a little, but an ambulance was on its way, and shortly the First Aider puffed up with the emergency inhaler. Michael had not forgotten how to use it, and by the time the flashing blue light turned into the car park he was calmer, out of immediate danger.

As the ambulance drove round the car park, PC Daley asked Michael if there was anyone they needed to call on his behalf. The patient pointed to his inside pocket, struggling to reach a mobile phone tucked in the depths of his anorak. It was an ancient device, of the sort that would court derision in happier circumstances, but the policeman fiddled around until he got a signal. Between them, with hand signals and pauses for breath, Michael managed to indicate Marnie's number, and scribble a few words on the back of the supermarket receipt.

It was a difficult call to execute. The officer was aware of the minister's widower status; he did not know the nature of the relationship between Reverend Michael and the recipient.

"Hello. My name is Police Constable Robert Daley."

Silence.

"Mr Michael Batty indicated that I should inform the owner of this number of certain circumstances."

"What circumstances?"

"Well, among other things, Mr Batty has been taken ill in the Denswick branch of Asda. An ambulance has just arrived to take him to hospital."

Silence again. Michael scrawled another few words on the scrap of paper.

"Mr Batty is indicating that you are not to worry and should stay where you are. Someone will keep you informed."

Marnie ended the call in disbelief. She should have known better than to believe things would turn out well. When had that ever happened to Marina Thorne? Marina. That was what Mick called her. A name that ought to command respect... but it seemed he didn't respect her after all. He'd put someone up to this. Rare tears ran down her cheeks. Hurt and disappointment overwhelmed the habitual staunchness. Marina curled up in her fiancé's old armchair, smelt his body in its fabric, and sobbed.

An hour later, the tinny ring of the doorbell brought her to attention. Should she answer or not? What if it was someone needing spiritual guidance or a funeral arranging? Eventually, she shuffled to the door, drying her eyes on her sleeve.

A pile of bulky plastic bags, surrounded by a pair of navy-clad arms, seemed suspended in mid-air. After a second's hesitation, she noticed a pair of legs below... and those were plods' feet, she could tell at a glance. A muffled voice said,

"Good evening. I'm Police Constable Daley. I rang earlier. Just thought I'd drop off Reverend Batty's shopping and fill you in on the situation. May I come in?"

Marnie was always wary of the fuzz but restrained the urge to kick this pillock in the groin. Was this a sick prank? Yet the chap seemed genuine. Reminding herself that she was now affianced to a clergyman, Marina altered her demeanour.

"Do come in, Constable. Let me help you with the packages."

PC Robert Daley, duvet, pillow and the rest were ushered through to the shabby sitting room and deposited on sofas and chairs. Marina sat neatly by the fireside viewing the policeman expectantly. She had not yet introduced herself or explained her status in this house.

"Er... Miss... er...?" attempted Robert.

Marnie stayed schtum.

"Are you a relative of Mr Batty?"

"Friend."

"I see. Well, Michael was in the supermarket when he suffered an acute attack of asthma. He didn't have any medication on him. The store's First Aider supplied an emergency inhaler, which alleviated the symptoms, but an ambulance was called as a precaution and he's been taken to hospital."

"But why are you here?" Marnie was not so naïve as to expect police attendance at every asthma attack.

"A call had been received due to an incident in the store." Robert did not want to wash the Reverend's dirty linen in front of this 'friend' until he knew a bit more about her. She was not what you'd call open or approachable. "Myself and a colleague responded to the call. The items I've brought were in Michael's trolley when he was taken ill."

"How did you know where to bring them?"

"I know Reverend Batty personally – in fact he conducted my wedding. He's a familiar sight in the community, him and his bike. Even those who aren't chapelgoers know who he is. Um... how long have you been friends?"

"Several years," was as much detail as Marnie was prepared to give, thinking of Mick's reputation. "He'd offered to put me up for the night as I have business in the area tomorrow, which is why he went to buy new bedding. I gather the spare room in this house has never been used since he moved in."

That should scotch any rumours before they started and keep things respectable, in case Robert Daley was loose of lip. Her tone made it clear that the conversation was at an end.

He got to his feet. "Right then, I'll leave you in peace. I expect Michael will ring you when he's feeling up to it. If you're worried you can ring the infirmary." He jotted a number on the back of a Christmas card, nodded farewell and left.

Marnie sat in silence for a while, assessing her options. Tired out, she lugged the new bedding upstairs to the spare room, made up the bed and climbed in, undressed, unwashed and unimpressed by her first night as an engaged woman.

15

Belinda knew there was a booking in the village hall diary for February, but couldn't recall the details. Since Dad's stroke five weeks ago her life had become focused on hospital visits and caring for Mum, Melanie, the library and the house. By mid-January, Doug had returned to Sunderland, where the job had been extended, Aidan was back at university and her daughter was being no help at all. This change in her darling was as much of a shock to Belinda as her father's terrible transformation from a sprightly and capable man to a pitiable cripple. Mum was coping admirably, but her daughter was not. Belinda's sister Fiona had managed to get across twice, which was nice, but the closeness the sisters had enjoyed when young had faded as their lives diverged.

"I'd love to help," Fiona would claim each time she rang, "but you know how it is. The NHS needs me more than Dad right now and I have every confidence that you're coping just fine. I'd only be in the way. You have your routines, I know, and Melanie must be a great help. You're so lucky to have such a close bond, and you're so much closer to Mum and Dad than I am."

Her sister tried not to mind – Fiona had a good career, after all – but it rankled.

With the diary open on the kitchen table, she took a break for tea and biscuits, trying to remember the circumstances surrounding this booking.

4th February – Saturday evening. Private party.

The details were not written in her own hand, but in Aidan's, and the contact number was not a local code. Dimly, she recalled that Aidan had taken the booking on behalf of a mate's family, which was throwing a surprise party, so everything was to be kept hush-hush. Her son had taken care of the hire agreement and the deposit and was coming home especially for the weekend, so it would be fine to leave everything to him. Each time they spoke on the phone, she was struck by his increased confidence and composure. At least something was going right.

The rest of the committee were nowhere to be found at the moment. Two of them were enjoying winter cruises, the Su's had gone to Hong Kong for a family wedding, another was swotting for Open University exams and John was still not back on his feet after his op. Responsibility lay heavy on Belinda's shoulders.

Dunking another ginger biscuit in her tea, she let tears run down her cheeks and drip onto the diary. If only she had someone to comfort her, but those on whom she'd depended now depended on her.

The door handle moved and a ringed knuckle rapped on the glass half-pane. A brilliantly bronzed face topped by orange and black hair craned in.

"We're back! Brought you a pressie!"

Patricia Street didn't wait to be invited in, but dumped an airline carrier containing a bottle of spirits onto the table before looking round for an empty socket and inserting a plug. A thin cable ran to the small electronic photo frame she was carrying.

"I've brought our holiday snaps for you to see. Ooh! Ginger-nuts. I had a fella with them once!" She hooted at her own joke and delved her hand into the biscuit jar. "Get us a cup of tea then!"

Belinda filled a cup and numbly returned to her seat. Patricia was on her third biscuit before she launched into a loud account of the holiday, punctuated regularly by cackles of laughter and itemised lists of the alcohol consumed. Only when her tale was coming to an end did she comment on Belinda's reddened features.

"Have you got something in your eye?"

Belinda dabbed her face with a pink tissue. "No, I'm OK. It's just that I've got a lot on my plate."

"Oh, tell me about it! I said to my Gerrard, I says, 'Everything's always down to me'. I think they'd all stay in bed all day if it weren't for me. Don't talk to me about having a lot on your plate! You've no idea!"

"Mm… mm" A hiccupping sob prevented more.

"You want to leave off that village hall an'all." The visitor was on a roll now. "Needs pulling down. Folk don't want to go to no brick shed to enjoy themselves. Bet it's got mice and rats and all sorts." She shuddered in disgust at the thought.

"Have you ever been inside?"

"Me? No way! My standards are way higher than that. Even when we go caravanning we only ever go to the top-notch sites – the ones with a club and a resident entertainer. We don't go in for no home-grown entertainment or roughing it. We like everything to be professional."

"But your children make their own music," Belinda exaggerated.

"Means to an end. They're only practising in'garage until they hit the big time. They came third in the Happy Vanners Talent Contest at Skeggie last summer, and our Sloane had only learnt the song a week before. They are *so* talented, though I say it myself."

The proud mother pulled herself up as she recalled what Belinda had said.

"Anyway, enough about me. What's your problem?"

"My father had a stroke just after Christmas."

"Oh, I see. Dead, is he? Well, it's for the best, I say. You don't want 'em lingering, do you?"

"No, he's not dead."

The tears flowed freely into the palms pressed against Belinda's eyes. For once, Patricia had no retort. Belinda took a deep breath and concentrated on the electronic photo frame, now displaying the cycle of holiday snaps for the third time.

"That's pretty," she commented, as a shot of crimson sunset filled the screen, then whispered, "He's partially paralysed, almost blind and can't make himself understood."

"Ooh, poor old beggar. Euthanasia, that's what I want if I ever get like that. Pull the plug, I've told my lot!"

She leant across the table and pulled the plug from the socket, wrapped the cable around the frame and made for the door. She turned. "Is there owt you want me to do?" Her expression did not bear out the generosity of the question.

"I'll let you know," Belinda answered weakly.

"Maybe I'll join that committee of yours, if it'd help!" Patricia let the door slam behind her.

A silent prayer ascended. "Please... NO!"

That said, malevolent thoughts took over. She emptied the crumbs from the bread bin into a basin, added two tablespoonsful of peanut butter, some shrivelled boiled ham from the back of the fridge, a tin of sardines, and mixed them to a paste.

Later, hearing Patricia's car drive away, she climbed over the fence, wriggled under the caravan and applied the mixture to the cracked tarmac. She pulled the plastic pipe away from the van floor and peered in. Her earlier food parcels had been consumed and there were encouraging signs of rodent traffic.

"Time for breakfast, my beauties," she muttered, wiping fingerfuls of the stinking mix into the hole before replacing the pipe. She must remember to remove it before the season for spring-cleaning caravans began.

*

By the time the first Saturday in February arrived, Dad had been transferred from Intensive Care to a rehabilitation unit fifteen miles away. Mum was coping less well as the days passed; there had been talk about care packages at a case conference, but nothing definite decided. Whenever Belinda wasn't working she was in caring mode, so when Aidan came home for the weekend she was only too willing to let him deal with the booking at the hall. She could sit with Mum while Doug took a turn round the supermarket.

*

Aidan was there at five o'clock to admit the hirer, a tall thin man with a waist-length ponytail who examined the posters pinned to the door as he waited at the top of the steps. Hearing footsteps, the man turned and extended his right hand.

"Ambrose Mulholland. You must be Aidan."

The boy was mesmerised by the man's presence. In the orange glow of the street lamps, the skeletal face seemed other-worldly, imagined, although the handshake was firm enough.

After a rushed housekeeping tour, Ambrose indicated that he'd like to be left alone to set things up for the evening and handed over the hire fee in a sealed envelope.

"But you and your friends are coming back, aren't you? I really need you here. Shall we say 6.30 prompt?"

Aidan gulped. It had all been arranged remotely and had seemed like a laugh at the time – a chance to earn a bit of extra cash, too. Now the time had almost come he was not so sure. He nodded and left, jogging home with the envelope of cash clutched in his fist, hoping his mates wouldn't kill him when they discovered what he'd let them in for.

Mulholland manoeuvred his battered van as close to the side exit as he could manage, and set about unloading its contents. Cameras, screens, backdrops, lighting rigs and floor mats came first. These were laid round the edge of the room, then folding workbenches with integral vices, boxes of chisels and rasps, electric grinders and blocks of wood a foot square. With difficulty, he inched in a black bin containing potters' clay, boards and tools, and finally, four easels.

He worked for half an hour to set up this creative studio. Each side of the hall was devoted to an art form: photography, wood carving, clay modelling and painting – space for sixteen artists, though it would be a tight fit once the models were in place. In the centre, the floor-mats formed a rectangle, illuminated by the lighting rigs.

*

Aidan was a good-looking lad, curly-haired, quite strongly built and glowing with youthful vigour. Once or twice, girls who fancied him had suggested that he could have been a male model but he'd taken their comments with a pinch of salt. He saw himself as more of a lumberjack type, which probably had something to do with his choice of degree subject. Still, when the offer came of £100 for an evening's work, he'd jumped at the chance. It was easy to persuade his old friend Solly to come long; then Jim and Dan had shown willing. They presumed the modelling session was a photo shoot for some 'in-your-face' fashion gear or sportswear.

By the time Aidan returned with his pals, the hall was filling with artists fiddling with their equipment, but having downed a few cans at Solly's house en route, the lads were quite relaxed and up for anything.

Ambrose strolled over as the group walked in, extending his right hand to each in turn. In his left he held a drooping roll-up. Aidan wondered whether to point out the No Smoking stickers everywhere – his mum would have a fit if she'd seen a cigarette in the hall – but decided to let things ride. Actually, it looked as if most of the people in the room were smoking too. Smelt quite nice really, kind of dreamy and surreal.

Talking it over on Facebook the following week, none of the lads could remember how it was that they each agreed to try one of Ambrose's special-blend herbal cigarettes. At the time, it had seemed the companionable thing to do. Here they were, all pals together, meeting new people, trying new things – isn't that what youth is all about? OK, this guy Ambrose wasn't what you'd call young from the look of his face, but he moved like a gazelle and seemed pretty cool. He held their attention without effort; the four young men barely noticed the other people seated and standing at tables behind their equipment, eyeing them up.

Eventually, conversations turned to the purpose of the occasion. Aidan was puzzled: he'd expected to see cameras, but why the art stuff?

Ambrose suggested they use the Ladies' powder room to change in.

Inside the tiny, square room there was nothing but a bench, a mirror and a flap-down baby-changing table. The lads looked at one another, giggled, and trooped out again. Everything was such a laugh. Ambrose was waiting outside and shooed them back in. His tone changed.

"Take off your clothes and leave them in here."

More giggling, this time more nervous and incredulous; whispered protests and hesitation. Aidan felt it was his responsibility to clarify matters.

"Er… you said we'd be modelling, so where's the clothes?"

"There seems to be some misunderstanding," said Ambrose quite coldly. "There was never any mention of clothes. This is what artists call *life modelling*. Now take off your clothes. You have made a commitment." There was something in his voice that demanded obedience, though his outward demeanour did not alter.

Giggling rather less now, they slowly dropped their trousers and removed tops and socks. With underpants in various stages of wear and tear, they suddenly felt very young and vulnerable.

"Pants too," Ambrose commanded, working hard to keep a straight face.

The boys stood in a row, clutching their genitals. It was reminiscent of the PE changing rooms at school.

"Now this is what's going to happen." Ambrose spoke sternly. "You'll be working in pairs." He studied their physiques. "Solly and Dan, you two are quite slender. You can be together. Aidan and Jim, you're a bit more beefy – you're a good match."

He offered them each another roll-up, with a look that did not brook refusal.

"All those people out there are professional artists and they've paid good money to hire this hall plus you four as life models. That's why you're getting a hundred quid each for a few hours' work. If you chicken out, there'll be some very angry artists – some of them with mallets and chisels. Even a paint brush can do a lot of damage in the wrong place." His tone was light enough, but his eyes were cold and the words held just enough threat to quieten the naked ones.

Ambrose picked up two sheets of paper which had lain unnoticed on the bench.

"Here we have pictures of two very famous pieces of art. Each involves the sport of wrestling. The first is an American painting, executed by Thomas Eakins in 1899." He held up a printout. It showed two dark-haired, naked men entangled in a wrestling hold on a light brown floor.

"Solly and Dan, this is what you'll be modelling."

They looked at each other. Each opened his mouth to

161

protest, but no words came. To wrestle like that fully clothed would be a lark. But naked? In front of strangers? Er... NO!

"You'll be fine," Ambrose went on. "It's the way things were done in classical times, and still is in many cultures. You're not ashamed of your own bodies, are you? Surely you're not prudes?"

Bravado won out. "No, we're not prudes! No – it's cool. Yeah, we often roll around naked for a laugh..."

Each of them took another drag on his roll-up. Ambrose handed the printout to Solly.

"Right. Go and take up your position on the brown mat."

Dan and Solly shuffled out, the latter at least able to shelter his private parts behind the paper. Ambrose turned to Aidan and Jim. He held up another printout.

"This is a much more famous work of art. It's got several names, but I'll refer to it as 'The Uffizi Wrestlers'. The original was a bronze statuette from ancient Greece, but that was lost, and the famous version is a Roman marble sculpture, probably from the third century BC, currently in the Uffizi Collection in Florence."

He turned the picture towards the boys. Their jaws dropped. Surely he couldn't expect them to do that?

These wrestlers, also naked, looked stronger, like bodybuilders, in fact. Aidan and Jim surveyed each other's physique with dismay. They weren't exactly skinny, but by no means toned and honed like those in the picture. One man was crouching on knees and one hand. The other hand flailed mid-air at the end of an arm being forced up and back by the upper fighter, whose body stretched across his opponent's back, one leg entwined with the other's. It looked like agony, and much too close for comfort.

"Off you go. You're on the green mat," ordered Ambrose abruptly.

He turned and went back to the big room. Jim and Aidan hesitated.

"Come on!" came from the retreating ponytailed head.

By now, Solly and Dan had almost got themselves into position, after many false starts and interruptions to look at the picture. Their pose looked a bit less painful – and considerably less intimate – than that of the Uffizi Wrestlers. Jim and Aidan balked.

A hip flask was thrust under Aidan's nose. He took a swig and passed it on to Jim. Neither had a clue what was in the flask, but they stepped onto the green mat with an approximation of confidence. It was decided that Jim would go underneath, with Aidan on top, forcing his opponent's arm back. It felt terribly wrong at first. Neither of them was gay – or they didn't think so, at any rate – and public school homosexual high jinks were unknown in state comprehensives. To have one's private parts pressed against another lad's naked nether regions just felt unnatural – though not altogether unpleasant. And a hundred quid was a hundred quid, when all was said and done, and no-one was going to die, were they?

Behind the easels at one end of the hall sat two elderly ladies, spinster sisters, both teachers of art in their day. Hattie Dewson had at one time lectured at a big art college in the west of England, while younger sister Penelope had been Head of Department at a renowned girls' independent school. On retirement, the two had set up home together in a Victorian house with space for studios and displaying their many creations.

Independently, each sister had arrived at the same specialisation: depictions of the male form. They spent much of their time and most of their pensions touring the galleries of the world in pursuit of this fascination. When at home, they used whatever means they could to produce their own work in any medium available. To have four young, nude male models was a rare privilege, and one for which they had been prepared to pay a high price. In Los Angeles they had scrutinised the

Eakin painting, looking for the effects of shadow and strain. The marble sculpture in Florence had made them long to stroke those firm buttocks; in fact Penelope had been forced to hold her sister's hand to prevent this happening.

Now, they were thrilled to have chance to create their own versions of both masterpieces. It was true that these young models did not have quite the muscular development of the originals, but the sisters were not aiming to produce copies. They would give their own interpretations of each piece.

As the young models were finding it difficult to adopt the correct poses, Hattie and Penelope decided it was their duty to help, being teachers of a sort. Working as a pair, they grasped limbs and appendages with surprising strength and assurance, pressing here and pulling there until each duo was correctly positioned.

"These buttocks are very like David's," commented Penelope as she gently adjusted the angle of Dan's hips.

"You mean Michaelangelo's David, of course?" Hattie checked, with a smirk. "Yes, they do have that same slender strength, but of course the stance has so much to do with the grace of the lines. These Uffizi boys are not really sturdy enough for their piece. Tense your back muscles, dear, so we can see some definition." She patted Aidan's bottom.

The youth tried, but couldn't sustain the effort for long. Most girls seemed to think he was quite fit, so who were these old biddies to complain? Anyway, could anyone maintain a pose like that for hours?

All this while, the photographers had been setting up the lighting rigs: different lamps for different effects to suit everyone's needs. The models didn't care. The lighting gave off enough heat to keep them warm, the sense of suspended reality helped by the smoke-scented atmosphere. The boys did as they were told and stayed still. Cameras clicked and rattled; flashlights flashed. Men in baggy trousers and grimy jackets knelt close, then distant, snapping views of the clinches from every perspective.

At the workbenches, wood carvers shaped rough outlines with electric saws, blades and rasps. At others, clay was slapped on boards until plasticity increased. One man studied a square block of soapstone, chisel in hand. Only the photographers were finding this easy – but then, that was why the artists had each been prepared to pay £200 for this rare opportunity. To produce a finished piece in five hours was impossible, but with photographs progress could be made back in their own studios. With any luck, Ambrose would repeat the event in a month or two's time.

Breaks were called every half hour. The models took the chance to bend and stretch, at first donning their trousers to move around in. There was wine for those who wanted it, coffee or lager for those who didn't, and a ready supply of roll-ups, all free of charge.

By the third break the young men decided they quite liked the feeling of nudity so didn't bother with their jeans. One or two of the artists were feeling hot and, envying the young men's freedom of movement, removed first their shirts and then their own trousers. This was no frivolous or salacious behaviour, they swore. It was for their art.

By 10.15, Hattie Dewson was down to her petticoat, a home-made garment in peach-coloured satin with hand embroidery at the bust and hem. Maiden lady as she was, this aspect of her creativity rarely saw the light of day, and she was delighted by the admiring glances she imagined were coming her way.

Hattie was seated just in Solly's line of sight. Swivel his eyes as he might, her vast but low-slung cleavage drew their focus like a spring on a gate. It was horrible! What was she thinking of? His discomfort was further increased when the woman rose from her seat and came close, squatting down to peer in detail at the way Dan's torso pressed him down.

"Of course, Eakin has his wrestlers wearing a sort of loin cloth," she told them, "but this is much more effective. Freer; more classical." She adjusted her position.

Solly snapped his eyes shut after an unfortunate glimpse up the skirt of her petticoat. He saw stocking tops and suspenders and so much that was worse. Not a thong, surely? He didn't think £100 was payment enough .

Mercifully, sister Penelope was wearing trousers, though she too had found the heat overwhelming and on top was down to her bra, a massive and utilitarian construction in white poplin. Paint brushes in a range of sizes were slotted beneath the straps for convenience; her breastbone and spare tyre were streaked with paint in black and cream and flesh tones in between.

The hall was booked until midnight and activity continued unabated, the atmosphere growing warmer and drowsier as the liquor and smoke increased. At eleven forty-five, Ambrose called a halt. The models eased themselves upright, clothes were pulled on and the artists began to pack away. Ambrose announced that another session would be booked for March and details forwarded online. The four models made their way to the Ladies', to dress and collect their pay. Ambrose strolled in eventually and handed them £80 each in used notes.

"But you said a hundred," Aidan protested.

"Yes, you'll get it... but not until after you've done the second sitting in March. Let's fix a date. Talk among yourselves and let me know." He walked back to the hall.

Miffed, but keen not to mess up the deal, the lads compared possible dates and selected an evening at the end of the month. They felt deflated and slightly conned, but still pleased with their night's earnings. Once they had their clothes on again, the indignities they'd suffered faded into insignificance against the promise of colourful tales to tell their mates back at uni.

Reluctant to go to bed, her mother had been having a weep, so it was almost midnight when Belinda passed the village hall on her way home from Denswick. Seeing the lights still on and cars in the car park, she stopped to investigate and save the hirer the bother of dropping off the key.

At the top of the steps she noticed a strange, rather pleasant smell, but this was forgotten when she saw a waist-length ponytail hanging down a long, lean back. The wearer turned, surprised at the sight of her, before striding forwards with a polite, "Can I help you?"

"Is it Ambrose?"

"Yes. And you are...?"

"Belinda. It's me – you remember! I was on the wood-carving course at the sculpture park."

Surely she wasn't so instantly forgettable.

Ambrose hesitated. He wasn't sure how much she knew and didn't want to drop anyone in it.

"Ah, I meet so many clients. Remind me again..." he prevaricated, to give the models time to adjust their dress. He was fully aware of Belinda's identity and relationship to Aidan. He was also aware that she would not approve of all the evening's activities.

"Mine was the snail..."

Ambrose continued to look puzzled.

"This summer, was it? Or the year before?"

"It was August. Last August. I enjoyed it so much. And you must remember Marnie, one of the other women there. We've stayed in touch and have become friends. She visited over Christmas. She'll be so disappointed to have missed you!"

"That name does ring a bell." Ambrose spoke slowly, as if thoughtfully, but still buying time. Marnie, as facilitator, would be getting a hefty cut of the night's takings.

Belinda paused. A thought had struck her.

"There's been a party here tonight – were you a guest? Or a parent, more likely? My son Aidan was coming – I thought I might give him a lift home."

"Ah yes. A party." He thought quickly. "It was an artists' party – as you can see." He gestured towards the materials being packed away. "I think the person who organised it had to leave early."

"I didn't know Aidan had any artistic friends," she said. "How lovely. I can't wait to see what he's done." Today's youth wasn't all bad after all. It would be something different to chat to Mum and Dad about during hospital visiting.

"I think most of the youngsters have left already," Ambrose lied. "You might catch him up if you hurry."

"Well OK then. Make sure you drop the catch on your way out, please." Belinda took one more fascinated look round, was struck by the range of the guests' ages, and started down the steps. She paused. Why was that old woman just wearing an underslip? Must be Alzheimers. Shaking her head, she climbed into the car and wearily drove the last quarter mile home.

Recognising his mother's voice, Aidan had ushered his friends into the Ladies' toilet cubicle. They wriggled into their clothes and, one by one, sidled out of the fire exit. Aidan went last. At a sprint, he weaved drunkenly across the car park, hoping this would dissipate the smell of smoke which clung to him, then across a field to their estate. By the time his mother had garaged the car and come through to the kitchen, he was in the shower. Dad was snoring in front of the telly and Melanie was fast asleep in bed. The £80 was folded neatly in his jeans pocket. He didn't bother to say goodnight.

Ambrose stood in the village hall kitchen doing calculations in a small notebook. He would come out of the evening's venture with a couple of grand profit, even after Marnie's cut.

It had taken a lot of thought and many hours on social media to set up, but over the years he had developed a sixth sense about the proclivities of his many contacts in the art world. Finding four young male life models willing to work together was a stroke of luck. He would be confirming the next session as soon as he knew the hall was available. The cost of hiring an inner-city venue would be sky high. These community buildings were a bargain – low overheads, see, with all the work done by volunteers. They'd saved him a fortune. At the back of his mind he had visions of a nationwide franchise in this sort of thing. He'd have to talk it over with Marnie sometime, although she was behaving all goody-two-shoes nowadays. Regarding the boys, he wondered about using them for more homo-erotic poses at a later date.

He pondered the possibilities as he swept the floor, as stipulated in the Conditions of Hire.

16

At one end, the hipped roof of Sallby Village Hall had been partitioned off to form a storage loft. In this space, a dark-haired young man of swarthy complexion lay on his stomach, breathing shallowly and eyeing the movement of the sweeping brush through a crack where electric cables passed through the floor. Six hours had been a long time to stay still. There had only been intermittent bouts of conversation loud enough to drown the sound of adjusting his position.

Dragomir Duric was spending his sixth night in the loft. This building was largely unoccupied, so most of the time he could move around freely. The timetable of weekly bookings displayed on the notice board outside had been useful in helping him organise a routine... his English was just good enough to make sense of it. Drago was hopeful of finding work soon, but in the meantime his den was clean, dry and well hidden. He found other places to go when the hall was in use, letting himself in and out with a key given by a well-wisher. Tonight's events had come as a shock.

With help from his cousin, he'd made the loft quite habitable. Most of the ceiling rafters had been boarded over years ago for some long-forgotten purpose and here, with a sleeping bag, pillow and foam mat, he whiled away his time, sleeping mostly, or listening to an old transistor radio loaned by the same well-wisher. He was trying to improve his English by listening to Radio

4, but it was difficult. He used the kitchen and toilet facilities when the hall was empty. The lightweight aluminium ladder was easy to slide up and down as necessary, and with the walls in the corridor being grubby already, the signs of his presence went unnoticed.

Now, desperately needing the toilet, he squirmed uncomfortably on the dusty floor, waiting for the guy with hair like a girl to leave.

There were no mice in the loft, but spiders aplenty, and sometimes the deafening twitter of the sparrows which nested between the tiles and the roofing felt. Every now and then a confused bird would struggle through a hole in the fabric, only to batter itself to death trying to escape the enclosed space. This time, before dusk, Drago had spoken calmly in his native tongue, stretched out on his belly, offering crumbs from his remaining sandwich. At last the bird had calmed, squatting in the shadowed eaves, mute and sullen, eyeing him with suspicion. Beneath its ruffled feathers a tiny heart fluttered in fear. The man had recognised that fear; of being trapped in an alien environment. He had felt it in on the cross-Channel ferry, flattened among a load of sawn timber.

His first attempt at stowing away had come to nothing. He was detected by the driver before the truck had boarded the ship; handed over to the French authorities and, as a clandestine, removed from the control zone. But he hadn't gone far. After a few weeks he'd tried again, this time with more knowledge of the way things worked. His transport was selected with care: a wagon bearing an English name and a company address in a northern city. Once at large, he planned to make his way to Denswick, where his cousin Stevan had made a new life for himself.

This time Drago had been lucky. The customs officials only searched one in ten trucks, and his was the ninth. He changed the SIM card in his phone and was able to make contact within hours of arrival in England.

His cousin had found a steady job as a window-cleaner's assistant, and lodgings with a young couple who had little money and a little house, which he was smuggled into under cover of darkness. The couple were poor, struggling on benefits to pay for what they needed, and were happy to keep quiet in return for cash. Drago, too, was welcome to take cover for a while. He'd spent as much time as possible outdoors and it had been in a park that he'd met Samantha, a beautiful girl whom he'd seen visiting her brother. The likeness between the siblings was remarkable, and it gave Drago the confidence to start a conversation. The girl had been feeding the ducks on a sludgy lake with slices of stale bread. It was love at first sight for Drago; the feeling intensified when he discovered Samantha had a small flat of her own.

Samantha was training to be a swimming instructor; her income was low, but just enough to survive on. The flat – a bedsit, really – was cheap, in exchange for unofficial caretaking duties at the hairdressing salon below. In truth, she found living alone more of a challenge than expected, and found herself spending most of her spare time at her brother's house a few streets away.

By the time she met Drago there, all pretence about his identity had been dropped. Their relationship burgeoned, and her kind heart went out to this exotic immigrant, so lonely and in need of nurturing. She was sure he was a good man, and gave him her all.

Soon they were sharing the flat above the hairdresser's. It was too soon for Drago to look for work, they agreed, so they lived in pinched circumstances warmed by young love and a sense of adventure. When Samantha began to suspect she was pregnant, they had been together for eleven weeks. Drago was overjoyed; to have a child was a privilege for any man. Now he would have a British child and a beautiful British wife. He would do the honourable thing and marry his sweetheart, but first he must find a job and earn money for his new family.

Things had gone black with a knock on the door, the authorities having been made aware of a foreign-looking bloke with a strange accent asking for work in the local builders' yard. There were few enough jobs for the streetloads of native workless, so there was any number of disgruntled unemployed willing to 'dob him in'.

Drago had gone without a struggle, embarrassed and dejected, and did not put up a fight against the inevitable deportation, although he vowed he'd be back to claim his child and his bride.

*

So here he was, lying on his stomach watching a long-haired man sweep the floor with a wide broom, and wondering how long it would be before he could a) have a pee and b) see his sweetheart once more. He adjusted his position yet again, trying to relieve the pressure on his bladder, afraid to move across the loft for the container he usually used in emergencies.

At last the sweeping ceased. Rubber-soled feet strode lightly across the floor, darkness fell at the click of a switch and the front door banged shut.

The fugitive struggled to his feet, stooping to avoid the sloped ceiling of his hide-away. He waited a moment: the slam of a car door; an engine igniting; the swish of tyres on gravel, and all was quiet. The sparrow crouched in the furthermost corner, head under its wing, as if asleep. Drago decided to let the creature be for now. He opened the hatch, adroitly lowered the folding ladder and scrambled down.

It was a relief to stand up straight and walk. A dim glow from an orange street lamp shone through the dusty windows, giving just enough light to move by. Emboldened, he went first to the Gents', turned on the light and made use of the facilities with relief. Barely had his flow begun when he heard the sound of a door opening. Light footsteps were followed by a short scream close behind him. He could not stop mid-stream, but instinctively turned, exposing himself and spraying the newcomer with urine.

Shock stilled Belinda's tongue. Fear filled her eyes. Urine soaked her skirt and splashed her boots. She looked into the frightened eyes of a young man caught in the middle of a private act. She had seen that look before, but not in the village hall.

Realising that she'd forgotten to collect the keys from the hirer and too edgy to sleep, Belinda had decided to pop back to the building in the hope of catching Ambrose before he left. She saw the last of the vehicles leaving, but noticed that a light had been left on, so let herself in to check that the hall had been left clean and tidy and flick the switch. It would save her a job in the morning.

Never before had she confronted an intruder. Never before had Drago felt so vulnerable. Never before had two dumbstruck strangers stood in the Gents' toilets at ten past midnight on a cold winter's night, mouths agape and afraid of what might come next.

The man trembled as he turned back to complete the task in hand. Belinda grabbed a paper towel and scrubbed at her skirt.

"Sorry, lady," the young man muttered. His accent was thick.

"Who are you? Did you get locked in?"

Her heart was thumping. She turned slightly and, glancing down the corridor, did a double-take. The loft hatch was open and the ladder down! Why? How?

Drago saw her reaction and had a brainwave.

"Little bird. A little bird. Up there. I try to... hold it." He mimed the action. Learning a language online is not ideal, and he had to think hard about his vocabulary.

"Very scared. It fly and hit head… hurt its…" He flapped his arms.

"Wings?" Bel supplied.

"Little bird has fear. Need door. I help it. I try…" His deep-set eyes looked sad.

She had only seen inside the loft once. Many years ago, one of the men on the committee had gone up there in search of old minute books and found those dating back to the hall's construction. At the time she had climbed the rickety ladder and poked her head through the hatch. Now, she wanted another look.

The stranger tried to divert her attention. "The bird. In kitchen, I think!" he pointed.

"We'll look in a moment." She was already half-way up. The man knocked against the ladder hard, almost toppling her. Was that deliberate?

She continued up until her head and shoulders were through the hatch.

A strong flashlight had been left burning. A neatly laid-out sleeping bag bore the impress of a supine body; books, a radio, jigsaws, a plastic bottle and a rucksack were plain to see.

It took Belinda's brain a few seconds to fit the pieces together: this chap was living in the loft. She felt, rather than heard, the flutter of wings beneath the eaves as her own fear pulsed in her ears.

Back at floor level she faced him, her eyes asking the questions.

"Lady! Lady! Please. I need stay."

"Why?"

"I am good man, not bad. But police find me, send away. I must stay. My girlfriend, she having baby but now no baby. Very sad. I sad also and must see her."

Bel could think of nothing to say. The young man's dark eyes brimmed with tears.

"I here before. We fall for love. Then I send away from UK. Now I come back marry her. My cousin he tell me baby gone. I need find her. Maybe we have more baby."

"But why are you here, in this loft? How did you get in?"

"Please, lady. Is secret. I not say or…" He mimed the drawing of a knife across his throat. "Kind people give me key. They say hide here for two, three weeks, then get job and room."

Belinda turned on the light in the kitchen and put the kettle on to boil. Reaching two green mugs from the cupboard, she glanced over her shoulder. The man had slumped against the wall, head hung low. Tears ran unchecked down his cheeks. How old was he? Twenty-two? Twenty-three? Not much older. Some mother's son; some boy who'd set off in search of adventure, but found love, sorrow and rejection. Her heart went out to him. She wanted to learn more of his story.

Pouring boiling water onto stale coffee granules, she asked, "What's your name?"

"My name is Drago. Dragomir Duric. I am from Serbia."

"Tell me what happened." She reached for the powdered milk, stirred in a spoonful and handed him a steaming mug. They moved into the bar area and pulled two comfy chairs up to a small table. The light from the kitchen shone through, giving a homely, intimate atmosphere. The radiators cooled down with clicks and rattles.

Belinda made a mental note to adjust the timer to keep Drago warm.

Haltingly, the boy (for he was little more) told his tale; of his life in Novi Sad, the second city of his country, which sometimes hosted a music festival. How, one year, a band of British-born Serbs had performed at the festival. Drago had got to know them, hung out together for a few days, he and his cousins Stevan and Hamid, and hatched a plan to explore the world together. Maybe they'd meet up with the band again… he thought they lived in Leeds.

176

The first time, they'd reached the Channel ports and two of the trio had immediately been turned back. Stevan had gone undetected and made it across. Hamid returned home, deterred by the risks involved. But Drago had waited, waited and watched, until eventually he too made the crossing to England, with nothing more than a few clothes and a sleeping bag in his rucksack, plus an address provided by one of the musicians. It belonged to a Brit of Serbian extraction, he'd claimed, who might provide shelter and a helping hand. And so the cousins had both, separately, come to rest in the town of Denswick. Stevan had already found work with a window-cleaner by the time Drago reached the town, and was living in relative comfort. Attempts to contact the musicians had been futile.

*

Bel noticed the black hairs on the back of his hands. As she considered her quandary, an almost 'out-of-body' detachment settled on her: she was perfectly calm to find herself drinking cheap coffee in this familiar place in the middle of a winter's night with an illegal immigrant and a trapped sparrow. She knew that she was, technically, in a vulnerable position. She knew instinctively, however, that she was in a position of power.

She held this man's fate in her hands.

Belinda believed in sticking to the letter of the law. Bel, on the other hand, was more pragmatic. What good would come of turning this young man in? Belinda was a sucker for a sob story; Bel wondered how she could turn the situation to her own advantage.

*

Drago was reaching the end of his tale. "Today a man say I can do job. Soon get money."

The job was at the new manual car wash that had appeared a few months previously on the car park of a closed-down pub near Denswick. Belinda had used it a few times herself. Operating out of a Portakabin with hosepipes, buckets, sponges, wash-leathers and an ancient mangle, a succession of men with tawny complexions, well-toned muscles and East European accents worked tirelessly from dawn to dusk. In a carefully choreographed sequence, three blokes at a time would squirt detergent, sponge wash, hose down, clean wheels and wipe dry. They even blacked the tyres and opened the car doors to wipe the sills... and all for £4.99. It was cheaper than the drive-through.

Rarely the same three men, Belinda had noticed, and there was always one who spent most of his time talking into his mobile phone as he worked. She'd wondered where they lived; Balkan accents should have been noticeable around Denswick, being primarily a white British working-class town, but they were never heard away from the car wash.

"Will they find you somewhere to live?" The answer was no.

"But when I work I get money. Then find my Samantha. She not live in same house now," he concluded sadly. After the loss of their baby, the girl had left the flat above the hair salon and moved back home to her parents, whose address he didn't know. They had made their daughter promise to end contact with Drago before agreeing to take her back, so the suitor's aim was to find a job and a home before throwing himself at the feet of his beloved. Then, maybe, she would defy her parents and marry him.

He spoke with such sincerity that Belinda was smitten. As a mother, as a woman, as a believer in love – his story convinced her, so much so that she almost forgot to ask again, "But how do you come to be sleeping in the loft of my village hall?"

"Kind lady and man say OK. Lady give me key, tell me what do."

Belinda was staggered.

"What are their names?"

"The man, he a priest, I think. He pray with me. I good boy, Christian – go to mass in Serbia. He pray. He good man. Lady give warm place and food."

There was no priest she could think of in the vicinity. The village church staggered on with a peripatetic, part-time vicar who had been in hospital with a nervous breakdown for the last three months, to her certain knowledge. The Catholic priest in Denswick, Irish to the stereotype, did not have a reputation for kindness.

"Who is the lady?"

"She his wife. The man..." Here Drago crossed his eyes momentarily.

This meant nothing to Belinda. Mind you, loads of people had borrowed keys for the hall over the years and not returned them. She really must get the locks changed when there was enough money in the kitty.

Tiredness and the oddness of the situation suddenly overwhelmed her. She must go home, but could not turn this young man out on the street.

"I'll come again tomorrow and talk about this. Maybe not tomorrow," – she had work and hospital visiting – "but soon."

The hall was rapidly losing heat now the heating had gone off. Drago could do with a hot water bottle, she thought, or even better, an electric blanket, though she doubted there was a socket in the loft.

*

On her way home she tried to pretend the meeting had never happened. If she hadn't returned to the hall she'd have been none the wiser and Drago's secret would be safe. But she *was* the wiser; her night was spent tossing and turning beside Doug, who broke off snoring to tell her to lie still. The secret of the village hall lodger nestled at the back of Belinda's mind, taking on a more romantic hue by the hour.

By the time Doug set off for the north-east and Aidan for Wales on Monday morning, the future mapped out for Drago and Samantha was rosy.

17

Just before midnight on 27th December, the Reverend Michael Batty had been allowed to leave the Accident and Emergency Department of Denswick Infirmary following his severe asthma attack, at the end of a day which had turned his life upside down. He sat in the back of a taxi too exhausted to decide whether the inversion was good or bad.

Good that he had found his Marina again; bad that he'd been caught technically shoplifting. Good that he'd been able to offer a listening ear and spiritual succour to his swimming instructress; bad that a member of his congregation had been summoned to arrest him. He had left Marina in an empty house, with no food and a comfortless bed. Would she still be there when he got home?

Would Robert Daley really deal with this discreetly, as he'd promised, or, once down at the cop shop, would he gossip and guffaw about the goofy minister? Would the Reverend Mick be even more of a laughing stock than he'd been before?

Being of a naturally pessimistic disposition, Michael expected the worst and usually got it, but the gods, or his God, had looked kindly on him that day. PC Daley took his faith seriously, though not much else. In addition, he knew a thief when he saw one, and he knew the minister was anything but. After Michael had gone off in the ambulance, Robert paid for the offending duvet out of his own pocket before loading the purchases in the back of the police car and delivering them to the manse.

The woman who answered the door took him by surprise. His copper's nose smelled someone from the wrong side of the law, but his Christian charity gave her the benefit of the doubt. Still, he'd be watching…

When Michael finally arrived home, discharged and feeling foolish, he heard her snoring loudly and peeped into the spare room, where she lay looking every inch a trollop. But she was *his* trollop, and she was still here.

He switched off the light and climbed the stairs to his own bed, exhausted and abashed but, for the first time in ten years, not lonely.

Over the next days and weeks they shared their stories and dreams, and Michael planned a discreet wedding to be conducted by a colleague from an adjoining circuit. Neither bride nor groom wanted a public fuss, but it was important to Michael that their union should be blessed and not altogether a hole-in-the-corner affair.

*

One Monday morning in mid-February, a small congregation gathered in Denswick Methodist Church. On the bride's side: Jolene, a one-time room-mate, Bud Baxter and Ambrose Mulholland. On the groom's: two church wardens (one of whom was Dorothy Simmons); his late wife Sylvie's brother and sister-in-law; PC Robert Daley and his wife; and Samantha, the swimming instructress. The organist made up in volume for what his playing lacked in accuracy.

Only the two ministers and churchwardens knew the hymns: 'Love Divine' to start, with Michael's favourite, 'And Can It Be…?', to end. He longed to teach the words to his Marina; to stand on the church steps and bellow at the top of his voice,

"My chains fell off,
My heart was free.
I rose, went forth
And followed thee!"

In his exultation, he could not tell where Marina ended and God began. With both of them by his side, Michael was sure he would be able to right the wrongs of the world. His voice cracked with emotion as he reached the finale:

"Bold I approach the eternal throne
To claim the crown
And Christ my own!"

Tears salted his lips. His heart hurt with joy and relief. "Thank God! Thank God!" Angels' voices echoed in his head. Trembling, he took his bride's hand as they turned to the congregation and walked away from the communion rail to the vestry.

The register signed and witnessed, a small buffet catered by the café over the road was uncovered, a non-alcoholic toast of sparkling grape juice offered, and the tension relaxed. It was Samantha who caught the bride's small posy of hyacinth florets; Michael had told Marina the girl's sad story, so the bouquet was aimed with care. Marnie had an idea.

A discreet taxi drove the happy couple to a honeymoon in a farmhouse close to Walla Crag. Their world had turned: they basked in love's sunshine by the chill glory of Derwentwater, strengthened by their union, fortified by a sense of completeness and ready to face whatever came next.

18

As a harbinger ray of spring sunshine streamed through the bedroom window, *Patreesha* Street nudged her husband. No response. She nudged again, a little harder.

"It's gonna be a nice day. You can get 'caravan cleaned."

Gerrard Street rolled onto his back and snorted. His eyes remained closed.

His wife's eyes studied the play of the sunlight chinking through the curtains. It was only a few weeks until Easter and so time to gear up for the caravanning season. There would be another talent show at Happy Vanners soon and you couldn't go anywhere with a mucky trailer.

Gerrard Street had other plans for his Sunday, such as sleeping for two more hours and watching sport on the telly for another six. If Patricia wanted the caravan cleaning, she could do it herself. Not that he'd ever say that to her face, mind. He'd got *some* sense.

He rolled back onto his side and made himself comfy. He wasn't that keen on caravanning anyway. It had always been the fishing that attracted him – from the inshore boats operating out of the little harbours along the coast, £40 for the day. As a way to escape the wife and kids, you couldn't beat it. Mind you, their Harley was starting to take an interest. Gerrard would have to knock that on the head if he were ever to get any time to himself.

Patricia tried again. "You could get all 'cushions out and aired in this sunshine while I'm cooking dinner."

The breathing at her side deepened. She prattled on regardless, formulating ideas for innovative titivations to the holiday home's décor. She'd always longed for the sort of husband who'd bring her tea and toast in bed on a Sunday morning, but she'd not found one, and Gerrard had been her third attempt, though the only one to give her children. He was alright in that department.

She rolled out of bed and trudged downstairs to make her own tea and toast. She could hear the blurt of TV from Sloane's room and electronic beeping from the boys'. They'd stay in there all day if she'd let them, but they needed to practise their music ready for the talent contests. She'd give them a couple more hours.

Sunlight streamed in, reflecting off the foil containers from last night's takeaway debris piled on the hearth as she drew back the curtains. The room smelt of curry and lager. Patricia opened a window, padded back to the kitchen and fished a black plastic sack from a drawer. While the toaster did its work, she collected the worst of the rubbish before dumping the bag outside the front door.

The caravan took up most of the front garden that wasn't already used as a car park. Even she had to admit that it all looked a bit of a mess at the minute, though at least the caravan hid those trees and bushes next door, which just encouraged birds, and with birds you got bird muck. She wouldn't have minded leaving space so she could chat over the fence to that Belinda woman once in a while, though. The van did form a kind of barricade... and that lass probably needed a bit of cheering up, what with her husband buggering off every week.

Back in bed with the tea and toast she flicked on the TV, quickly locating a re-run of the nation's favourite talent show. As a determined wannabe showbiz mum, Patricia scrutinised every detail of texture, tone, colour, pose and voice, identifying star potential amongst the motley assortment of singing nail technicians, acrobatic hoodies and ageing, toupéed balladeers. Whatever star quality was, she had no doubt that her own offspring possessed it in cartloads.

An hour later, she was restless again. Toast crumbs made her cleavage itch and the sheets gritty. Her spouse had slipped back into the deepest of slumbers and even when the sun shone through the uncurtained window right onto his eyelids, it was obvious that cleaning the caravan was not on Gerrard's Sunday morning agenda.

"I'll do it myself, as per usual," muttered his martyred wife, who nurtured the delusion that she alone held the family together.

Donning a pinafore over a denim boiler suit from her eighties' heyday, floral wellies and yellow rubber gloves, equipped with buckets, brushes, squeegees, hosepipes and an array of cleaning chemicals, she sashayed out of the front door to confront the five-berth Meadowlark Superior, now tinged with colour where the winter weather had stained the white walls and roof with a greenish bloom. She circled the trailer, planning her onslaught. *Inside or outside first?* Patricia wondered. When her inspection took her to the boundary side, she was surprised by the amount of tree debris on the ground beside the battered fence. She dragged out a couple of stout, short branches but didn't ponder on how they came to be there. This tidying up decided her. She would start with the outside.

An hour later, the sun glinted on the Meadowlark's glasswork and shimmered off its sides, and Patricia needed an audience for her achievement. Time for the kids' music practice and a brew.

Fifteen minutes after this, the Street Fytas assembled in their 'studio' psyched up to making this Sunday special, as instructed by their mother.

Imagine, if you will, the wondrously complex, bewildering harmonies of 'Bohemian Rhapsody' as performed by the rock band Queen. Recall the ever-changing chords, tones and rhythms, the inventive lyrics, at once unfathomable and profound. Now imagine, if you can bear it, those same notes, lyrics and harmonies delivered in a series of staccato yells and glissando shrieks by three untalented and tone deaf schoolchildren. Where Patricia heard the former, the rest of Sallby heard the latter.

Upstairs, barely stirring, Gerrard Street pushed his head further under his pillow. Downstairs, heartened by the enthusiasm evident in her offspring's rehearsal, Patricia girded her loins for an onslaught on the van's interior.

Warbling garbled snatches of the Rhapsody under her breath, she rummaged in the hall drawer for the key. She was still singing as she turned it in the lock and threw open the caravan door.

The stench knocked her back. Her gorge rose to her mouth. She heaved. Bluebottles lay dead on every surface; a few moved somnolently on curtains or squirmed in cobwebs. But the smell...!

Patricia tried to step inside but was again driven back. What appeared to be beads were everywhere. Yellow sponge spilled out of the banquette cushions which Gerrard Street had unwisely left *in situ* over the winter. Tiny fragments mingled with thousands of tiny black ovals.

"Gerrard!" Her scream was loud, but not as loud as the wailing of electric guitars from the garage.She banged on the van walls and yelled again.

*

"That band is truly dreadful," thought Belinda next door, as she turned up the volume on her elderly CD player. She had

been concentrating on learning the lyrics of a new song while ironing Melanie's school clothes. Belinda had come across an unfamiliar disc when vacuuming under her daughter's bed the previous week.

The cover picture showed faces masked in white made up to look oriental, and the words *The Mikado* suggested this didn't seem Melanie's type of thing at all; even less so when her mother played it to test for 'appropriateness'. Catchy tunes, clever words which didn't make a lot of sense to her, yet she'd found herself listening to it several times when she was alone. One song in particular had struck a chord. It could have been written for her: must have been put there on purpose, as a reminder to reinstate the malevolent mantras.

She experimented to see if her own voice could block out the din from next door, and surprised herself, for though one singer will never make a chorus, her vocal force was improving.

It sounded as if someone next door was hammering, or was it drumming? That family really were inconsiderate Sunday morning neighbours. It was time to refresh her campaign.

"As some day it may happen that a victim must be found.
I've got a little list… I've got a little list
Of society offenders who might well be underground,
And who never would be missed – who never would be missed!"

She sang pointedly, eyes narrowed. Yes, the entire Street family would go on her list. As she pulled another shirt from the ironing basket, her mind worked on lines of her own.

"There's the pestilential children who cannot play the guitar
But who screech and wail and holler just to please their dear Mama…"

She had them on her list. They sure would not be missed. She smiled as she sang along and enjoyed the ironing for the first time in ages.

Over the fence, though shaken, Patricia Street was a determined woman as she looked down at the Keep Calm and Carry On pinafore that protected the front of her boiler suit. Hysterics never worked with Gerrard. True wartime grit was called for.

Holding the tea towel over her nose with one hand and a long-handled brush in the other, she climbed into the caravan. Her wellingtons crunched over the desiccated droppings. She bashed the brush against the doors and cupboards (which Gerrard had failed to leave open as recommended in *Caravan Monthly*). The only sound was the intermittent hum of a dying insect. No mice... so why the droppings?

The smell was stronger as she passed the sink. Another step, and she unlatched the door of the minute bathroom. This stank even more. She shut the door, leaned her head outside and yelled her husband again. Again, Gerrard burrowed deeper into the bedding. Patricia, feeling sick, scurried to the steps and gulped in fresh air.

She hated mice – was terrified of them, though of little else. What were husbands for, if not to deal with vermin and protect their wives from rodentine horrors? Was Gerrard to be a failure in that department as well as in so many others?

Her fear was out of all proportion, she knew. The merest glimpse of mouse fur was enough to set her heart pounding; her legs would carry her up onto the nearest table or out through the door, her mind empty of everything but revulsion. And if she should glimpse a length of skinny tail... oblivion seemed the only option.

Standing well clear of the van, she banged on its sides with the sweeping brush. Nothing. No scurrying, no squeaking, no Pied Piperish columns of vermin leaping down the caravan steps. She tied the tea towel across her face, bandanna-style.

Emboldened, back in the caravan, she opened the door beneath the neat kitchenette sink. Hurled back by the stench, she glimpsed an enigma even as she staggered. Hundreds upon hundreds of snail shells were piled up around something dark.

She slammed the cupboard shut, her head swimming. Snails? No inkling of an explanation came to her. She vomited a little out of the door, breathed deeply and once more yelled, "Gerrard!"

The Street Fytas had moved on to a more lyrical number. Maybe Jermyn would come to his mother's aid.

"Jermyn, sweetheart. I need you!"

In the garage, hearing his mother's call quite clearly, the eldest son responded *sotto voce*,

"Duh... We're rehearsing!"

He tutted at the others and the musical siblings set off on a double-volume rendition of 'We Will Rock You' complete with stamping feet.

*

Next door, having completed the ironing, Belinda thought she might do a spot of pruning in the spring sunshine. Doug had already gone down to help Dad out with a few odd jobs, so she rooted out her gardening gloves and secateurs.

Meanwhile, over the fence, some colour had returned to Patricia's cheeks. She needed to see those shells again... at present, she couldn't believe what her eyes had told her.

Inching open a tiny drawer, she reached for the torch she knew would be there. A little juice left in the battery allowed a yellow beam to shed some light on the snail shells, all empty. Holding her breath, she moved the beam a fraction. Mounds of dark fur gleamed dully in the dim light. Two, three... no four at least; a tiny snout and a knot of thick rats' tails – all crawling here and there with maggots.

It is impossible to say whether the scream, the yelp, the leap or the vomit came first.

Belinda, just exiting her own front door, heard the noise but could see nothing for the caravan on the other side of the fence. The screams continued in gasps, interspersed with yelps and a retching sound.

"Hello! Is something the matter?"

No reply. As the lamenting and heaving continued, she left her own front gate and trotted along to her neighbours'. From there she could see Patricia Street, in a rather odd get-up, curled over on the tarmac, howling and shuddering, face buried in a red cloth.

Common decency forced Belinda through the gate to crouch down beside the woman. At the back of her mind, the refrain of *"I've got a little list..."* rang a warning bell that somehow, this was all her fault.

✳

Paroxysms of shock and revulsion rocked her neighbour's equilibrium. She was making no sense, prattling about snails and tails between retches.

"Shall I take you inside, Patricia?"

At the shake of the woman's head, the saliva dangling from her lips swayed back and forth. Belinda dabbed it away with the Keep Calm and Carry On tea towel. Urged at last to her feet, Patricia allowed herself to be led out of the gate and round to Belinda's kitchen, where she was dosed with a few drops of Rescue Liquid in warm water. Without comment, Belinda gathered that her rodent feasts had proved attractive to the vermin. Later perusal of the Ratrid packet explained their search for water. She felt a faint twinge of guilt, which didn't last.

Ten minutes later they sat calmly at the table, sipping camomile tea in silence until, with a sudden show of resolve, Patricia stood up.

"I need to make a call."

Belinda led the way to the lounge and pointed to the house phone.

"Have you got a Yellow Pages?"

This was produced. Belinda tried not to eavesdrop on the call… or calls, she thought, although she imagined they were to next door. The tone on this end was quite businesslike – all traces of shock had disappeared.

"I'll be off your hands in fifteen minutes." Patricia returned to the kitchen and sat down. No further information was volunteered as they sat listening to the Street Fytas' muffled din until at last, their mother went to the Lowes' front door, opened it and left without a wave.

Belinda couldn't resist a peek from behind the net curtains. A taxi had pulled up at the kerb, followed a few seconds later by a low-loader which came to a halt outside next door. Two men climbed out of its cab. Together, in silence, they manhandled the caravan into position, attached a large hook to its towing bracket and winched the Meadowlark Superior aboard. Within minutes it was well secured. As the convoy of two pulled away, the woman in the back seat of the taxi was tapping a number into her phone, which had been in her dungarees pocket all along.

*

The driver of a police patrol car passing through the estate took note of the low-loader, which bore a strong resemblance to the one he and his partner had followed up on the moors last summer, and ran a check on the vehicle. This time the livery was plain to see: *DunCrushin: Denswick's Premier Metal Recycling Company*. The Farm Watch squad would be calling on DunCrushin very shortly.

Within a very short time, the Street family's caravan was wrecked. Likewise the Street Fytas' musical ambitions and the holiday plans of Tyson Dunne, Managing Director of the aforementioned DunCrushin.

It was some hours before Gerrard Street tripped over the bag of rubbish on the step and noticed that both his caravan and his wife were missing. He would have been hard pressed to say which he was gladdest to be shut of.

Next morning, a red and white *For Sale* notice was visible through the gap where the caravan had stood. Belinda cheered inwardly and stepped jauntily to the tune of 'As Some Day It May Happen' as she made her way to the village hall, carrying a plastic container of freshly baked cake for the lodger. This time, she smiled to herself as she walked.

19

Solly Mann's parents had taken themselves off to the
Maldives for a month, making the most of an unexpected
legacy that had come their way. Their son had made the most
of their absence by returning home from university to engage in
a variety of extra-curricular activities not normally associated
with undergraduate mathematicians of banal tendencies. So
much was done online nowadays that Solly was confident his
absence from the *Groves of Academe* would go unnoticed.

The Manns lived in a big house on the leafier fringes of
Denswick, six miles from Sallby, thus it was easy for Aidan,
Dan and Ben to join Solly 'on retreat' without fear of crossing
paths with their own families. The two gigs at Sallsby Village
Hall would rely on a little bit of luck, but confidence in their
own good judgement – typical of young men everywhere – made
them blasé. The rest of the time they'd just sleep late, catch
up with their assignments when necessary, watch *Countdown*
and chill out. They'd put their names down for *Bargain Hunt*
already and would conduct research by watching afternoon
TV. The money they earned from the gigs would give them a
kick start in a business enterprise of their own, the nature of
which was, as yet, undetermined.

The new venture proposed by Ambrose and Marnie was
something different...but definitely not for parents to know
about. They'd be doing good, for sure, and earning some useful

money. Best not dwell on long-term consequences. You never got anywhere if you weren't prepared to push boundaries and break free of red tape. Ambrose had convinced them of that, and Marnie swore she had all the equipment and knowledge necessary to make it work. All the lads had to do was turn up at the village hall as required and perform.

✳

Belinda struggled on to keep the village hall functioning and even managed to persuade a few other committee members to attend a meeting by holding it in the pub in Densfield. She'd reported back on the bookings – just enough detail to make the minutes of the meeting sound official. The pressure was off for a while, at least. The others were happy in their ignorance of what needed to be done... Belinda only worked part-time after all. They'd become used to the treasurer's absence from meetings; the chair passed on his presumed apologies as a matter of course.

She had reached an accommodation with Drago whereby he could stay in the village hall loft, discreetly, in return for a few odd jobs and a slice of his wages. In return, she would furnish him with a few home comforts, some of which remained unspecified.

As the days went by, the young man's plight took on a more and more romantic hue, for he was far from home and family. The illegality of his presence paled into insignificance beside the poignancy of his lost love and mis-carried child.

Doug was away most of the time and seemed more distant when he was home. There was no-one who was prepared to listen to her worries and no word from Marnie since her visit had been cut short by Dad's stroke. That hurt. Melanie had turned into a teenage stereotype of the sulkiest kind – nowhere near the daughter her mother needed right now. That hurt.

And Doug seemed in no hurry to return to life as normal. That hurt, too. She hadn't the energy to argue or complain. In truth, she couldn't wait for him to leave on Monday mornings so she could check on Drago.

Her illicit secret, he gave meaning to her current existence. The rest was duty. She needed Drago for herself. He provided an outlet for her motherly nature: she'd always prided herself on her maternal instinct. Taking this unfortunate boy to her bosom, baking him an occasional cake, she told herself, were only natural. Any mother would do the same.

*

Drago's job at the hand car wash was exhausting, tedious and paid below minimum wage, cash in hand. It had been agreed between them that thirty percent of his earnings would be adequate to pay for the electricity, water and Belinda's acquiescence. That money, paid in coins and used notes, was dumped with the other cash at the bottom of Belinda's wardrobe. She would get round to sorting it soon, once she'd made the appointment with the bank. Some of the cash was spent on buying paint, brushes and other DIY materials. People assumed she was doing a bit of decorating at the village hall in her spare time. The rest of the committee, relieved that she hadn't asked them to help out, acquiesced from a distance.

That suited Belinda. The more people kept their noses out the better. John the treasurer still lingered, a heart attack having followed close on the heels of the varicose vein operation. It wouldn't be proper to write him off just yet, though. News of his condition leaked out from time to time, but Derek Spinks had still not managed to relax his mother's grip on the paying-in book or the village hall accounts.

With luck, it would all sort itself out before the Charity Commission got tough. Eliciting middle names and dates of birth from new members to complete the form each year was hard enough; cooking the books would be a whole new ball game! She must deal with it some time, but not just now.

*

All the cool kids, Melanie among them, had taken to setting off for school at 7.30am, but what they did between then and nine o'clock was a mystery.

By 7.35am, Belinda was letting herself into the village hall by the back door, energised by the knowledge of Drago's presence. Closing the door carefully behind her, she became aware of a noise. She froze, trying to identify the sound. Was it weeping? She tiptoed forward to where the young man sat sobbing, head in hands, his tears dripping unchecked onto the table.

Bel walked up behind him and gently laid her hands on his bare shoulders. The shoulders were broad and muscular, tinged with a dark fuzz which continued down the long back to the unbuttoned jeans. The shoulders shook with sobs.

Bel's hands seemed to move of their own volition, strengthening, stroking and caressing as a mother's hands caress her child, a lover's her beloved.

The dark head lifted and the man turned in his seat. Dark eyes, deep and wet as mountain tarns, were raised in search of her own, but found them not. The man turned away again. The stroking continued.

He leaned his head back against her as she stood behind him. Her hands moved forward, stroking, stroking across the rough chest, up to the neck, the earlobes, the scalp. Down, over the nipples: hard; erect. Towards the waistband: tempting; forbidden.

He swivelled in his seat, turning the chair noisily. His face buried itself between her breasts; hirsute hands clasped her

197

buttocks as the sobbing reached a more violent pitch. Her arms wrapped themselves around the head. Her own chin rose; her eyes shut tight; her head flung back.

At the same instant, she noticed the bird's corpse.

"Mama! Mama!" he howled. *"Prevara prostitutka!"*

Even in Serbo-Croat, the words were recognisable.

What was he saying? That his mother was a prostitute? That she, Belinda Lowe, Mrs Ordinary, was a prostitute? And a prevaricating one?

But worse than *prostitutka*: he had called her *Mama*! It was Bud Baxter all over again. She felt the blood rise to her cheeks; stepped away, unable to look him in the face.

*

The black dot of the sparrow's one visible eye seemed to wink at her. The bird's neck was awry; the temptation to set it straight, to smooth the ruffled feathers and give the creature a decent burial, was too strong to resist. Tipping the fruit loaf out of its container, she folded the creature's wings, wrapped the body in a shroud of paper towels, laid the package in its plastic coffin and sealed the lid.

Businesslike, she moved into the kitchen, made coffee and handed it to the man, whose sobs had subsided when the stroking stopped. His eyes still sought for hers: still they failed to find them. His fingers searched for hers as he took the mug, but were evaded. He could not understand the sudden coldness. She who had been so warm, so comforting...

Drago wept, not for his mother, not even for his lost phone, but for his lost love and lost dreams, dreams that had evaporated in this very hall just eleven hours earlier, in an episode of which Belinda was ignorant. She indicated that he should clothe himself, still avoiding those eyes; saw a T-shirt discarded on a chair; smelt it; tossed it onto the table. He had expected her to take it home to wash and dry. They usually came back, neatly ironed, within a few hours.

She sat down opposite him, shoulders back, face deadpan. Emotions battled for dominance: pride had the upper hand at the moment. Coolly, she asked the reason for his tears.

His halting English was difficult to comprehend, interspersed as it was with sobs and heaves, but she recognised the name Samantha somewhere in the explanation.

The name would go on her list.

Changing the subject, she asked him for the rent. It was Drago's turn to be shocked. Yes, he'd agreed to pay her something, but he'd not expected to hand over actual cash every week. To his way of thinking, he was earning his keep by painting the skirting boards. He had other methods of payment in mind as well – his cousin had told him that old English women were eager to please and easily satisfied. He fished a couple of £20 notes from his back pocket and held them out to her. She indicated that more was needed – only nodding when five notes lay on her upturned palm. As her fingers closed over them, his left hand cupped hers from beneath and his right from above. Her hand was captured. Involuntarily, her eyes flicked to his: were captured also. Her heart pounded. Resolve and pride succumbed to folly, compassion, and a smidgeon of desire.

*

He wondered how much she knew about the events of the previous night and whether his faltering English would do justice to what he was about to describe. Snivelling, stumbling over his words, Drago reported the scene observed through the crack in the loft floor.

Some time after dark, he'd been relaxing on his bed when he heard a vehicle arriving, then footsteps up to the door.

Swiftly and silently, he'd lifted the ladder and closed the hatch in a well-practised move, before settling down to peer through the crack and see what was going on.

As curtains were drawn and lights came on one by one, he could see the top of a woman's head, blonde, short-haired. She was wearing a winter coat. Next time she passed beneath him she was dressed all in white – such a uniform as he had seen worn by beautiful nurses in American hospital dramas on TV. Her movements were brisk and businesslike.

Another vehicle arrived; the sound of rattling wheels rotating on changing surfaces, hushed voices and manly footsteps. Something was trundled indoors.

Two men: one, thickset and shaven-headed; the other, taller, wearing a hat and long, dark overcoat. They seemed to be working to a plan.

Twenty minutes later, the hall had been transformed into a clinic. Wheeled screens divided the space into cubicles. The one in his view housed an examination couch such as those used by doctors and therapists, and a medical trolley in stainless steel, which was topped by mysterious items in sealed bags. A folding chair; glossy magazines; a folded white garment lay neatly on the couch, with two chairs placed at a small, square table. A bottle of wine, two glasses, a small posy of flowers and a disposable camera added to the mystery.

Drago was baffled. Tired from his work and weary of peering through floorboards, he had rolled onto his back and tried to sleep.

*

Unobserved from above, five feet below, Marina Batty had adjusted her nurse's cap and smoothed the starched, white uniform. This project meant a lot to her, but if it went wrong she could lose everything. Without the pressure from Daryl

Baxter and Ambrose Mulholland, Marnie would have backed out when she married. But they had too much on her: she couldn't take the risk.

During her spell in prison, she'd thought long and hard about using her professional knowledge in less sordid ways. She had a lot to give, and now, as a minister's wife, felt a calling to bring comfort and support to those in need. She had identified a need; she had cogitated and consulted, planned and persuaded. She was confident that it could work. She was less confident that it was entirely legal, but no-one was likely to tell. Anyway, as far as Marnie was concerned, people were free to do what they liked with their own bodies. There was not much she didn't know about what the 'experts' call *Sexual Health*. Contraception, disease, abortion – she'd seen it all, though her grasp on the physiology of conception and pregnancy was based more on avoidance than formal education.

Let nature take care of all that. Her role tonight was to start the balls rolling, in a manner of speaking, and make people happy. Who could quarrel with that? Michael was unaware of the plan, but she was confident that in essence, he would be wholeheartedly behind it –and what he didn't know couldn't hurt him.

Marina's preparation had been thorough: having first identified Samantha as a potential beneficiary, and Samantha having been at the wedding, only a confidential little chat was needed to convince the swimming instructress that the scheme must be above board, emanating as it did from the minister's wife. Word soon got round among the yearning, childless singletons of Denswick and its environs (though Samantha always swore she'd told no-one).

Marnie had met each young woman for coffee and a chat, explained the procedures, handed over a green leaflet issued by the Denswick Hospital Trust's Department of Genito-Urinary Medicine and stressed the statement on the back: *The benefits of knowing a positive result usually outweigh the drawbacks*. It was, she made clear, the client's responsibility to be checked out for potentially harmful sexually-transmitted diseases.

The girls had all known grief or rejection, but why should they lose hope of motherhood? They were sufficiently liberated to know they could choose an alternative path to barren spinsterhood. £500 was a lot of money, but nothing in comparison with the charges made for official Artificial Insemination by Donor treatment. The girls had begged or borrowed to raise the cash.

As far as the men went, she'd thought about involving the Serbian, but decided against it and told him, by text, to vacate the premises for the evening. Unfortunately, the arrival of the text message had been heard only by the spiders in the kitchen drawer, where the occasional cleaner habitually deposited any lost property she found.

Mr and Mrs Mann's cruise having now reached the South Pacific, the four students were raring to go. Ambrose had roped in Bud Baxter plus Sam and Vic, the shoe-fight transvestites, whose mothers would be happy at the suggestion their sons had fathered a child, even if the babes themselves would never be dandled on grandmamas' knees.

Solly, Dan, Aidan and Jim had each taken a little trouble to disguise his appearance. Nothing drastic – but enough to have made their mothers weep had they been present. The chaps would get £200 each for the two sessions… much more than the £35 maximum permitted by law.

Arriving together in Mrs Mann's rather swish runabout, they were directed to a cubicle apiece to familiarise themselves with the set-up. Ten minutes to look at the magazines, and by the time the nervous young women arrived, the men were up for the task ahead.

Candy Dunne was the first to walk in. She needed a sibling for her darling Job, who regularly asked for a baby sister. Her husband's behaviour at Job's birthday party had scandalised both families and broken her heart, yet since the separation her longing for another child had been overwhelming. Things got even worse when Tyson was remanded in custody, awaiting trial for his part in a countywide farm machinery insurance fraud scam. There was little hope of reconciliation. Job's mother did not want to play the slag herself and go with just anyone. She wanted her ex to think someone else had loved her enough to give her a child. When the gossip mill spread word about this baby-making opportunity, she'd decided to give it a go.

Gone were Candy's flash car and superior tone. She barely raised her eyes high enough to notice that no cobwebs dangled from the rafters before being seated at one of the tables with a glass of wine. Candy thumbed through a glossy *Motherhood* magazine as more women arrived and were seated at a table apiece, eyes averted.

At a signal from Bud, the men took their places opposite the women. Pseudonymous introductions were made, more wine poured, and each couple photographed cheek-to-cheek and smiling. The cameras were handed to the women to keep and develop as they saw fit.

Marnie insisted on the photos. It was the not knowing that hurt a child. Not knowing why she was thin when her mother was voluptuously built. Not knowing why she had blue eyes when her mother's were brown. She had no evidence that her mother had even *conversed* with her father. She was determined that any infant conceived as a result of this operation would have this one luxury: a photograph of the two parents together, looking happy, sharing a drink. Every child deserved that, at least.

When the couples were ready, the men returned to the cubicles, to fill the turkey basters waiting in sealed bags to receive the product of their self-stimulation. At a quiet cough from behind each screen, the women entered and readied themselves on the couches. Some chose to administer to themselves, while others preferred Marnie or the partner to press the plunger. Most of the women wanted the father to be present at insemination and the hoped-for conception; the men looked coyly at the magazines while the procedure took place.

Up in the loft Drago had dozed until roused by the sound of a voice he recognised. He returned to the spy hole. The view was restricted to an area about three metres in diameter immediately beneath him: half a couch; a magazine open at a double-page spread of a naked woman with pendulous breasts; some sort of barrier, and a young man seated at a table, drinking wine and conversing with someone out of Drago's sight. Drago was certain: the young man was speaking to Samantha. Soon she walked beneath him and stepped out of her underwear. The man was close by.

Drago couldn't make out what was going on, but there was no doubt that his beloved Samantha, for whom he had hidden in this chilly loft for seven wintry weeks, had taken off her pants for another man. He couldn't watch anymore, but climbed into his sleeping bag, buried his head under the pillow and wept silently.

He had been through all this agony, discomfort and deprivation for nothing.

Next morning he woke with a start, cold and dying for a pee. His sudden movement had startled the sparrow, which fluttered around in panic before crashing into the raised hatch, breaking its neck and tumbling through to the floor below. Belinda had discovered the sobbing man just five minutes after this second loss.

By the end of Drago's tale, trying to sort truth from fiction and bad grammar left Belinda's head in a mess. She was tired, bewildered, and her hand had been captured by an illegal immigrant who depended on her. She tried to tug it free, but the grip tightened. She tried to look away from those dark eyes, but hadn't the spirit. She knew she was a sad, middle-aged woman with too much on her plate. She had a family to take care of and... and... all this!

Belinda rose from the chair, pulled away her eyes, her hand, grabbed the plastic box, the T-shirt, her coat, and strode determinedly out of the door, which slammed behind her. The man shrugged, dried his eyes and made himself another coffee to take up the ladder with a piece of the new cake. He was asleep before Belinda reached home.

Her stride shortened as the distance from the hall increased. She slowed, not ready to face the normality of home, of stripping the beds on a Monday morning, checking up on Mum and Dad and getting ready for work. Drago's story could not, surely, be true? Maybe she'd misunderstood his ungrammatical, accented English. Yet the sob in his voice persisted in her ear. That alone rang true. Let the tale be fabrication or not, there was no doubt of the man's grief. But why was the bird dead?

Despite this question, her soul failed to break free of the hypnotic darkness of the tear-filled eyes. The firmness of the hand that had captured hers was tangible. Surely, a throb of love had passed between them, though her sensible mind told her she was being hoodwinked. Belinda was the captive; the fugitive the captor. She knew it, deep down.

So did he.

*

As the washing turned in the machine, knees weakening, she sank onto a chair left awry in the kitchen. Tears rolled down her cheeks and dripped onto the checked tablecloth. Up-ending the carrier bag, she inhaled *his* body smell, burying her face in the T-shirt, using it to dry her eyes, pretending it belonged to Aidan, or Doug…but knowing it did not. Absentmindedly, she set the blue-lidded box on the worktop, poured hot water onto instant coffee and allowed herself five minutes of self-pity.

She tried to think of Drago's mother. After all, he was a son first and foremost, just as Aidan belonged to her more than anyone else. Her mind's eye washed with an image of her son's face atop the Serbian's naked torso. She blushed with guilt at the thought.

The rattle of the letter box was followed by a knock on the front door. Drying her eyes, through the glass panel she could see the new post lady in her red Royal Mail polo shirt and gilet. A handful of junk mail and bills was thrust at her chest when she opened the door. The woman nodded at the letter box.

"'s full. Can't get this lot in."

Po-faced, she turned on her stoutly booted heel. The gate clicked behind her before Belinda grasped what she'd said.

Protruding from the letter box, jammed part-way through, was another padded brown envelope. There had been so many of them she'd lost count, yet she didn't recall a rush of bookings in the village hall diary. The package ripped a little

206

as she tugged it out. Her heel kicked the door shut. She laid the brown envelope on the third stair, thinking she really must check up on things soon.

The junk mail – an old-folks' cruise offer and multiple money-off vouchers for products she would never buy – joined the pile on the table. The bills she stood, unopened, behind the kettle.

She straightened her shoulders and took out a clean dishcloth. Putting stuff away, wiping surfaces: a fail-safe step back to efficiency mode. First she would make up Melanie's packed lunch for tomorrow. She had some tortilla wraps in the cupboard, she knew, and there was bound to be some sort of filling in the fridge. She took another of her blue-lidded storage boxes from the cupboard.

Tomorrow's lunch sorted, she cleared the worktops, putting everything in its proper place: fridge, cupboards, or bin. Spray, wipe and move on, up and down the cupboard doors, polish the window and mop the floor. All in order. All clean, fresh and wholesome. Just like her family.

At the sight of the envelope on the stairs, the wholesome feeling evaporated a little, but wave of tiredness and hopelessness overwhelming her, she lay down on the sofa and flicked through the television's daytime dross. Hypnotised by drug-riddled siblings swearing at their desperate, deranged mother, Belinda was lifted to sleep on a balloon of relief: maybe her own family was quite normal after all.

Somewhere in her dreams swam the malevolent mantras, the little list. They swam in the same pool as Job Dunne, her father, snails and a hairy-handed Aidan speaking in a foreign tongue. Surrounding the pool was a forest, which the dreamer recognised as being the Welsh home of her ancestors. She struggled to speak the new language but her voice was drowned by the harmonies of a male voice choir singing 'Cwm Rhondda'. She tried screaming and kicking at the choir, until she jerked awake to find herself on the carpet. Her toes hurt. She was exhausted. The dream skittered away to who knows where, like a mouse in a pantry.

She lay there for a while. Tears seeped from behind closed eyelids. When they reached her lips, she licked them off. She reached for the remote control, pressed a button, and again let herself wallow in other people's misery.

*

The padded envelope was added to the growing heap in her wardrobe. She must clean it out soon. A jumble sale in the hall would be a good idea, if only she could persuade someone else to join in. Belinda had enough unwanted gifts and knick-knacks to fill a table. Thinking about this was a change from dreaming of Drago and worrying about Dorothy, her mother, her father... her husband, her children... the Charity Commission, the menopause... blocked drains ... paying-in books ... Drago.

20

The following day Belinda made up her mind to try once again to wrest the village hall account books from the bony hands of Sybil Spinks. The grapevine had it that, although physically more or less back to normal after the heart attack, John had never fully recovered from the anaesthetic administered for his varicose vein operation. He was now at home, with carers going in four times a day. Son Derek was keen for both parents to move into residential care, but John and Sybil were resisting. Belinda could wait no longer: it was time to confront the situation. She would visit the treasurer at home and get hold of what she needed before it was too late.

She was opening the front door when the telephone rang.

"Mrs Lowe? This is Jasmine Struthers from Truetrust Academy. I'm phoning about your daughter Melanie. I'm afraid you need to come to school right away."

Belinda was baffled until she remembered: Denswick Comprehensive had fallen foul of the latest educational experiment and been academised. Her knees buckled. "What's happened?"

"I'd rather not discuss it over the phone, Mrs Lowe. If Mr Lowe is available, he should come too."

"No... he's working away. I'll be there in twenty minutes." She hung up.

Her mind went blank. Her daughter in trouble? Never! Melanie was a good girl! Dim recollections of the girl's tantrum in the garden centre bruised her certainty, but maternal loyalty triumphed. *Perhaps she'd had an accident, or been taken ill. Why hadn't that Struthers woman explained?*

*

She drove to the school in a trance but did a double take as she drove past an expensively-wrought sign trumpeting the school's transformation with an engraving of a knight in shining armour. *What's that all about?* she wondered.

The furniture in the foyer was unrecognisable. Gone was the dingy beech and blue tweed that had served generations of teachers and parents. Behind a chrome and glass partition, a minion dressed by Tesco was touching up her nails. The receptionist looked up with a quizzical expression.

"I'm Mrs Lowe, Melanie's mother."

Deadpan face, deadpan voice. "The Head's waiting for you. Come this way."

Blankly, Melanie's mother followed her down the corridor. The receptionist stopped outside a door labelled, "Jasmine Struthers Director of Studies." Belinda knocked and opened the door.

"Mrs Lowe is here."

The Director of Studies' office was already full. An arc of stern-faced individuals, on chairs of chrome and silver-grey, focused intense, disapproving eyes on the new arrival. In the corner, a uniformed Police Community Support Officer ignored the subdued chatter coming from her radio. The Director rose to her feet. Although she extended her hand towards Mrs Lowe, it was only to gesture towards an empty seat which faced the arc.

Terror silenced Belinda. She tried to engage eyes with someone – anyone – but all eyes were expressionless. Ms

Struthers began to introduce the others present, but Belinda's mind registered only one.

"This is Anthony Montano, Chief Child Protection Officer for Denswick Borough Council." A man with auburn hair and long, crossed legs nodded in acknowledgement.

Blank bewilderment. Her eyes asked the question, 'What's this all about?' Her voice asked, "Is Melanie OK?"

Ms Struthers cleared her throat, "How do you expect her to be, Mrs Lowe?" She crossed her own slender legs and sat back, waiting.

"She was fine at breakfast." Belinda's voice sounded tinny, false.

"But how did you expect her to be at lunchtime?"

"Well, the same. Is she ill?"

"Your daughter is traumatised, Mrs Lowe."

"By what?"

"Melanie has been traumatised by the packed lunch you prepared for her, Mrs Lowe. She suffered an acute anxiety attack which required attention from paramedics. There is also the possibility of her having contracted some avian disease which could be potentially life-threatening, as well as a possible spinal injury. An ambulance was called and your daughter has been taken to Denswick Hospital in the care of her Pastoral Head of Year, Ms Jeggings."

Anthony Montano, looking more down-at-heel than his name and job title suggested, leant forward to speak. When he did, his voice was ponderous.

"Child abuse is the scourge of our times, Mrs Lowe. Every week, members of my staff are shaken to the core by the perverted methods used to inflict physical and psychological damage on young people. When the damage is caused by the child's parent, there can be no hiding place for the perpetrator."

Belinda agreed wholeheartedly, though she only gave a slight nod in Mr Montano's direction.

"But what has all this got to do with Melanie? Has someone been abusing her?" A sob caught in her throat. Her chest tightened. She found it difficult to inhale, and sat back. Still the flintstone cold eyes glared. Why would no one explain? Her eyes flicked from one face to another, looking for help. None came.

Eventually Ms Struthers broke the silence. "Melanie is in the habit of bringing a packed lunch to school. Is that correct, Mrs Lowe?"

"Yes. I always make it myself."

"Always, you say? In that case, could you tell me what you prepared for your daughter's lunch today?"

Belinda's mind went blank. She tried hard to remember.

"Well, I packed it up yesterday because she sets off so early for school nowadays. Let me think... it was a wrap of some sort. You know the sort of thing. One of those tortilla pancakes you get from the supermarket. Kids seem to prefer them to proper sandwiches."

"Well, Mrs Lowe, Melanie's lunch box certainly contained a 'wrap'." Ms Struthers hesitated for a millisecond before articulating the last word.

Anthony Montano took over the questioning. "Mrs Lowe, you have confirmed that Melanie's packed lunch was prepared by yourself and consisted of a wrap. Did this 'wrap' have any filling?"

"Well yes, of course. Are you saying that the wrap made her ill? Has she got a tummy upset?"

"Well, I can confirm that the wrap is at the centre of our investigations. I'd like you to think back and tell us in detail exactly what you gave your daughter for today's lunch."

Belinda tried to think back. She could see the contents of her kitchen cupboards in her mind's eye. No, it wasn't anything out of a tin. What was in the wrap? Cold chicken? Yes, she was almost sure of it. Although... there had been a pack of turkey slices in the fridge as well. It was one or the other, she was certain. And a Satsuma ...and crisps.

"It was poultry of some sort, with mayonnaise and a bit of salad, some fruit I'm sure. And crisps, I admit."

Maybe the Food Police were after her for not sticking to the school's Healthy Eating Policy, to which all parents had been instructed to adhere via the academy's online newsletter. She acknowledged that salted potato crisps were now considered to be the work of the devil...but not child abuse, surely?

"Hmm." Mr Montano's consideration was long, low and slow. He leant forward. "How do you define 'poultry', Mrs Lowe?"

"Well... it's birds, isn't it? The sort you eat. Cooked."

"Ah! You say the poultry in Melanie's wrap had been cooked?"

"Well of course." Belinda was beginning to lose patience. "What do you think I am? Do you think it was raw? You must be mad!"

"Well, Mrs Lowe, we do have doubts about the sanity of one person in this room," (her outburst had not gone down well with the PCSO) "though I'm no psychiatrist, of course." She covered her back.

Ms Struthers took the lead once more. "Mrs Lowe, I will recount in detail the events in the school restaurant this lunchtime. As you see, my secretary is making notes of this interview."

She indicated a slim, gelled young man in a sharp suit, notepad balanced on an angled knee. He nodded solemnly at Belinda.

"And just to make sure you understand the seriousness of the situation, I must point out that this meeting is being recorded."

The Director of Studies adjusted the equipment on her desk, uncrossed her legs, drew breath and began.

"Here at Truetrust Academy, we pay great attention to the food experiences offered to our students. The vast majority opt for the ample and healthy meals provided by the academy's own kitchens and sponsored by Food Emporia: Truetrust Academies, or FETA. This invaluable resource enables us to keep costs low, to help busy working families. The new, enlarged assembly hall doubles as the dining room. The décor is smart, and the ambience carefully nurtured to ensure a sophisticated nourishment experience which will equip our young people for the high-flying futures we expect for them. Truetrust's student restaurant bears little resemblance to the noisy school canteens of your day, Mrs Lowe.

"However, as with Melanie, there is still a residue of students who choose not to take advantage of this opportunity to eat high-quality meals at low cost in gracious surroundings. These young people eat their packed lunches in the same space but at a different level… in fact they eat their lunches on the stage."

Belinda was silenced. She hadn't known the packed-lunchers were segregated… but then Denswick Comp had only become Truetrust Academy at the start of this school year. She wasn't sure she liked the idea, but the government claimed it was progress…

Ms Struthers cleared her throat. "Ahem. The stage is, of course, elevated, and the students who eat there are kept under observation quite easily by the Nutrition Supervisors patrolling at the lower level. They are also in full view to the remainder of the diners."

Still Belinda had nothing to say.

"The polite and calm dining experience of my students, Mrs Lowe, was shattered at exactly 12.24 this afternoon when your daughter screamed shrilly, spat out the contents of her mouth, kicked over her chair, flung her lunch box into the wings and leapt off the stage in a paroxysm of hysteria. She fell to the floor retching and wheezing, unable to communicate in any coherent fashion.

"The academy's First Aider was summoned immediately, but already there was pandemonium on the stage, where Melanie's friend Chelsey had been hit in the face by the wing feathers of a decapitated bird. A sparrow's head was later found in the hair of Benjamin Jepson, the young man sitting opposite Melanie. Another student, Jermyn Street, was caught in the eye by the flying plastic lid and has also been taken to hospital in the same ambulance, for treatment to a lacerated eyeball.

"All the screaming caused panic at the lower level. Many students rushed forward to help the girl who had fallen from the stage, in their haste knocking down and trampling Mrs Althea Lodge, one of the Nutrition Supervisors and aunt of Ms Jeggings.

"In the commotion, the glass on the fire alarm was smashed and the whole school had to be evacuated. By the time a second ambulance had been called for Mrs Lodge, the fire drill carried out and all 1,367 students checked in their class registers etc., seventy percent of them had still not taken their lunchtime refreshment. Lessons proceeded at the usual time, but I can tell you, Mrs Lowe, that unfed teenagers do not make attentive students. At present, the corridors are being patrolled by the entire Senior Management Team, which is dealing with misbehaviour and rowdyism at levels never before experienced at Truetrust Academy. We are grateful for the swift response from PCSO Heather Banks, here." She gestured to the stout woman in uniform, who nodded grimly.

Belinda had taken in very little of the tale. In fact, she had still been mulling over the idea of the packed-lunchers eating on the stage when her brain registered the word, "Sparrow". Thereafter, Ms Struthers' speech had been drowned by the klaxons sounding in her own head. It took some time to recall when she had last seen a dead sparrow… it didn't seem too long ago, somehow… or where. As the truth dawned, an icy chill crawled through her body. At the village hall, she had wrapped the dead sparrow in a paper towel and placed it in the blue-lidded plastic box. She could not remember what came next.

Ms Struthers continued. "Investigations showed that the sparrow had been wrapped in an off-white paper towel, very similar in colour to the supermarket tortilla wraps you mentioned earlier. So similar, in fact, that your daughter – yes, your daughter, Mrs Lowe – engaged in conversation with her friends as she was – raised the 'wrap' to her mouth without noticing anything amiss, and took a strong bite.

"It was the feathers, followed by the crunch of beak, which caused the poor child to spit out the contents of her mouth, which, unfortunately, landed in the hair of the young man opposite, with whom Melanie has an on/off relationship, and who currently favours a rather long and unkempt hairstyle."

"Dear me."

"Is this making sense to you, Mrs Lowe?" The Director of Studies stopped, leaned forward, looked around at the assembled meeting, hesitated a little longer, before saying with a wry smirk, "I can see from your expression that it is."

Belinda's voice was faint.

"I look after Sallsby Village Hall. Or at least, I'm Chair of the Management Committee. Yesterday, when I went to check the building, I found a dead bird. It must have got in somehow and been unable to get out. I wrapped the bird in a paper towel and put it into a Tupperware box I had with me at the time. But I can't remember what I did with the box after that. Honestly!"

"Well you know now, Mrs Lowe. You gave it to your daughter for lunch!" Ms Struthers' sarcastic tone did nothing to amuse the others in the room. Mr Montano decided to take hold of the reins.

"I'm afraid I have no choice but to take this further, Mrs Lowe. As the victim's mother, you seem disturbingly unconcerned about her condition. You have also failed to explain the presence of a packet of salted potato crisps in the lunch box. I must ask you to accompany me to my office in the Social Services building on Dewdrop Way. We will leave your car here. And we would like to speak to Melanie's father with some urgency. Do you have his work number?"

No, she didn't... had only a vague idea of his whereabouts, it seemed. Reluctantly, she checked on her own rarely used phone for Doug's number. The PCSO, Ms Struthers and others wrote it down: further evidence of familial dysfunction. To Belinda, they were signing her death warrant.

"I've got to go to work. I need to open the library at two o'clock." She glanced at her watch. Everyone else looked at the large clock on the wall. Both indicated five minutes to two. She had five minutes to get to work and open up.

"You continue to demonstrate a callous disregard for your daughter, Mrs Lowe. Most mothers would be at A&E by now. You need to notify your employer that you must absent yourself from work this afternoon... and possibly for considerably longer."

"Of course I want to see Melanie! I'm just confused, and can't believe this is happening. I can't lose my job though... give the council an excuse and they'll close Denswick Library in a flash."

A stout man in a well-worn suit, who had sat quietly throughout, swelled his chest, lifted his head and introduced himself.

"I'm Councillor Bernard Tuke, Chairman of the Board of Governors at Truetrust Academy. My special interest is the welfare of children and I am Chair of the Schools, Children and Young Persons' Overview and Scrutiny Panel. I also sit on the Libraries Committee. From this meeting I will be going directly to another at the Town Hall, at which the future of the remaining libraries in the borough will be discussed, along with arrangements for staff redundancy and redeployment. You haven't done yourself any favours, Mrs Lowe."

Councillor Tuke lapsed once more into silence and deflated back into his chair, his florid face grim.

Before long, the meeting broke up. Belinda was allowed to telephone her boss to plead family crisis before Mr Montano ushered her out of the building. The PCSO stopped them in the car park.

"I'm on lates tonight. I'll be round your house for a chat later. And I'll want to talk to your daughter." Stern, she climbed into the waiting squad car that had arrived at her summons.

In the car, Belinda tried to engage Mr Montano's eyes, but he stared determinedly ahead throughout the journey. Her head seemed to have turned to mush: she had no words; no explanation; no excuses; no hope. And she had had no dinner!

"I need something to eat," she announced, confirming the illusion of a self-obsessed and uncaring parent Mr Montano had formed on first sight of the mother, "and a cup of tea."

Once in his office, the man relented and requested tea and biscuits. Minutes later, sipping her own drink, Belinda watched as the secretary set a cup in front of her boss and picked a stray hair from his jacket with a familiarity bordering on lust. Feeling a warmer glow and drawing the chair up to his desk, Tony Montano clasped his hands and leaned forward.

"Tell me about your relationship with your daughter."

*

It took until after 3.30 to persuade Anthony Montano that Belinda's mental condition posed little threat to her daughter's wellbeing. There were gaps in the mother's story, to be sure, and he was not entirely convinced that the sparrow's death had been accidental. Nevertheless, safeguarding children, not wildlife, was his priority.

The phone lines between Dewdrop Way and Truetrust Academy had been busy throughout the interview. It appeared that Melanie had suffered no lasting physical damage but an appointment with a counsellor would be in the post within days. Ms Jeggings was supporting her aunt as she sat in the waiting area of the hospital's Medical Imaging Department, in expectation of an X-ray on her crushed ribs. Ms Struthers herself was on her way to collect Melanie from A&E, whence she would deliver the child to the emergency contact address held by the school, to be left in the care of her grandparents.

This information was relayed to the girl's mother by the attentive secretary. Feeling drab and dumpy, Belinda wondered how to go about explaining things to her parents. When she reached their bungalow, Melanie was nowhere to be seen.

The girl's grandfather was trembling and pale. A thick veil of disbelief and bafflement hung between daughter and parents. Belinda was good. She was their rock, their support. Belinda took care of people. She managed things; tended to their needs; organised whatever needed organising. They had believed her to be utterly stable and benign. They loved their granddaughter, but could barely recognise the tear-stained waif deposited by the headmistress. The explanation offered had been curt and unfeeling. As soon as Ms Struthers left, Melanie had paid no heed to their entreaties and flounced for home herself.

No-one offered to put the kettle on for Belinda. How could they not? The kettle symbolised normality and civilised conduct. Her knees gave way; she sank to the sofa. No-one spoke. No-one looked at her. No questions or explanations were forthcoming. She rested her head on the cushions and sought oblivion. It was not long in coming.

Two hours later, she noticed that someone had covered her with a blanket. It smelt vaguely of Febreeze and dead dog, but it was the sliding slam of a van door that had gatecrashed her mental void. The click-clack of a front gate, three loud thumps on the unlocked door, and by the time she was fully awake, Doug stood with eyes steaming down at her.

"What the 'ell's been going on?"

Where was the placid, gentle man she was wedded to?

"What the effing 'ell are you doing lying there asleep while our daughter's running round half-naked?"

Had he been drinking? She was sure she'd caught a whiff of ale as he yelled.

"I bin working all morning – just nipped to t'pub wi''lads for us lunch – and I gets this call from some posh bird, telling me mi daughter's been traumatised and tekken t' 'ospital." Belinda hated it when Doug lapsed into matespeak – he spoke quite grammatically as a rule. She tried to speak but no sound came.

"I've 'ad to leave mi pie and pint, let'lads down 'cos I'm 'only spark on 'job, and drive 150 miles – brekking 'speed limit *and* I've 'ad a drink – and what do I get home to?"

No-one dared hazard a guess.

"This little trollop having it off in'shed wi'yon lad from next door, while 'er mother's fast asleep on 'er granddad's settee!" He thrust forward a weeping, haphazardly dressed Melanie, who'd been lingering in the doorway. "Explain yerselves!"

He flung Belinda's feet off the sofa and sat down. "An' put t'kettle on. Mekk us a coffee."

This version of Doug was unrecognisable, but the coffee was made instantly and handed over. Melanie had curled up in the corner behind the TV, aiming for invisibility.

"What do you mean, 'Having it off'?" her mother ventured.

"What do you think I bloody mean? I've bin t'ospital, school, library – no sign of either o' yer. Even went to 'village 'all an' all. That scrawny lass from Christmas were there. Then I went home and found this…" he nudged the girl with his foot, like a turd he was trying to wipe off "… stark naked in'shed wi' that Street lad. Didn't 'ear me comin' an' I copped for the lot!"

The traumatised father was shaking from head to foot. Other adults in the room observed the veins bulging in his temples and feared a seizure was imminent. His angry eyes brimmed with unshed tears.

Belinda's mother had a clear thought, for once. From the sideboard she extracted a decorative candle in a box labelled, *Waxomatherapy: light a candle to your troubles and feel them slip away.*

A box of matches, kept nearby in case of power cuts, was produced. Within seconds the dead dog smell was overpowered with that of something called, according to the box, Vetivert, or burning wood, according to Doug.

"Mekks mi wanna puke. I'm working mi guts out up there, trying to mekk enough money to keep yon lad at uni and 'er in smartphones (another toe nudge at the girl) – and you can't even feed 'er properly or keep an eye on 'er!" He flung his cup aside. "I've 'ad it wi' you lot!"

He slammed out to pace the narrow path of the front garden. An elderly woman in a beige coat passed the gate, watching him.

The throwaway line 'that scrawny lass from Christmas' jarred even amidst the other horrors of the day, but Belinda couldn't deal with it just then. The comment sought a quiet place at the back of her mind, where it could fester till given air. 'Had it wi' you lot!' squeezed in beside 'scrawny lass'.

She pulled herself together and Melanie to her feet. Maybe the candle was working. (She must write to Waxomatherapy in anticipation of some free samples.) Perfunctory pecks on the cheek for Mum and Dad, coats and bags gathered, the door closed quietly behind them. They climbed into the van and waited for Doug to cease his pacing. It would all turn out to be something and nothing, Belinda was sure.

The bungalow returned to peace, quiet and resumed confusion.

"Oh dear, oh dear, oh dear," was all the walls heard until cocoa time. The occupants knew enough to be baffled, but not enough to begin to understand what was happening to their family.

✻

Doug followed his wife into the house in Dapple Grove. She pointed to the electricity bills Derek Spinks had dropped off some weeks earlier.

"I was just about to see if I could get the village hall accounts from Sybil Spinks when Mrs Struthers rang," she ventured. "I just dropped everything and went to the school."

Melanie had by this time trudged indoors.

"It's MZZZ Struthers, for Heaven's sake! God, you're *so* unliberated. Her husband's not even married to her. He's married to Mrs Hickstart, and they've got two twins in Year 7 but everyone knows she's a lezzer and only likes playing hockey and watching girls in the showers, so it's OK."

No response sprung to either parental mind beyond, '*What is the world coming to?*'

Sobs, repressed all day, could be held back no longer. "I thought Melanie was dead!"

✻

He did not hold out his arms in comfort as she'd expected, but went out the back to close the shed door, which swung wildly

222

on its hinges in a strengthening wind. He pottered outside, pulling weeds, emptying last year's pots – anything to avoid her weeping and that obscenity which had once been his little girl.

*

It was dark before he came indoors again. The girl had cried herself to sleep in bed; her mother, likewise, in the bath. He called.

"Belinda! Get yourself out of there. You'll catch cold."

She stirred, came to and clambered out, shivering. By the time she climbed into bed, he was waiting up with a cup of cocoa and a hot water bottle. He no longer sounded like a stranger.

"You'll have to take her...you know...to the clinic."

"What clinic? She won't actually have done anything, Doug. She's too young. It will just have been a game of 'You show me yours and I'll show you mine'."

"I saw them! It was everything. She'll have to go to the clap clinic."

"But they're children! I don't think she even likes Jermyn Street. It can only have been the once, anyway. It's Ben she likes." Ben was clever, clean-cut and an all-round star: a suitor to encourage.

"Take her!" he insisted. Belinda kept quiet.

"That family – the lot of 'em – they'll go with anything that moves. Animal, vegetable or mineral!" He was undressing, turned away from her, and didn't notice her puzzled expression as she tried to think of vegetables and minerals that moved of their own volition. And another seed was sent to the festering hole: how did he know?

"I'll have to be up at five so I can be back on the job at eight. It'll be down to you to get it sorted." He clambered into bed and faced away from her. As an afterthought, he half-turned and patted her thigh through her nightie.

"You will," he murmured.

When PCSO Heather Banks and her hobbo Grant Hall stopped by at 21.30, the house was in darkness. They went to check out the pub instead.

*

On the first Tuesday of each month, it was a pie and a pint at the Bucket and Shovel for Tony and his mate Guy from the Environmental Health Department. They talked about motor sport, the best routes to take from A to B, the price of petrol and the latest football debacle. Rarely about work, and never about families.

But the tale of the sparrow sandwich was a tale worth telling and, that evening, Tony couldn't resist. To be fair, the borough's Chief Child Protection Officer was minded to accept the mother's version of events: that the child had taken the wrong plastic box from the fridge. And he took care not to mention names or identifying features. He was, however, a lively raconteur with a gift for embellishment, and there was soon a substantial party of listeners-in. The remaining questions – how the bird met its demise, why it had been wrapped and stored so carefully, and what else might be in the refrigerator – remained tantalisingly unanswered and an exhilarating topic of speculation.

Guy Dance had not reached such elevated Local Government heights as Tony. He had come to rest on the middle rungs of the Environmental Health career ladder, spending a lot of his time checking the state of the grouting in fish and chip shops, with occasional forays to follow up reports of foreign substances in shop-bought pies. When things were slack and he fancied a trip out, he'd rummage through his files on premises where food was served only occasionally, to see where he could carry out a quick inspection and take advantage of lunch in a country pub nearby.

Thus it was that the very next day at 9.15am, Guy dialled the number of the council's contact for Sallby Village Hall. Bird ingress was a serious business and potentially a major health hazard in a public building, and the RSPB had let it be widely known that sparrows are a 'species at risk'. This was Guy's chance to get his name in the papers – maybe even bring a prosecution. It said on the council database that Sallby Village Hall was a charity. Even better. There was nothing the papers liked better than to dish the dirt on so-called do-gooders. Let there be so much as a sniff of bird muck or mouse shit, Guy Dance would slap an order on the place.

He'd noticed that the contact person was female. A Mrs B. Lowe. A woman. He wasn't too keen on them, despite being married to one, brother to two more and father to three wannabes. Too cocky by half, the lot on 'em. Guy blamed it all on The Queen, The War, The Pill, Tights and Tampons. Teach a woman to drive and she thought she were your equal. The rest just followed on.

The voice that answered the phone did not sound confident. Good. It encouraged him to adopt his most officious tone and soon, an appointment was made for him to inspect the hall that afternoon. He looked forward to the inspection with a determination bordering on glee.

He'd 'ave 'em! Let 'em try any more sparrow shenanigans, and he'd 'ave 'em! He was a bird lover, was Guy.

*

Oddly, Belinda slept soundly the night after the meeting, both from exhaustion and fear of waking. Doug's warm and heavy presence kept the bed cosy; she felt perhaps a little less alone than had become the norm.

Waking, it took seconds to notice that her husband had already left for Sunderland, then to recall the horror that was yesterday. It was all something else that had to be tucked away, to be dealt with later. There was no way she could imagine tracking down the 'clap clinic' – though there was probably a leaflet on it somewhere among her items for display at the library. But what would it *really* be called?

Her mind played with the possibilities as she dressed. The idea of her little girl being at risk from a sexually transmitted disease was nonsense, of course. It never took root. It was some horrible fantasy of Doug's brought on by drink and exhaustion. All would be well when Melanie came home from school. They could have a laugh about Dad's over-reaction. Belinda smiled fondly at her own memories of snogging spotty youths behind the bike sheds at Melanie's age. This episode was a storm in a tea cup, she was sure. Best ignored.

The girl herself had been up and out by 7.30, showered, fed and groomed to perfection. She could brazen out the infamy, flaunt yet another sexual conquest, and *at last* take advantage of the academy's in-house catering. How she'd hated her mother's packed lunches, even though they did mean she got to sit with Ben Jepson. His mother was some kind of vegan freak, so maybe it was time to persuade Ben that her beansprout salads damaged brainpower. Melanie would do some research. Then they could both leave the stage and leave Juvenile Jermyn to eat with the other saddos.

Alone at home, her mother took time to regroup. Some exercise time; a little yoga and meditation. She remembered the malevolent mantras as the woman in the beige coat floated into her mind's eye. Jermyn Street was added to her little list, along with Ms Struthers and that Tuke bloke. Malevolence accomplished, Bel dressed coolly, applied some lipstick, admired herself in the mirror and prepared to face the day.

She really must go to see Sybil Spinks. A neighbour from Curlew Close, returning John's long-overdue library books some days ago, had mentioned that moving the couple into residential care was under discussion. Yet again she was delayed by the ringing phone. Someone from Guidance, it sounded like, wanting to meet her at the hall that afternoon. She felt the merest tinge of puzzlement as to why the hall was the specified venue... but she hadn't time to dwell on it. Determined to do battle with Sybil before it was too late, she made Curlew Close her objective.

A faded detached villa, Sphynx Lodge nestled at the blunt end of a cul-de-sac. The number of *For Sale* signs on the close took Belinda by surprise; Sphynx Lodge alone boasted two.

There was no sign of movement behind the bland curtains. The doorbell chimed unanswered. Mail was piled up on the porch floor. Cardboard boxes stacked on worktops were visible through a side window. As she peered on tiptoe, with a rumble and squeal of brakes, a maroon removal van nosed its way onto the drive and three men in brown overalls climbed out. The gaffer looked at her quizzically.

"Are you'family?"

"No, I'm a friend. What's going on?"

"If you're a friend you'll know, surely." The gaffer eyed her with suspicion.

"I've been trying to get in touch with the people who live here but their son's not answering my calls."

"Oh aye?" He turned from her and began instructing his men on where to begin. "There's no point 'anging around 'ere. They're not in."

"Where are they?"

"Not my job to know that, missus. We've to clear everything, that's all I know. Some stuff's going to storage but most of it'll be straight to the saleroom or the tip. And now if you'll let us get on…"

"I need something from inside… it's really important."

"Can't 'elp you, love." He moved forward and opened the front door.

Belinda pushed past him, muttering, "I only need the accounts…and cheque book… and there's bound to be some cash John didn't get round to banking…"

By the time she'd spotted the bureau in the dining room, the gaffer was on the phone to the Safer Neighbourhoods Team.

PCSOs Heather Banks and Grant Hall had just begun their shift, grumpy after their long stint yesterday, which had culminated with a brawl outside the pub where they'd been checking up on the latest gossip and warming their toes. They didn't get much call to visit Sallby, but had just managed to scrounge a lift to the end of the close.

Belinda was still riffling the bureau when they arrived. Had she tried to leg it, the three removal men had between them agreed to detain her by force, if necessary. This woman was attempting sheer daylight robbery! Their jobs would depend on her not getting away with it. Heather and Grant immediately recognised the woman rummaging through the drawers of a mahogany bureau.

Heather's voice was peculiarly treble. "And what do you think you're doing, Mrs Lowe?"

The intruder froze. She recognised the voice. Her heart leapt as her mouth slid into top gear.

"Well, it's very awkward, you see. Mr Spinks has some money and a cheque book that I need because he keeps the accounts you see, but he's been ill and Sybil won't let me have them and I've asked Derek but she won't give them to him either and so what am I to do? It's the law, you see, it's a condition. John usually takes care of the bills for me and I don't know where they are but the water and electric will be cut off if Derek doesn't give me the money and then where will martial arts and the toddlers be? Everything will go to pot if Derek doesn't give me the cheque book and some money!"

Last night in the pub the PCSOs had debated the state of the sparrow woman's mind without reaching any firm conclusion. They withdrew into the hallway.

The woman seemed to think it made sense, but Grant and Heather were thinking along the lines of a mental health referral.

Or maybe it was just an act to obscure her true purpose. Maybe Mr Spinks was the father of her children and she was his mistress. That would account for him paying the bills. She'd mentioned toddlers, so it sounded like the girl from yesterday wasn't the only product of the union.

Had she said, 'Marsha, Lars and the toddlers'? Quite outlandish forenames for Sallby, but it was amazing what went on in these villages. And who were Derek and John? Sybil – must be Mrs Spinks – had found out about her husband paying the bills and the kids (at least five by the sound of it), and had decided to call time on their cosy little arrangement.

It took the PCSOs only a few minutes' subdued discussion to agree that this was the most likely scenario. Deciding not to call the Adult Care Service just yet, they strolled back into the room, where Belinda had reached the bottom drawer without finding what she was looking for. She paused in her rummage through used envelopes and rolled-up string.

"I can't find them anywhere. But they must be here!"

"What is it you're looking for?"

"All the financial stuff… money, cheque book, bank statements, accounts, insurance. I can't manage without them."

Grant thought he had a way with women. "OK, love. I can see you're upset. Tell me if I've got this right. Mr Spinks keeps you going with money, but is married to Sybil."

Belinda nodded distractedly.

"He takes care of all the bills and makes sure there's money available when you need it."

She nodded again.

"And Mrs Spinks knows of this arrangement."

"Oh yes. He's been doing it for years. At least thirty. He would never let us down."

Thirty years? She must have been one of those groomed teenagers one hears so much of, Grant surmised.

"And Marsha, Lars and the toddlers rely on him as well?"

"Well of course. Where will they go if the bills aren't paid and there's no power or water?"

Heather, meanwhile, had been running more checks on Belinda's identity. She pulled Grant back into the hallway.

"It turns out she lives on Dapple Grove with a husband and two others – an eighteen-year-old son as well as the girl. They must've kept Marsha, Lars and the toddlers off the radar, somehow. Wonder if the little'uns are twins."

Grant sidled back cautiously.

"Tell me a bit about yourself, Mrs Lowe. What family have you got?"

"Well, I've got a husband but he's in Sunderland. And Melanie, she's fourteen. And Aidan's at university, and a mum and a dad…" Her eyes filled with tears as her voice trailed off. She gulped. "They live in Denswick. And a sister…"

"Tell me where Marsha, Lars and the toddlers are."

"At the village hall, of course!"

The mental health option was looking appropriate.

"Why would they be there?"

"They need the space! And without them there'd be no money so it would all have to end. Can't you see that? I need you to help me find the money and the books, not ask stupid questions."

Grant and Heather could tell that the woman's anxiety levels were dangerously high. (They'd been trained to spot it, and given some tips on how to defuse potentially confrontational situations.) Looking at things dispassionately, it seemed likely that yesterday's carry-on was not a one-off event. Mrs Lowe was clearly deluded. Delusion is a psychological condition, not a criminal offence, but it was their job to make sure that no crime was committed while she was in this state. It was time to take her home.

Gently but firmly, they raised Belinda to her feet. They explained the need to let the removal men get on with their job and reassured her that they'd do what they could to resolve the matter and get back to her. As a special favour, they'd check out Marsha, Lars and the toddlers at the village hall to make sure everything was OK.

Belinda soon found herself walking through the village towards her home, flanked by the two homely but firm officers. One or two passers-by who knew her presumed there'd been a break-in at the village hall. A few who didn't had heard about the events in the school dining hall the day before, and assumed she'd been arrested.

Desperate for sleep, as soon as they reached Dapple Grove Belinda sank onto the sofa while Heather made herself at home in the kitchen, making hot drinks and biscuits for them all. The conversation was turned to general topics. As Grant laid a blanket over Belinda, Heather found the remote control and clicked on an antiques-based programme.

"Just relax and take your mind off everything, love," she said. "We'll take a look in at the village hall while we're here... see what Marsha, Lars and the toddlers are up to."

"Fun 'n' Fitness this morning and Guidance this afternoon," Belinda slurred, as she passed from waking to sleeping.

The officers closed the door gently behind them, then stood on the path trying to interpret Belinda's last words. *Guidance* for Marsha, Lars and the toddlers, eh? That suggested that Social or Mental Health Services were already involved.

Fun 'n' Fitness could mean anything, but it sounded as if that's where they would find the mystery children.

*

Ten or twelve vehicles stood in the muddy field that passed as a car park, but the front door of the hall was firmly locked. Grant and Heather trudged round to try the fire exit, and finally a back door which opened with the turn of a knob.

Inside, buggies and strollers draped with blankets and dangling dummies were parked haphazardly in the vestibule. Mothers, grandmothers and the odd father sat round the edge of the big room, engrossed in adult conversation about water births, immunisation and whether or not paternity leave was a good thing.

At the entrance of the PCSOs, two bright young women interrupted their rendition of *"I'm a dingle-dangle-scarecrow"* to a small group of interested mums and tots.

The taller one asked nervously, "Can we help you?"

The officers tried to play it cool, implying that visiting parent and toddler groups was part of their core strategy, aimed at increased understanding of community issues. The conversation was edged around to the relationship between the play leaders and the people who ran Sallby Village Hall.

It emerged that contact was minimal: when the group was set up, the chairperson had checked they had proper insurance and enhanced disclosure. The shorter of the women kept the Toddler Group accounts and popped the rent through the treasurer's door in cash every three months or so, but as they had their own keys there was no need to meet up. Occasionally the Belinda woman dropped by with toilet rolls or washing-up liquid, but that was all. They had no complaints.

Casually, Heather Banks asked, "Do you keep a register?"

"Yes. Do you want to see it?" A flash of concern about data protection was doused and the book handed over.

The officers searched for clues as to the whereabouts of Marsha and Lars, but the names weren't there.

Some of the parents were not happy to see the Fuzz prying into Toddler Group affairs, especially as the PCSOs did not explain their presence. One or two who were already acquainted with Grant and Heather felt particularly vulnerable. Tiny fists were soon stuffed down the wadded sleeves of tiny, hooded coats. Screaming children, wrenched from favourite toys, were dumped in buggies or hauled outside to be strapped in mammoth safety seats. Neither parents nor children had had their £2-worth, and there'd be something to say next week, you could bet on it. The play leaders were left to clear away on their own.

"We're looking for two children called Marsha and Lars. They may be related to Mrs Lowe, who we believe is the Chairperson of the Management Committee of this hall. What can you tell us?"

The women looked at each other blankly. "Never heard of them."

"Mrs Lowe distinctly told us that Marsha, Lars and the toddlers were at the village hall."

"Yes, they're both twice a week. Martial Arts is Tuesdays and Fridays after school. I bring my son. But there's no Lars or Marsha there, I'm sure of it."

Heather glared at Grant. "Idiot!" she hissed. "Martial Arts! I told you that's what she said. Are you deaf or what?"

Grant looked abashed but had to save face.

"Hmm. Can you tell me, ladies, what would happen to your group if this building were to close?" A note of authority had crept into his voice.

Not more cuts! No one had given a thought to who owned the village hall. Grant certainly hadn't, before he opened his mouth.

"Oh no! Don't say that! We'd have nowhere to go."

Grant was reluctant to admit this corroboration of Mrs Lowe's assertion. "Hmm. I see."

Heather chimed in. "As a matter of interest, the rent – you say you pay it direct to the treasurer. Where does she live?"

"It's a he: Mr Spinks. He lives at the other end of the village – Sphynx Lodge. I've never met him. I just pop the money through the door and he sends a receipt in the post, though he seems to have missed the last few times. We keep the books properly. You don't think we're fiddling them, do you? I can show you if you like, but they're at home." She would worry about that for the next week, until a bigger misfortune shoved it from her mind.

Heather was keen to get out of there, but Grant was reluctant. He hesitated on the threshold.

"Not at the moment. We do have some concerns about the village hall but at this stage we're just making enquiries." He paused slightly, nodding his head towards Emily's muddy car. "That Volvo over there. Belong to one of you, does it?"

"Why? What's wrong?"

"You're driving on illegal tyres. Inadequate tread."

Now Emily, too, had something to keep her awake that night.

Leave 'em worried was Grant's motto.

The officer turned on his heel and strode away, with Heather jogging to catch up.

By the time the mums with older children met at the school gate that afternoon, it was common knowledge that the women who ran the Toddler Group were either paedophiles or racketeers.

21

Belinda was wide awake and at the hall in time for her appointment with Guidance. She still found the choice of venue puzzling, but Drago would be out at work so the meeting could be held without fear of interruption. And she had nothing else to fear, she was confident of that. Anthony Montano had accepted her version of events; Melanie seemed perfectly fine, and Aidan would soon be home for the Easter vacation. Her world was secure. Further guidance was unnecessary.

The kettle had just boiled when Guy Dance arrived and introduced himself. As she shook his hand her eyes lighted on the Denswick Council identity tag which hung from his lapel. She was surprised by the name, but shaken by the words *Environmental Health Inspector*.

"Can I get you a coffee?" She edged towards the kitchen.

"That won't be necessary, thank you. If we could just get on..." Guy didn't want to spend too much time alone with this weirdo. He just wanted to find some evidence and scarper. She looked too normal by half... but then the best criminals always did, didn't they?

They sat at the same table Belinda had shared with Drago just two days earlier. In fact, she realised, this was exactly where she had put the sparrow into the box. She camouflaged a shudder by rubbing her arms and apologised for the cold.

"I didn't think it was worth heating the whole hall for a short visit."

Guy ignored her comment and surveyed the room, then ticked boxes on a list in front of him. Clearing his throat, he explained his duty to inspect premises used by the public, especially those where food may be served or prepared. He explained Belinda's duty to keep the place in good repair and free from vermin; to provide evidence that food hygiene procedures were followed. He recounted tales of mass sickness traced back to damp tea towels laden with prodigiously breeding bacteria, dried repeatedly over hot radiators. He inspected the hand-washing facilities in the kitchen and behind the bar as he spoke of fried fish outlets which used the basins as receptacles for uncooked chips. He prodded, he swabbed, he scraped. His eyes searched for gaps where a slender mouse might sidle, for cracks and cloths which brimmed with bugs.

He was disappointed to find no fault with the kitchen but, keen to expose some wrong that would justify the expense of coming all this way out of town, he set off to explore the rest of the building. Belinda waited anxiously at the table.

Guy tugged at the radiator guards and found them securely fastened to the wall. He bent to stroke the ancient floorboards, full of knocks and gouges, inspecting his fingertips for splinters. None found. No feathers, no droppings, no birds, dead or alive.

The inspector was beginning to lose heart. He noted the stepladders safely stored; the laminated set of instructions for their use; the No Smoking and the Keep the Noise Down notices; the well-labelled fuse box and the covered sockets. He checked the stability of the stacked chairs on their trolley and found none toppled. He opened the padlocked cleaner's cupboard – no problem there, either.

About to give up, he spotted a glimmer of light beneath the front door, and made a note. He measured the gap and judged that a very small mouse – or maybe a shrew – might squeeze itself into the hall that way. He would have something to say about the need for a brush strip, but that wasn't really enough to satisfy him.

If Environmental Health was to assert any authority, he needed to find something serious to pin on her, and Guy was a ferret of a man. Looking up, he spotted a hatch, high up on a corridor wall. Its geography told him that there must be a loft above the lounge.

Without asking Belinda, he located the long pole used to draw down the loft ladder. Belinda sat in terror as he removed his jacket and began to climb.

The game was up! There would be an investigation. *Another* investigation. Panic set in.

She could hear him moving overhead; wanted to follow him up and feign surprise. Instead, unable to sit still any longer, she went outside to search for litter in the car park.

Shortly, the inspector appeared at the back door, briefcase in hand. She approached him in terrified silence.

"Just one little thing, Mrs Lowe." He mentioned the gap under the front door and instructed her to go to a DIY store for a strip that would keep mice out. "Not that I found any evidence of rodents. I was aware, however, that there was a high level of birdsong audible in the loft. I suggest you get your roofer to check the felting. We don't want any bird ingress, do we now?" He smirked, disappointed, but relishing the strain he'd put her under. He relented a little. "On the whole, Mrs Lowe, you seem to run a tidy set of premises. I won't issue any notice *on this occasion*. Just see to those little matters within the next month or two, if you would, and I'll be back to check."

He'd left her puzzled, he could see, but Guy knew she was hiding something. That loft was unnaturally clean. She'd obviously had a clearout before he arrived.

Next time. He'd get her next time.

As soon as the sound of the inspector's car faded away, Belinda pulled down the ladder. How had he not seen Drago's camp? She clambered up and peered in. The space was empty, except for the generations-old gym bench. No sign of the lodger. No sign of his cosy nest. No footprints in the dust... in fact, there was no dust. Drago and his stuff were gone. Her young man (as she liked to think of him) had left without saying goodbye...after everything she'd done for him. Relief washed over her mind; loss stabbed her heart. She sat down at the small square table and sobbed, overwhelmed with both.

The council van in the car park did not escape the notice of grown-ups passing the hall on their way to collect infants from school that afternoon. One of them, who worked part-time at the Chinese takeaway, recognised the driver as he pulled away. Before the little ones reached home after their day's education, local wisdom had it that not only was the Toddler Group in trouble with the police, but the village hall was under investigation by Environmental Health as well. When the big kids got home, supplementary information had it that the woman who ran the hall had, the previous day, tried to poison her daughter. They'd heard it from the horse's mouth: the daughter herself.

There would be fewer attendees at Martial Arts and Toddlers over the next few weeks.

22

Having seen what he had seen through the crack in the loft floor, and with his pet sparrow dead, Drago had seen no point in staying.

He'd expected to find cultural differences between the British and his own people. In general, the English in particular were thought to be rather odd by continental standards, and yet people like him kept coming. Maybe it was curiosity that drew them to this cold, damp island. But was it really worth all the effort? He'd almost made up his mind to go home, before he thought of his lovely Samantha.

He would confront her and demand an explanation. It was better to know the truth than spend the rest of his life wondering, though he no longer knew where she lived.

His mind kept replaying the glimpses of the night before. The woman in white intrigued him – the one who looked like an American nurse. Seen only from above, she seemed familiar somehow. As he lay there musing, another face came into his mind's eye. A man's face. The man seemed inextricably linked to the woman in white.

Drago scrolled down the short list of numbers on his phone, which he'd recovered from the drawer late last night after the clinical proceedings were over. He had a feeling that he'd find the answer there. *Chapel man*: that was it. The woman was married to the chapel man. They had both been so kind to him, although he suspected that this was not their real name. Drago's cousin Stevan had put them in touch; there'd been some link or other with Stevan's employer.

Drago's thumb hovered over the *Select* button. He pressed and waited.

The "Hello" was terse. Marnie had tried to forget the man in the loft. The woman's voice, however, was enough to convince him that the chapel man's wife and the American nurse were one and the same person.

He explained his need to move out of the village hall and his desperation to speak to Samantha again. The voice instructed him to go to work as usual and await instructions.

Around lunchtime, Marnie took a ride past the car wash on Michael's bicycle and stopped across the road. She waited until no customers were around before texting the immigrant again.

"Behind the chapel after work."

Knowing that Sallby Village Hall would be unoccupied that lunchtime, she pedalled the four miles and let herself in. Knowing the building well by now, it took only half an hour to remove all trace of the lodger and stow his gear in the outside meter cupboard for collection.

Marnie deduced that the Serb must have seen the business conducted the previous night, and was sorry for his hurt. Still, business was business, and it was time he sorted himself out, anyway.

The first AID clinic had been very successful, grossing over thirteen grand for the two-session course of 'treatment', paid in advance. Of course, Ambrose, Bud and the others had no idea that the girls had paid so much for their sperm; the men had received more than the official medical rate, so were satisfied with what had been agreed. Then there had been overheads, of course: secondhand clinical couches, trolleys, plus disposables, but she reckoned she'd cleared a good eight grand profit.

It was money she didn't want or need. She'd give Drago £500 to help him set up home with Samantha (who had been demanding rather too much spiritual succour from the Reverend Michael for his wife's liking). Each of the donors could have an extra £50, by way of an introductory bonus. The chapel would receive an anonymous donation – not enough to arouse suspicion, but enough to sort out the problems with the drains.

She'd keep a thousand for herself, in case things ever went wrong with Mick. Maybe she'd take out one of those ISA things. The thought gave her a thrill: never before had Marnie thought of opening a bank account.

The rest of the money would be stuffed through Belinda's door in a padded envelope. Marnie was having the time of her life and, after all, she had another AID clinic arranged for a fortnight's time. Her waiting list was getting longer by the day.

Michael Batty believed his wife to be developing a wellbeing outreach group for young women. He was delighted by the recently increased size of his congregation, and put it all down to the gusto of Marina's efforts, being unaware that regular attendance at Sunday morning service, plus first refusal for the chapel on any forthcoming baptisms, were conditions of membership of the Wellbeing Club.

In his ignorance Michael was, at last, a happy and fulfilled man and he thanked God hourly.

*

Glad to get away from domestic issues, next day Belinda hoped for a busy afternoon at the library. At the start of her shift, an athletic-looking newcomer approached the recently installed triangular desk (the removal of customer-facing staff being the latest edict from Denswick's Culture and Leisure Department). The woman took her time examining all the notices and posters displayed, then, dissatisfied, flicked through the rack of leaflets on the wall.

"Can I help you?"

"Maybe. Do you have anything about places to hire? Church halls and that? For groups and classes."

"I think I have a few leaflets about Sallby Village Hall, somewhere." She made a pretence of searching.

"Don't bother," said the woman. "They've closed it down."

"Oh really? Who have?" Belinda's heart paused. "When did that happen?"

"Yesterday. T'police. They're investigating 'Mother and Toddler Group – folk reckon it might be a paedophile ring. And it's failed an Environmental Health inspection." She edged closer. "The woman who runs it's been arrested for child abuse. It's all ovver 'village."

The librarian gave a squeak of horror and sank onto the wheeled swivel chair, which skidded away from her on the polished floor. She reached out for the desk to steady herself.

"My 'usband, he runs 'Martial Arts classes there. 'As done for years. Now 'e's nowhere to go. My 'ubby, he's not surprised. Always thought there was summat odd about the 'ole set-up. But it's the kids I feel sorry for, them as 've been training for their exams and belts an' that. All that work for nothing. Our Liam," she swelled with pride, "'e's got 'is black belt now. Learnt it all from 'is dad." She leant back, happy to be the bearer of both scandal and success story.

Belinda kept quiet. This woman would find a place on her little list, along with her treacherous husband, with whom for fifteen years Belinda had enjoyed a friendly and co-operative working relationship, or so she'd thought.

She couldn't lose Martial Arts. Where would the hall be then?

The door swished shut behind the woman.

Paedophile ring? Child abuse? All round the village? Belinda wept quietly.

*

In her beige coat and unobserved behind the Large Print Romantic Fiction, Dorothy Simmons had been listening in. She'd been watching Belinda all her life, but had never seen the lass cry since she was in her pram. Her observation had been driven by bitterness, although, Christian woman that she was, Dorothy would have claimed merely to be taking an interest in the younger person's welfare. Dorothy did not have a daughter, but if things had worked out differently when she was younger, maybe she would have done. One the same age as Belinda, who had her father's slightly bowed legs and toothy smile. As it was, her son Dave was all she had, and he were as much use as a stick of celery when it came to keeping her company and talking about stuff. He was just like *his* dad. Awkward. And since he'd broken his leg, there was no living wi' 'im.

Dorothy always softened at the sight of tears, and ever since the new minister got married she'd felt more inclined to judge others kindly. She'd been very suspicious of *him* for the first three years, but the invitation to his wedding had won her loyalty. It had been a long time since anyone made Dorothy Simmons feel important.

Hefting three stout volumes under her arm, she waddled to the self-service Swipe and Stamp machine, which she got wrong every time. Knowing Belinda's involvement with Sallby Village Hall, she would admit overhearing the bad news and maybe get to know the truth behind them. She'd love to have some new gossip to share at the Cup of Cheer Club the next afternoon. It would make a change from grumbles about ailments, government and inadequate bus timetables. Not that she was a scandalmonger, of course. She smoothed her hair, put a smile on her face and approached the Swipe and Stamp.

"Hello, dear. I can see you're upset, but could you help me with this machine?"

Belinda looked up, startled to find she was not alone. She fumbled in her pocket for a tissue and dried her eyes, wondering how much the woman – God, it was Dorothy! – had overheard.

Eyeing her silently with suspicion, Belinda took the library card, ran it through one part of the machine and waited for the sliver of paper extruded by another. She didn't feel inclined to chat to the woman who'd been stalking her for thirty-odd years.

Dorothy, having got so close, couldn't miss the opportunity to make verbal contact at last.

"Bad news about that hall in Sallby. Isn't that where *you* live?" The question was disingenuous.

"Mmm. Probably all just rumours, I'm sure."

"Terrible how some people gossip." The old woman gathered up her books and dared a slight smile. "Hope you feel better soon." She fumbled with her gloves as she pushed the door open. "Goodbye."

Belinda was stunned. After all this time, why was Dorothy being nice to her? No good would come of it. But then, what good ever came of anything? The rumours were out there, and Belinda Lowe, respectable wife, mother, library assistant and servant of the community, was at their epicentre.

The library was now empty. Taking from her drawer a lost library card to conceal her unauthorised access, she ran the words *Clap Clinic Denswick UK* through a search engine on one of the public computers. No results found. She would need to find the correct terminology.

*

At about the same time, Teenage Sexual Health Practitioner Tracey Jubb was installing herself in the Medical Room at Truetrust Academy, aka Denswick Comprehensive, on one of her twice-weekly visits. She hated this aspect of her work, having been moved from Smoking Cessation in the Area Health Authority's latest restructuring. Tracey didn't like teenagers, and she certainly didn't like to think of what they got up to in their spare time. But a job was a job, and Tracey had mouths to feed so, school by school, she displayed her leaflets, handed out protection and pretended not to be judgemental.

This was not the practitioner's first consultation with Melanie Lowe. Tracey blamed it all on *The Mikado*. Since rehearsals began in September, no fewer than fifty percent of the operetta's cast had knocked on her door. This common feature became apparent when a list of rehearsal times and cast members was posted on the notice board outside the Medical Room. Tracey harboured a niggling suspicion that the adjacent sexual health counselling poster had been misconstrued as a complementary therapy for the thespians. When Nanki-Poo brought Yum-Yum along for a Couples' session, her worries had been confirmed. This time, however, Yum-Yum arrived alone.

"Come on in, Melanie."

*

Mealtime that evening began in silence, despite the mother's forced attempts at flippant chat. There was no eye contact, no closeness, no encouragement to mention *the big issue*. Setting the cutlery together on her empty plate, from her pocket Belinda withdrew a folded piece of A4 paper, covered in black and green print. She cleared her throat. Her voice came out two tones higher than normal.

"I've brought you this." She cleared her throat again, terrified. "After what happened the other day... you know... with Jermyn... I thought perhaps we should have a little talk."

Melanie ignored the leaflet. "'Bout what?"

"Well, you know… boys."

The girl raised an eyebrow but continued to push burger and chips around her plate.

"I'm sure Dad was mistaken about what he saw, but… you know… if ever you need to ask me anything…" She trailed off.

"Why would I ask you? Anyway, I know everything."

"Well, you might think you do…" She was trying to be gentle and open, but it was *so* difficult.

"We do it in school, for heaven's sake. I think the teachers know more about sex than *you* do! Doh!"

Her mother's internal voice mused, *That's probably true, but what is it they know that I don't?*

Aloud, she said, "What your dad thought he saw…" She just couldn't find the words.

"You mean, what he *did* see." The girl's tone was an offended brag. She stood up and pushed her chair back.

"Surely not, Melanie? You probably don't understand as much as you think."

Why was her daughter rolling her eyes as she pushed back her chair?

"You're *so* patronising!" The girl gave a final shove and picked up the TV remote. The strains of the BBC news intro filled the room.

"But do you realise… you might get pregnant." Her mother struggled to stay calm.

"Not possible." Melanie feigned interest in the issue of female bishops being debated on screen.

"You see, you don't know as much as you think, Melanie. You're still a child."

"Yes I *do* understand, and I know it's not possible. Miss Jubb sorted me out."

She turned up the sound and briefly flirted with the idea of becoming a bishop herself, whatever one was.

"What does Miss Jubb teach?"

"Sex."

"Just Sex?"

"Well yeah! She's an expert. She's in the Medical Room. What's a bishop?"

"How can she have sorted you out?"

Surely they didn't do lunchtime abortions nowadays?

"Morning-after-pill. Everyone gets them. She does condoms as well, but no-one uses *those*. They're gross. Why *shouldn't* a woman be a bishop?"

She ran upstairs to Google the word *bishop*, leaving her mother trembling with failure and the loss of her child's innocence. Having read a definition of the word, the girl quite fancied being a bishop. The uniform would certainly make her stand out in a crowd, which was the essence of celebrity.

Belinda cleared the plates and returned to the TV, flicking through the channels until she found something noisy enough to drown out the screaming in her head. She stretched out. Eventually, she slept.

Seeing her mother thus a couple of hours later, the girl left the house carrying a heavy bag. Her eventual destination was her grandparents' bungalow, but she might make a few detours en route that no-one needed to know about. She was thoughtful enough to leave a note:

Gone to stay with Gran and Granddad till Dad and Aidan get home.

23

Granddad was impressed with some of the girl's habits. They reminded him of his National Service years: early rising, obsessive cleanliness, plenty of spit and polish. Well, not the spit. He lay in bed listening to her pattering around the bungalow, remembering his days of young fatherhood. There had been no showers then. A lick and a promise before the girls were packed off to school and a bath once a week if they needed it. Now, it seemed, Melanie was unable to leave the house without three fresh coats of nail varnish and lip gloss, though she was a pretty little thing without any embellishment.

He convinced himself that Melanie's form teacher scrutinised her class's deportment and grooming in much the same way as, in his corporal days, he had inspected his platoon. Sadly, the poor man was wrong.

*

The girl had very good reason for rising with the lark and leaving for school before her grandparents were up and about. As one of the leading players in the forthcoming production of *The Mikado*, attendance at early morning rehearsals was imperative. The buffing, brushing and glossing was all part of a star's morning routine. Appearance was all in the construction of charisma.

At 7.30 each day, the Sallby contingent of the cast met at the Jepsons' gate. Ben's father, renowned locally as a keen participant in extra-marital sports, had unselfishly agreed to be morning taxi-driver while rehearsals lasted. Felix Jepson was oblivious to both the pubescent sexual tensions suffusing the vehicle each morning and the fact that it had already been noted, locally, that young Ben was his father's son in more ways than one.

Deposited at the school gates, Yum-Yum, Nanki-Poo and two anonymous members of the company chorus manoeuvred their way past the cleaners and caretakers who buffed, brushed and polished in their own fashion, and made straight for the Drama Studio. There, the long-limbed, luscious new drama teacher, Miss Montgomery, and the oh-so-handsome, oh-so-gentle Head of Performing Arts, Mr Reubens, were developing a splendid working relationship. The power of the rapport between the two teachers was inspirational to their students; aspirations, emotions and hormones soared along with the youthful voices. Even Jermyn Street had unearthed his latent musicality, once persuaded that volume was not the be-all and end-all for a member of the chorus, and Sloane's sinuous moves obscured her insecure grasp of the complicated lyrics.

Whether the students gathered each morning for the love of music, drama and the D'Oyly Carte operettas; whether the dedication of their teachers would bear fruit on stage; and whether their exam grades would reflect their enhanced cultural awareness, were all debatable. It was incontrovertible, however, that by the end of the production's run, the *The Mikado*'s cast would all be considerably more worldly-wise than their peers.

*

As the performance dates drew closer, after-school rehearsals continued until 6pm. Gerrard Street did the homeward run to Sallby. Neither driver questioned why the Lowe girl no longer travelled with the others, but each gradually became aware that her mother was now alone in the house in Dapple Grove. Both men sensed a potential opportunity, but Gerrard was more conveniently situated to take advantage of any opportunity that might arise.

Belinda spent part of each evening with her parents, hoping that her daughter might deign to leave the spare bedroom and speak to her. Meanwhile, she held circular conversations with her mother and gave practical assistance to her father, who was as recovered from the stroke as he was ever going to be. She also needed to spend time at home, to attend to village hall business, hope for calls from Aidan or Doug and retain her sanity. Alone in bed each night, it was not her husband that she longed for, but the dark-eyed young foreigner with hairs on the back of his hands.

*

This same young foreigner had, after leaving the village hall cleaner and smarter than he'd found it, spent a single uncomfortable, unlit night, silent and still, in an attic at Denswick Manse. It was important for the minister to be kept in the dark.

Knowing that Dave Simmons was still off work, Marnie needed a day to track down the young man's cousin. The minister's wife had only exchanged after-service pleasantries with Dorothy Simmons since the wedding, so a home visit was called for.

Her once brassy hair now a sober shade of pale brown, Marnie dressed conservatively for the occasion. This went down well with the older woman, whose favoured fashion options were always beige, baggy and nondescript. The personal visit, which she took as recognition of her unstinting labours on behalf of the chapel, pleased her. Luckily, Mrs Batty timed it to coincide with David's latest hospital appointment, which had been alluded to on the chapel threshold the other day.

Marina had made it her business to find out how this church-and-God thing worked, who was who and who did what to whom in the organisation.

Now, she praised the churchwardens' diligence in their duties, was stunned by the good done in the community on the chapel's behalf, the high standard to which the building was maintained, their readiness at all times to support weddings and funerals. The wardens were all marvels and Marina was in awe.

After this pump-priming, conversation naturally took a more personal turn as Marina subtly elicited something of Dorothy's history: how she had once been sweet on a young man at work who had been snapped up by a younger, prettier girl; how she'd met Wilf Simmons on the dodgems at a travelling fun fair; how, being twenty-seven at the time and afraid of being left on the shelf, she'd married him within months and rued the day ever since. Their first child, a girl, had survived only a few days.

"It was very hard," she hiccupped as she wiped her eyes. "I had our David a couple of years later, but you never get over something like that. Now Wilf's gone – that's a blessing. I know it's a terrible thing to say, but he was a difficult man. I'm happier without *him*, but a daughter would've looked after me in my old age."

Marina sighed sympathetically. "You still have David, though."

"He's like his dad. A hard man. And since he's broken his leg, there's no living with him.

"His wife was lovely – Pauline – but he's ditched her and his two kids. That's why he's living here with me. She threw him out and I don't wonder. I miss her and the little 'uns." The tissue came into play again.

"Tell me about the children."

"Our Lauren's ten and our Kyle's seven. Nice kiddies they are. Take more after their mother than him."

"Is there no hope of reconciliation?"

"Not if Pauline's got any sense. Turns out he'd been having a bit on the side. This woman turned up here one day saying she was a friend of Dave's. Pauline was in the bathroom mixing up a blue rinse for my hair and came out to take a look. 'Who are you?' she says to this woman – all suntanned she was, with coloured streaks in her hair and that."

Dorothy rarely had chance to get things off her chest and although she hadn't taken to the minister's new wife immediately, the relief of sharing the stored grief secured her loyalty for ever.

"Who was she?"

"Called herself *Patreesha*. Pauline said, 'As far as I know, Dave hasn't got any friend called *Patreesha*.'"

"'Well, you know different now, don't you, love?' she came back, quick and hard-faced as you like.

"Well, Pauline – I could see she was upset – she went back into the bathroom, poured the blue rinse down the sink, then put on her coat and took the *Patreesha* woman outside. That was the last time I saw my daughter-in-law."

Dorothy breathed deeply and paused to control herself. "It's no wonder my hair's a mess!" She reached up a hand and tweaked a permed curl.

"Next thing I knew, David turned up with a suitcase, saying Pauline had thrown him out because of a *misunderstanding*."

The tears had run their course now and the sobs were muted. The women spoke quietly about the temptations faced by those who cleaned the windows of domestic properties; the weakness of men, and the modern-day lack of respect for marriage vows.

But Dorothy hadn't finished.

"So I let him sleep on the settee. Have to keep it quiet from the council. He'd already broken his leg falling off a ladder – it was a really bad break, had to be pinned and all sorts – it just wasn't healing properly. So he's here, all day, every day, with his great leg sticking out across the room for me to trip over. Then, would you believe it, that *Patreesha* turns up again? This time she's wearing a right get-up: dungarees and wellingtons, even though it was a sunny day. Said she'd left her husband and had decided it was Dave she wanted. Ooh, I *was* upset, especially being a chapel warden.

"Well, you could tell that David wasn't expecting it. 'But what about your children?' he asks. 'Never you mind them. None of your business,' she says.

"I just sat there while they argued. Anyway, she could see there was no room for her here, and she'd none of her things with her, so he gave her some money to find a B&B and sort herself out. From what I gather, she collected her stuff next day when her husband and the kids were out, and found herself a little flat in that new development where the pithead baths used to be."

This was the longest conversation Dorothy had shared for years.

"David's at the hospital now. We're hoping they'll take his pot off today so he can get back to work. He'll need physio, of course. That young chap Steve who helps him has done his best, fair dos, but David's worried about all the customers he's probably lost."

"Ah, Steve! Is his real name Stevan? He cleans the windows at our house." Marina's patience had borne fruit. "I was wondering when he's due round again – they're looking very

253

grimy and we don't have a ladder to do it ourselves. You don't happen to know his routine, do you?"

"Well no, but I think David wrote his number down for me somewhere in case I needed it." Dorothy pushed herself up from the high-seat chair and sorted through the papers propped up behind a dancing lady on the mantelpiece. She found what she was looking for on the back of an overdue book reminder from the County Library Division.

Marina took out her own device, looked at the card and entered the number she needed.

It took no more than two minutes to bring the visit to a close without being abrupt. Both women had got a lot out of the conversation.

Within half an hour it had been agreed that Dragomir Duric would take refuge at Stevan's place in Bath House Court. In earlier times, the dwelling would have been called a bedsit. Being in a newly erected seven-storey block, designed around a communal garden with the old colliery's winding gear as a sculptural centrepiece, it was advertised as a studio apartment. Either way, it was tiny.

24

As spring intensified, Belinda made use of her days off to prepare for her family's reunion. Aidan would be home soon, and Doug had promised to spend a full week with the family. In the garden, she sat on her carved snail, weathered to grey now, watching the sparkle of sunlight as a breeze ruffled the pond. Everything would soon be back to normal, she felt sure. Things weren't *so* bad. A few minutes' yoga breathing, a bit of positive thinking, some vigorous tidying – that would sort it.

The time had come to clear out her wardrobe.

Grabbing a trio of black sacks, she bounded upstairs and flung open the bedroom window. The sharp air and scent of imminent growth spurred her sense of purpose. The garments on their hangers were lifted from the rails and tossed onto the bed. The topsy-turvy pile of shoes went on top, one by one, but Belinda soon realised she did not possess enough shoes to make a pile so big. At its foundation lay another pile, made up of brown padded envelopes, a calico bag and a blue-lidded bucket.

At sight of the bucket came the immediate grip of fear. Both Denswick Borough Council's Licensing Department and the Air Ambulance people might, even now, be investigating a fraud, a fraud committed by someone using the name Belinda Lowe. A sunbeam shone through the window onto the bucket and the calico bag, illuminating their grubby whiteness and with it, her failings.

Eyeing the containers with suspicion, she spent the next hour sorting the clothes into piles – Keep, Jumble, Recycle and Bin – but no matter how long she tarried over the task, the bulging envelopes, bucket and bag did not disappear from the bottom of the wardrobe.

The blue-lidded bucket she recognised dimly. It smelt of a cold Christmas night and was very heavy. Up-ending it onto the floor she knelt to count the grubby, small-denomination coins and the occasional £5 note. At last, the money stood in wobbly piles on the carpet. She totalled and retotalled till she got the same figure twice. £121.21, plus three euros, a supermarket trolley token and a Canadian dollar. *Who would do that?* she wondered.

Throwing the calico bag aside, she added the cash to the pile of padded envelopes that had come through her letter box over the months. There'd been more than she realised. Puzzling over them had been one more stress that she just couldn't handle and, as each one disappeared from view, it had also disappeared from her consciousness. If she thought about them at all, it was to assume that one of the hall's regular hirers, knowing of the treasurer's hospitalisation, had delivered the rent to the chairwoman instead.

Moving her knees to avoid the ridge beneath the carpet, one by one she emptied the envelopes and gasped at the flurry that tumbled to the floor. This was more than overdue rent. She sat back on her heels, exhaling through pursed lips.

Head dizzy, heart pounding, she leant back against the bed. She had extracted £400 in rent from Drago on top of his free labour in redecorating the hall – probably worth another grand. She was already struggling to think how she'd explain those things away when the committee eventually reconvened.

Yet here, on her bedroom carpet, was an unexplained £41,000 that was nothing to do with her.

Going to the police was out of the question. They'd battered her door down for no good reason back in the summer; they had her in their deluded sights for child abuse, and she'd not yet got over her close shave in the *pilgarlic* debacle. No. She could not ask the police to investigate.

Was someone testing her honesty? Was it drug money? Could Doug be a dealer, pretending to be working in Sunderland whilst all the time peddling crack cocaine and trying to launder the money through the village hall accounts? She entertained the possibility for a while but, nah! Doug possessed too little imagination and too much decency for anything so exciting. It could certainly be nothing to do with Aidan. He was a golden boy, and he would be coming home soon. As for Melanie, who could tell what she'd do now she'd hooked up with Jermyn Street?

At the same time, a mental image of Marnie floated through on a cloud of disgruntlement. It was hurtful that her supposed new friend had not been in touch since Dad's stroke. Belinda could have done with a friend right now.

It felt like a burglary in reverse. She recalled the police break-in and wondered if that was when it all began. Perhaps the window-cleaner's mate, the one who'd leered at her and called the ambulance, had riffled the drawers and found a spare key. Maybe *he* was the drug dealer, and he'd stashed his loot in *her* wardrobe. She looked in the mirror and tried to see herself as a gangster's moll, but no. She just looked like someone's mother, someone's daughter, someone's wife who worked in the library: drab, dull and depressed, but not at all degenerate.

None of the possible explanations made sense. She and Doug had joint accounts. It was one of their *things*. Total trust, she reminded herself, although, somehow, she must keep this windfall from him.

Slowly, putting off more decisive action, Belinda returned the Keep clothes to the wardrobe and filled the three black sacks until they bulged. She toyed with the idea of concealing the money there, but what if some poor charity shop volunteer came across it and was arrested? No. This was her problem and she mustn't lumber anyone else with it. She didn't want the money for herself, and she didn't want it on the premises. Who knew when the police might see fit to batter her door down again? How on earth could she explain it away? She might be able to wangle the Drago income through the books, but not £41,000.

When the shock was subsiding a little, her mind turned to ways she might dispose of the cash in more creative ways without arousing suspicion.

Doug wasn't much of a gambler, but on Grand National day he'd go down to the betting shop in Denshill and place £20 each way on a horse chosen at whim. Although his wife had never been inside, she would watch the comings and goings with interest from the car and had never recognised any borrowers from the library among the clientele. The bookies' was no longer a woman-free zone: that was apparent from her surveillance. As Belinda knew nothing about gambling or horses, she'd never win anything. She could lose a lot of money that way, and she could start that afternoon.

Once the idea had taken root, she did some research. The television pages told her which racecourses were operating that day and running *Bookmakers Denswick* through a search engine provided the addresses of seven betting shops where she could place a wager. Excitement bubbled up with more force than anything she'd felt since enrolling on the sculpture course, almost a year ago.

Over a lunch of oatcakes and cream cheese, she prepared her backstory, plotted her route and chose her runners. Starting slowly at first, she'd spend just £100 at each gambling outlet, so as not to arouse suspicion. She'd select names according to a different theme each day. She'd liked Geography at school, so took that as her first.

In case of nosey staff or punters, her gambling persona was visiting relatives in the area with her elderly father, who'd always liked a bet but couldn't get out much nowadays. It was the only pleasure left in life for the poor old chap, so who was she to deny it? The fictional relatives would always live in the next-but-one village along (Belinda being aware of how, when a woman tripped in Denshill, within the hour all Sallby would know who'd pushed her).

She didn't need to feign ignorance of the procedures in a betting shop, and timidity added to the authenticity of her story. Usually, the old man's bets were placed by her brother, she'd say. Adrian, she said, had recently suffered a catastrophic but not fatal climbing accident near Grenoble. (A poster print of that area, displayed in the travel agent's window near the library, had attracted Belinda throughout the winter.) The other punters were only too eager to help this poor lass, who'd brought her dad away to ease his worry, despite her own, and was doing her best to keep his spirits up. And she weren't a bad looker, either.

By the fourth establishment, Bel was gaining confidence. There were plenty of nags named for geographical connections: River Eden, Seastrider and Brummy Strumpet attracted her money, among others. She moved between the betting shops, in villages heard of but never visited.

Against all expectations, a few of her choices made good, Brummy Strumpet coming from nowhere to romp home at 33:1 in the 2.30 at Doncaster. This was not what she'd hoped for. By the end of the afternoon she had considerably more cash than she started with, but felt exhilarated. There was no harm in it, Bel concluded. It was just a bit of fun and it filled the loneliness, a little.

Stopping off at the supermarket for some bread, her attention was caught by the gaudy billboards and posters promoting lotteries and scratch cards. She'd never taken any notice of them before, but quickly identified another, even simpler, way to ease her burden. She spent another £100 on various opportunities, including £50 worth of National Lottery tickets. She'd have to watch the Saturday night TV programme to see if she'd won; that would be a new experience. The silver paint was easily scratched off the numbers and symbols. Deflated, she handed six cards back to the cashier, leaving the store with a small profit on the exchange and fifty lottery chances still to play.

Belinda was not normally a woman to fantasise, but sinking into sleep, Bel played with the notion of spending the money herself. That night, she dreamt once again of the ruined cottage, deep in a Welsh wood, and of a dark-eyed foreigner who dwelt therein.

*

Behind spiked railings along the main road on the edge of Denswick stood a compound full of motorhomes and campervans for sale or hire. Doug and Belinda had sometimes craned their necks as they drove past, speculating on prices and where they would take the family if they could afford to buy.

Next day, the librarian set off for work an hour early and, for the first time, drove through the open gate between the railings. Thirty or forty imposing, bus-sized vehicles were on display, diagonally fanned out in a semi-circle on the broken tarmac. Under a grey sky, the window of a green-doored Portakabin glowed dimly with yellow light. Inside, the Managing Director of PD RoamerHomes Ltd, Phil Dunne, sat twiddling his thumbs as he acknowledged the folly of pretending that this was a viable business. The winter had been dreary, with no money around for high-priced holiday homes, mobile or static. A couple of the rental models were hired out for three months to elderly couples off to travel overland in search of sunshine in the Middle East or North Africa, but the way things were politically, he had low hopes of ever seeing the motors again. Even families planning to holiday in Britain were holding back.

Now that his brother Tyson was banged up, Phil could no longer rely on backhanders or dodgy dealing to keep the bills paid and the loan sharks off his back. Phil needed a sale, and he needed it soon.

When a knocking disturbed his thoughts, he ignored it. *Kids who ought to be at school*, he thought. At the second knock, he rose and unlocked the door. A shortish woman in her forties looked up at him. He raised his eyebrows but did not smile. No pound signs revolved in his mind's eye.

"Are you the person to speak to about the motorhomes?" Belinda asked uncertainly.

"Aye. What d'you want to know?"

"I'd like to have a look at some, please."

"Buy or rent?"

"Ummm... well... not sure. It all depends..."

"Depends on what?" Phil wasn't going to waste time trudging round in the cold with this woman if he could help it. She was wearing a wedding ring. Why wasn't she with her husband? Phil was a traditionalist; he liked a woman who knew her place, and that place was firmly under a man's thumb. (This conviction was largely theoretical, Philip having rarely glimpsed daylight from under his wife's very large, red-taloned *Pollux* since their nuptials some eleven years earlier.)

"On whether I like what I see." Bel was a woman of substance. No jumped-up salesman in a Portakabin was going to talk down to her. Shooting him a steely glance, she stood her ground.

Phil recognised defeat when he saw it, tore himself away from the fan heater hidden beneath the desk, slid on his jacket and collected some keys from a locked cabinet.

"You'll be wanting the lower end of the price range, I expect."

"Not necessarily." Her response was tart. "I'd like to look inside several, consider the features and arrange a test drive."

Phil opined silently that this woman's husband wasn't giving her enough ironing and hoovering to do. Test drive indeed! It was nippy out, so he took her to the nearest van, a Happilarks Wandalonga model, with its domed frontal lobe accommodating a full-sized double bunk above the cab. After a few desultory gestures, he sat himself down on a tweed-covered banquette and let the woman organise her own viewing.

She was less than impressed. Her £41,000 had already increased by a few hundred pounds and who knew where it would end when the lottery was drawn at the weekend? She'd buy tickets from most outlets within a five-mile radius of Sallby. Surely one of them would come up. Bel wanted something better than the Wandalonga. It was only a bit of fun, anyway. She deserved a bit of that, after the year *she'd* had.

Being pressed on price, Phil quoted £32,490, although he was anxious to explain the benefits of easy monthly payments. He did not, of course, mention the APR of 11.9%.

"It would be cash," said Bel, "but I was thinking of something more luxurious than this one."

Phil trudged back to the office to pick up the keys for a Nomad Libertine, though he had no faith in this woman's authenticity. She was a time-waster, if ever he'd seen one.

Leaving the compound with five minutes to spare, Bel had a fair idea of which motorhome she would choose to buy if this were real, and had a bagful of promotional literature with which to while away her lonely hours. *It's only a bit of fun,* she reminded herself again.

At work, she logged onto the council's employee intranet as usual, expecting a few routine emails and instructions. Blaring red from the screen, a special notice for all Library Service staff spelt out proposals to transfer the buildings and contents to a private trust over the next few months. Early discussions suggested that the new trust would reduce staffing by ninety percent but in return, and in the new spirit of localism and the Big Society, offer unlimited opportunities for volunteering and unpaid work placements, helping the jobless to gain skills which would lead to useful paid careers in a range of public and private sectors. It was a win-win situation! The existing workforce would be granted opportunity to take voluntary redundancy or apply for work with the new organisation. The trust would have the exciting chance to reshape the library service with an emphasis on paperless provision of reading material focused on job skills, economic regeneration and online self-led research facilities for other areas of interest. Acres of forests would be saved and the pollution caused by paper manufacture reduced. Almost as an afterthought, the communiqué mentioned that it would also save the council £900,000 per annum (plus another possible £185,000 if the mobile library service was also axed) and help to balance its budget.

The email was accompanied by several attachments for librarians to print and display. There would, of course, be full public consultation online and public meetings to be held in the city at 4pm on the following two Fridays, venue details TBA.

So this was it: the end of her career and the end of the library. OK, she was no high flier, but she took pride in what she did. The thrill of yesterday and the anticipation of the test drive were wiped out.

With a heavy heart she printed and displayed the notices, as instructed.

The news was soon out: most users had some family connection with council employment in one form or other; Twitter and Facebook carried the news from work to home in seconds. People who had never been inside the building made it their destination that morning, and moaned to Belinda about loss of services and the exorbitant imposition of council tax as if it was all *her* fault. Few commiserated about the loss of her job.

No one said, "Ooh, yes. Put my name down for a couple of shifts without pay."

People were cross, very cross. But they all knew that apathy was what the council relied on, and that, in the end, apathy would triumph. It was a done deal.

That evening, Melanie did not extend the courtesy of leaving her temporary bedroom during her mother's visit. Subdued, Belinda explained the situation to her parents, who took the news as further evidence that the world as they knew it was coming to an end. There had always been libraries. But they did not make a profit, and this avaricious new world was sending them to the dogs.

Their granddaughter's fleeting presence, whilst not exactly a burden, was causing them a degree of disquiet they could well do without. Her extended school hours demonstrated laudable diligence on the part of her teachers, but Gran and Granddad were fearful that the child was not getting as much sleep as a growing girl needed. They were loath to speak of this to Belinda, whom to Melanie was anathema.

Belinda had planned to entertain her parents by recounting her visit to the motorhome forecourt, but had lost all interest. Local TV news carried a feature on the library closure. There was no getting away from it. Using expected calls from Doug and Aidan as an excuse, she escaped as soon as she could, to nurse yet more wounds in private.

25

Dragomir Duric had been quite happy lodging in the loft and enjoying the tender ministrations of the older woman. Life with his cousin was more cramped and boring, though between shifts at the car wash Drago did earn a few extra pounds cleaning windows. Dave Simmons would soon be back at work, and the pair worked all daylight hours to maximise their income while they could.

To some extent, exhaustion numbed the hurt Drago felt at his sweetheart's conduct, which he could not begin to fathom. He had decided it was only fair to confront Samantha and give her chance to explain, so he waited for the minister's wife to arrange a meeting.

Samantha had taken some persuading to join the clientele of the Artificial Insemination by Donor clinic at Sallby Village Hall, and only went along with it to support her sister-in-law, who Samantha's brother had abandoned for life on a North Sea gas platform. Messages to the family made it apparent that he had no intention of returning home in the foreseeable future.

With some relief, within a fortnight of their visit to Sallsby, both Samantha and her sister-in-law knew they had not conceived. Despite paying for two AID sessions, Samantha was not sure she'd bother turning up next time, yearning as she was for her hairy-handed lover.

Reverend Michael had completed his twenty-week course of one-to-one swimming instruction and each Wednesday joined the lunchtime public swims although (as he explained to his wife over breakfast) they did not 'float his boat' in the way the hands-on instruction had done. Instead, he joined twenty or thirty of the 'retired or redundant' persuasion ploughing shallow furrows up and down, up and down. As Michael's fitness improved, he learnt to circumnavigate the pairs and trios of gossiping women who oozed through the chlorine solution and kept their hair dry. Not one of them recognised the minister; without his dog collar and wearing goggles which concealed his wandering eye, he felt invisible. Sometimes it was Samantha's turn to sit on the tall lifeguard's chair watching over the swimmers. He would smile and wave, just the once, and experience that warm glow of admiration. Now it was Marina's turn for lessons, though never having been inside a swimming pool before her marriage, she was a reluctant student. Nevertheless, she went along with her husband's wishes and kitted herself out with a subdued little line in swimwear from the supermarket. Michael had put her name down for classes with Samantha and this would be her fourth week.

She was not comfortable in the water but persisted. The lessons were all part of her journey from the margins of society to full community membership. Marina wanted to be one of the crowd, to join the dry-haired women, the flabby and the bony, as they chatted through their weekly thirty lengths, but for now she floundered the widths with the instructress's support and encouragement. This day, as the lesson drew to a close, she delivered the message that Samantha had been longing to hear.

"My window-cleaner asked me to let you know that his cousin's back."

At the news, tears overflowed from the soft blue eyes.

"Does he want to see me?"

"I believe so, but Stevan said something about finding a private place to meet up."

The full lips trembled.

"If you like, I could open up the chapel for half an hour in the morning without anyone knowing. Shall I tell him eight o'clock?"

Relief and grief merged with guilt for losing faith in her lover's loyalty, but a meeting had been arranged. Samantha nodded. She would be there.

*

Many of the flats in Bath House Court had been snapped up by members of the travelling community which, dealing solely in cash, had been less affected by the economic crisis than other sectors of local society.

Every vacant field, every demolition site within a ten-mile radius of the town, was purchased by the travellers within days of going on the market, if not before. They were either developed with gypsy cash or left to bloom with burdock and willow herb. The council certainly couldn't afford to make use of them.

With the demise of the National Coal Board and the disappearance of its successor from common sight, until the bottom fell out of the nation's finances no-one had got round to selling off the piece of land where the pithead baths once stood. Cleaning up contaminated land, whilst laudable in theory, was expensive.

The entrepreneurial gypsies and travellers had their own code of conduct. Never slow to exploit an opportunity, when the land came on the market they put in the first and only sealed bid. This bid arrived in the council's Asset Management

Department in an envelope embossed with the company address of a famous London law firm, well known to the council from the various appeals against rejected planning applications. Money was no object. Further bids were discouraged as a defence against allegations of discrimination.

Drawings were quickly prepared, corners cut, and the development erected in record time. Soon the travellers had acquired a near-monopoly of short- and medium-term rental accommodation in the little town.

Standing in one day for her husband at a meeting of the Denswick Organisation for Community and Interfaith Local Enterprise (known as DOCILE), Marina made it her business to identify the key players among the caravan dwellers. Before the round-the-table introductions were made, she addressed the chairman in person.

"Please bear with me. I'm new to this," she said demurely. "Would you advise me, please, on the correct way to refer to the different sections of the community? The last thing I want to do is offend anyone."

The chairman was fiddling with his hearing aid and missed the request. An unsmiling, broad man with straight eyebrows and scarred knuckles assured her that she'd find out as the meeting progressed.

The chairman retrieved his hearing device from the carpet and tweaked out bits of fluff as he called the meeting to order. Introductions were made too fast to remember, but she did catch the word gypsy when the unsmiling man spoke.

"You prefer to be called gypsies rather than travellers – is that right?" Marina assumed an earnest demeanour.

"Depends on who you ask. I represent the gypsy community – but some call themselves gypsies when really they're only travellers. It depends which family you're talking about... there are some trouble-makers among the travellers but most true gypsies are honest, law-abiding folk like anyone else, struggling with discrimination and poor facilities, trying to live in peace with their families."

There was a shuffling of feet at this, but no comment. The minister's wife thanked the man with a sweet smile.

A portly, red-faced chap in a black dress and hat, who had introduced himself as Father Dermot O'Hanlon, incumbent of Our Lady of Sorrows Roman Catholic Church, leant forward.

"Very good church members, the gypsy community," he chipped in. "Very generous. The travellers too," he added as an afterthought. "They're all God's children and they're all welcome at our Lady of Sorrows." Father Dermot was wary lest news of his interjection leaked out as far as the smaller, unauthorised sites that had sprung up on the green belt around the town. He was too old to tangle with a baseball bat.

Much of the priest's spare time was spent settling squabbles over who owed what to whom, which trailer was allowed on which site, and whose traveller son had tried to take advantage of whose gypsy sister or daughter. Outright internecine warfare was sometimes tricky to avert and he was quite familiar with the visiting hall at the local prison.

Over the years, this had taken a heavy toll on Father O'Hanlon, who, it must be said, was no stranger to the bottle. A life of celibacy and drink had not contributed to Dermot's happiness nor deepened his spirituality, but he stayed true to his vows and away from choirboys.

He was happy to count the gypsies and travellers among his flock. Indeed, on the rare Sundays that they did actually travel, his congregation shrank to a mere handful of devotees. They had a true and generous faith in Dermot's Lord, and without their contributions, Our Lady of Sorrows' finances would have been in a pickle. Father O'Hanlon and local gypsy king Patrick Kevin McVeigh (known as Pakamac behind his back and Mr McVeigh to his face) had an effective pastoral relationship: the priest listened to Pakamac's confessions and Mr McVeigh negotiated the terms of any atonement he was prepared to make.

The priest acted as go-between to forge contracts or solve disputes between gypsies, travellers and the settled community. Marina had divined this within weeks of her arrival in Denswick. She had also divined that the Father had no time for Methodists, with their temperance and tolerance, or for her husband in particular. Subtly, she soon made herself useful as Michael's regular representative on DOCILE. It established her as a force to be reckoned with, something her husband had never achieved, though precisely what the organisation itself had ever achieved was tricky to define and a mystery to most.

There was often talk, at meetings, about the significance of the E in the acronym. E for Enterprise. This was what Denswick needed. Marnie had ideas, but for now, the only local enterprises that thrived were the Indian takeaway, the hand car wash, illicit drugs and Bath House Court, where turnover was brisk.

The minister's wife had her heart set on securing a two-bedroom apartment for Drago and Samantha; space for a nursery would give them hope for a better start second time round, she thought. When *Any Other Business* was reached on the agenda, Marina praised the landlords of Bath House Court.

"Whoever they might be," she said, "they deserve our thanks for investing in such a versatile and valuable piece of real estate. The development," she continued, "is proving a boon to hard-working young couples and singletons trying to set up home, free of whatever shackles or encumbrances have held them in check hitherto."

Bath House Court was social housing along the popular Public and Private Finance Initiative lines. The private part was a hundred percent provided by the travelling community; it was, however, Mr McVeigh alone who decided which of his people may invest in the business, who vetted the tenants and, occasionally, attended meetings of DOCILE on his community's behalf.

271

Marina needed to convince the gypsy king that she was sympathetic to his way of life and in awe of the close bonds within the travelling brotherhood but, as a newcomer, she would need help in winning Mr McVeigh's confidence. The key lay, therefore, in paying court to Father O'Hanlon, who would also be a tough nut to crack. For this, she needed to feign an interest in his faith.

As the meeting drew towards its usual unproductive close, she introduced the daring concept that the committee should focus on its declared aims: the representatives must themselves learn about one another's beliefs, values and culture if they were truly to take the lead in a cohesive society

"I've taken the liberty of preparing a formal proposal, if that's OK," she said, looking round for consent. This took DOCILE by storm. Astounded by the woman's effrontery, one of the minor local politicians on the committee mumbled something about incorrect procedure.

The secretary, struggling to keep up with interjections and digressions for the minutes, tactfully explained the reality that rambling discussions were usually followed by deferral to the next meeting of any decision requiring action.

"However," she announced efficiently, "DOCILE's constitution allows any member to table a formal proposal. Mrs Batty did telephone me some days ago to ask if the matter could be added to the agenda, but I'm afraid I'd already sent copies out with the minutes. It's entirely my fault that this has come as a surprise to you all."

She turned to the chairman, whose hearing aid had chosen that moment to detach itself from his ear again.

"As this is my error, I'd be grateful if you'd allow the proposal to be dealt with, Mr Chairman."

Mr Chairman could tell he was being asked for permission about something, but not what. He nodded his assent while trying to locate the lost device with his toe.

Marina launched her campaign. "As a newcomer to the area, I've been struck by the tolerance and diversity in evidence on this committee. As a new minister's wife, personally, I feel the need for instruction on the different ways of life, the different beliefs and values that we each represent."

She had them with her opening sentence, despite murmurings about full agendas, procedural irregularities and other commitments. She pressed on. When she'd finished, everyone sat back. Most were searching for a way out.

The minister's wife had raised their nape hairs by suggesting that the *I* in the acronym – I for Interfaith – should become real. As a starting point, each member of the group should call on Father O'Hanlon to take the lead by providing instruction in, and elucidation of, the Roman Catholic faith. Coming from the wife of a Methodist minister, this was astounding.

There being no known Muslims in Denswick, an imam from the nearby city of Dencastle had been dragooned onto the committee. He was uncomfortable with the proposals but could always invent a prior engagement. A Hindu woman who worked at the Jaipur Star takeaway attended meetings when she could. Darren Gould, Pastor of the Rejoice with Jesus! Evangelical Church, which met once a month at the disused cinema-cum-bingo hall, was excited by Mrs Batty's proposal. He had no doubt that, when the time came for Rejoice with Jesus! to enlighten the committee on the fount of his church's evangelical zeal, each and every DOCILE member would clamour to be Born Again. The elderly councillors at the meeting pursed their lips at Marina's suggestion, wanting to keep religion out of the group's proceedings altogether. They preferred to focus on the Community Local Enterprise aims, though not one of them had ever offered a viable suggestion. The Quaker teacher was undecided and would wait for God's guidance.

The response was lukewarm from all except Pastor Darren, but bewilderment stopped their mouths and there were no

273

objections when the date was fixed for the following Monday afternoon.

When the time came, only the Quaker schoolteacher, the evangelical pastor, the woman from the Jaipur Star and the Methodist minister's wife were free to attend the tour of Our Lady of Sorrows. Father Dermot, a little the worse for a bottle of ouzo once donated as a raffle prize, was feeling self-important. His was the One True Faith, so it was his duty to pontificate.

The Quaker teacher asked searching ~~questions about th~~e nature of the divine and the woman from the takeaway showed her face for half an hour, long enough to be puzzled by the super-sized image of a crucified man. No wonder Our Lady had Sorrows!

Pastor Darren was, briefly, deflated, for he had failed to see the Light of God within the tipsy old priest. Yet he soon determined to Rejoice with Jesus! at the opportunity presented by the DOCILE initiative, and give it his best shot. He suggested his own church as the venue for the second Fact-and-Faith-Finding tour, and hoped the councillors would all make it. Their souls would be awakened by the dazzle of Light.

The minister's wife had years of experience to draw on: experience of extracting what she needed from a given situation. When Father O'Hanlon expounded on the need for confession and absolution, she turned the conversation to the difficulty of keeping on the straight and narrow, when straying offered so many more attractions. She urged admiration for those who struggled, who climbed back onto the path of righteousness after each fall.

"For example," she explained, "I know of a young man – a Christian, I believe, a hard worker persecuted in his homeland for fighting for a fairer society – who has gained entry to this country, not claiming benefits but depending on kind acquaintances for shelter…"

The assembled group felt that inner glow of kinship with these *kind acquaintances.*

"He's already spent six weeks living in a loft but, despite his hardship and longing for freedom, cannot find a proper place to live. He has a sweetheart, a local girl with a sad history, who works in the public services. He is desperate to find shelter for this vulnerable young woman he loves so much, the woman he wants to marry and have children with. But what chance do they have in these dreadful times…?" Her voice broke and she paused to compose herself. "And to think we call ourselves a Christian country. But ignore me… I just feel so sorry for him, after what he's been through." She rummaged in her handbag to avoid the committee's eyes.

Father O'Hanlon enjoyed officiating at weddings; he was well known for turning up at every reception whether invited or not, for who would eject the parish priest? His eyes lit up at the thought of another.

"I might," he told Mrs Batty, "I just might know of a little place that's vacant just now." He tapped the side of his nose conspiratorially. "Just leave it with me. I'll have a word with the landlord and get back to you." A slight belch released the ouzo fumes which were giving him heartburn.

"Oh thank you, Father. You have such a kind heart!" Marina shook his hand warmly.

"No problem. No problem at all." He turned away, consciously thinking of the troubled young couple and the babies he might get to baptise, and unconsciously wiping his hands on his soutane.

Within three days, Patrick Arthur McVeigh had given his assent, a bond plus one month's rent in advance had been paid, and Drago was established on the sixth floor of Bath House Court. Mrs Batty had been established as a woman who got things done. Samantha was left to explain her conduct to her sweetheart and her second departure to her parents.

26

It had been a winter of winds and torrential rain, so working days for Stevan Duric were infrequent. He was once more second fiddle to Dave Simmons and finding it hard to afford the rent. Stevan climbed the ladders while Dave limped around at ground level, collecting payment and tips. This bred resentment in the younger man, so whenever his boss had to attend a physiotherapy appointment, Stevan invited his cousin to work a shift. Doubling the number of windows cleaned meant double the money. Stevan and Drago shared the extra between them.

Drago had also taken on as many extra shifts at the HandCarWash as he could get, but it was still difficult to pay the all-inclusive rent on his new home. To make it easier on his tenants, Mr McVeigh included the cost of utility bills in their one monthly payment; they got a better deal that way, he assured them.

Mr McVeigh also helped his tenants by adding them to his occasional workforce. His business empire included not only Bath House Court and the HandCarWash; he had connections with PD RoamerHomes and McRoofers of Denton, and was currently negotiating terms for buying out DunCrushin Scrap Retrieval. The young Patrick had done plenty of hard graft in his time, but now he preferred to direct operations from his office, situated next to the entrance in Bath House Court. He always kept a lookout for new ways of deploying his labourers.

One night towards the end of March, the gales returned. Trees blew down in parks and gardens; streets were littered with debris, and children's trampolines sailed high like blue and yellow UFOs unseen in the dark. Slates and tiles slid down roofs and balanced on cracked gutters.

At daybreak, a team of McVeigh's men toured the villages in their wagons, chainsaws at the ready. By the time householders saw the light of day, the timber was stacked in neat piles and concealed under a loose tarpaulin at the rear of the Elegance compound, to season over the summer.

The early-morning tours also gave the men chance to spot any damaged roofs and report back to Mr McVeigh by phone. Around breakfast-time, other trucks would happen by the affected homes. Sharp-eyed drivers would assess the damage and knock on doors to express their concern. The patter was always the same, with some variation in the authenticity of the Irish brogue in which it was delivered.

Still in their dressing gowns, bleary-eyed, the householders were first bemused, then shocked. It took time to make sense of what the caller was saying. They would totter out onto the path and follow his pointing finger to stare at the roof.

"I'd hate for you to be killed if one of them tiles fell on you, lady (or sir). They're in a very dangerous state. It's lucky for you we were passing. Yours being so urgent, we can postpone the job we were on and get yours fixed by lunchtime."

One or two residents had the presence of mind to ask for a written quote. *Their* tiles were left to teeter on the gutter edge.

"Cash in hand, £50 per tile. You won't get a good job done cheaper than that, kind lady. Don't worry if you've no cash in the house – I'll drive you to the cashpoint myself. Can't say fairer than that now, can I?"

No physical coercion was applied and, greatly relieved to have survived a close shave with death, each fortunate victim felt constrained to take advantage of the kind offer.

﹡

Like thousands of others, Belinda had lain awake half the night listening to the sounds of the gale and the ominous noise of slippages from the roof, only falling into a light doze as the wind calmed. It seemed moments later that she was woken by the triple chime of the doorbell. She pulled on her warm plaid dressing gown and ran a comb through her hair. Confident that her rebellious daughter had at last come home, she ran lightly downstairs to the front door.

The grizzled man on the step wore a navy donkey jacket and pull-on hat, which he touched subserviently as the door opened. Immediately, he launched into the patter.

"Lovely lady, so sorry to have got you out of bed but we were just passing by and spotted that you might be in danger. It would have been wrong of us to drive on."

"Well thank you, but what danger?"

"You'll have heard the terrible winds in the night, lady. Terrible damage they cause, winds like that. Terrible damage."

"Where?"

"We were right to stop. I can tell you don't know."

"Know what?"

"The danger you're in, kind lady, danger from the damaged roof. Won't you step outside here and let me show you."

Belinda hesitated, aware of her bare feet. She leant forward to look up to where he pointed.

"Can you not see the tiles? If they fall they could kill you. Do you see, lady? It was our Christian duty to stop and let you know, to keep you from danger."

Yes, Belinda agreed to step outside and inspect the damage and fetched her slippers from the cupboard under the stairs. Three tiles had come loose and were hanging precariously over the gutter above the step.

"What a stroke of luck, kind lady, that we spotted it! One

breath of wind, even the door slamming, could have brought that down and killed you stone dead!"

"Well, thank you for taking the trouble. I'll have to ring the roofing chap."

The man nodded roadwards, to where his mate's silhouette was just visible at the wheel of a flatbed truck bearing the insignia *McRoofers of Denton*.

"Let me check, but I think we might have three or four of the exact same tiles on the back of the truck!" Would she agree to be their first customer of the day?

"Will you be wanting to ask your husband first, lady?" the foreman asked considerately.

"He's away at the moment." Belinda's reply was less considered. The man knew he'd got the job.

Having checked, the grizzled chap confirmed that yes, they did just happen to have the identical tiles on the back of the truck – another stroke of luck. It would all be done by the time the lady was back from the cash machine.

"No, we don't take cheques, dear lady, but we can run you down to the cash machine if that would help."

"No thanks. I'll just get dressed and drive myself down."

While the men rattled their ladders into position, the kind lady quickly dressed. She locked the doors and windows, dimly aware that she hadn't had time to think this through, but she couldn't cope with a leaking roof on top of everything else. Belinda made a mental note of the truck's registration number as she drove away, congratulating herself on her caution but failing to write it down.

By the time she returned, the job was done and the ladder back on the flatbed. The man held out his upturned palm as Belinda counted out ten £20 notes. *A lot of money for half an hour's work*, she mused but didn't say, noting, as he folded the notes, that the roofer did not have hairs on the back of his calloused hands.

She hesitated before closing the door. There was something else that had to be done.

"The village hall round the corner: I noticed on my way out that some ridge tiles are damaged. Could you take a look at those, please?"

The man was wary. Who would pay? He knew that payment by committee was a long job, likely to be made by cheque. McRoofers of Denton didn't handle cheques.

The man agreed to look at the hall roof and come back with a price. It was Pakamac who would make the decision on taking the job or not. Belinda closed the door, wondering how she could make the payment for the hall roof without arousing suspicion. She had all that cash in the wardrobe, but no legitimate explanation for it being there.

27

The gales occurred only a few days before the opening of Truetrust Academy's production of *The Mikado*. Of her family, only Yum-Yum's brother knew of her forthcoming stardom, for the girl had deliberately created a persona far removed from reality. If none of her family came to see her performance, it would prove to both staff and students that she was unloved and rejected, battling against all the odds to follow her passion and bask in the limelight.

It was like something off *The X Factor*... in fact she had discussed the possibility of forming a duo with Jermyn and applying for the next series of auditions, though she'd rather team up with Ben. Going in with Jermyn, she risked being subjugated to the whims of the other Street Fytas, and she'd always be an outsider.

Sloane Street and Melanie did not get on. The younger girl was used to exercising manipulative control over her father and brothers, but Melanie could threaten that power, especially since Dad Gerrard had started doing odd jobs for Mrs Lowe. Sloane begrudged that. Sloane missed her mother, and she missed the Happy Vanners competitions, the prinking and preening, the girly stuff her mum was so keen on. Even the Street Fytas' rehearsals were lacklustre since they became a one-parent family.

Truth be told, Belinda didn't think much of Gerrard Street, but there are times when a woman needs a man and a man needs a woman, and Gerrard's needs were stronger than most. Having three kids to care for he needed help, not least with the ironing and Sloane's impending puberty. With this in mind, he thought about running his mower over next door's grass once in a while. Over the fence, Belinda had acknowledged that this would be a godsend. She currently had no intention of taking in ironing – though with her job disappearing, who knows what she might have to do to make ends meet?

While Gerrard was working in her garden one day, the PCSOs paid a visit to Mrs Lowe's address. Their stated aim was to enquire about Melanie's wellbeing, but privately they were keen to discover anything to confirm their belief that the library assistant was a wrong'un. Yes, they had their sources and knew that Belinda Lowe was regarded locally as a pillar of the community, but there'd been many a public servant who hid behind a cloak of respectability to promote her perversions.

It was a normal domestic scene that greeted them at the house on Dapple Grove, a greenfinch singing on the breeze-stirred cherry tree while the man of the house mowed the lawn in the afternoon sunshine.

"We've just come to check up on how your daughter's doing after all the upset," Grant explained over the whirr of the electric hover mower.

Gerrard Street stopped mowing. "What upset?"

"Has no one told you? Is your wife around?"

"No, she's gone. I don't know anything about any upset. What's happened?"

"Your wife should have told you, sir. Where has she gone to? When will she be back?" This was Heather.

"She won't. She's sodded off and I'm not expecting her back. Good riddance."

"I see. May we see your daughter then?"

"She's staying late at school, rehearsing for some play or other. What upset?"

"The mix-up over her lunch box." Heather was cagey. The less they gave away, the more likely he was to spill the beans on his wife.

Gerrard had heard a little about the lunchtime riot from Jermyn but had been concentrating on the football at the time. It had gone in one ear and out the other.

"Kids run wild all the time. They get over it." Gerrard didn't like the police sniffing around ... not that he had anything to worry about, as far as he knew.

"And your wife – if you don't mind, we'd like a little chat about her." Heather was all sweetness. "There have been a few upsetting incidents recently and we wonder how she's bearing up."

"Don't ask me! She's always been keen on getting her own way. Headstrong, like. She's buggered off... took the caravan an'all. She's a crazy tart!"

"And your daughter?"

"Still at school, I told you. I'll be picking her up in half an hour. Nothing wrong with her."

He gripped the *Start* handle and recommenced the slow trudge up and down the lawn, making it clear that the conversation was at an end.

Grant and Heather had got what they came for: the mother was a crazy tart who'd buggered off weeks ago, taking the family caravan. They knew a few trailer parks in the area. Did Mrs Lowe have connections with the travelling community? That would be a new twist. A stroll round the unauthorised sites for a look-see was called for, when they got chance.

Passing Sallby Village Hall, they noted with interest two men loading weathered pantiles onto a flatbed truck, but it soon slipped their minds.

✳

While Gerrard Street was mowing her front lawn, Belinda had been baking a couple of quiches and a batch of cherry buns. Half, she would take to her parents: the rest would go to the Street chap in repayment for his work. She hated cutting the grass herself so it was a fair swap.

Gerrard mowed the remainder of the lawn feeling resentful. He missed Patricia in the way you miss a verruca when it's gone. Mind, she'd been good at looking after the young'uns – give the crazy tart her due. He'd never thought she'd just walk away from them.

Dirty washing was piling up around the house. He gathered it randomly together from time to time and stuck as much in the machine as would fit, but it never looked right when it had dried, somehow. He lacked that mystical understanding of laundry known only to women. Gerrard had no interest in honing his own domestic skills.

The lawn completed, he reached in his pocket for a pair of rusty secateurs and began deadheading last year's roses, which straggled, brown and papery, over the fence. The remnants of fallen blooms formed a squelchy mush beneath his feet. He was pensive, weighing up the possibility of engaging Belinda Lowe as a stand-in for his wife. With the library due to close, she'd soon be out of work. Loads of time on her hands. That girl of hers was staying with her grandparents, by all accounts. The lad had left home and the husband too, as good as.

Gerrard straightened his back and eyed his reflection in the front window. Still a full head of hair, not much of a paunch if viewed from the right angle… yeah, he could still cut it with the ladies, he reckoned. The Lowe woman would be a pushover.

Not that he wanted commitment. Nothing like that. Just some domestic help, a few home comforts… and maybe the odd bit on the side. She'd be gagging for it, at her age.

He'd talked himself into it. Clipping the secateurs shut, he walked round to the back door, rattled the handle and walked inside, wearing his most disarming grin.

The smell of fresh baking brought a tear to his eye, in memory of his long-dead grandmother. Neither his own mum nor Patricia had gone in for home cooking, preferring to "leave it to the professionals," as they said. Culinary conversation in the Street household rarely strayed further than comparisons of M&S and Sainsbury's ready meals.

Belinda was at the sink, washing the utensils. She saw the tear in his eye. Poor chap must be missing his wife. She gestured to a chair at the kitchen table, handed him a steaming mug and pulled out a stool opposite.

Her opening was tentative. "Must be hard, with three children to care for." She reached for the oven glove hanging from a hook on the door.

Gerrard said nothing, but sipped his coffee, savouring the scent of the quiches cooling on a mesh tray on the worktop. The face of his grandma was as clear as day in his mind's eye. Not that she'd ever made quiches... but she'd been a dab hand at bacon and egg flans.

More tears came to his eyes as memories of his childhood flooded in. Life had seemed – no, was – so simple then.

Belinda reached over and patted his hands, which were grubby but slender-fingered.

"It *will* get better," she assured him.

He lifted his head and directed the moist beam of his eyes into hers. He grasped her hands, oven cloth as well.

"You're a wonderful woman," he ventured. "So capable."

Belinda glowed with satisfaction. She had always prided herself on her capabilities. The cherry buns, having reached a state of perfection, glowed golden under the oven light. Using the glove, she lifted out the tray.

"So capable and so fragrant," smiled the quite-good-looking neighbour, who perhaps was a man of discernment after all, she admitted. Gerrard inhaled deeply, slipping back in time.

The appreciation was making Bel feel coquettish. She ventured a flirtatious glance. "There's plenty more I'm good at," she simpered, making wide eyes in his direction. *What are you doing?* Belinda's voice was faint in her ear.

He was wondering if she'd be good at cosy chats about periods with their Sloane – that's what was really bugging him – that, and the ironing. But needs must when the devil drives.

"So … what else are you good at?" He tried out a saucy wink.

Belinda began to feel flustered but Bel overruled her prudery. "It depends what you're looking for."

He laughed. "Well, right now I'm looking for a nice warm cherry... bun." He pointed at the largest one, still burning hot in its tray. "I like hot stuff."

They snorted, laughing at themselves. Bel began to think Gerrard was quite something.

Suddenly his face resumed its serious expression. "No more hot stuff for me though, now that Patricia's gone. I've got to put all my attention into keeping things stable for the kids."

"How've they taken it?"

"They don't say much, but the heart's gone out of them. It's Sloane I feel most sorry for, what with puberty coming and all that. A girl needs a woman's touch."

He chanced a wary glance at Belinda's expression. It was hard as nails. This might be more difficult than he'd thought. Silence ensued.

Soon, the buns were cool enough to touch. She took one between thumb and forefinger and held it six inches from his mouth, tempting him, laughing quietly.

He leant forward to within an inch of the cake, lips parted. His eyes flicked up to hers and back to the bun.

"What an offer." His voice was throaty now. His teeth sank into the warmth, tongue seeking out the smooth sweetness of the glacé fruit.

Mouth full, he looked her in the eye. "You're just like my grandma. She was a teaser, too."

Belinda failed to hear the second sentence. His grandma, for Heaven's sake!

She caught sight of the distorted reflection in the glass of a cabinet door. Her hair was mussed from the heat of the oven, but otherwise she didn't look too bad for her age, surely? The guy must be forty if he was a day, so his grandmother would have been eighty or ninety by now.

Gerrard saw her changed expression and knew he'd blown it, for the time being. The spell was broken, and Belinda kicked Bel out of her head. Matter-of-factly, carelessly, the cook turned to remove the rest of the baking.

"Mmm! Smells delicious."

"It's only a quiche. Hardly *cordon bleu*."

She made sure no eye contact was possible, and Gerrard was stumped. Not known for staying power, he got up to leave.

"Here, take the buns and a quiche – but don't put the lid on until everything's cool."

She held the door open, watched him shuffle out and struggle to unlatch the gate with one hand. She did not offer to help. He turned and caught her eye.

"I meant to say… your girl did well the other night. They all did."

"Well at what?"

"The show! You know… *The Mikado*. Star quality, that one. I was looking out for you there but must have missed you." He began to walk away then paused. "It was good to see your lad looking so well." Did she know he'd been back? From the look on her face, he didn't think so.

Her expression didn't falter. "Thanks." She nodded brusquely and slammed the door shut.

※

Why did she not know? Her daughter had been in a show! And Aidan had been there to watch. When he was supposed to be at university! Were they ashamed of her, their own mother? How could she not have known? Had her own children disowned her?

She felt a constriction in her chest; was unable to inhale, try as she might; back through the door to the garden, gasping for air; fell to her knees by the pond, shoulder hurting where it knocked against the wooden snail, which toppled and cracked. She lay prone. From the ground, the atmosphere seemed easier to breathe: greener, earthier, sweeter. Eyes closed, she concentrated on the air slowly re-entering her lungs. Her skin was cold as ice, corpselike. This latest realisation could not be borne. She breathed, but longed for oblivion. It would not come.

※

Time passed, who knows how long? There was no dealing with anything anymore. So she wouldn't bother. She would just lie there, though it was chilly on the stones. If only she had a blanket. She tried to sleep, there, where she lay. Let them find her dead. It was time for the easy way out. She'd given life her best shot and failed. Might as well give up.

She could hear the phone ringing inside the house but let it continue until the caller gave up. Every few minutes it rang again. Why would no-one leave her in peace? But there was no peace in these ice halls of hell. It rang, time and time again, relentless, intrusive, obsessive in its insistence, until at last she succumbed to its urgency. Stiffly, she pulled herself to her knees. The snail had lost its head and she mourned the loss for what it signified. Grasping anything she could for support, she stood and slowly edged her way back inside. The ringing had stopped, but would soon start again.

It took ten minutes. By now warming a little and sipping a hot drink, Belinda picked up the receiver cautiously.

"Belinda, thank goodness I've got hold of you. I've been trying for ages. It's Anita. Whatever's going on at the village hall?"

The reply was non-committal.

"A customer's just come in and said there are no tiles on the roof. I thought I'd better ring and ask what it's all about. I know I've not been able to get to meetings recently so I'm a bit out of touch. Have we got a grant? When's it all going to be finished? We need some work doing on the shop roof so if the firm's any good will you ask them to call round here? I know you'll have done plenty of research and found someone reliable... I just wanted to say well done for sorting it all out." The voice tailed off, aware that it was getting no response.

No tiles on the village hall roof?

Did she care?

She should do.

It was her duty.

But did she?

"Sorry, Anita. The line's really bad. I can tell it's you but not what you're saying. I'll call you back."

She ended the call and laid the receiver on the windowsill. Stopping first in the kitchen, she grabbed four of the cherry buns intended for her parents before climbing the stairs slowly and seeking comfort from the duvet. Beneath its tented mound, she stuffed the cakes into her mouth one by one, relishing their sweetness in the search for oblivion.

*

By the time the weathered red pantiles were missed, most of them had found their way atop the splendid barn conversion nearing completion in a field half a mile from the road between Denton and Denshill. Bearing as they did the lichen and smoke stains of ninety years, the tiles blended perfectly with those on the crumbling grey limestone farm buildings, constructed two centuries ago from rocks picked by hand from the land. Patrick Kevin McVeigh had a good eye – and the knack of spotting an opportunity. When his two roofers had called for instructions on the job at Sallby Village Hall, he needed no pause for thought. Those tiles were just what he'd been looking for to complete his latest acquisition in the traditional manner.

The converted barn stood alone in a big field, with room for a sizeable site behind the house. He'd put up some nice ornate gates – he was fond of big gates and big dogs, was Pakamac – moved a trailer or two on and started the build. When that was complete, he'd invite selected members of his family and the wider travelling community to take up residence. Sometimes, living in a house got too much for the missus so he'd keep a couple of trailers for her, too. He planned to face the council with a *fait accompli*. What with the closeness of family bonds, the need for the children's schooling, the desire to integrate into mainstream society and the special emotional needs of his wife – well, Patrick's expensive lawyers would make mincemeat of the poor sods pleading the council's case if retrospective planning permission was refused.

As for the roof, it would be finished in a day or two, with a team of men working on it as long as daylight lasted. The weathering being genuine, no passer-by could tell the tiles were newly fixed, so when Grant and Heather heard reports of a roof-full of pantiles going AWOL, their eyes never lighted on Mr McVeigh's retirement home. They dimly remembered seeing the tiles being loaded outside the hall, but thought better of mentioning how they'd witnessed a daylight robbery and walked on by.

Patrick McVeigh was delighted with the way things had fallen into place.

28

As March drew to a close, the DOCILE scheme for interfaith enlightenment inched its way forward with a formal invitation from Rejoice with Jesus!

Only Darren was excited at the prospect, although it was inconceivable to the pastor that others on the committee might be less enthusiastic. Whilst it had been tricky to arrange a full-blown evangelical service midweek, Darren's fervour was strong enough to persuade an impressive congregation of sixty born-again souls to Rejoice with Jesus! at the old Odeon on a damp Wednesday afternoon.

There was singing, there was clapping, there were random Praise the Lords! and Hallelujahs! aplenty from the audience which swayed in front of the big screen, from where a toupéed, glinting-toothed American filled them with fear of the Lord's wrath and the imperative joys of being saved by Jesus, reinforced by drum rolls and guitar riffs from two musical reborns on stage either side of the screen. Impromptu prayers and exhortations from the front four rows (which seated the congregation with room to spare) echoed around the vast auditorium.

Darren's long, straight legs stalked the aisles where ice cream and popcorn had once been sold, his eyes bright with a messianic gleam. He urged his guests to cast off their inhibitions and let his Lord into their hearts. This really mattered to Darren: at stake was not only the salvation of the DOCILE souls, but also the salvation of the Denswick branch of the Rejoice with Jesus! Evangelical Church.

Just ten days after DOCILE's visit to Our Lady of Sorrows, the owners of the former cinema-cum-bingo hall had given Rejoice with Jesus! notice to quit. The premises were to be demolished, the land sold for development. In an ironic twist of fate, in so energetically promoting his church's value to the town, the pastor had prompted its downfall.

Father O'Hanlon was close to Patrick McVeigh, and might even, over a glass or two in the presbytery following the tour of *his* church, have shared misgivings about the impact Rejoice with Jesus! might have on the young Roman Catholics of the Denswick diocese, and thus on his own diminishing congregation.

This confidence coincided with two of the gypsy king's daughters, within earshot of their father, discussing the attractions of Rejoicing with both Jesus and the entrancing Pastor Darren, whose preaching and fervent eyes they had accidentally sampled one evening outside the fish and chip shop.

Patrick loved his daughters dearly and guarded them fiercely. On the spot, he made up his mind that neither they nor any of their many siblings would Rejoice with Jesus! in his lifetime or for many years beyond it.

His solicitor made the necessary enquiries about ownership of the Odeon and arrangements for its immediate purchase at an attractive price for the vendor, a mere pittance for Pakamac. His architect exhumed the drawings for Bath House Court and set his surveyor to work on adapting them to suit the new site. Within days, a full application had been submitted to Denswick Council's Department of Planning, and several quiet words had been spoken between Mr McVeigh and the political members of DOCILE, to ensure that no objections would be raised during the consultation stages. He might also have a word with a debtor who worked on the council's IT systems, to see if a glitch to the online public access Planning Portal could be induced.

At the service, of the half dozen DOCILE members squirming on the fifth row, only one was aware of the threats to the evangelicals' place of worship. The other five were as shocked as the congregation when the big screen went dark, a spotlight beamed onto the stage and, clothed in black, to an ominous beating of drums, Pastor Darren strode on.

Clutching a wireless microphone the size of a tennis ball, he began.

"We who are born again, Rejoice in The Lord!"

"Hallelujah! We rejoice in Him!" his flock responded in unison.

"Brothers and sisters in Jesus. While we Rejoice in the Son of God and His Goodness, it is with a heavy heart that I must share sombre tidings with you all."

Darren broke off, knelt and said a quick prayer before rising to gaze out over the neatly-seated throng. A ripple of concern and fear ran along the four front rows.

"The Lord has presented us with a great challenge. Are we up for it?" he yelled, lifting his open hands skywards.

"Yes!"

"The Lord is testing us. He is testing the truth of our rebirth. He is testing the power of our expanding army of re-born souls! Are we strong enough?"

"Yes!"

There was some mumbling between the responses from those wishing the pastor would get to the point.

"Brothers and sisters in Jesus, I have to tell you that our church is to be cast out of our home as the Children of Israel were cast out of their land."

A gasp ran along the front four rows. Most of those on the fifth were puzzled.

Darren explained the property owner's decision to evict Rejoice with Jesus! at short notice. His congregation was stunned. The sounds of weeping could be heard here and there from the church's less stoical members.

"Brothers and sisters in Jesus, let not your hearts be heavy. We are an evangelical church. The Lord is challenging us to go forth and evangelise. By closing these doors to us, He is telling every one of us to go forth from this place and spread His Word.

"Rejoice in Jesus! brothers and sisters, for He has commanded us. Go Forth! Spread The Word. Shout it on the shop fronts and on the football fields; in the public houses and the old folks' homes. Proclaim His love in the libraries and in the council chambers; in village halls and betting shops, dog tracks and bowling alleys; in schools and hospitals, playgroups and youth clubs. Broadcast your salvation in triumphant tones on city streets and country lanes!"

What began as a ripple of response swelled to a roar. All sixty evangelists rose to their feet, randomly shouting, "Praise the Lord! We accept the challenge!" Darren conducted the throng and boomed into the microphone.

"We will shout thy name from the rooftops, Lord, and bring our earthly brothers and sisters to join us as brothers and sisters in Christ!"

Another roar of assent followed. The congregation was still on its feet.

On the fifth row, the DOCILE members were stunned. Even Pakamac was feeling nervous about the fervour just unleashed. In his seat next to the aisle a very rare event was taking place: Patrick Kevin McVeigh was doubting the wisdom of his own actions.

In the mind of the Methodist minister's wife, a new train of thought had been sparked. As the impassioned evangelists filed out of the building with tearful backward glances, Marina Batty lingered. She had a suggestion for Pastor Darren.

29

It was early evening when Belinda crawled out from under the duvet, driven by hunger. She boiled herself an egg and ate it with a slice of stale bread, thickly buttered, while debating the wisdom of contacting her parents. When the phone rang, she answered without thought, heart momentarily uplifted in the hope it might be Aidan calling. At least *he* was still her boy; at least *he* still loved her, she was sure.

It wasn't her son, but her father, desperate to know how to handle Melanie's latest tantrum and his wife's decline.

"I'm not feeling too well, Dad, I've been in bed all afternoon. What's all the fuss about?"

"The girl's carrying on about no one loving her. Something about being humiliated. I don't understand what she's talking about half the time. Mind you, I blame the school, keeping her there till nearly midnight doing extra classes every couple of nights. It can't be good for her – for any of them. A growing girl needs her sleep."

Belinda concurred.

"I didn't know about any extra classes. I'm sure they wouldn't keep them there till midnight."

"That's because she's living here and you're not. You never talk to her. We're piggy in the middle and we're sick of it. It's not fair, Belinda. I thought better of you than this!" Dad's outbursts were rare but frank, more so since the stroke, and all the more cutting for their rarity.

Not fair of *her*! Was it fair of *them* to lure her treasured child away with lax discipline? The option of adding Mum and Dad to her little list fluttered like a butterfly round the rim of her thoughts before being flattened with an imaginary rolled-up newspaper.

"I've got to go. I'm not well." She hung up, leaving her father upset and helpless in the face of all this feminine malfunction.

The morning's post still lay on the mat inside the front door. Maybe there would be something pleasant – a surprise Thank You card from a hirer or an invitation to a party, perhaps – though she'd never received either before. She shuffled through the pile: junk, junk, water board, seed catalogue, notification of changes to council services. Bottommost in the pile was a cream, windowed envelope of some quality. It was addressed to the Chairperson, Sallby Village Hall, c/o 18 Dapple Grove, etc., but it was not this that made Belinda start. It was the black crown in the top left-hand corner, arched over a portcullis edged by chains, and the words House of Commons in bold black type.

Her first, instinctive reaction was guilt. The government was on to her! The Charity Commission had gone straight to the top! She sank onto the bottom stair, trembling. Her saner self, audible somewhere at the back of her head, told her the Charity Commission had nothing to do with the House of Commons; it had its own methods of dealing with transgressors.

The louder voice at the front of her head shouted, "Run!" She resisted, and sat a little longer.

An envelope as important as this demanded a paper knife. She prolonged the dread by searching the desk drawer. Dread was better than accusation. Her fingers lighted on a souvenir from New Zealand, brought back from an international conference once by her sister. It was fine and sharp and made of pale wood. She studied it, took a deep breath, and inserted the point under the flap.

There were two letters. The first was from her local Member of Parliament, Bob Topliss. Belinda had never met him, but knew his face from the local papers. He was one of the old brigade, having once worked at the local pit, and was probably on his way out at the next election.

The first letter referred to the second, which the Hon. Topliss had been asked to forward to the person in charge of Sallby Village Hall.

The second, longer and more pompous at first glance, was from the office of Miles Baxter-Hatton MP, Junior Minister for Communities and Social Cohesion.

Belinda gasped. Her hand shook. The prose was complex, something to do with consultation, with particular reference to maximising the services provided by volunteer-run community facilities such as village and community halls.

"On a more personal note," the letter concluded, "I recall your enthusiastic support for my ideas when our paths crossed last summer, and invite you to join the Northern Focus Group to develop the concept of Broadening Experiences in Local and Community Halls." It was signed with a flourish.

She was asked to confirm her acceptance in writing by 30th April, after which details of the first BELCH meeting would be circulated. Travel costs would be reimbursed.

The bushes at Hepworth House, kneeling on the folded towel, chisel in hand, marking out the pilgarlic crest. Again, the surge of elation, the smell of damp earth, the scrape of metal on metal as she worked. Then the shame. This might be Baxter-Hatton's revenge. He had unearthed her culpability and the letter was a

lure, precursor to an exposé, as she had exposed him!
She could write 'Not known at this Address' on the
envelope. 'Return to sender.' But Baxter-Hatton would
have his ways of tracking her down.

She tucked the letter behind the bread bin with all the others. She'd make time to think about it once Aidan was home.

Belinda needed to get out of the house, away from the phone and the letter. Collecting the hall keys from the drawer and the *Betting Chronicle* from the kitchen table, she set off on foot to clear her mind.

The sight of the tile-free roof took her unawares. She'd tried to block Anita Su's call from conscious thought, convinced it was a wind-up or exaggeration, but even in the dusk of early evening the building looked ravaged. She could make out the holes in the felting under which sparrows nestled and chirped. If only Guy Dance were here right now. He'd surely give her some praise for taking action. A collage of Drago's dead pet, the Serb's broad, hairy back and Anthony Montano's face slotted into place in the revolving picture show of her mind's eye.

Ravaged: the word seemed apt. Her logical brain told her it could be fixed. Her emotions told her it was beyond repair, a metaphor for her life. Stolen, maybe; more likely, thrown away through carelessness and her own love of self.

She hadn't got the energy to fix either of them. She reached the hall breathless, made a hot drink and sat down with the paper and a pencil. She knew she'd chosen Drago's chair, the one he'd used at their last meeting. She sniffed the upholstery, trying for one final breath of his body's aroma. Satisfied, she opened the paper and studied its contents. Tomorrow she would place a few bigger bets and splash out on the scratch cards. Might as well be hung for a sheep as a lamb.

It was nearing midnight when she returned home to find Doug on the doorstep. A frightened call from his father-in-law had brought him at speed from Sunderland, without his house keys. The one hidden for emergencies was missing.

Belinda, who had chosen her runners and was determined to place her bets first thing next morning, was not particularly pleased to see him. She unlocked the front door with barely an acknowledgement. She was already resenting his presence, his acting as if he owned the place.

He asked where she'd been.

"I could ask you the same thing," she retorted.

"You know where I've been, and why I've been there." He tipped out his pockets, allowing a few coins and a small bundle of £20 notes to fall onto the sofa.

"Huh! Money. That's all you care about."

"How can you say that?"

"Because you've gone. You've left us. You've left me to cope and I can't."

"That's rubbish and you know it. I'll ask you again. Where have you been?"

No reply.

At this moment a pair of headlamps pulling into next door's drive flashed their beam through the uncurtained window. Doug drew a sharp breath.

"With him? That jerk from next door?"

At first, no reply, then, "He's not a jerk."

Doug took the answer as an admission of guilt. He left the house, calling over his shoulder, "I'm going to collect my daughter!"

"She's my daughter too!" yelled his wife.

"No one would guess!" The van door slammed shut; the engine revved; he reversed at speed onto the road and disappeared from view.

*

She was asleep by the time he returned, bringing their daughter and her belongings with him.

In her dreams she climbed an insurmountable hill, dragging behind her unidentifiable impediments which kicked and screamed at every step. As she neared the summit, she saw that the hill had a roof, supported on tall pillars, pillars built of fools and horses. She was glad to wake. Glad to see that although there was an indent in Doug's pillow, the man himself was absent from the room.

She rolled over and smelt the pillow. Subtly, its familiarity gave her comfort; barely discernible but real, like the faint green tinge of a newly-sown lawn. Her face was still buried in his scent when the door creaked a little further open. Balancing the tray on one hand, he pulled back a curtain to let the sun in.

"Come on. Sit up."

She did as she was told, trying to settle her hair into something acceptable.

"Thank you." She munched the toast and jam in silence, waiting for him to speak. She waited a while longer. She sipped the tea and winced at its heat.

He just stood there, watching. At last, he twitched his head in the direction of the girl's room.

"She's still asleep."

"Mm."

"There's been a call for you. Someone wanting to book the village hall. I said you'll ring back."

"Righto."

She began the second slice of toast and held out her empty mug. He took it from her. "Want another?"

"Mm."

She heard him go downstairs, his stockinged feet soft on the carpeted treads; heard the click of the kettle's switch and the sound of water returning to the boil. This time he was carrying two mugs. He perched his behind on her dressing-table stool to sip in silence.

"About the village hall," she ventured.

"What?"

"Someone's stolen the roof." Her composure ended with the sentence, eyes filling with tears, voice a childish whine, the whine of a brat whose favourite toy has been broken.

"Don't talk daft. How can a roof be stolen?"

"You'll see."

If he didn't believe her, she wasn't going to argue. It wasn't worth the effort. She slid down the bed again and turned on her side, dismissing him as he had dismissed her sorrows.

He was out by the time she got up. He hadn't left a note and she wasn't going to ring his mobile. She'd had enough of pandering to people who didn't care about her.

＊

Doug paced the long grass around the perimeter of the building, looking for signs of fallen pantiles. Every now and then he paused, stroked his chin and shook his head. He didn't know what else to do. For once, his wife was *not* making a fuss about nothing.

He knew how hard she worked for the village hall... though he didn't know why. He knew how important it was to Belinda to ensure its survival... though he doubted anyone else felt the same. He did not know about the missing bank books and accounts, the bags of money stashed in her wardrobe, or the pile of neatly addressed envelopes stacking up beneath the letter box at Sphynx Lodge.

He stooped now and then to pick up a sweet wrapper or plastic bottle and headed for the bin by the back door, just as a car pulled onto the field. A slightly-built man wearing a Denswick Council name tag climbed out and walked towards him.

"Pleased to see action's being taken to address the problem of bird ingress," said the man, stretching out his hand in greeting. "Guy Dance. Public Health Inspector, Denswick Council."

He first glanced over one shoulder, then the other.

"What have you done with the tiles? They were all in excellent condition – I made a note when I was last here. Put them in storage, have you? Good idea. Leave 'em lying about and some thieving bastard's bound to make off with 'em." His tone was genial with a touch of smugness.

Doug's silence passed for assent. The two shook hands.

"You can see how the little blighters have got in, can't you? It only takes a small hole or two and you'll have a flock of 'em roosting up there. They're an *at risk* species, y'know, though it's difficult to believe, the mess they make." Guy paused for breath. "Mrs Lowe about?"

"I'm her husband. She's not well."

"Sorry to hear that. Any idea how long the job's going to take?"

"What job?"

"The re-felting and replacing the tiles."

"No. She didn't say. I've been working away. Only come home 'cos she's not well."

"No problem. Get her to give me a call when it's done and I'll pop out and give the hall its hygiene certificate. Nice to meet you. Hope she's well soon."

Guy's polite and helpful tone belied his inner resentment. He'd felt sure the woman would have ignored his instructions and given rise to a closure order. Damn it. Still, the roof was currently in an incomplete state and there was plenty of scope for things to go wrong. Guy would keep his fingers crossed. He really needed to close something down if he wanted to keep his job.

30

Aidan's mother could tell he couldn't wait to come home. His last few calls had been positively enthusiastic. He'd even asked if things were OK at the village hall.

"Fine," his mother lied.

Before Doug left again for Sunderland, she told him, "See! He does miss us. He does, I know it. A mother can *feel* it."

He climbed into his van and let the window slide down.

"Everything will be OK once he's home," she insisted. "I'll ask him if Melanie's said anything about this carry-on with Jermyn."

Doug knew better than to tell her she was wrong.

"Aidan's very mature for his age," she told her mother later. "He'll tell me anything that's cause for concern."

Belinda's father kept his mouth shut. His daughter was deluded when it came to that lad. He'd long suspected it, but now he knew it for a fact, having spotted his grandson from a bus in Denswick when the lad's parents thought he was in Wales. George had been on the way to see his chiropractor when he spotted Aidan, with a couple of other young men, turn in between a pair of tall stone gateposts as the bus passed by. There was no doubt – the lad was conning his mum and dad.

Lying on the practitioner's couch, he'd explained that his daughter was having a tough time, sure enough, but everyone has tough times every now and then.

"Things aren't too rosy for me and Gwen either. This is no time for our daughter to crack up – she needs to pull herself together. I'll keep my mouth shut about the boy for now, but you can be sure I'll give him what-for when I get him in private. He'll be home for Easter soon."

The chiropractor agreed with his patient: a spot of National Service would make a man of the boy, if only the government would see sense and bring it back.

On Dapple Grove, the atmosphere between mother and daughter was tense; the full truth about Melanie's involvement in *The Mikado* had not yet been addressed. The girl sent frequent texts to her brother.

NVR SPK 2 MUM BOUT MKDO.

MUM TRIDE2POYSNMI

To be honest, Aidan had never given a thought to whether his sister had told their parents about the show. He'd just assumed Mum would be there on the night.

"I thought even Dad would have made the effort," he'd said after the performance. "Gran and Granddad would have enjoyed it too. Why didn't they come?"

"Because they're old and haven't a clue what's going on half the time. They all care about themselves more than me."

Aidan had ignored this as one of Melanie's pathetic efforts at attention seeking and walked away, to where Solly was waiting in his mum's car to drive him back to uni en route to his own. They all needed to put in a full week before the end of term.

*

Melanie was determined not to repent the error of her ways. What was OK for Aidan was OK for her, right? She had fallen hook, line and sinker for the brief postings she'd seen on his Facebook page. Aidan's typing had never been great.

TRICKY STUFF WITH HOLLY ROWAN AND ASH ALL IN THE BEG NOW

His sister was jealous. She realised her brother had mistyped the penultimate word. He'd had three of them in bed at the same time!

"Isn't Rowan's a boy's name?" she gasped inwardly. Her brother was becoming more exotic by the day. Ash could be male or female, but she disliked Holly already – stuck-up cow!

The Facebook page carried photos of girls' bottoms, panties showing beneath hitched-up skirts. These pictures were all taken from behind, Aidan having been a mere observer at the feast of flesh, but Melanie didn't notice that. It looked like her brother was getting some grown-up action and his sister wanted a share.

*

"Help me clean Aidan's room?" Belinda asked her daughter two days before the student was due home. She hoped that, like before, they would share confidences while they worked. The girl edged into her brother's room, a limp duster held between forefinger and thumb.

"Cleaning's gross. I'm gonna have a maid when I grow up," she muttered.

"That'll be nice, love." Her mother avoided confrontation as she washed the window with a chamois leather, checked that the clean sheets had not developed wrinkles and that no flies had laid their eggs on the window frame since yesterday.

"What shall we have for dinner when Aidan comes?"

"Dunno."

"What would you like?" Belinda was trying too hard. "You choose and we'll cook it together. It'll be fun."

She moved to the mirror hanging on the wall.

"Not bothered."

Belinda balked as a photo of a massive-bosomed brunette with no knickers slipped down the wall from its hiding place behind the mirror, disturbed by over-enthusiastic polishing. With a gasp but without comment, she screwed up the paper and shoved it in a drawer to dispose of later. One of Aidan's mates must have put it there as a joke.

Trying to get close to the girl was a waste of time, but it would all be fine when Aidan came home. Shoulders back, she forced a smile.

"All done," she announced.

The girl slunk out, still holding the unused duster between finger and thumb.

*

Doug was in Sunderland for a few more days, so they would have the boy to themselves for a while. Melanie had scores of complaints about mum to divulge. She counted them out on her fingers to Chelsey on the way to school on the last day of term.

"There's giving me a dead sparrow sandwich, for a start."

Chelsey had heard it all before.

"Mmm." Chelsey was looking over her shoulder for Ben Jepson, who was chatting up some girl from Year 8 ten yards behind them.

"Mum's a weirdo. Aidan knows that already. He'll see she's getting worse."

"Mmm." Ben Jepson was fingering the girl's long auburn plaits.

"I'm thinking of moving to Wales," announced the abandoned sister. "To Aidan's flat. He won't mind sharing his room. It'll be great. He'll be thrilled when I tell him."

"Are you sure?"

"Yeah, we get on really well and his flatmates are really really cool. Jude, one of them's called. He's got this beard – it's

307

a hoot. I won't mind doing the cooking. I can make omelettes and everything. I'll do the shopping after school."

"They won't just let you in any school. They'll need to see your parents." Chelsey tried to be realistic.

"I'll say Aidan's my guardian – our parents have been killed in a plane crash or something."

"Oh." Chelsey gave up.

"I'm learning Welsh too. Listen."

Chelsey listened.

"*Maes parcio.* That's car park."

"Mmm."

"*Araf.* You see that on the roads. It means slow or something."

"Right."

"And... listen to this... *Ysbyty.*" (She pronounced it WHYZBYTEE.)

"What's that mean?"

"Hospital. If anyone asks directions to the hospital car park, I'll be able to help them." Melanie glowed with pride in her linguistic prowess, but Chelsey wasn't listening. Ben Jepson and the girl with plaits were snogging in the bushes beside the school gates. The shards of Chelsey's shattered heart were ground even smaller.

*

That evening, Melanie turned a deaf ear as Mum chatted to Dad on the phone.

"I thought we could take a picnic to the sculpture park. It will be lovely to show you all where I carved my snail." No one had noticed the decapitation.

"Don't start making plans. He'll want to do his own thing." Doug was down-to-earth.

"He'll love it – all those trees! He'll be able to identify them for us."

"Hmm. He'll have some studying to do and he'll want to see his mates."

She protested. "He'll want to see us too. Spend time with those who love him." The desperate upward inflection turned her sentence into a plea. It was unthinkable that things had changed forever.

*

When the time came, the lad wouldn't hear of his mother picking him up from either the rail or bus station.

"I'm a grown man, Mum. I don't need you fetching and carrying me about. I think I can find my way home by myself." His tone was decisive.

She wanted to explain that she needed to be needed, but the words wouldn't come. Instead, she gave in meekly.

"Oh, alright then. What time will you be here?"

"Not sure – some time Friday or Saturday, probably. Don't make any meals for me – I'll see to myself."

The tears welled up, too many for her to blink away.

"OK. Bye." The quivering voice revealed her disappointment.

"Mum's being manipulative again," he told his housemates. "I've a good mind not to go home at all, but there's someone else I need to see so I'll have to."

*

By bedtime on Friday, Belinda and her daughter had emptied the box of chocolates they'd bought to share with Aidan and replaced his favourite DVD in its box. It had been waiting on the player, ready.

The girl took herself upstairs at ten. Downstairs, Belinda dialled her son's mobile number. Maybe he'd had an accident or something. The call went straight to voicemail. She sent a text imploring him to get in touch, before climbing the stairs herself.

*

At the time the message was received, Aidan's phone was in his jeans pocket. The jeans were roughly folded beneath his T-shirt, underwear and trainers in the Ladies' at Sallby Village Hall, only 500 metres from his mother's loving arms.

This was to be the last official gig for the life models, and the artists were demanding a longer session than planned. That didn't bother the lads too much. The Dewson sisters had already booked them to model in their own home studios at a very attractive rate, travel costs included. As for Hattie and Penelope, their bodies had been finding the endless tours abroad exhausting and they needed to rethink their strategies for viewing the male form.

The differing physiques of the four young men offered endless opportunities for original art. The sisters wanted to break out from copies and interpretations of great works and unleash their own, boundlessly increasing creativity.

"You know, Penelope dear," Hattie said to her sister as they packed their equipment at the end of the evening, "if we find the boys satisfactory, we ought to think of hiring them longer term."

"What's in your mind, Hattie?"

"We have plenty of space at Da Vinci House. Even with our studios and galleries, there are some rooms we rarely use and two big attics full of junk."

"I don't follow you, dear."

"Why don't we convert those attics into twin bedrooms for the boys? Then we could put them up overnight – or even longer if we're working on a major piece."

Penelope found her sister's idea quite titillating, but tried not to get too excited.

"We'll have to look at the financial side of things, of course," Hattie cautioned.

"I'm sure that if we cut down on overseas trips we'll be able to manage." Caution was not second nature to Penelope.

The sisters would mull over the practicalities on the way home.

*

Belinda checked her phone repeatedly during the night and the following morning. It was difficult to resist the urge to ring round the hospitals. He didn't come the next day. His sister barely left her room. His mother wept. His father promised to give the lad a piece of his mind when he *did* turn up.

31

Easter Sunday in Sallby that year commemorated not only the resurrection of Christ, but also of the Rejoice with Jesus! Evangelical Church, whose members would be, for the first time, holding a service at Sallby Village Hall. The incredibly helpful wife of the Methodist minister had shown Pastor Darren round the building just a few days earlier, and although both were perplexed to see a tileless roof, each had taken it as a sign that the evangelists had been sent by the Lord to help restore the building to its former glory. And Glory there would be, Darren was certain.

To be sure, the space did not offer the capacity for expansion in numbers that Darren hoped for, and setting out the creaky chairs took quite a while, but the building was homely and, more importantly, cheap.

The minister's wife had explained that, although she was not herself in charge of the hall, she was very good friends with the person who was. Mrs Batty would make sure all relevant permissions and insurances were in place. All Darren had to do was arrange car shares so the members of his flock could get out to Sallby.

Marnie was delighted. At last she'd be able to contact Belinda with the new booking, and casually drop news of her own marriage into the conversation. She nursed a secret glee. Since the wedding, her future was secure and she had felt no need for the money made by the various village hall enterprises. There would be no more special events. Michael trusted her always to do the right thing, and although Marina herself thought the enterprises were for the public good, that might not be enough for her husband, who had already suffered enough at the hands of narrow-minded jobsworths.

Marina's conscience was clear, for every penny of her share of the profits had been stuffed through Belinda Lowe's letter-box to be used on the village hall. She was gleeful at the prospect of her friend's response and at the sight of the bare roof. The money was obviously being put to good use. She felt sure that Michael would be proud of her Christian act and its benefit to the community.

In the call, she would explain the Rejoice with Jesus! Church's predicament, convinced that Belinda would be delighted by the regular income for the hall – all above board and thoroughly respectable. Marina tried ringing for most of Saturday until late at night, but the line was always busy. It would have to wait until after the service – not the best, but the only option.

Meanwhile, she had one more scheme to work on. A few swimming lessons ago, Samantha had spoken of her sister-in-law's longing for her absent husband and desperation for a child. Marina wanted to find love for Bud Baxter, who had once, in his cups, spoken of how *he* longed for a wife and family. All this longing! It had been a simple thing to make sure that the abandoned wife was paired up with Bud at the AID session. Now she just had to work on ensuring the individuals kept bumping into each other until the two became one. The minister's wife had come to realise that, given the opportunity, she had the ability to make things happen. She had no doubt that, within months, Michael would be officiating at another wedding.

*

Easter Sunday, Doug was home, grim-faced but pretending things were OK. Chocolate eggs adorned the breakfast table, but the foil wrappers remained untouched. They barely spoke; all was numb, all subdued behind the meaningless dusting and tidying.

Their daughter slouched downstairs around noon, only to isolate herself inside headphones on the sofa. Her right thumb flicked incessantly between the buttons of her mobile, her eyes rarely straying from its tiny screen.

No one heard the click of the gate or the rasp of the key in the door.

"Mum! Dad! Anyone in?"

Belinda ran from the kitchen, arms wide to receive her beloved son. Instead of Aidan, her open embrace encircled a blonde woman, youngish, whose face was vaguely familiar. Over the blonde's shoulder, her eyes questioned Aidan's before spotting the small boy holding her son's hand.

"Mum, Dad… This is Candy. We're getting married!"

The young man looked overjoyed. He swelled with pride. "We're having a baby!"

Belinda staggered back slightly, relief, hurt, shock and horror fighting for supremacy. Glancing down, she saw the little hint of a swell on the woman's belly. Two months gone at most, she guessed.

Melanie skidded downstairs into the awkward silence.

"Who are you? Who's that kid? What're they doing here?" She punched her brother's shoulder.

"This is Job. I'm going to be his dad."

Doug found his voice and his manners. "You'd better come in. Aidan didn't mention he'd be bringing guests."

He ushered them into the living room. As the woman walked ahead, he noticed the hearing aid in her left ear before

314

glaring at his son to indicate his fury. Belinda and her daughter were left to blink back their tears on the bottom stair.

"He says they're getting married." The mother struggled to hide the sob in her voice. "She's pregnant."

"She can't be. He can't get married. I'm going to share a flat with him!"

"Oh no you're not! What gave you that idea?"

"I could look after him. I'm ready to leave home anyway."

"Get a grip, Melanie. You're still a child. You don't matter to him now. None of us does."

Stunned by this dreadful realisation, mother and daughter sat in silence, glued to the step. Their world had changed forever. It was the shock of a bereavement, or even worse: they had been superceded. Mothers know it must come, and Now is never the right time. But how? But when? And where had she seen that woman before?

The name – Candy – rang a bell, and at the thought, the clangour of the village hall fire alarm rang in her mind's ear. Malevolence crept stealthily from the shadows; the memory of the brassy woman's superior tone and crass haughtiness flooded back. Job Dunne's party booking. She thought of her not-so-little list and remembered the name at the top.It took an hour to hear the creatively expurgated version of the story. How the couple had met at a party at the village hall – the one Aidan and his mates had come home for specially. How the couple had fallen in love instantly. How Aidan was *sooo* proud of his sweetheart, a survivor of marital domestic abuse and desertion, coping with recently-inflicted partial deafness, raising the delightful Job on her own, the loss of her home, smart car and sophisticated way of life thanks to bent coppers and incompetent lawyers, accepting all without complaint. She was not far short of a saint and the family would be privileged, he was sure, to have mother and child move in with them.

The prospective grandparents scarcely spoke. They weren't the type to rant and rave in front of a stranger, though the blow hit them like a canonball in the midriff. Yet they lived on. Melanie eyed the blonde soon-to-be-sister-in-law and scorned her visible dark roots and chipped nail art. What would she tell Chelsey?

Two more places were laid at the tea table, discussion deferred until after the boiled ham and cheesecake, which Job wasn't allowed in case of allergic reaction.

Aidan's parents didn't know where to start, but it *did* have to be discussed. The young couple insisted that this was *'for keeps,'* that they knew what they were doing, that everything would be just fine.

"But what about university?" The boy had been the first potential graduate in the family. Their hopes had rested on him.

"Well, it's not what I expected anyway. And there aren't any forests round here... and Candy wouldn't want to move away. It would disrupt Job's education." The young man took his future responsibilities as a father very seriously.

"But it's disrupting your own education," Belinda pleaded. "All that effort passing your exams! All that money wasted!"

"And what do you think you're going to live on?" This was Doug, who was really getting quite cross. "Do you work, Candy?"

"She's a PA." Aidan spoke up proudly.

"I worked for my ex so I'm on Jobseekers' now." Then, muttering as if to herself, "There's no way I can get a job – I have to be here for Job if he's not well."

"How did you manage before?"

"I took him with me! It was his dad's office so it were alright. And the ex-mother-in-law had him sometimes if I had to go out, but she's not having him now."

"And Candy was poorly when she was expecting Job, weren't you, darling?" Aidan stroked his love's head fondly. "We need to look after her and the baby."

"So I'll ask again… what are you going to live on? Because *I'm* not keeping you! *Your* mother's just lost her job, too. We've paid your tuition fees for the year, so you can bloody well get back to Wales when term starts and take your… *fiancée*… with you. And her kid!"

"You don't mean that, Dad. You're a good father. I hope to follow in your footsteps and be a good one to Job and the baby. Anyway, I'm thinking of going into property development. There's money to be made."

"Only if you've got money to invest. How much have you got?"

"How do you mean?"

"Money? Saved? To invest?"

"I thought we could go into business together, with *your* skills."

"Dream on, Sunshine! If this is you being responsible, God help the kid. I've been working away from home, every hour I can get, to keep you, your sister and your mother fed, clothed and housed. And you expect me to say, '*Oh, how lovely, two strangers and a foetus to provide for!*' as well? And I thought you were the clever one of the family!"

This reception was not what Aidan had hoped for: the family had not taken his Candy to their hearts as readily as he'd expected, and she was looking quite flushed; Job was cowering behind the sofa pretending to be a cat.

"Where are you living now, Candy?" Belinda asked. There just was not enough room at Number 18 for the three of them, but they ought at least to consider the options.

"I'm still in the house, but it's owned by Tyson's business so everything's got to be sold. They've found a buyer. Me and Job have to move out within the next two weeks."

"Don't want to move!" yelled Job. "And I don't want to live here. It stinks!"

"That's just Melanie's perfume," Aidan reassured him. "I grew up here and it was just fine. You'll soon get used to it."

"Won't."

"We just haven't got room." Belinda was quietly pleased to hear Aidan's childhood had been 'just fine'.

"Mum, I've something else to tell you. I've been doing some modelling... earned a bit of money that way. And I've just heard from the people who use me that I can go and live with them some of the time. There'll be room for Job and Candy here while I'm working up in Leeds. Then when I come home, Mel can go to Gran and Granddad's. I've got it all worked out!"

"No-one's having my room!" Melanie had found her voice.

"Modelling?" Doug's face was purple. "Modelling? What sort of bloody modelling?"

Aidan explained as vaguely as possible, sensing that telling the whole truth could be hazardous. He was concerned by the colour of his father's face and the throbbing veins visible on his temples. His mother, on the other hand, had turned white, and sat, hands clasped on her lap, still as alabaster. Melanie stood in the doorway and pulled her tongue at the little boy, who was unimpressed.

Doug walked out into the garden, fists clenched. They could hear him using a hammer to check the strength of the fencing panels. A cracking sound revealed a weak spot. More followed. Belinda started to think about new fencing.

It was Candy who breached the impasse.

"Pick up your toys, Job." The boy had brought a few Lego bricks and a remote-controlled truck with him. It was just like his real dad's truck. "It's time we were getting home."

Civility returned. Belinda fetched the coats, checked for anything left behind, and accompanied Candy and Job to the door, inwardly pleading that her own boy would stay. But no. He followed his new family down the path, turning to wave as the gate clicked shut behind him.

His mother and sister took themselves to bed. His father soon discovered just how weak the fencing was. When it got dark he came inside, logged on and browsed fence merchants' websites until 3am.

He was due back in Sunderland at eight. Seeing his wife sleeping soundly as he left, he lifted the telephone receiver from its dock and laid it on the arm of the sofa. She needed her rest, and he didn't want her disturbed by any more nonsense about that village hall roof.

32

The small red hatchback sat at the roadside for an hour before Phil arrived to open the gates. The wife had been giving him earache about money as usual, and the motorhome entrepreneur had been forced to admit that the business's days were numbered. The revelation did not go down well. What with a six-week cruise booked and skiing a must for the winter, Mrs Dunne was not going to accept the situation in silence.

The hatchback's owner had been bothering Phil like a gnat you just can't swat. He'd lost count of the inspections and test drives he'd let her have. A time-waster, he'd said from the start, and his patience was running out.

The car followed him through the gates and she was by his side before he'd opened the office door.

"I've come about the Happilarks Safari Supremo."

Phil sighed. "You've already test driven that twice."

"I want to buy it."

This had to be a wind-up. No way could she afford the fifty-four grand.

"Do you want another look?"

"No. I've decided."

In the office, Phil broke a tacky cobweb as he fished details of various easy-purchase options from the filing cabinet. He tossed the brochures onto his desk.

"You need to take a look at these." His voice was sullen. "How much deposit have you got?"

"No deposit."

He thought as much. This woman was a slate short of a roof if he wasn't very much mistaken. He regarded her blankly.

"I'll pay cash."

Phil could hear only the blood pounding in his ears.

"Let's see it, then."

"First, I want to give my car in part-exchange. How much will you offer?"

So this was her game. Trying to offload her runabout, then do a bunk. But a sale was a sale, and Pakamac could easily offload the hatchback – no bother. He eyed the red car through the window.

His chest swelled with magnanimity. "I'll give you a couple of grand off the price of the Safari Supremo."

"Done."

He gaped.It was worth four, easily.

"How long will it take you to get the cash?" Maybe the cruise could be saved in the nick of time.

"I have it with me." Belinda left the Portakabin office and slowly moved the car beside Phil's own company vehicle. Back inside, she tossed a brown envelope onto the desk.

"There's the logbook and MOT. There's three months left on that. It'll be a good buy for someone." It felt as though, with the document, she had passed half her life over to PD RoamerHomes.

She went back to the car, returning with a calico bag bearing the emblem of a charity for the homeless. Hefting it onto the desk, she lifted out a muddle of brown padded envelopes, which she up-ended one by one.

Rubber bands held the notes together in bundles of mixed denominations, each totalling £1000. Methodically, she counted them out one by one, pushing aside the telephone and other desk paraphernalia to make space. When the desk was full, she used the top of the filing cabinet.

She stopped when fifty-two bundles were laid out.

"What about insurance?" Phil ventured.

"It's all sorted. I've spoken to a broker who's given me a quote. As soon as I've got the documentation, I'll give them a call and pay by card."

Phil wanted to believe this was not a scam, that he could go home that night and tell his wife to pay the balance on that cruise. He longed for a night at the pub when he could stand a round for his mates instead of sloping off after a swift half on his own.

"Is there something I need to sign?" Bel was getting impatient.

He fumbled about in his desk. He'd not sold a motorhome for so long that he'd forgotten where the paperwork was kept. Eventually, he thrust the form under her nose. She signed, and passed her pen to him. He added his signature in a daze, trying to suppress a grin of satisfaction, and held up the keys.

"I'd like you to make that call to your insurance company now, if you don't mind."

If the woman were criminally insane, as he suspected, he didn't want to get caught in the flack when she ran amok in the Safari Supremo.

"Use the desk phone if you like. I'll wait outside." He eased his way to the door and slid out, to prevent the wind disturbing the bank notes.

Five minutes later she joined him on the forecourt, holding out her hand for the leather key fob.

"Would you just help me unload a few things from the boot?"

He nodded and opened the lid. Two large suitcases, a roll of bedding, a plastic crate of kitchenware, what looked like a decapitated wooden snail and several shopping bags of

322

foodstuffs covered the flatbed behind the front seats. She stood to one side while he transferred them into the Supremo.

With some difficulty she clambered into the driver's seat, started the ignition and slammed the door shut. The window glided down.

"Where are you off to?" Phil shouted above the purr of the engine. He'd better have some idea in case the Feds came calling.

"Just somewhere I once lived – over to the west!" she called, as she pressed the accelerator, turned a perfect semi-circle and drove out past the spiked railings. She pipped the horn twice in triumphant farewell.

Deciding on a quick call at the village hall, Bel moved up through the gears, ignoring waves and hoots from passers-by. She needed to put some miles behind her before she was due at work for her final shift. From tomorrow, Denswick Public Library would be administered by three squabbling volunteers, none of whom was willing to do any cleaning or put out the bins. Good luck to them, Belinda thought, although Bel decided to add their names to her little list, which was not so little now.

*

Dianne Dewsbury had been trying to apologise to Belinda for days, but every time she'd tried to make contact the line was engaged. Dianne had a lot of explaining to do which really ought to have been done face to face, but what with one thing and another she just couldn't be bothered to catch up with everything that had happened at the village hall while she and Alan had been on their cruise.

As Belinda was steering the motorhome out of Denswick, Dianne left yet another message on the answerphone at 18 Dapple Grove, Sallby.

"Belinda, it's Dianne. We're back – but I'm off again tomorrow – Joanne's twins are due in the next few days and of course she wants her mum there with her. I don't know how long I'll stay but I won't come back until I'm sure she can cope.

"The thing is, Belinda, there's something I forgot to do before we sailed. I hope it hasn't caused too much trouble – but I'm sure you'll have it sorted anyway, knowing you. Before John Spinks went in hospital he brought the village hall accounts and bank books round to my house. Asked me to pass them on. I think you were visiting your son at uni… and what with packing and sorting out the cats, I put everything in a drawer and forgot all about it. I've just come across the folder when I went to put my passport back. Totally slipped my mind.

"Anyway, just to let you know they're all safe. Catch up in a month or two. See you!"

*

Along the tree-lined road to Sallby, a seventy-two-seater coach had been unloading two classfuls of twelve-year-olds into the drizzle outside the swimming baths. There seemed to be something else hindering traffic flow, too. Bel slowed to a halt.

Voices cackling like lightweight goslings and swiping each other with swimming kits in rucksacks and carrier bags, the youngsters were being herded back onto the bus by their teachers. The kids didn't want to go – it was much more interesting to watch the carry-on taking place on the pavement.

Edging the motorhome forward, Bel could see a brightly coloured rectangle waving in the air in front of the children. It bore some sort of printing in blue. The rectangle seemed to be fastened to a wooden broom handle.

The scene unfolded further as another car crept past the stationary coach and the motorhome edged forward. An elderly woman in damp beige was waving the placard energetically in the path of the students, the message *REJOICE WITH JESUS!* written in blue felt pen on yellow card. Belinda could make out the old woman's voice, which proclaimed in wavering tones,

"God loves you all! Rejoice with Jesus and you will be saved! Suffer the little children to come unto me, He said. Go to him, children, and be born again!"

As Bel waited and the teachers struggled to control their pupils, two uniformed officers strolled up with little sense of urgency, having been summoned by the pool manager. Grant Dalton and Heather Banks eyed the scene and the woman in beige wryly.

"Right. Back on the bus, all of you!" Grant's instruction carried some weight with the pupils. The children began to file back up the coach steps.

"Who's that old woman, sir?"

"Is she mad, miss?"

"Will they lock her up?"

"That's Naomi Simmons's grandma!"

"They'll put her in a cycle attrick hospickle."

"What's that?"

"In Densfield behind the egg factory."

"No! What's a cycle hat trick?"

At the door of the swimming baths, pool attendant Samantha wanted to know the reasons for the delay. She was expecting another coachload of young swimmers in fifty minutes and couldn't afford to get behind time. The two PCSOs appeared to be speaking sternly to the woman, who Samantha vaguely recognised from the Over-Sixties Slow and Sure sessions held each Wednesday lunchtime.

Despite the fine rain, the woman continued shouting her message of salvation to those on the bus, while a passing tractor-and-trailer combination distributed fodder beet onto the highway as it avoided the blockage.

At last, one either side of her, the community support officers began to walk the demonstrator back in the direction of Denswick. Disheartened, her resistance was weak, but she was still protesting as the trio moved towards the Safari Supremo. A message on her radio distracted PCSO Heather, who stopped for a moment.

Still talking, a metre in front of the motorhome the woman looked up through its windscreen. For just a second, her eyes met Belinda's. Recognition was immediate and undeniable.

Despite her position as chapel warden at Denswick Methodist, Dorothy Simmons was an ardent fan of the Evangelicals' Pastor Darren. It lifted her spirits to Rejoice with Jesus! in between her more conventional devotions, and she had happily swelled the front-row throng for the midweek service in the old Odeon. On hearing the handsome young man urge his followers to proclaim God's message on the streets and in the old folks' homes, Dorothy just *knew* she had something to offer.

"It will give me another purpose in life," she told the pastor. "Reverend Batty won't mind at all. He'll support me all the way."

Pastor Darren hadn't been sure that Dorothy's image matched the one he was trying to convey, but reminded himself that, being by age closer to God's Kingdom than he was, the worshipper had the right to follow His call in any way she chose.

Now, Dorothy carried out a sidelong examination of the vehicle. It was certainly one up on the little hatchback.

Heather Banks had stepped aside into the trees and was talking into her radio. Her eyes signalled to her partner that there was a more urgent matter to attend to. She ended the call.

"It's Clement again," she told Grant.

"What's he up to this time?"

She smirked. "Using his mobility scooter in a threatening manner... again."

"We've got to go to another incident now, Dorothy." Grant tried to convey the seriousness of the situation.

"Take yourself home and have a cup of tea. Don't get upset, but you can't just approach children and start shouting at them nowadays. There's child protection to think of."

"Protection? That's what I'm trying to do. Protect them from sin and keep them safe with Jesus. They need to know that God loves them all!" Her defence reached only Belinda's ears.

She leaned across the passenger seat and called out,

"Would you like a lift home?"

What are you doing? asked Bel's voice.

Belinda was feeling guilty about the malevolent mantras and the old woman's place near the top of the list. Dorothy hadn't been doing any harm, after all.

The demonstrator nodded and dabbed her eyes with a hankie while Belinda climbed down, helped her into the passenger seat and laid the placard in the back of the van.

The hold-up had cleared, leaving several squashed beet on the tarmac, and the vehicle continued along the road to Sallby. Dorothy was feeling both relieved and frustrated, not to mention intimidated. After all, she'd only spoken to this young woman once, even though she'd been keeping watch since the day Belinda was born.

Moving up into third gear at last, the Safari Supremo passed the jumble of Truetrust Academy's flat roofs in the distance. It flashed past the ornate new gates, then braked sharply as four young teenagers in sloppy school uniform stepped into the road, shouting over their shoulders at an old man in flat cap and muffler.

The old chap's mobility scooter followed close behind the youths, nipping at their heels, swerving left and right as he herded his truanting descendants up to school.

The Safari Supremo had stalled with the emergency stop. Belinda pressed the ignition and moved off, turning left off the main road to follow signs to Densfield and Sallby.

"I don't live out this way."

"Don't worry. There's something I need to do before we can be on our way." Bel's tone was civil rather than compassionate.

"I don't do very well on buses." The older woman was beginning to feel a bit queasy, and very warm. "Fancy calling the police on me like that... a woman of *my* age."

Visibly upset, she took a clean handkerchief from her pocket, using it to wipe her nose and dab her eyes. She unfastened her coat, her taupe cardigan and the top button of her acrylic blouse.

On reaching Sallby Belinda swung past the boarded-up pub, which now carried a *To Let* as well as two *For Sale* signs, and headed for the field beside the village hall.

"I just need to check on something." She jumped down and disappeared from view. Dorothy sat listening to the birds in the hedgerows and wondering if the constant plea in her prayers – that someone should offer her loving kindness – had at last been answered. Over her shoulder she eyed her placard. It had taken her an hour to make, using her grandson's felt pen and coloured card, and left her own sweeping brush without a handle.

Also over her shoulder she spotted the two suitcases. They gave her pause for thought, but she knew she'd not be able to make it back home from this field on her own. She'd left her handbag at home to free up her hands for the placard and had only her bus pass in her pocket. Few buses ran through Sallby.

There were no other vehicles in the car park. Good. Bel breathed deeply, calming herself as she surveyed the building. The stripped roof was damp from several hours of fine drizzle but she refused to contemplate the implications.

She wiggled the key right, then left, as always. It turned. Almost timidly, she slipped into the hall and pulled the door to.

Quite tidy. The tea towels were grubby, but she let that pass. Her footsteps echoed as she crossed the sprung planking, eyes lifted in search of cobwebs. She spotted a few and left them to the spiders.

The smallest key opened the padlock on the cleaner's cupboard. The room was tiny –full of half-used tins of paint, toilet and kitchen rolls, stepladder, brushes, mops and buckets.

Bel grabbed a handful of paper towels; spotted a near-empty bottle of turps on the top shelf and reached it down. She dumped everything in a flip-top bin by the back door.

She looked under the bar for the battered cardboard box where globe-shaped tea-light holders were stored. A few still had gobbets of wax at the bottom from the last time they were used. She tossed them into the bin and pushed the box tidily back in place.

Once more she sat in Drago's chair. There was no smell of him now.

The cupboard was still unlocked. Returning, she took a small box from the cluttered window ledge, closed the door and clicked the padlock shut.

She would leave by the back door; stepped out; hesitated, and set one foot back inside. She took the box from her pocket, used it, and dropped the flaming match into the bin. The door blew shut as she walked away.

In the loft, Hamid Duric lay very still. His cousin had warned him about this woman, the one he had spied on as she walked beneath the crack in the loft floor.

In the bin by the door, the match smouldered between the paper towels and the plastic bottle.

*

329

Sitting quietly in the passenger seat, Dorothy lost her bearings as the motorhome wound its way along the country lanes, but ten minutes after leaving Sallby Village Hall it became clear that the vehicle was not travelling towards Denswick. There was no conversation; the old woman was beginning to feel humiliated by the silence. That feeling turned to fear when the Safari Supremo swung onto the motorway sliproad, following signs to Huddersfield, Manchester and the North West.

Her throat dried. Efforts to point out the driver's mistake came out in a croak.

"Not this way... Want to go home..."

No response, though Bel gripped the steering wheel tighter and hunched further forward, eyes flicking between the rear view mirror and the thundering traffic in search of a gap large enough to slide into. She found one between a coach taking pensioners on holiday to Rhyl and a small white Aygo, whose elderly driver's choice of speed was evoking much frustration in the vehicles behind.

Settled into the gap, Bel sat back and exhaled slowly.

"Taking you for a little run," she said. "Bit of a treat."

Still she did not glance to her left. She stared ahead, alert to the swervers and the road bullies, her heart pounding, excitement and uncertainty swamping Belinda's silent inner protests.

"Erm... I don't travel well. I get sick."

"Suck a mint." Bel pointed to her handbag in the foot well. "There's a packet in there."

Dorothy did as she was told with a whimper. Her protests silenced, she sucked on the white peppermint, which offered some comfort and stilled her tongue. Bel put her foot down as the motorway climbed higher.

Dorothy had stopped whining, deterred by the warning flash in the younger woman's eye that forbade argument. The scenery sped by: the cooling towers of ageing power stations; warehouse-sized furniture outlets; in the distance, housing estates teetering on steep, bleak fellsides, until the road left behind the cities and remnants of industry and rose over the Pennines. The Supremo slipped effortlessly between the juggernauts' thundering wheels to the outside lane. Bel sat back, revelling in the power under her control.

From time to time, a whimper was suppressed between crunches on the peppermint. The old woman's countryside jaunts hitherto had been limited to rural parks and, on special occasions, the grounds of stately homes. Lamb was something she bought at the butcher's. Now, she found herself counting the sturdy, black-faced creatures which gambolled alongside their grubbier, more stolid mothers cropping the turf and heather on the bulbous moors.

Bel's airways opened and, her spirits soaring at last, she began to sing.

> *"And did those feet in ancient time*
> *Walk upon England's mountains green..."*

Mutual suspicion faded away. They exchanged a glance and wary smiles.

> *"And was the holy Lamb of God*
> *On England's pleasant pastures seen?"*

They both knew all the words and improvised the concluding set of chords in unison. The two women were briefly united in spirit and travelled on in companionable silence until eventually, Dorothy dozed.

*

As they approached a sign for Hartshead Moor Services, the old woman opened her eyes and chanced a question.

"Is that where we're going?"

"Nope."

"Please tell me where…"

"Mystery Tour! Pensioners like them, don't they? I'm giving you this one free. Thought you'd be pleased."

The driver's eyes narrowed unnervingly. Dorothy kept quiet. The coach in front struggled as the road climbed even higher, slowing down the Safari Supremo. The lull prompted a question from Bel.

"Why have you been stalking me for the last thirty-odd years?"

Dorothy was stunned.

"Stalking you? What do you mean?"

"Ever since I was ten. Wherever I go, you're there, peering at me like some creepy voyeur."

Forget the hymn singing. Bel had dropped any pretence of kindness.

"Did you have an affair with my father?"

"I've never had an affair with anyone. I'm a God-fearing woman, and in my day people didn't run around with other people's husbands like they do now." Dorothy was not enjoying this mystery tour at all. "I'd like to go home now, please." She flapped her hand in front of her face to cool her emotions.

"Tough. I'm not letting you out of this van until you explain why you're fixated with me." Anger was coursing through Bel's veins, the end-product manufactured by months of malevolent mantras.

"I'm not fixated." Tears flooded the faded grey eyes. "I love you as if you were my own child." The voice was a whispered sob.

"Why? Why me? What right have you got to intrude on my life?"

"I've never intruded! It's just not true. I'm just interested in you because I had a daughter, but she died."

Belinda checked herself, briefly. "Lots of women lose babies." Bel's granite heart had not softened.

"My little girl was born on the same day as you."

That was baloney.

"How do you know when I was born?"

"I was in the next bed to your mother in the maternity hospital. We were friends."

The tears coursed freely down the faded cheeks.

"What was she called?" The tone was seething.

"The same as you."

This was spooky. Definitely sick.

"But we gave you different second names. Yours is Flora, isn't it?"

Belinda nodded.

"My little girl's was Dawn."

There could be some truth in the story, Bel had to admit. Few people knew she was a Flora.

The Aygo having fallen behind, an articulated juggernaut forced its way into the gap and kept pace with the Safari Supremo, just two metres from the rear bumper. The truck's windscreen and the driver's gesticulating fingers behind it filled Bel's rear-view mirror. Her head thumped; her ears rumbled with the rotation of the thundering tyres. The pounding in her chest was getting stronger. She could feel her own hysteria mounting.

Taking her eyes off the Rhyl-bound coach, she glared at the weeping old woman beside her.

Dorothy was thinking that at least with their David she knew what to expect. Perhaps a daughter would have been just as harsh. They drove in silence for a while, with Dorothy emitting deep sighs and dabbing at her lip.

"I really am feeling quite queasy," she admitted eventually. "I think you need to stop the bus."

"It's not a bus. Have another mint." The driver offered no sympathy. "So who was your baby's father? Was it my dad?"

"No, no, of course not! I got married when I was twenty-eight. Met a chap on the dodgems at Densfield fair – Wilf. He was a miner. Big. Strong. Could look after himself. But he was very possessive. A difficult man to live with."

Dorothy's face was sad, disillusioned, a fleeting flashback to the dawning of this insight in the early years of her marriage. "Then I had our David a couple of years later. We wanted more children but it never happened. I never had another little girl."

Her breathing was more laboured now; anxiety was turning to distress.

"I need one of my pills."

"Take one then."

"I haven't got them with me. I never expected to be going on a bus ride!" She was desperate for air. "Please take me home."

The voice was starting to whine and the driver found it irritating.

"Pull yourself together. I can't just turn round on a motorway."

"Oh." More dabs with the hankie: across the forehead; round the temples, along the upper lip. She continued her story.

"Our antenatal appointments always seemed to be at the same time, so we got to be friends. We'd chat away and imagine what our babies would be like. There was none of this knowing the sex before it was born in those days. Your mam and me, we used to joke that if one of us had a girl and the other a boy, maybe they'd get married one day." Her tone was gentle now, the impending sobs building up in her chest. "But Wilf didn't like me to have friends."

Bel was sceptical. How come she'd never heard of this so-called friend of her mother's?

"Then, after my baby was born, they wheeled me into a ward, and later they put Gwen in the bed next to me, both of us with our baby girls in those little plastic cots by the bed, born fourteen hours apart. It was a lovely coincidence, we thought."

A deep sob reverberated against the windscreen.

"We made a pact. Every year, on their birthday, we'd meet up, just us and the babies. I knew I'd have to keep it quiet from Wilf. He'd never have agreed to it."

The old woman was playing for sympathy. The story was probably a pack of lies.

"Then on the fifth day, I woke up to feed my baby, and she was dead. Stone cold in the cot by my bed." It was years since she had wept like this. "Wilf, he blamed me. Said I can't have been looking after her properly. The doctors said it was a cot death. No explanation. She just stopped breathing."

Bel was fighting hard against her own emotions. She was a mother, after all. She did have some empathy, but no way was she going to give in to compassion.

"Your mum and dad were very kind. After a few weeks they brought you round to our house, let me hold you and give you a cuddle – but Wilf sent them packing. Told them to keep away. So I'd lost my baby and I'd lost my only friend." She gasped back a sob.

How come Mum and Dad had never spoken of the dead baby? This had been *her* moment, *her* time, *her* escape, yet somehow this creepy old crone had inveigled a way into *her* life once again, made *her* feel guilty. As if *she* was to blame.

"I've got palpitations." The whining voice started again. "I need my angina spray."

"I suppose that's at home as well?"

"Mmm." Her breathing was more laboured now.

Belinda could sense panic overwhelming Dorothy's common sense.

"Keep calm. We'll sort it out."

The concern in her voice was forced. Bel pushed consideration aside. Time to recalculate. *Time to ditch the bitch*. By the time they reached the services, Plan B had taken shape.

✳

Out of the motorhome, Belinda ushered Dorothy between the parked vehicles and sat her down at a table in the self-service café.

"Tea or coffee?"

"Tea, please."

"Wait here."

Dorothy waited, a little cooler now, calmer away from the thunderous traffic. She fiddled with the plasticised menu cards falling from their stand, her mind back in 1969 with its joy, hope, sorrow, and the pain which still endured.

Belinda put the mugs of tea on the table.

"So why did I see my father coming out of your house when I was ten?" The ring of truth in Dorothy's tale did not answer the big question.

"I didn't know you had." Dorothy thought for a while. "He only ever came once. It must have been then.

"In spite of everything, your parents sent a birthday card for my Belinda every year. I thought it was very kind of them and it helped keep her alive in my heart. Usually, I got to the post before Wilf did. One year though, it must have been on her tenth birthday, he opened it. Carried on something awful – about interfering busybodies gloating over our dead baby. It was nothing like that, I knew.

"I cried a lot and it all calmed down, or so I thought. Then one day, around four o'clock, your dad knocked on the door. He'd come to apologise. Apparently, Wilf had gone round to the factory and called him outside. Threatened to have him beaten up if either he or Gwen came near our house or sent a card again. Your dad was scared – he's not a big chap like

Wilf – but he had the guts to come and explain in person why there'd be no more cards for little Belinda Dawn." She paused. "No one else ever sent one."

The tea was sipped in silence. Belinda was forced to acknowledge her misconception. Maybe Dorothy wasn't as bad as she'd believed. Yet the fulfilment of her own transformation, the goal of her malevolent mantras, was so close... she couldn't back out now. One sign of weakness and it would all have been in vain. She'd be back to meek, little, put-upon Belinda, with a hussy for a daughter, a modelling stepfather for a son and a grandkid on the way, not to mention a village hall going bankrupt... and burning down!

No. Bel would have to see this through.

"I need the toilet." The statement broke what had become an awkward silence. Bel thought quickly.

"Righto. We passed the Ladies' on the way in. I'll show you."

Taking her elbow, she helped Dorothy to her feet and steered her towards the café's exit.

"I need to get something from the van," she muttered as she walked away.

Minutes later Dorothy reached the front of the queue in the Ladies' and settled herself in a cubicle. She became aware of a conversation by the washbasins; one of the voices sounded like Belinda Lowe's. Then there was silence, except for the sounds of running water and super-fast hand driers.

Eventually, she emerged from her cubicle, washed her hands and slid them between the blowers. Turning, she noticed the blue and yellow placard on its broomstick handle leaning against the wall.

Her gasp caught the attention of a young woman at the front of the queue. "A woman with short hair left it there. She said someone would know it was hers..." she trailed off.

Dorothy's palpitations returned. She grabbed the broom handle to support herself and tottered out muttering, "I need some air."

The women in the queue tutted at one another before silence returned. Dorothy struggled past the café to reach the exit. On the concourse, her placard caught the wind and the eyes of a few people as they scurried past, but no one stopped.

Hundreds of vehicles were parked in front of her, but few motorhomes were apparent. Belinda must mean her to proclaim her message to the travellers, she surmised. Lifting the placard higher, she began in a wavering voice,

"Rejoice with Jesus! Let him take your burdens from you so you may be born again into righteousness!"

The comers-and-goers gave her a wider berth as her tone became more desperate. Where was Belinda? Where *was* she?

Bel was in the driver's seat of the Safari Supremo, considering her options. Decided, she started the engine and revved around the car-park, giving the aged evangelist a toot on the horn as she sped past, en route for the westbound carriageway. The toot attracted Dorothy's attention as the motorhome disappeared from view.

Veined legs buckling beneath her, the old woman sank slowly onto the damp, grey flagstones. She could only wait for Jesus to take her home.

*

As the Safari Supremo rejoined the motorway, a dark grey Honda which had seen better days entered the service area from the eastbound carriageway. The three travellers, all wearing dog collars beneath their casual jackets, were returning to their circuits in the eastern counties from a Vocation course on Safeguarding near Wigan. In the back seat, the Reverend Michael Batty was bursting to share wonderful, personal news with his fellow clergymen, but for fear of intruding, waited patiently for a suitable pause in the discussion of the course's relevance.

Having been persuaded by his wife that every modern clergyman must possess an up-to-date, mobile electronic multi-function device, Michael had recently become a fan of the text message, deeming them, he considered, more cost effective and less intrusive than actual calls. This day, as the Honda travelled eastwards past the outskirts of Manchester, Michael's phone had beeped. He knew just enough of the device's workings to appreciate that the sound signalled receipt of a text message, and after pressing several wrong buttons, managed to open it. *"DONE A PREGNANCY TEST. POSITIVE. HALLELUJAH! M XX."*

A few days earlier, Marina had commented that she was putting on weight, but neither of them ever dared hope that they would be blessed with a child at their time of life. They had never spoken about it. It would have been greedy to want more than the love and fulfilment they had found so tardily. Yet there was no mistaking the meaning of the text.

Michael was almost afraid to rejoice; memories of the loss of Sylvie and their child swirled in his head at the same time as joy and thankfulness at this second chance of parenthood. As the driver of the Honda searched for a space to park, conversation in the car paused just long enough for him to say,

"I've just heard that my wife is pregnant!"

Before leaving the vehicle, the colleagues shared a prayer of gratitude before walking inside, past the Rejoice with Jesus! placard leaning against a wall. A small crowd had gathered round something on the concourse, but in their excitement at the wonderful news and the proximity of tea and cakes, the clergymen paid scant attention.

*

She took a break at Birch Services, then kept her foot down all the way to the North Wales coast road.

As the traffic eased, she began to reflect on Dorothy's story. It was sad, without doubt. She was touched by Mum and Dad's kindness to their friend in her grief; by the way her father had faced up to the thuggish Wilf. How could anyone threaten to beat up Dad? He was kind. He was gentle and long-suffering. He knew right from wrong. He had not run away when threatened. Like Doug, who had not run away when his business was struggling. Like Aidan, who had taken pity on an abandoned woman and brought her into their own home... or tried to. But she couldn't be like them. She had no more strength left. She had to keep driving.

The smoke-grey sea on her right, patched with charcoal and navy, glinted and sparkled as the clouds scudded across the sun. The further west she went, the more she anticipated the embrace of the mountains on her left until, leaving the main road at last, she found the lane that led up high to the special place, the place where the treecreeper lived its quiet life, where the water flowed damply over the moss-blocked mill-race and the stones whispered the message, "Welcome home!"

She pulled the vehicle into a clearing until it was invisible to passers-by on the track. Cutting the engine, Bel lay back, closed her eyes and inhaled deeply.

They would never find her here.